The Splinter Men came through the mist like black-clad wraiths, silent even down to the soundless slap of their feet.

They looked alive, almost. Their pale skin and expressionless faces were little different from those of living Nidalese, and if there was a whiff of old blood and chill earth to them, it was no worse than might cling to any gravedigger. But the burning hunger in their dead black eyes betrayed them, and the splinters driven like wooden stitches through their lips told their name.

Isiem had hoped there might only be four Splinter Men, corresponding to the four empty shacks ringing the central hut, but the gods did not choose to smile on him there. At least a dozen of the maimed murderers streamed toward them, dragging two other bloodied, apparently insensible people. Through the dense fog, Isiem couldn't see if their victims were alive or dead, but in either case the two of them hardly looked able to stand up on their own, let alone offer any resistance. They'd be of no use in a fight.

The Splinter Men seemed to think the same, if they thought anything. Twenty yards away, they let their victims fall to the ground. Focus returned to their hollow eyes, and they raised their heads like blind men hearing music. An awful yearning contorted their dead faces as they turned in wordless unison toward Ascaros.

They said nothing. No threats, no demands. Abandoning their victims, the Splinter Men simply rushed toward the shadowcaller with their long knives drawn . . .

The Pathfinder Tales Library

Nightblade

Liane Merciel

paizo

Cover art by Maichol Quinto.
Cover design by Emily Crowell.
Map by Crystal Frasier.

Paizo Inc.
7120 185th Ave NE, Ste 120
Redmond, WA 98052
paizo.com

ISBN 978-1-60125-662-1 (mass market paperback)
ISBN 978-1-60125-663-8 (ebook)

Publisher's Cataloging-In-Publication Data
(Prepared by The Donohue Group, Inc.)

Merciel, Liane.
  Nightblade / Liane Merciel.

    pages : map ; cm. -- (Pathfinder tales)

  Set in the world of the role-playing game, Pathfinder and Pathfinder Online.
  Issued also as an ebook.
  ISBN: 978-1-60125-662-1 (mass market paperback)

  1. Wizards--Fiction. 2. Magic--Fiction. 3. Good and evil--Fiction.
4. Imaginary places--Fiction. 5. Pathfinder (Game)--Fiction. 6. Fantasy fiction.
7. Adventure stories. I. Title. II. Series: Pathfinder tales library.

PS3613.E727 N53 2014
813/.6

First printing October 2014.

Printed in the United States of America.

To Ron and Lauren,
for letting us borrow the best writers' retreat in the world.

N
Steaming Sea
Barrowmoor
Nidal
Mindspin
Mountains
Molthune
Backar Forest
Pangolais
The Beast's Lair
Fiendslair
Cettigne
Uskwood
Umbral Basin
Ridwan
Menador Mountains
Pezzack
Barrowood
Cheliax
Devil's Perch

Chapter One
Plague Birds

That's the last of the stevedores," Ena said. The hooded dwarf unfolded herself from her perch atop the lintel of a barrelmaker's shop, collapsed the miniature spyglass she'd been using to watch the warehouse in the distance, and swung down to the street with a nimbleness that seemed at odds with her stocky figure. "We'll give them a few minutes to clear out, and then it should just be us and the night watchmen around the warehouse." She raised an eyebrow at Isiem, the gesture almost invisible in the shadows of her hood. "You're sure you can handle them?"

"Two untrained men with cudgels?" the Nidalese wizard asked dryly. "I should hope so."

"Without killing them, please," another of their conspirators snapped. She was a tall woman, almost as tall as Isiem himself, and although the red scarf wrapped around the lower half of her face masked her features, he guessed she had some elven blood. It was in the inflections of her voice, the litheness of her movements—and her peremptory tone. He'd never met the woman before, and the rebels recognized no ranks, yet she commanded him like a servant.

But it wasn't worth the argument. It had been just over a year since Isiem joined the rebellion in Pezzack, and in that time he had learned that the rebels were an impossible bundle of contradictions. Merciless and merciful, crude but idealistic, largely disorganized yet capable of orchestrating sophisticated attacks.

Their assault on the warehouse was one such operation.

For years, the provincial town of Pezzack had been a nest of rebellion against the diabolists who controlled Imperial Cheliax. Its remoteness and the natural barricade of the mountainous, monster-infested wastelands to its east made it difficult for Queen Abrogail's agents to control. Despite two fiery assaults, infighting among the rebel factions, and an ongoing campaign by the Chelish navy to starve the resistance into submission, Pezzack remained effectively free.

That naval blockade was the reason that Isiem stood out here, shivering on a frigid winter's night, amid a ring of accomplices whose names and faces he did not know. Other than Ena, they were strangers to him, and he to them. Hoods and masks hid their faces; an illusion guised his own. None of them used names. If Chelish agents or insurgents from a rival faction caught one of them—as had happened before, and would happen again—that unlucky captive would have little to betray.

The only thing the conspirators shared was their goal. Ena's informants had whispered that something terrible was secreted in the crates that the stevedores had just unloaded into the loyalist-controlled warehouse on the water. What it was, the informants hadn't known, but it was deemed dangerous enough that Ena had contacted the best in the rebellion for help.

"I wasn't planning to kill the watchmen," Isiem said, sifting through the spell components arranged in his top pocket for easy access. He didn't need to re-sort them—he knew them all with calm, sure familiarity—but the ritual soothed him in the quiet moments before action. "I'm well aware that it does no good to turn their families against us. Besides, it's hardly necessary. They pose little obstacle to our goal."

"Likely to be bigger problems inside," Ena said. "Still don't know what, though. The devilers won't leave valuables unguarded, but they won't use obvious guards either. Whatever's protecting their goods, it's hidden and it's not living. They didn't have any extra guards on the ship, nor meals carried down to the hold. My spies saw nothing. Might be the cargo itself is the danger."

"We should burn it," one of the other masked conspirators interjected. His voice, like the half-elf's, was unfamiliar to Isiem. Ena seemed to have reached farther afield than usual in putting together this night's crew. "Bar the doors and burn down the whole warehouse."

"That is a *profoundly* stupid idea," Ena said. "Profoundly." The dwarf stretched her legs and started toward the warehouse, melting in and out of the shadows effortlessly in her mottled gray cloak. "Let me remind you: the point is to find out what the devilers are doing. If their cargo is valuable, we want to steal it and sell it. If it's not, we want to find out what their plans are. We can't do that if we burn it, now can we?"

"And the rest of the warehouse is filled with food," the woman in the red scarf added. "That's what raised our suspicions initially. How often do ships carrying food get through Governor Sawndannac's blockade? She's been trying to starve the Pezzacki into submission for months. But even if it was a ruse to ensure we'd take in their cargo, the fact remains that the warehouse *is* stocked with food. We can't waste it."

Chastened, the man offered no answer. Ena didn't seem to want one. The dwarf turned back to them long enough to hold one finger up to her lips, under her hood, then pointed to the right side of the warehouse and held up two more. With that, she slipped off to the warehouse's left side, facing the water, where a smaller side door stood beside the large loading doors. The dwarf crouched against the wall, working on the padlock that secured the smaller door.

Isiem went the other way. He could see the watchmen coming; their lanterns cut bright lines through the night's salty fog. They kept close together, sheltering themselves against the dark. Their oiled cloaks were beaded with damp, their hoods pulled low so that he could not see their faces.

Not that he needed to. As the watchmen passed a narrow alley between two warehouses, Isiem struck. He sifted a pinch of fine sand from a pocket, letting it trickle to the ground while he spoke the words of magic that would send his unknowing victims into slumber.

As its last word left his lips, Isiem's spell seized the watchmen. Without a word of protest, they slumped gently into the fog.

Isiem swiftly bound and gagged the men. They woke as soon as Isiem stuffed the rags into their mouths, but were too startled to offer much resistance. One after the other, he pulled the struggling watchmen into the alley and out of casual view. Morning would find them stiff, cold, and scared—but they'd live to see the new day, and that was all the kindness he could spare them.

At his signal, two of the other conspirators took up the guards' badges, cudgels, and fallen lanterns. Raising their lights to cut through the night, the false watchmen took up the patrol. They'd maintain the illusion that nothing was amiss, and serve as a first line of warning if some outside threat should intrude.

Isiem went around to the waterfront side of the warehouse. Ena had forced the lock on the small office door. The dwarf eased the door open and waved Isiem and the woman in the red scarf forward, slipping ahead of them into the warehouse. None of them carried a light; either by magic or by the innate gifts of their blood, they could see well enough by the misty moon.

Shelves and pallets filled the warehouse in towering rows. Pezzack was not a large town, and its warehouses were modest, but even so it was disorienting for Isiem to see corded bundles of salt cod stacked higher than his head, or rows of hanging hams like impossibly fat, salt-crusted bats crowded in a roost. The pungent aroma of garlic mingled with the spicy fragrance of the long, wrinkled red peppers that the Pezzacki called "rooster's beak"; under it all was the earthy odor of the cured meats that filled most of the visible space.

"Where's their bloody secret cargo?" Ena muttered, stopping amid a cluster of hams. The dwarf pulled a small charm out from under her jerkin: a single-pointed blue crystal wrapped in silver wire and hung from a leather thong. She slipped it from around her neck and let it dangle from her fingers, watching it intently through the dusty gloom.

After a moment, the crystal vibrated, then pulled toward a few unassuming wooden boxes stacked under a heap of grain sacks. "Magic," Ena grunted in satisfaction, putting her charm back on and tucking the crystal under her shirt. "There'll be something more than carrots and onions in those boxes, I'll wager."

"Be ready," said the woman in the red scarf. She drew a longsword with a smooth, blued blade. Another crimson scarf wrapped its hilt, but the pommel was bare, and on it Isiem saw a sword-and-halo etched in gold. Iomedae's mark.

"Help me with these sacks," Ena told Isiem, grabbing one end of a sizable bag.

It must have weighed over eighty pounds, and the dwarf's short stature made moving it awkward. Isiem hoisted the other side with a grunt, helping Ena ease it to the floor. He tipped his chin at the woman who stood poised with her sword. "She could help, instead of trying to stare down this barley. She's probably stronger than either of us."

Ena snorted. "That's what paladins do. Look noble while the rest of us do the heavy lifting." She raised her voice, directing two of the other conspirators: "Get the next sack."

Minutes later, with the grain sacks piled on the floor, Ena pried open the top box under the paladin's watchful gaze. She brushed aside a layer of straw and sacking, then paused and stepped back slowly. "Wizard. Come here."

Isiem came forward. The box was packed tight with bones, all painted black. Most appeared to be the bones of large birds, although he couldn't tell whether they were from eagles, vultures, or some rarer breed. He'd never been a great student of the natural world.

Alongside those bones were others that seemed to be the fleshless hands and arms of some small, clawed creatures. Kobolds, perhaps; Isiem judged that they were slightly too small, and the claws too developed, to belong to goblins. They, too, had been painted entirely black.

He picked through the bones. They had been stacked in neat, careful rows, nestled together to conserve space. Gummy, necromantic preservatives stained their joints and the crevices under the hands' hooked claws.

"What is it?" Ena asked tensely.

"Undead of some type, I think. I've never seen ones quite like this." Isiem shrugged, stepping back. "Open the next box."

The next box contained more black-painted bones, as did the one beneath it. The final box, however, held something different under its coat of yellow straw. Hinged glass cases, each filled with dead birds, gleamed inside.

Isiem picked up one of the cases. It held eight birds ranging in size from crows to sparrows, and it felt strangely light in his hands. A whiff of funereal spices—frankincense, sandalwood, Osirian black resin—hinted that it, too, bore some necromantic spell. A curled copper shaving on each of the birds' eyes, and a sprinkling of salt in their feathers, told him what that magic was: a rite to stave off decay.

More cases of dead birds filled the box. Isiem peered more closely at the one in his hands. The birds' throats looked swollen, as if they'd all swallowed eggs that had lodged in their gullets, and there seemed to be a dried, flaky residue about their nostrils and the sides of their beaks . . . But even though his magic allowed him to see clearly in the dark, it was impossible to be sure through the glass.

Curiosity pushed him to open the case, even as caution pulled him back. Isiem didn't recognize the necromancy at work here, nor could he identify the disease that had killed the birds—if what he'd seen *was* a disease, and not some poison or side effect of the pre-servative spell—but he wanted to. Pezzack had little to interest a wizard of any real skill, and less to challenge one; Isiem had spent much of the past year mired in boredom. This was a mystery, and that pleased him.

He didn't want to kill his collaborators for the sake of his own curiosity, though. Or himself. Glancing over at the Iomedaean, Isiem asked, "Can you cure diseases?"

She nodded silently.

"Good." Isiem turned to Ena, who had taken up a seat on the barley sacks and was chewing a piece of purloined ham while she watched. "Warn the others not to come in here, please. I'm about to do something very stupid, I suspect."

"That's always promising." The dwarf stuffed her slice of ham into a pocket and stood up. "Try not to actually do it until I get back. Don't want to be surprised any more than I have to."

She disappeared amid the warehouse shelves, returning moments later with a satisfied nod. "It's done. I told them not to come back in until I give leave, whatever they hear in here. The three of us will have to handle whatever you're about to unleash."

"Nothing, I hope." Isiem unlatched the case. Even as he grasped the glass lid to lift it, however, a clatter and rustle from the bone boxes told him that his hopes were for naught.

"So much for that," Ena said, reaching into her cloak. Spinning on her left foot to face the boxed bones, she pulled out a small, spherical glass bottle that sloshed with liquid. The dwarf did something to it—Isiem couldn't see what—and flung the glass ball at the boxed bones.

With a crystalline tinkle, it exploded into a cloud of thick, fragrant fog. Bones rattled and scratched against the boxes' wood as if a dozen skeletons were dancing a jig within the mists. The undead were rising.

The paladin strode forward, her shield raised with one gauntleted hand and her longsword shining radiantly in the other. The fog glowed around her like a sunlit cloud—and then it erupted into a second flurry of motion, this time from the inside out, as dozens of avian skeletons hurtled up in a lace-winged flock. They hurled themselves into the paladin's face, threw their bodies against her shield, bashed against her armored legs. The sheer momentum of the skeletal flock drove the woman stumbling backward. Her red scarf fell away, confirming Isiem's suspicions that she was a half-elf.

"You were wrong," Ena said, letting a second glass ball tumble back into her cloak. She sidestepped around the chaos, looking for an opening. A pair of hooked knives flashed in her hands, reflecting the blue fire of the paladin's sword. "They're not undead. That fog is holy water, and it isn't doing anything to them."

"I can see that," Isiem said through gritted teeth.

The black-boned birds weren't attacking the paladin. She was only an obstacle to them, and they whirled past her like windblown leaves parting around a tree trunk. What they wanted—what drew them and drove them—was in the glass cases at Isiem's feet.

They swept toward him, sieving the air with their whistling wings. Between the birds' naked ribs, the skeletal kobold hands dangled like stirrups, twitching as they neared the cases and their cargo of dead birds.

As they drew near their goal, the flock funneled into a tight formation: a vortex of bones spinning toward Isiem. His hood blew back as they approached. Dust stung his eyes, blurring the oncoming skeletons into a single dark cloud.

He could still see them well enough to kill them, though. Squinting through his tears, Isiem focused on a spell.

The wizard plucked a tiny crystal cone from a pocket. Holding the cone to his lips as if it were a war horn, Isiem whispered an incantation through the polished stone. As he spoke the last word, he pointed two fingers in a V directed at the flock of winged skeletons and the paladin still caught in their midst.

The half-elf threw herself to the floor, not a moment too soon. Wintry cold and bitter frost blew from Isiem's crystal, smashing into the skeletal birds. Several of them burst apart immediately, blasted into pieces by the elemental force of the cold. Shards of their bones ricocheted off the walls and embedded themselves in the hanging hams like hellish peppercorns. Others froze and fell to the ground, where their ice-rimed bones shattered on impact. A few flapped away at the edges, slow and lopsided under sudden coats of ice. Ena pounced on the crippled birds, smashing them to the ground with a box lid and stomping them under her boots.

In seconds, it was over. The paladin picked up a discarded piece of straw-flecked sacking and scooped the last of the struggling skeletons into it, then dropped the whole bundle into one of the empty boxes and put the lid back on. "I don't think these were made to fight," she said, while knotting a rope around the box. Its lid thumped with the captive skeletons' efforts at escape. "They had some other purpose. Do you know what it was?"

"I have a guess," Isiem said, "but it's only a guess."

The half-elven woman rubbed her forehead, where a long red scratch disappeared into her dark auburn hair. With the scarf gone, she was a handsome woman, with high cheekbones and a strong square jaw. Not girlish, and perhaps not beautiful in the traditional sense, but possessed of a calm certitude that drew the eye. "I expect you'll want to study them, then." She examined her sword for dirt or damage, found none, and sheathed it. "Can you do so safely?"

"I should be able to." Isiem plucked a shard of black bone from the side of a ham. He could see no sign that the meat had been contaminated, but he pulled out a small knife and carved out the flesh around the puncture mark anyway. One never knew what taints such creatures carried. "Help me collect the pieces, please."

It didn't take long to collect the larger bones. The smaller fragments, however, had been scattered across the warehouse by the force of Isiem's icy blast, and spotting them among the piles of spilled grain was tedious work. After the better part of an hour, they still hadn't gathered all the pieces, and Ena began to cast meaningful glances toward the door.

"We should go," the dwarf said. "It'll be sunrise soon, and someone might come to check on the watchmen. No need to linger looking for bone scraps. We've got enough."

"I'd like to find them all," Isiem said.

"Why?" Ena pushed down her hood, rubbing at a nick above her left ear. Short brown stubble covered most of her head, but scars from a long-ago explosion left irregular bald patches across her scalp and eyebrows. "You can't cover up that we were here. The devilers are going to know that anyway. All you'll do is maybe get yourself caught."

"I won't get caught." Isiem showed her one of the little balls of resin he kept tucked in a pocket. An ivory eyelash was embedded in the gum, its pale arc barely visible. "Not by any ordinary watchman. And if they've got someone capable of breaking through my magic, we'll have trouble whether or not I stay to pick up these bones."

"What makes the bones so important?" the half-elven paladin asked. "Why risk yourself over them, even if you do have a spell to hide with?" She had wrapped the red scarf around her face again, concealing every-thing but her eyes, so Isiem could not be sure of her expression.

He heard no suspicion in her voice, though, only hon-est curiosity, and so he answered honestly in turn. "I think they're plaguebearers."

"Plaguebearers?" Ena recoiled. She eyed the toppled boxes nervously, scrubbing a hand against the front of her jerkin as if trying to rid herself of some invisible stain. "When were you planning to warn us?"

"When we left." Isiem shrugged. "The paladin says she can cure diseases, and I don't think the plague is directed at us, nor do I think the sickness escaped from its bonds. In my estimation, we are in little danger. Nonetheless, I'd rather not risk ordinary Pezzacki if we can avoid it. I've been wrong before."

"Who's it meant for, then?" Ena asked. "They sent it to us."

"The strix," said the paladin. Her dark eyes hardened above the scarf. "Birds, not people. Those dead birds in the cases are meant to carry sickness. The winged skeletons were meant to . . . disperse them, perhaps?"

"Something like that," Isiem agreed. "The preserved birds hold the sickness, and the skeletal carriers see that it reaches its intended victims. The cases were not opened, so the plague should be contained. That's my theory, anyway. It's only a theory. I'll need to study them." He waved them toward the door. "In the mean-time, I'll try to find the rest of these bone fragments. Don't wait for me."

"We'll meet at the usual place when you're ready," Ena said. "Two days?"

"Two days." Without waiting for Ena and her taller companion to leave the warehouse, Isiem resumed his search for the scattered pieces. A cold draft through the door told him when they had gone.

Hours later, stiff-backed and bleary-eyed, Isiem looked up to see soft gray light spilling through the warehouse's small, filthy windows. Morning was upon him. His spell of disguise had long since faded, and although he wasn't sure if he'd found all the bone shards in the warehouse, there was no more time to look. He had to go now, or risk being seen and recognized when the sun rose high enough to show his face.

The boxes were already stacked and waiting by the warehouse doors. Isiem cinched the neck of the sack he'd been filling and dropped it atop the heap. He plucked a few strands from a knot of horsehair in his pocket and let them float to the ground, weaving a short incantation between the falling threads.

From shadows and sea fog and five scattered hairs, a mottled black horse arose. It stood patiently as Isiem loaded the cases onto the black horse's back, covered them with sacking and fastened the bundle in place with crisscrossed ropes, then took the animal's bridle and led it out to the streets of Pezzack.

Off in the distance, blurred by fog, the small lantern-lit boats of fishermen pushed out to the cold black sea past the creaking, floating hulks of Docktown. Across the way, a baker's hearth threw a warm orange glow like a lighthouse in the mist. No one else was awake or abroad. Fog swirled over the ruts in the town's dirt roads and slicked the cobblestones of its few paved streets. It enclosed Isiem in a gentle haze, lulling him toward somnolence.

Until he rounded a corner and found himself abruptly face to face with a child.

The child was eight, ten, something like that. Boy or girl, he couldn't tell. Wide brown eyes, a smattering of freckles, a dirty wool cap pulled low over protruding ears. A puff of startled breath escaped the child's lips and hung white in the air between them.

Their gazes locked, and in those huge waif's eyes Isiem saw a fatal flash of recognition.

His illusory disguise was gone. It was his true face that the child saw. And that face, Isiem knew, was difficult to forget. As filled with colorful eccentrics as Pezzack was, a near-albino Nidalese from the Uskwood still stood out. There was only one such man in this part of Cheliax, and that one was known to be wanted.

He would be remembered. If the child was a loyalist—as some were, even in this rebellion-rife border town—Isiem could be reported. Then the Hellknights would come, implacable in iron, and the tensions in Pezzack would explode.

If the child was a spy for one of the other rebel groups, Isiem's position wasn't much better. The Galtan faction, led by a madman named Habar Curl, was always looking for proof that his rivals were insufficiently pure in their dedication to the cause. The slightest whiff of cooperation with Imperial Cheliax was enough to earn a beheading, as far as they were concerned, and tolerating a Nidalese traitor went far beyond that. There was no question that if he caught Isiem's friends, Habar Curl would bend their necks to his blade.

The safest course, therefore, would be to kill the child. It would be so very easy in the sleeping silence of the town. The mists would hide his bloody work; the sea would swallow its aftermath.

But Isiem hesitated, and the child spun on his foot— *her* foot?—and in a swirl of rags and skittering footsteps, vanished into the night.

Isiem didn't pursue. Swallowing a mixture of relief and fear, he tightened his grip on the black horse's reins and turned down his own path through Pezzack. Once again, quiet closed around him, broken only by the muted clop of the horse's hooves and the clacking of bones inside the boxes it bore.

It was not a loud sound, but that clacking filled the wizard's ears with echoes. Other places, other bones. Pangolais. Nisroch. Westcrown.

He had enough of those burdening his conscience already. Deaths filled his memories: friends, enemies, victims of fate and circumstance. Some had been avoidable. Most had not.

As he turned down the last twisting alley to his temporary refuge, Isiem wondered about tonight's encounter. Was it sparing the child or killing him that was the mistake?

He didn't know. He couldn't. Such knowledge was not for mortals in this world.

But there was only one choice that he would not regret. And as he stepped into the quiet darkness of his borrowed home, leaving the budding dawn behind, Isiem knew that he had made it.

Chapter Two
The Nightblade

Two days later, the paladin came to Isiem's door.

She wore a curly black wig over her real hair, and she'd donned a wicked-looking false scar that twisted her nose to the side, but he recognized her immediately. Her stride was the same, long and loping, and she had made no effort to disguise her height. More obviously, she still carried the sword she'd had in the warehouse, and it still displayed its Iomedaean mark proudly.

"You're not trying very hard," he observed as he let her in. Out of habit, Isiem glanced up and down the alley before closing the door behind his guest. He saw no one.

"I don't have to," the paladin replied with a shrug. "Nobody's looking for me. I can't say the same about you." She regarded him with a cocked eyebrow. "You let the child live."

"Does that surprise you?" Isiem asked, nettled. "I would have thought you'd approve."

"Did I say I didn't?" She moved into the room, looking around skeptically. There wasn't much to see. Isiem had moved into a small chandlery squeezed between a tannery and a butcher's yard. The candlemaker had been caught up in the conflagration of Second Ashes; whether he'd met his death in the raging fires or at the end of a rebel's knife, no one knew, but when the smoke had finally settled, nothing was left of the man but charred bones. His brother had collected his molds and any other equipment worth salvaging and had offered the building for rent.

Small, remote, and besieged by the smells and sounds of the stockyard, the shop had languished, unwanted, until Isiem moved in. It had suited his needs perfectly, but it was hardly a welcoming place. A stained wooden table held Isiem's traveling spellbooks, a cheap lamp, and a small collection of arcane equipment. The boxes from the warehouse were stacked along a wall, covered by a canvas sheet. Other than Isiem's spartan cot and the worn, shapeless pillow beside it where Honey slept, there was nothing that marked it as a home.

The brindle dog had been sleeping on that pillow when the paladin came in. The last year had been hard on Honey. Suddenly, it seemed, she was old. Cold mornings gave her an aching, stiff-hipped walk, she was mostly deaf, and both her eyes had developed the cloudy glow of cataracts. Isiem wasn't surprised that she failed to notice the woman until their guest was already inside. Once she finally did, her only reaction was a startled woof, a glare, and an indignant return to her nap.

The paladin chuckled softly. "Quite a fearsome guard you've got." She moved away from the dog and pulled at a corner of the canvas, peeking at the boxes underneath. "Did you find out what the birds' bones were for?"

"I expected to give that information to Ena."

"She's busy." The half-elven woman dropped the canvas and turned back to Isiem. "It occurs to me that I never introduced myself. My name is Kyril. I serve Iomedae, the Inheritor."

Isiem inclined his head. "Thank you. I'm—"

"Isiem, a Nidalese wizard in exile. Born somewhere in the hinterlands, trained in the Dusk Hall of Pangolais, assigned to the Midnight Guard of Westcrown, then sent to Devil's Perch. Where you feigned your own death, abandoned your homeland, and fought to keep the strix from being eradicated by Imperial Cheliax." Kyril's smile was brief and superior. "Ena told me much about you. We've been friends for a long time."

"It seems you have the advantage."

"I like to know who I'm dealing with. As much as I can." She shrugged and glanced back at the canvas-draped boxes. "So . . . what *are* they?"

"More or less what we thought. Magical constructs built to spread disease among the strix. Mindless, but ordered to scatter shreds of those sick dead birds among the strix's suspected hunting and nesting grounds. They were painted black for concealment against the night sky, and their claws were enchanted to amplify the plagues in those corpses."

"Do you know who made them?"

Isiem shook his head, frowning. "Not with any real certainty. I believe the skeletons were done by a wizard in Egorian, or one who trained there. One of my early teachers was from that city, and she taught me a similar preparation of preservatives to be used in necromancy. I never found much use for the formulation, though. Some of the materials are too difficult to procure elsewhere. So your wizard, I think, must have trained in Cheliax and had access to the ports and apothecaries of Egorian. The plague birds, by contrast, came from Varisia—but that's only a guess based on the distribution of species, and some of the banding patterns on the blackbirds' wings."

Kyril stroked a thumb over the radiant sword symbol engraved on her pommel. "Would you be able to find the creator? The necromancer?"

"Not without more research, and some questioning in the field. Given time, however, I believe I could." He said it neutrally. It was no secret what methods of "questioning" a Nidalese was likely to employ, and he did not expect a paladin to approve.

"In Egorian?"

"I've given it some thought."

She nodded slowly, dark eyes narrowing. "Yes, I can see why. It's a mystery, isn't it? More than that, it's a challenge. And it gets you out of Pezzack, a town that may become decidedly unsafe for you soon."

Isiem gave her a lopsided little smile. It was true that he was in danger here, but he didn't expect her to care. "You sound like you want me to go."

"I do," she said, "but not to Egorian."

"No?"

"No." Kyril turned the chair away from Isiem's desk and straddled it, pushing her sword out of the way with the unconscious ease of long habit. "I have another task that calls for your expertise. A bigger mystery, a greater challenge. And, if you care, the chance to do a larger good. If not, the chance for considerable wealth. We're willing to pay for your time."

A sarcastic reply leaped to the tip of Isiem's tongue, but he held it back. Much of what she said rang true: he *was* looking for a challenge worthy of his skills, and he *would* likely have to leave soon. If Kyril had already heard about the child who'd seen him, then imperial authorities and rival rebels would soon hear the news as well. He'd successfully evaded all his enemies thus far, but only because they hadn't known he was still living in Pezzack. Once they did know, they'd come looking with magic, and no false-face illusions would save him.

And there was, in truth, little reason to stay. Pezzack was a poor and charmless town, and he'd grown disillusioned with its incompetent rebellion long ago. Only two things kept Isiem in this place: his friendship with Kirii, the *rokoa* of the Windspire strix, and his dog Honey, who had gotten far too frail for the hardships of the road.

Kyril saw him looking at the sleeping old dog. "We can find a place for her."

"I have one," Isiem replied. He'd decided on that the night before, while thinking about Egorian. "Tell me about your task."

"Eledwyn," the paladin said. "Do you know the name?"

"No."

"Mesandroth, then. Do you know that one?"

"Yes." In the Dusk Hall he'd had a friend—a young sorcerer named Ascaros—who was distantly descended from that infamous, long-gone wizard. Even among the Nidalese, Mesandroth had been legendary for his cruelty and his mastery of magic. He'd commanded extraordinary power, and worked jaw-dropping feats, in another age.

For that reason, and others, Mesandroth's legacy remained strong in Nidal.

"Eledwyn was one of his apprentices." Kyril paused, then amended: "Not 'apprentice,' exactly. She was an elven wizard whom he lured into his service. Although outwardly loyal, she planned a secret rebellion against her master. He wanted to use her, and her research, to find a path toward immortality—and Eledwyn had no wish to help him."

"What happened to her?"

Kyril shrugged. "Her rebellion never came to pass. Mesandroth learned of her treachery and crushed her before she had a chance to execute any of her plans. But we believe that one of her secret workshops—a place called Fiendslair—may have survived, and with it some of the research she developed to destroy him. That research may be extremely valuable to our cause."

"The rebellion in Pezzack?" Isiem affected a lightness he didn't feel.

The half-elf gave him a flat look. "The rebellion against House Thrune," she said. "The rebellion against the diabolists who hold Cheliax in thrall to Hell."

"There are some who'd say I'm not much better," Isiem pointed out.

"None on this expedition." Kyril leaned forward, her voice dropping urgently. Her breath smelled faintly of sweet cloves. "We need you. Mesandroth was Nidalese. Eledwyn was not, but she was trained in his methods and worked at his behest. A Nidalese arcanist is crucial to our expedition."

"And I'm the one you can get."

"You're the one we can *trust*."

"I'm honored, but—"

She held up a hand. "Don't answer now." Pushing back her chair, the half-elf stood. "Take some time. Not too much, because I don't know that you *have* too much, but consider your choices carefully before you make one. Our cause is good. So is our coin. And there may come a time, soon, when you find it useful to have friends."

Kyril strode to the door and paused, checking her wig and false scar with light, careful touches to ensure her disguise was still in place. Then she put a hand on the doorknob and gave Isiem a last look. "We'll wait three days for your decision. You know how to reach Ena?"

He nodded.

"Send word to her. If we hear nothing after three days, we'll take your answer as no. I would prefer it wasn't, of course."

"What do you hope to find there?" Isiem asked, just as the woman began to open the door. "In Eledwyn's workshop."

Kyril shut the door again, cutting off the thin line of sunlight that streaked her face. She glanced over a shoulder, her expression impossible to read. "A weapon."

"What sort of weapon?"

"I don't know." For an instant, her jaw tightened and her brow creased; then the flicker of apprehension was gone. "My compatriots can tell you more. Eledwyn called it a 'nightblade.' That's all I know. That, and she wrote that it was capable of destroying empires."

The hint of hesitation in her voice intrigued him. "That's what you want, isn't it?"

"It is." The paladin turned away. "Yes." Then she opened the door and was gone, her last word hanging behind her.

Isiem went to Windspire the next morning.

He rode, although it would have been easy enough to teleport himself there with a spell. The wizard wanted the time alone to think. The day was clear and brisk, with a salt wind at his back, and the solitude cleared his mind. The smoke and clamor of Pezzack receded, vanishing behind the line of ill-kept watchtowers that was meant to guard the town against the strix.

As the miles rolled by under his horse's hooves, the coastland's tough grasses and thorny bushes gave way to barren hills and wind-sculpted stone. Hour by hour, the ascent grew steeper; the road dwindled into a goat track and then vanished altogether. By twilight, the red and black claws of Devil's Perch were distantly visible against the shadowy silhouette of the Menador Mountains, and Isiem had made peace with his decision.

He dismounted from his horse and, with a word, unraveled the magic that bound the black steed to him. The animal disappeared, and Isiem began another short incantation. With the last word, he stepped forward, and passed through an infinite instant of aching, surreal emptiness to arrive abruptly in Kirii's tent.

The rokoa was pouring tea from a kettle when he appeared. For the smallest of moments she froze, then straightened deliberately and turned toward him. Perfumed steam shrouded her face and threaded through the black feathers of her enormous, folded wings.

"It is rude to come into private rooms without warning," she said. After a year's practice, her Taldane was very good, although the clicks and whistles of strixtongue inflected her speech heavily. "Even for friends."

"I'm glad you still consider me a friend." Isiem shook off the lingering disorientation of his spell—teleportation was seldom *unpleasant*, exactly, but it did take a moment to adjust—and offered her a formal obeisance, hands clasped in front of his chest as he bowed.

When he raised his head, Kirii was smiling. It was a peculiar smile: the gesture was not natural to the strix, and the rokoa's small, sharp teeth gave it an unintentionally predatory cast. But the awkwardness itself was touching. From the beginning, their friendship had been founded on such halting, clumsy gestures of goodwill.

"I do," Kirii said. "But I also know that many in Windspire do not, and I cannot fault you for coming here in secret. The *itaraak* might have given you a sharp welcome."

"Despite all I've done for them." He'd meant to say it lightly, but a note of bitterness crept into his words.

"Yes." The strix's odd, pupilless eyes fixed on him, their gold-on-gold striations pulsing slightly. Geometric tattoos covered Kirii's face, masking her youth behind the dignity of a full rokoa. Although Isiem knew his friend had come to her position as a bright-burning idealist, a year of carrying her people's spiritual burdens seemed to have dimmed her early fervor. She seemed more cautious, more measured, less the impetuous young firebrand he'd known. "My people are proud. They do not welcome reminders of their debt to an outsider, and they are quick to believe they won their victories alone. Pride, and suspicion, make them doubt you now.

"We won on the battlefield, but our enemies strike at us from hiding. On all sides we are beset by face-less evils and treacheries. All the itaraak know of their foes is that they are human—outsiders, like you. Some say you are in league with the soldiers of Cheliax. That is true, if not as they mean it. You do work with the Chelaxians, and sometimes the itaraak see it."

"I work with rebels to help your people, yes. They've helped you again, by the by." Isiem briefly described what he'd found in the warehouse with Ena and Kyril. At the end of his tale, he handed over a small, flat box: one of the black-painted avian skeletons and one of the plague birds, sealed safely in glass and with ward spells, along with a copy of his notes on their enchantments and likely purpose. "We disrupted this attempt, but there may be another. It might be wise to prepare a cure, or an antidote, for whatever plague their necromancers had planned."

Translucent membranes sheeted across the rokoa's eyes in a sideways blink. "This I will do." She accepted the box uneasily, putting it aside quickly and shaking her fingers as if to rid them of invisible filth. "And you? You speak as if you are leaving."

"I am."

Kirii nodded. It was another learned gesture, although less affected than her smile. She did not ask why he was going. It was, Isiem supposed, explanation enough that he'd had to teleport into her tent instead of walking openly through Windspire. He had *saved* the strix—not only their lives but their ancestral home-lands and the very identity of their tribe—yet instead of greeting him as a hero, they regarded him with con-stant distrust. "This is your farewell?"

"It is." He paused, fidgeting with the knots that tied shut one of his pouches of spell components. "I have one last favor to ask."

"Ask."

"My dog. Honey." The words caught in his throat, soft but jagged, like a wad of warm resin rolled in sharp glass. "She's old, and she doesn't have long left. Will you care for her?"

"The warbeast that could not fight? I remember that one." Another sideways blink. After a pause, Kirii ducked her head in a quick, bobbing nod. "Yes. I will do this."

"Thank you." The rokoa's tent was the safest place Isiem could imagine for his dog. It was warm, secure, and well guarded, and although it *was* perched on the top of a flat spire that rose fifty feet above a chasm, that hardly mattered for a dog so old she could scarcely be coaxed past the doorstep to make water.

Whatever remained of Honey's days, she would live them out comfortably, and that was the best gift he could give the friend who had retaught him the joy of life amid ashes.

"It is Windspire who should thank you," Kirii said, "but as they will not, I will give the goodwill that should have been yours to the beast."

"I'm grateful." Isiem bowed his head again, more deeply this time. "Truly. I have been honored to know you."

Kirii's nostrils flared in half-feigned alarm. "You are not going away to *die*, I hope."

"So do I," Isiem said wryly. He took a scroll from a hollow bone case at his belt and unfurled it. "But whatever happens, I doubt I'll return to Devils' Perch. You'll have to find another liaison to the rebels."

"A difficult task. Perhaps for the best, however. It may serve well to have an itaraak in that position." Kirii sighed in contemplation, then shook her head. "I do not like farewells. Go, Isiem. Go, knowing that without you Windspire would be nothing."

He did.

The spell on his scroll brought him back to the chandler's shop, where Honey was snoring on her pillow in the dark. It was late, and the town was sleeping. Isiem summoned a spark of light to break the blackness, dimming the magic so that it would not disturb his dog.

She hadn't touched the food he'd left her that morning. The sight of the meat and gravy congealed in its bowl made Isiem's heart sink.

He knelt beside her and buried his face in her fur. Honey lifted her head and licked at his cradling arm. Her tail thumped sleepily against the floor.

It felt profoundly wrong that he should have to leave his friend in the twilight of her days. It felt like a betrayal. But he couldn't take her with him, and he trusted Kirii to care for her. The selfishness of forcing Honey onto a road she could not walk would be far crueler than leaving her behind.

Isiem sat helplessly on the floor and breathed in the dusty sweet scent of her fur, and when he could no longer hold it in, he wept.

When dawn broke, he took her to Windspire.

Chapter Three
Companions in the Light

That night, under cover of darkness, Isiem went to find Ena.

The dwarf didn't keep a home in Pezzack, as far as Isiem knew, but she did have a few regular haunts. The primary one was the back room of a nameless tavern that catered to laborers visiting from the new silver mines. The owner was a friend to the rebellion, and his workers often caught bits of tavern gossip relevant to Isiem's dealings with the strix. They knew of his interest and, for a new pair of boots or a jug of decent beer, were usually willing to tell him whatever they'd heard.

They also knew of his relationship with Ena, and when he crossed the threshold into the tavern's smoky warmth that evening, the barkeep nodded to the back room's door. He was a former mountain trapper, a big gruff fellow who'd lost part of his right foot in an accident a few years ago. A passing strix had dropped a waterskin, saving his life, and he'd never forgotten.

"Got that black beer you like in back," he said. The code phrase meant Ena was in the back room, and she wasn't alone.

"Thank you." Keeping his hood low, Isiem passed a table full of muddy-booted dwarves and a seamy-faced woman with thin brown hair who sat alone in the corner, staring listlessly into a jar of cloudy grog. He pushed open a door that sagged on hook-latch hinges and went down three short stairs. Rough brick walls hemmed him in, brushing close against his sides.

At the bottom of the stairs he came to a cellar walled with more bricks. Beer barrels and enormous, brown-fogged glass jugs of homebrewed wine sat on the floor. Wooden racks against the walls held dusty bottles bearing the seals of more expensive vintages. It had been years since the last drop was drained from those bottles, but the inn's owner kept them in their racks as a remembrance of better days.

And to hide a secret door. Isiem lifted the second-to-last bottle from the left on the third shelf. Part of the wooden support had been carved out under it, creating a gap just large enough to fit a man's finger. He slipped his in and pulled up, then out.

The wine rack slid toward him, bringing a section of the brick wall with it. Isiem stepped through the gap and into a cramped, oddly configured room where Ena, Kyril, and four unfamiliar men sat around a makeshift table.

The oldest of the men appeared to be about fifty. Tall and broad-shouldered, he carried himself like a soldier, although he wore the divided yellow robes of a traveling Sarenite priest. He had a short, neat beard of brown streaked with white, and his bright blue eyes twinkled with good humor. A sheathed scimitar hung at his side.

The other three men seemed to be together. Their apparent leader was a lean, smirking half-elf in a weather-beaten cloak. Over his chest sat a bronze clasp depicting a snake across a shield. He had black eyes and a black beard and, Isiem was willing to wager, an equally black heart. Although rarely worn so prominently, that shield-and-serpent clasp marked its wearer to knowledgeable eyes as an agent of the Aspis Consortium. Isiem had never dealt with the Consortium personally, but he had heard much about its workings from his one-time mistress, Velenne. He distrusted the man immediately.

Thick-necked thugs sat on either side of the Aspis agent. One was tall and one was short, but both had the dead-eyed, incurious faces of men who dealt in violence for a living and were not overly particular about the recipients of their trade. The short one's arms were covered with colorful, obscene tattoos; the tall one wore wire-rimmed spectacles and chewed an unlit cigar. They looked up as Isiem entered, glanced in unison at the man he presumed to be their employer, then returned by studying the newcomer.

The tall one cracked his knuckles. Both of his ears were knotty stubs of scar tissue. They made peculiar bookends to the expensive, delicate spectacles. The glasses confirmed Isiem's suspicion that these were members of the Aspis Consortium; no ordinary thug would be able to afford such costly lenses. "You the wizard?"

"Yes," Kyril answered before Isiem could speak for himself. "Isiem of Pangolais. He has been invited to join our expedition as our advisor on matters arcane."

All eyes turned to Isiem.

The wizard pushed his hood down slowly. He had not expected to be confronted with an audience, and he needed a moment to gather his thoughts. Revealing himself bought a little time: with his unusually pale complexion, near-black eyes, and long ivory hair, he was distinctively Nidalese, and the reputation of his people could give hardened killers pause.

It did these. The Aspis agent and his heavies drew back visibly as Isiem pulled an empty chair to their table. "Tell me what you hope to achieve."

The Sarenite cleric leaned forward, steepling his fingers under his neatly trimmed beard. "Kyril told you some of it already."

"Some." Isiem glanced at the paladin, who nodded in guarded acknowledgment. "She told me that you were seeking one of Eledwyn's sanctuaries, and that you believed there might be a weapon inside. A 'nightblade,' she called it. But she didn't know what it was. Do you?"

"Not exactly," the older man admitted. "I've devoted my life to studying Mesandroth Fiendlorn's work, yet I know very little about him. He sought immortality, we know that. One of the avenues he pursued was possession. The question that intrigued the archmage was: if a demon can possess the body of a man, why should a man not possess the body of a demon? In such a form, he could be immortal.

"Of course, if such a thing were possible, it would undoubtedly corrupt the mortal soul beyond all recognition. Bodies shape our beings, just as words shape our thoughts. Putting a mortal soul into a demonic shell would no more grant true immortality than undeath would. Very possibly, it would grant less.

"Perhaps unsurprisingly, however, that didn't seem to concern the archmage. Mesandroth devoted considerable resources to exploring this possibility. Eledwyn aided him—but she also plotted against him. Her own research into the far planes revealed a weapon that was particularly lethal to fiends. Devils, demons, and daemons alike were destroyed by its wrath. She wrote that 'the terror took them, and the oozing death . . . and the one sound that came from all their drowning throats, the one song they could muster, was a howling hymn to ruin.' She called it a 'nightblade,' and hoped it would destroy her unwanted master. Her workshop was somewhere in what is now the Umbral Basin between Molthune and Nidal. We intend to find it."

Isiem arched an eyebrow. "So you want to venture into the Umbral Basin in search of something that could make a host of demons shriek a 'hymn to ruin.' That strikes you as prudent?"

Ena shrugged. The stubbly headed dwarf leaned back far enough to prop her hobnailed boots up on the table, angling her legs so that her feet were nearly in the short thug's face. "A thing like that, it could be useful."

"It could be *profitable*," the Aspis agent said. He rubbed a thumb over the golden snake on his cloak clasp. "Think of the buyers. Crusaders in Mendev. Freedom fighters in Cheliax and all their devil-cursed colonies. Governments mopping up after demoniacs or Lamashtan cultists. The demand across the world market would be incalculable. That's why we bank-rolled Teglias." He nodded his chin in the direction of the yellow-robed cleric. "Piety is well and good, but it's results we want."

"Profit?" Isiem regarded Kyril with open surprise. "That seems beneath a paladin of Iomedae."

The half-elven woman flushed. "We may not share the same reasons, but we do share the same goal. The Aspis Consortium is financing our expedition in return for information and, possibly, a specimen nightblade. Their money affords us a chance to strike a real blow for the liberation of Cheliax. I believe that's worthy."

Ena lifted her head, studying Isiem over her crossed boots. "It's not like you to be squeamish about allies. I figured *they'd* be the ones to hesitate about *you*. Glad Kyril wouldn't take my bet after all."

"Explorations are expensive," Teglias said. If he shared any of Kyril's hesitations, he did not show them. The bearded cleric's demeanor was smoothly matter-of-fact. "Without Aspis sponsorship, I should never have been able to expand my search beyond the temple library. Ganoven and his men are here only to ensure that our patrons' generosity receives its fair reward. They are not to influence the course of our investigations or interfere with our work. I assure you, they will stay out of your way."

"Absolutely," Ganoven agreed with a smirk, drawing Abadar's scales across his chest to mimic a piously sworn oath. "You won't even know we're here."

Isiem ignored the Aspis agent. He directed his questions to Teglias. "What do you need me for?"

"I am a historian," the priest replied, smoothing the front of his yellow robes with a palm, "and I've made a particular study of the lore surrounding Mesandroth Fiendlorn. Reading about magic, however, is a poor substitute for living it. We need a wizard. In particular, we need a Nidalese wizard. The traditions of Pangolais have changed very little in the millennia since Mesandroth tasked his apprentices with unlocking the secrets of immortality. The arts they used may be similar to those you've studied."

"Why should I help you?" Isiem asked.

Ena snorted. She dropped her boots off the table, thudding them to the ground one after the other, and thrust a stubby finger at Isiem. "Don't play coy. You want freedom for Cheliax as much as any of us does." She shot a meaningful glance at the Aspis toughs. "More than some, I'd wager. You've spent a year risking your life to keep the strix free. Your *life*. And for what? We've been thinking too small. We intercept boxes of bones in Pezzack while the devilers field armies to bring whole nations under the black and red. We'll never get ahead that way. The rebellion needs something big. This could be it."

"I can't promise our journey will be entirely safe," Teglias added, "but we've taken all reasonable precautions. Ganoven has arranged for us to travel with a caravan for part of our route. Once we split off, we'll be on our own, but Ena and Kyril are quite capable of handling most hazards we might encounter on the road. Ganoven will bring Pulcher and Copple"—he nodded to the tall and short heavies, respectively—"and so we should be well equipped for swords."

"Prefer my hammer, if it's all the same to you," Pulcher said. "Or the knife." He held up the big, sawtooth blade he'd been using to pare his nails, then grinned and went back to work. A small pile of dirty yellow nail shavings had already accumulated on the table in front of him. He pushed his unlit cigar from side to side in his mouth as he trimmed.

Ena stared at him, her face a study in fascinated disgust. After a moment she shook her head and gave Isiem a shrug. "There you have it, then. Swords and hammers and a knife only slightly dulled by peeling thumbnails. You'll be safe as a babe in its cradle."

"A well-paid babe," Isiem said. "So I was told."

"So you were," Teglias agreed. He rose, gesturing to the others. Isiem didn't move. "That is best discussed privately, however."

The others filed out. Pulcher left his pile of nail trimmings on the table, and spat his chewed cigar onto the floor as he left. Ganoven stopped abruptly, clicked his tongue, and pointed to the soggy thing as if correcting a dog who had dropped a retrieved fowl too soon. With a heavy, theatrical sigh, Pulcher stooped and picked up his cigar, carrying it gingerly between his fingers as they departed. Copple's malevolent chuckles trailed them out of the room.

When they were all out of sight, and Ena had closed the secret door behind them, Teglias sat again. "I have more than a location for the library," he said, holding Isiem's gaze steadily with his clear blue eyes. "I have a key. It's damaged, and very old, but I believe it's authentic and still functional. Would you like to see it?"

It was plain that the cleric wanted to show it to him, so Isiem inclined his head in a slow nod. He *was* curious. "Do the others not know about this?"

"They know it exists. I haven't shown it to the Aspis agents. Ganoven insists he should be permitted to study it, but I see no reason to indulge him. If he had any real arcane expertise, it would be another matter, but—well, you've met him. His pompousness is rivaled only by his ignorance. Such is the price we pay for Aspis money.

"Kyril advised me against showing it to you, either . . . but I want you to know how much we are in earnest." Teglias unlatched his satchel and withdrew a long, scabbardlike case of hardened leather. It had a curious latch: brass and red copper worked into the winged angel-ankh emblem of Sarenrae.

The priest flicked it open and withdrew a corroded black key, as long as Isiem's arm from elbow to wrist. The metal was melted and misshapen in places, and there was a toothy gap in its handle where a jewel or some other piece seemed to be missing.

Isiem took the key from Teglias's outstretched hand. "What happened to its bearer? Its condition doesn't suggest anything pleasant."

"You need not be concerned about that," the Sarenite said, crossing his arms and watching Isiem intently. "The key wasn't damaged until long after Eledwyn's stronghold fell. Someone tried to prevent the place from ever being reopened."

"I'm sure they had good reasons," Isiem said.

"They had reasons, yes. Good ones? Maybe, maybe not. But tell me: what do you make of the artifact?"

Isiem turned it over. The light was not good, and he lacked most of his tools, but he did have a glass with him. He took it from its padded pocket and held it to the key.

Under its tarnish and the corrosion of ages, the metal was silver. Its intricate piercework and the care with which it had been crafted spoke of Nidalese work. For thousands of years, the silversmiths of Pangolais had applied the Kuthite expertise with small blades to work metal into airy, intricately carved forms. No one else could match them in the art.

A few of the diamonds in the key's shank had survived. From the shallowness of their crowns and their large culets, he could see that they were of an antique cut popular in Pangolais nearly a millennium ago. That cut had been occasionally revived by later fashions, though, and was not indicative of the piece's age.

The slight reddish cloudiness to the stones suggested they originated from the Menador Mountains near Ridwan, however, and that *did* confirm the key's antiquity. Diamonds had not been found in that desolate land for centuries. The handful of gems that its mines had ever produced were prized by Zon-Kuthon's faithful, who said they were stained by the blood of their god. Such diamonds were said to possess extraordinary magical resonances.

Isiem had never had the opportunity to confirm those rumors for himself, but in that moment, holding that ruined key, he believed them. In the few minutes he'd spent studying the piece, he had become aware of an uncomfortable aura pervading the key. A simple cantrip confirmed it: the key was heavily enchanted, and that enchantment was soaked in evil.

"It appears to be authentic," he said neutrally, returning it to Teglias.

The Sarenite accepted the key with no sign of discomfort and returned it to its locked case. "Then you'll join us? There is real knowledge to be found in this place. Real magic."

"And real danger." Isiem didn't care much about money, in truth, but he *did* care about having leverage within the expedition. Having held that key, and sensed the malice embedded in its metal, he wanted a fuller say in their decisions. Particularly if some of them were likely to be fools. "I don't intend to risk myself cheaply."

"How much do you want?"

"The Aspis agents are, I presume, partners in your venture?"

"Yes."

"Then I'll take a partnership stake. Equal to theirs."

"That's an ambitious demand." The cleric coughed out an unconvincing laugh. "They've claimed a sixty percent share. I *can't* give you an equal stake."

"Renegotiate with them. Or find another wizard." Isiem stood, starting for the door, but the older man waved him back down.

"I'll try," he said tiredly, pinching the bridge of his nose. "I make no promises. Why is it so important that your stake be equal to theirs? Why not ours?"

"You're idealists. They're mercenaries."

That earned a weary chuckle. "As are you, I suppose. Fair enough that you should want to let them do your bargaining for you. But the Aspis Consortium has already put a considerable investment into our endeavor. They'll argue that you haven't done the same."

"True. I haven't. But their contribution was in the past, and mine is what you need to move forward. I think I have rather better leverage." Isiem folded his hands calmly. It wasn't a show: he felt a great serenity within, as if he'd rolled the dice of fate and was waiting for the multiverse to give him an answer. Whichever way they fell, he'd be content.

"There is that." Teglias rested his chin on the heel of his hand, regarding the Nidalese wizard across the table. The candles flickered between them, stirred by the cleric's sigh. "I'll put it before them. Again: I make no promises. But Ganoven needs a success to rise in the ranks, and he was the one who first suggested recruiting you."

Isiem blinked. He'd assumed it was Ena who'd brought him in. "Ganoven?"

"It's almost impossible to find a renegade Nidalese wizard," Teglias said. "You, of all people, know how difficult it is to escape the Umbral Court. Those who survive as apostates do so by lying low enough to evade notice and hiding in remote corners of the world." He waved at the tavern around them. "Such as Pezzack."

"How did *Ganoven* know I was here?" Isiem asked. He'd never met the man in his life, and although he considered himself a wizard of no small skill, he wasn't remotely powerful enough for his reputation to have spread so widely.

"The Aspis Consortium sought out your former mistress in Egorian. Her connections to Nidal are well known. She suggested that you might be amenable to our proposal."

That, too, surprised him, but not for long. True, Velenne had no love for the Aspis Consortium, but she'd always been open to bribery—especially if the bribe was delivered in private by a handsome young man. "And so you came to Pezzack."

"So we came to Pezzack," Teglias agreed. "Kyril knew Ena from their work together in the rebellion, and Ena vouched for you. Events in the warehouse confirmed you were someone we could use. Your study of the key is another proof of your ability. Does that satisfy your curiosity?"

"For now."

"Good. Then let me ask some questions in turn: What do you know about the Umbral Basin? Were you taught anything about Mesandroth during your time in Pangolais? Anything that might have escaped the notice of outside historians?"

"I've never been to the Umbral Basin," Isiem said, "although everyone knows its reputation. It has fallen under Nidal's shadow, but because it is not truly a part of our nation, we don't control it, and the darkness runs wild there. Shadows poison the land and warp its inhabitants. Masterless magic bends the rules of the ordinary world without purpose or reason. It is not a place we go."

"Can you control the forces there?" Teglias asked.

"Perhaps. Some of them. No one wizard can hold back the full force of a shadowstorm, nor turn aside an army of night ghouls. But I should be able to influence the smaller things, and hide us from the larger."

The cleric nodded. "And Mesandroth?"

"I know very little." Isiem hesitated. "I may have a source who knows more."

That made the priest's gaze sharpen. "Might this source be willing to help us?"

"Perhaps. For a price. It's been a while since we spoke."

"Then I suggest you make contact and find out." Teglias stood. "Meanwhile, I'll break the news to Ganoven. I imagine there'll be wailing."

"Good," Isiem said.

He didn't go back to the chandler's shop. The bare spot by his bed where Honey's pillow had lain was too hard to look at. Isiem had abandoned the place in favor of a dockside tavern, where he rented a tiny room on the second floor, alongside stevedores and foul-smelling whalers. The common room was a constant tumult of off-key singing, drunken arguments, and the occasional brief brawl. Now and then a tittering prostitute would tiptoe past his door with a client, or a group of inebriated friends would drag up a fellow insensible with drink.

The noise of so many people living their lives outside his door only accentuated Isiem's sense of solitude. He had never been part of their world. Under a mask of illusions, he could pretend otherwise for a while . . . but he never really belonged, and he was acutely aware of the chasm between them.

Few friends had graced his life, and none had stayed. Kirii, the strix, whose obligations to her people had consumed her from the moment she inherited her mother's position as rokoa. Velenne, his teacher and first lover, who had pushed him to find his own freedom outside Nidal. Honey, his dog, held back by age and frailty.

And going back further, back to his earliest memories of childhood at the edge of the Uskwood, there had been Ascaros. Inseparable as children, loyal to each other even as students in the Dusk Hall, they'd finally broken in the bleak, rain-swept city of Nisroch.

In Nisroch, Ascaros had learned the full measure of what it meant, exactly, to be one of Mesandroth's descendants. From birth, the young sorcerer had been cursed with a gift of magic that ruined his body with every spell and would, eventually, kill him. In Nisroch he learned that his ancestor had deliberately seeded that poisoned magic into his blood, intending for him to suffer that fate—unless he managed to follow the twisting, torturous path Mesandroth had laid out for his children to prove their worth and escape their doom.

The key to that path, however, was a living creature: a captive shae, nearly as old and evil as the archmage who had bound him.

Isiem had wanted nothing to do with Silence, as the shae called himself. Embittered by his servitude, the creature had worked for centuries to destroy every one of Mesandroth's descendants who called upon him for aid. He promised to do the same to Ascaros.

Yet Ascaros had thought it worth the risk, and the cruelty, of prolonging Silence's slavery. Just for a time, he'd said. Just until the shae taught him how to evade his ancestor's curse.

It had ended their friendship. Not in a fight, not in anger or recrimination, but in the quiet slow distance of disillusionment. They grew apart, and after they left the Dusk Hall to pursue their separate assignments, they never spoke again.

Isiem didn't even know if his friend was still alive. Nevertheless, he plucked a strand of fine copper wire from his pouch of spell components and held it stretched between his fingers. The tavern was not solidly built, and the delicate wire trembled with the vibrations of other people laughing and dancing and quarreling in the common room beneath him.

He closed his eyes, drew a calming breath, and focused a thread of magic into the wire. *Ascaros,* he sent, then paused. There was so much he wanted to say, so much he feared to ask. But the magic was limited, and fading already. *I am following the trail of Mesandroth's work. Can you help? Will you?*

Chapter Four
Terms

Ascaros's answer came immediately. The sending blunted emotion, stripping away all but the barest hints of the sentiments that accompanied the words, but even so the spell carried a sense of surprise and, close after it, a flash of malicious mirth. *Isiem! How delightfully unexpected. I might help. I am in Ridwan, binding beasts. Come. Let us talk terms.*

The spell evaporated before Isiem could reply. He had not prepared another casting, and so he sat back on his heels, letting the copper wire fall from his nerveless fingers.

After a while, he picked the strand of wire up, coiled it into a neat loop, and replaced it in its pouch compartment. He did it mechanically, fingers moving without thought.

It was so strange to hear from Ascaros again. Ten years and more had passed since last they spoke. There was still an echo of the boy he'd known in his friend's voice, but the man had become harder, crueler, more assured. He sounded like a master sorcerer—and if he was in Ridwan, binding shadowbeasts for the glory of Zon-Kuthon, he had to be.

And not just a sorcerer, Isiem reminded himself. As much as Isiem might like to pretend otherwise, Ascaros was very much still a shadowcaller, blending arcane magic with the divine power of the Midnight Lord. Unlike Isiem, Ascaros had not abandoned that part of the Dusk Hall's training. Forgetting that could be deadly.

Isiem sat alone in the dark, thoughts in turmoil, for the better part of an hour. Then he unfolded his stiff legs, collected his cloak, and left the boarding house to wander Pezzack.

Aimlessly he roamed the town's muddy, rutted streets. He had no destination in mind, but it seemed only fitting, when he looked up from the shadowed roads, to find himself standing in front of the alehouse where he'd met Ena and her companions the night before.

Isiem pushed open the door. This tavern was quieter than the other: there were no raucous songs and precious little laughter, just the grim silence of men and women drinking to forget their days of backbreaking labor.

Through the gray huddle of the crowd, Isiem spotted the familiar splotchy dome of Ena's fire-scarred head. She sat alone, near the back of the room, nursing a dented metal tankard. The wizard made his way to her table, drawing out a chair on the opposite side.

The dwarf scowled reflexively as she looked up, although the scowl faded into a look of almost comical surprise once she recognized him. "What are *you* doing here?"

"Drinking," Isiem said.

Ena shot a pointed look over the empty space in front of him. "Need a drink for that."

"I'll get one later." He glanced at hers. It was a dark, oily-looking brew, decidedly unappetizing. "What would you recommend here?"

"Leaving," the dwarf replied with a humorless chuckle. She hoisted the tankard and took a long draught, setting it back down with a thud. "But if this is all you can afford, the grog's not bad. No, that's a lie. It's awful. But it's strong enough that you won't *care* it's awful after the first swig." She cocked a bristly eyebrow at him. "I meant what I asked, though: what are you doing here? Never knew you to take much comfort from a bottle."

"I never have," Isiem replied. He seldom touched wine, and never drank to excess; stoicism was too deeply ingrained from his years at the Dusk Hall. All Nidalese were taught from childhood that pain was not to be numbed, but embraced as the gift of their god. And while that particular piety was more often repeated than obeyed, the habit of sobriety had stayed with him.

"Then why go to a tavern?"

"I wanted to think."

"Funny, that's what most people are trying to escape." Ena drained her tankard and banged it on the table until a harried-looking barmaid came to replace it. She flipped the woman a silver shield, waved away an offer of change, and set to work on the new one. "What'd you want to ponder? Pay a copper for your thoughts."

"Do you even bother to carry coppers?" Isiem asked, amused. The coin she'd given the barmaid had to have been triple the worth of the swill she was drinking.

Ena snorted. "No. Do you?"

"I can't recall the last time I had use for one."

"Well, I'm surely not paying for your secrets in gold. Suppose you'll just have to tell me for free."

Isiem's lips twisted into a skewed, half-conscious curl, somewhere between grimace and smile. He directed it at the tabletop, tracing over some of the old scars in the wood with a fingertip. Confiding his uncertainties to Ena felt uncomfortable, like making a confession to a priest outside his faith . . . but carrying those doubts in silence was harder still.

"I had—*have*—a friend who probably knows more about Mesandroth Fiendlorn than any man alive," he began. "He's one of the archmage's descendants, maybe the last one alive with any gift for magic. Separated by centuries, of course, but that seems to matter less with Mesandroth than most."

"You think he'll help us?"

"He has suggested that he might."

"Do you trust him?" When Isiem didn't answer immediately, Ena nodded knowingly into her tankard. "Ah. So it's like that."

"He's Nidalese."

"So are you."

Isiem shook his head, keeping his gaze fixed on the tabletop. Someone had begun carving his name into the wood and never finished the job. Later patrons' beer had spilled into the letters, cementing dirt and soot into a filthy, illegible black inlay. It was a strange form of immortality; he wondered if the original carver would have been pleased. "I am and I'm not. I left. Ascaros stayed. He's in Ridwan now, binding shadow-beasts. That's not an easy task, and not one trusted to the impious. It means he's powerful and stands high in the favor of the Umbral Court."

"Do you think he'll betray us? Betray you?"

"I don't know," Isiem replied. "When we were students, I kept his secrets and he kept mine, but that was over a decade ago. Old loyalties fray quickly in Pangolais, and the Umbral Court does not tolerate apostasy. If he's one of them now, then yes, I would expect him to try to bring me in."

Across the room, a halfling was loudly berating a toothless old man who was nearly as short as he was. The old man's nose was redder than a crushed raspberry, and his hands trembled with the delirium of the longtime drunkard, but the halfling was giving him no mercy. Isiem couldn't tell why the halfling was so upset, but his screeching gave them cover to talk more candidly.

Ena leaned closer so she could be heard above the din. "And our mission? The nightblade?"

"He might try to retrieve the weapon for his own use, or to advance in the Black Triune's favor. I doubt he would give it to the Kuthites without something in exchange. Ascaros was never particularly devout. But if the weapon exists and is useful, it might hold value as a bargaining chip, so that is a possibility."

"Could we stop him?"

Isiem's hand stilled over the illegible name carved into the table. He shrugged his long ivory hair off his shoulders. "Maybe. When we were students, he was less skilled than I. But ten years is a long while, and he's had the benefit of an extraordinary teacher in that time. One of Mesandroth's own servants."

"And he stayed in Pangolais, while you went into exile." Ena toyed with the chain of her amulet, winding it around her fingers and dropping it again. She never lifted the blue crystal into view, though. In this place, it would have been unwise to flash cheap costume jewelry, let alone enchanted gems. "Who's got the advantage on that count?"

"Most likely he does. Field experience is of no small value, and I've had plenty of practice since leaving . . . but I doubt Ascaros has been idle in the intervening years. He's had access to the Dusk Hall's libraries to continue his studies, the intrigues of the Umbral Court to sharpen his wits, and the trials of Ridwan to hone his mastery of the arcane."

"That's good," Ena grunted. One of the tavern workers had finally chased the shouting halfling and his hapless victim outside; the dwarf lowered her voice to compensate.

Isiem did the same. "Good?"

"He's not stupid and he can handle himself." She took another drink. "I say invite him to join us. Could be that all he wants is a chance to escape Nidal, like you did. Maybe that's why he's reaching out to the exile. And if I'm wrong, and he means to turn against us, we'll deal with that when it happens."

"Are you comfortable with the chance of being wrong?" Isiem asked.

Ena shrugged. The seamed corners of her eyes crinkled in a suggestion of a smile that didn't quite reach her mouth. "Your friend will choose as he chooses. That's on him. It's not in my control, nor yours."

"It *is* within our control to allow or foreclose certain choices, though."

"So it is." The dwarf looked into her tankard, swirled the last few drops around, and set it aside. She stood, dropping a final silver coin into the mug, and straightened the cloak on her shoulders. "But where would you be today if someone had closed off that choice for you?"

Alone in his room the next day, Isiem unraveled the copper wire and hooked it around his fingers. Outside, twilight was waning into night. He had not lit any candles, and the fine web of copper was almost invisible between his hands.

He breathed into the gloom, seeking the tranquility he needed to shape his magic. When he found it, the wire shivered in his grasp. Isiem twined his spell around its vibrations, amplifying them into the ether until they could carry his words across the world.

What are your terms? Tell me, and we will consider them. I will not go to Ridwan.

Again it seemed that Ascaros had been waiting for his message. His old friend's reply came swiftly: *It's "we" now? Curious! We must discuss this. But if you won't come to Ridwan . . .*

Without more, the sending ended.

Isiem disentangled the wire from his fingers and wrapped it back into its ball. Exhaustion weighed down his shoulders, although he had done nothing all day but study his books and cast this single spell.

The prospect of sending yet another message to Ascaros was wearying. It seemed that the shadow-caller intended only to toy with him; Isiem wondered whether he had ever had any real intention of helping. It seemed unlikely. And while Isiem had no claim on his friend's loyalty anymore, that disheartened him all the same.

He put the copper strand back into the divided pouch that held his spellcrafting tools. As Isiem slid the glimmering metal into its pocket, however, he felt it suddenly vibrate. An instant later, Ascaros's voice filled his mind. The shadowcaller had woven his own sending.

If you will not come to Ridwan, what of Barrowmoor? Tomorrow. Midnight. Meet me.

Isiem hesitated. The rocky hills of Barrowmoor, located in the desolate high reaches of northern Nidal, were widely considered taboo. The horselords of old were buried there, encrusted in charcoal and bone, and it was said that they did not rest easy. In Pangolais, they derided such superstitions as the foolishness of unlettered provincials—but they never set foot near Barrowmoor, either. There was nothing *there*, other than those ancient graves, and no reason for any civilized Nidalese to go.

But that was precisely why it might be the only safe place in Nidal for him.

Yes, Isiem sent back. *I will meet you in Barrowmoor. Tomorrow at midnight. Alone.*

After a night of troubled dreams, Isiem woke early. He washed his face, rinsed his mouth, and broke his fast on day-old bread and a boiled egg—a sparse meal, but all he could force himself to choke down. Anxiety and excitement twisted together in his stomach. It was hard to think of anything other than the meeting at midnight. The words of his spellbook blurred into gibberish; he could hardly force himself to follow them.

He did it anyway. Tonight, of all nights, he could not be caught unprepared.

It was difficult to know *how* to prepare, though. The wizard's curse was that he had to study his spells in advance; unlike a sorcerer, whose magic was born in the blood, his power derived from meticulous preparation and conscious control of the arcane. It could not be altered once set, and it had to be prepared well before he expected to use it.

Isiem wasn't sure what he might need to confront in Barrowmoor. There was a chance that Ascaros would betray him, of course; there might be a trap laid by the Umbral Court. But other dangers lurked among those numberless graves, and those were harder to foresee.

Folklore made no mention of undead among Barrowmoor's black hills, which added to Isiem's unease. Deadly and powerful as the walking dead could be, they were in many ways a known threat. Vague tales of curses and blighted luck, on the other hand, told him nothing of use.

After considerable thought, Isiem chose a complement of defensive spells. He had no desire to stand and fight in Barrowmoor. Concealment, deflection, retreat: those, irrespective of his adversaries, would serve the wizard best if events turned against him. He immersed himself in study, letting the day slip by.

Beyond his spells, he had few defenses. Most of Isiem's equipment had been lost or destroyed shortly after his defection from the Dusk Hall, and a year's exile in Pezzack had given him little opportunity to replace it.

The only significant piece he'd acquired was a simple platinum band set with five equally spaced rubies, each one dark and tiny as a miser's heart. He'd taken it off the bloody, broken fingers of a mercenary wizard that he'd found spying invisibly around Windspire. Once Isiem unraveled his spell and revealed him to the itaraak, they'd gagged the man, thrust a spear through his hands, and thrown him off the high stones of Devil's Perch.

But not before Isiem claimed his ring.

Crafted in Egorian, it bore the mark of House Leroung, but as far as Isiem could discern, it was not an infernal focus. For a Chelish wizard's tool, it was fairly innocuous. The ring held a single arcane spell, ready to be released at a command.

It reassured him to have a retreat so close at hand. Rubbing a thumb over the ring's small rubies, Isiem removed a silver bowl from a wrapping of soft deerskin. The bowl's flat bottom had been polished to a mirror sheen. Around it, densely inscribed arcane runes rose in spiraled rings upon the bowl's walls.

He stared at those sigils, lost in memories of similar runes written in the pages of gray-leaved books, until midnight was nearly upon him.

A few minutes before the appointed hour, the wizard shook off his remembrances and picked up the pitcher that held his drinking water. He filled the bowl with clear water until all the runes along its sides had been submerged, then lit three candles in a semicircle around it. Kneeling on the floor, Isiem gazed down at the flickering reflections of light and water and silver and reached out to his magic.

He wondered what Ascaros would look like now. He wondered if he'd even recognize his friend well enough to find him with the scrying spell.

Isiem had never so much as glimpsed Barrowmoor. But as he channeled arcane energy into the mirrored bowl and its sunken runes, a ghostly image of that forsaken place began to appear in the water. There was no mistaking it for any other place in the world.

Against a backdrop of moonlit mountains, a vast expanse of rough mounds stretched farther than the eye could see, bare and black and studded with bones. The smallest of the mounds were twenty feet across and ten high; the largest were three times that size. All of them were covered in lattices of ancient charcoal logs, eroded but intact, and many were crowned by crude towers built of more logs steepled together. It must have taken an astonishing effort for such primitive peoples to build those mounds, then burn entire groves of trees into charcoal and layer them over the graves of their lords in such elaborate patterns—but they had done it, and done it again, hundreds if not thousands of times.

Even through the miniaturizing effect of Isiem's mirrorbowl, the age of the place was palpable. No mist softened its charcoal-encrusted barrows; no clouds dimmed the starkness of the starlight on its stones. Ancient as they were, the long-dead horselords had been Nidalese, and it seemed fitting that their graves wanted no pity.

One figure moved among the barrows. Moonlight limned his raven curls and glimmered along the chains of silver and steel threaded through his formal black attire. His face was devoid of both color and emotion: white as freshly exposed bone, expressionless as a torturer's mask, it was the perfect visage of an Umbral Court agent.

Ascaros.

Ten years had changed Isiem's old friend. The last hints of vibrant red had drained out of his hair; the last traces of merriment were gone from his mouth. The boy had hardened into a cold, proud man, not tall but imposing nevertheless. All signs of weakness had been purged from him. Even the bandages that had once wrapped his withered left arm were nowhere to be seen. The shadowcaller held his black staff in a hand that looked as strong and healthy as the other.

His eyes were the same, though. Isiem released a breath he hadn't realized he was holding when he saw that. If Ascaros's eyes had been the empty, infinite black of the shadow-claimed . . .

But they weren't. The sorcerer's soul was still his own.

Unsettled by the intensity of his relief, Isiem withdrew his scrying. The vision of Barrowmoor faded back into water and cupped candlelight.

He snuffed the candles, emptied the silver bowl's water back into the pitcher, and thumbed the rubies of his ring again. Then, with a thread of sweat prickling cold down his spine, Isiem spoke a word of magic and stepped into the infinite hanging nothingness of the ether.

To Barrowmoor.

Chapter Five
The Sorcerer in Shadow

Barrowmoor was cold.

Not cold as winter was cold, or frost or wind or rain. It was an unearthly chill that reached up through the earth and seized at the soul, and made Isiem wonder if, perhaps, those ancient burial mounds were lairs of the undead after all. He could think of nothing else on Golarion that could create such a deadening freeze.

If there were such hungry shades abroad in Barrowmoor, however, they kept out of sight. Ascaros walked alone among the charcoal-caged mounds. His umbral robes melded into the darkness, creating the impression that the sorcerer drifted bodilessly between the hills.

As Isiem stepped out of a barrow's shadow into the cool gray moonlight, Ascaros saw him and lifted his black staff in greeting. Mirth edged the surprise in his voice. "You came!"

No one else was in view, and Ascaros had not shouted, yet Isiem winced at how his friend's words carried through the barren hills.

"I came," he agreed grimly, almost in a whisper. He thumbed the rubies on his ring, turning it around uneasily toward his palm.

"Then you must truly need my help." Ascaros climbed down from the barrow he'd mounted, moving smoothly over the enormous charcoal logs. He stopped fifteen feet from Isiem, folding his pale hands around his staff. "Whatever for? Your sendings were so vague."

"A necessary limitation of the magic." Isiem hesitated, looking around. He couldn't shake the feeling that unfriendly eyes were on them, and the fact that he could see none only added to his mistrust of the place. "Can we speak frankly here?"

"Of course. Why else would I have chosen this place? It's scenic, but I know how reluctant you are to return to Nidal. With good reason. I would not go back to Pangolais, were I you."

Isiem brushed the shadowcaller's advice aside with a wave. "Have you ever heard of a woman named Eledwyn? She would have been one of Mesandroth's apprentices."

Ascaros's dark eyes narrowed sharply. His grip tensed on the staff, then relaxed slowly as he made a brittle, unconvincing laugh. "So. It's not my revered ancestor's work you want, but his underling's."

"They're intertwined," Isiem said.

"I know that." Ascaros sat on a charcoal log, arranging his robes over his knees and then resting the staff across them. Behind him, the ruins of a primitive talisman-tower thrust its broken outline against the moon. A handful of relics dangled from the tower's remains: skulls, painted gourds, and pale flint blades hung from ropes of ancient, dirt-knotted horsehair. "Yes, I know of Eledwyn. She was one of the first to rebel . . . and one of the few that Mesandroth dealt with directly. If you're seeking her, you may be disappointed. I don't think you'll find much but grief and ashes in whatever remains of her workshop."

"Do you know where that is?"

"Don't you?" Ascaros laughed again. "This won't be much of an expedition if you have no idea where to go."

"My companions learned of a place called Fiendslair. They believe it to be somewhere in the Umbral Basin."

"Correctly so." The shadowcaller looked past Isiem, gazing across the rocky expanse of Barrowmoor and all its forgotten kings, then turned back to his childhood friend. "But the Umbral Basin is a very large place, and very dangerous. Tell me about these companions. Not Chelaxians?"

"Not as you mean them. They are Chelish, but they have no loyalty to House Thrune. On the contrary: most are rebels, or not opposed to working with the rebellion."

"Who are they? What do they want from poor, long-dead Eledwyn?"

"The leader is a Sarenite cleric. An idealist, I think, but pragmatic in the service of those ideals. There's a paladin of Iomedae, and a dwarf with a fondness for traps. Preferably traps that explode. Then there's an Aspis agent, and his two bodyguards. And myself. What they want—what we all want—is a weapon that might be used against fiends. Something to break the diabolists' stranglehold on Cheliax. They call it a nightblade."

Ascaros stroked a gemmed cuff that peeped from under one black sleeve. Isiem hadn't noticed it before. It was made of silver that had been cut and hammered into the shape of a flayleaf garland. Onyx and moonstone cabochons gleamed amid the wiry stems.

The silversmith had clearly been Nidalese, but flayleaf was an odd inspiration for such a crafter. The plant was a powerful narcotic, commonly used to deaden pain. It was not favored in Pangolais. Yet there it was on Ascaros's wrist.

Isiem wondered what magic the bracelet held. Clearly it was enchanted with *some* dweomer; he didn't believe Ascaros would have worn it otherwise. But what?

The shadowcaller caught Isiem's look. One corner of his mouth curled in a thin smile, and he straightened his sleeve fastidiously, hiding the bracelet again. "Do you trust them?"

"Pardon?"

"Your allies. Do you trust them? Capturing you would earn considerable favor from House Thrune. Enough to get quite a few rebels' sins absolved, I would imagine."

A breeze skirled across Barrowmoor, rattling the talismans on the tomb poles. There were no fires on the hills, yet the wind carried a ghostly, impossible odor of woodsmoke and rancid, burning grease.

The gust tugged Isiem's long ivory hair loose of its bonds. Faintly irritated, he pulled it back and tied it again. "They will not betray me to House Thrune. Nor to the Umbral Court. You, on the other hand . . ."

"You believe I might?" Ascaros asked softly.

"The thought has crossed my mind."

"Of course it has." The shadowcaller ran a thumb along one side of his staff, where runes were cut deeply into the ebon wood. He turned it toward Isiem, tipping it up so that the cloudy moonlight touched the sigils and allowed his former friend to see.

The marks designated the staff's bearer as a master of the Dusk Hall and a favored agent of the Umbral Court. Isiem felt an old familiar tingle of fear at the sight of the pattern; it was one that every student soon learned to dread in Pangolais. But his voice stayed even. "You've moved up in the world."

"I've had the benefit of a good teacher." Ascaros turned the staff's sigils away. Again a tight, thin smile touched his face and was gone.

"Silence? He must be nearing the end of his ten years' service. Have you freed him as you promised?"

Slowly Ascaros shook his head. His lips parted; then he hesitated, seemed almost to flinch, and closed his mouth. After another stretch of quiet he said: "That creature is . . . more evil than you can know, Isiem."

"I can guess," the wizard said dryly. "I was there when you met him, remember."

"Yes." This time Ascaros did flinch. He closed his eyes for a heartbeat, then shook away whatever thought or memory had come to him. "But what he said then barely touches it. I used to think demons were the vilest creatures to walk Golarion. I know better now. If I

73

ever free him, it'll be so I can hurl him and his accursed mirror directly into the Eye of Abendego."

"But you used him all the same." Isiem gestured toward his old friend's staff and the tenebrous robes of his office. "Quite successfully, it seems."

"Seems," Ascaros echoed. Another long, uncomfortable silence fell between them. Another gust of wind whistled through the barrows, creating a haunting not-quite melody. It sounded like the singing of ghosts.

The shadowcaller grimaced and bowed his head. Abruptly, his bone-white skin darkened and wrinkled like paper held over a flame. His hands knotted into gnarled, bony claws sheathed in dead gray skin. Most of the black curls on his head vanished, leaving only a sparse, bedraggled fringe about the base of his skull. His nose shriveled into a desiccated twist of flesh. As the illusion that had masked his true self faded, he stood before Isiem revealed as a man more dead than alive.

"He could not stop the curse." Ascaros's smooth tenor had been replaced by a ruined, crackling rattle: a mummy's voice. His eyes, yellow-stained and rheumy, were slow to focus on his friend's. "Silence gave me power, but he could not—or would not—lessen its cost. I stand high in the courts of Pangolais, yes. But I am dying, Isiem. Faster than ever before."

"You've asked the clerics for help?" Isiem asked quietly. What his friend had become horrified him, but he was Nidalese, and his first response was to hide all that he felt.

Ascaros's answering laugh was bitter. It hissed through the gaps between his shrunken, fanglike teeth. "The Kuthites? They tell me to embrace it. To revel in the uniqueness of this pain, and in the power that it affords me. Their lips get moist when they speak of it. No, I think it is safe to say that they have not much interest in helping me find a cure."

"I imagine the cleric leading our expedition would be willing to help an ally. I cannot promise he will be able."

"I'd hardly expect such luck." With a scowl at his own withered limbs, Ascaros renewed his masking illusion. Once again, he appeared as the man he might have been, instead of the monster he'd become. "It would be entirely too much to hope that one of the two or three living priests in this age who might counter Mesandroth's magic would happen to be in your party. Of course, if I'm wrong, I'll happily sing hymns of praise to the Dawnflower. But my expectation is that Eledwyn will have come closer to breaking her old master's spells than your cleric can."

"Then you will aid us?"

"I will come with you." Ascaros closed the remaining distance between them, leaning on the tall black staff as he picked his way down the hillside. "My assistance is contingent on my being permitted to enter Eledwyn's workshop alongside the rest of you."

"I'm not certain my companions will want an agent of the Umbral Court coming with us."

"They can swallow their qualms or go without my aid." Ascaros shrugged. "But, in this matter, I am an Umbral agent in name only."

"Explain, please."

"They wouldn't help me." Ascaros swept a hand across the front of his silver-hooked robes. His upper lip curled into a snarl. "The Umbral Court chose to leave me like this. To *exploit* me like this. I don't feel, when it comes to my ancestor's curse, that I owe any particular loyalty to Pangolais. This is for myself, Isiem. I'm going to save my own life. Of course I'll tell them otherwise, so they'll permit me to leave. But make no mistake: I go into this with my own interests at heart."

"Seldom have I been so relieved to hear such bald selfishness," Isiem said wryly. "Is there any risk that the Umbral Court will learn of your motives and pursue you?"

"Only if I'm stupid or clumsy. I don't believe you've ever known me to be either."

"Not especially, no," Isiem agreed. "Even without worrying about Nidalese hunters at our backs, though, it is likely to be a dangerous journey."

"Really." Ascaros's tone dripped acid. "Dangerous? An expedition into the Umbral Basin to find a laboratory where a half-mad wizard experimented on demons? Surely not."

Isiem acknowledged defeat with a rueful little nod. "Fine. Do you know what the dangers *are*? Our information is sadly limited on that point."

"The woman wanted to kill demons. I imagine it would be safe to assume she kept some available to practice her attempts—why else would she call the place Fiendslair? I would further imagine that Mesandroth freed them when he killed his traitorous apprentice and cast her work into ruin. It would fit his sensibilities. And as demons do not age or starve or die—unless they kill each other, as these may well have—I expect we'll find some waiting for us inside. Presuming we *get* inside, which may be quite difficult in itself. Mesandroth was a man with many enemies, and one well versed in wards. He taught the same caution to his underlings."

"What sort of wards?"

"The first line of defense will be concealment. But that, I think, is something I would prefer to discuss in the company of your scholar-cleric." Ascaros stretched languidly. He lifted the spiked chain that signified his allegiance to Zon-Kuthon, god of darkness and pain, studying the twisted steel with pointed intensity. "Are you satisfied that I came to you in good faith? Will you let me join your little expedition?"

"I'm satisfied as to your goodwill," Isiem said, "but it's not for me to let you join. I can, however, take you to meet the others. Come."

"*Two* Nidalese? You must be joking." Ganoven stalked furiously around the perimeter of the tiny room, undeterred by either crowding or clutter from his display. He kept a hand on the hilt of his rapier, pushing the weapon out behind him so that its scabbard twitched like the tail of an angry cat. "Are they *both* going to demand full partners' shares? Why not just cede the whole damned expedition to them?"

Lacking any better options for privacy, the party had crowded into the rented room that Kyril and Ena shared in Pezzack. The place was intended for laborers who needed little more than a mattress between long days of work, and it was small with just the dwarf and paladin inside. With all of them crammed in, there was hardly space to breathe. Isiem sat cross-legged alongside Kyril on one of the room's lumpy straw mattresses. Ena and Teglias shared the other. Ascaros stood in a corner. Ganoven, who had been the last to arrive, had nowhere to go, which visibly added to his irritation.

The Aspis agent had ordered Pulcher and Copple to stay outside. Ostensibly they were to guard the hallway against interlopers, since there was no room for them inside, but Isiem thought that Ganoven had also done it simply to show that he could. The black-bearded half-elf seemed to be obsessed with social ranks. Any slight to his standing rankled him badly, and it seemed that he viewed this whole meeting as just such an insult.

No one else seemed to be concerned by his ire. Teglias regarded the shadowcaller with the same compassionate gravity that Isiem imagined he'd show a repentant parishioner seeking forgiveness for some minor sin.

"I understand you're descended from Mesandroth Fiendlorn," the cleric said.

"Yes," Ascaros said. He had retreated behind a wall of icy reserve. His face looked so like a mask that Isiem had to remind himself that it literally *was* one; the illusion mirrored its wearer's Nidalese reserve with uncanny precision.

"Do you think that will help us on this expedition?"

"It might. It might hinder you just as much, or more. Mesandroth was fond of setting tests and traps for his blood, and he had no mercy for those who failed to prove themselves worthy. My presence may trigger challenges that would not exist for you otherwise."

Ganoven snorted. "Are you trying to persuade us to take you or to leave you behind?"

"Neither." Ascaros gave the Aspis agent a flat look and dismissed him, returning his attention to Teglias. "I want you to know what you'll be getting."

"I believe we have a fair sense of that." Teglias exchanged a glance with Kyril, who nodded almost imperceptibly. The cleric turned back to Ascaros. "What's your price?"

"Not a partnership share." Ascaros folded his hands atop each other, wrapping both around his rune-scribed staff. The gems studded into his flayleaf bracelet were luminous under the black cloth of his sleeve. "I will take whatever of Mesandroth's work, or Eledwyn's, may be useful for my needs. I doubt there will be any overlap with your interests."

"What if there is?" Ganoven snapped. He'd chosen to wear blue velvet slashed with crimson today, and while his outfit was doubtlessly the height of fashion in Egorian, its starched ruff and puffed sleeves looked ridiculous next to Ascaros's umbral robes and Teglias's simple, practical tunic and trousers of undyed cotton.

"There is not," Ascaros said coolly. "I'm told that you seek a weapon to use against fiends. If that is true, your goals and mine have no conflict. What I seek in Eledwyn's lair has nothing to do with the work that interests you."

"What *do* you want?" Ena had been darning a pair of ancient woolen socks while listening to the others converse. The socks might have been beige, once upon a time, but long use had faded them into a shapeless, distinctly unappealing brownish gray. Isiem had a suspicion that she kept them around just to annoy Ganoven. If so, it was clearly working. The Aspis agent stiffened and raised his nose a notch whenever he chanced to look in her direction.

Ascaros didn't seem to notice the byplay between Ganoven and the dwarf. "Before he tried possessing demons," he said, "Mesandroth sought immortality through living undeath. Not as a lich is undead, or a vampire, but a hybrid that could take their longevity without giving up its soul.

"He did not wish to risk himself in these experiments, of course. He chose to infect his kin instead. The earliest of them, seeking favor as his apprentices, may have accepted the touch of undeath willingly. At the very least, it's possible that they had more insight into what was done, and how, and with what opportunities to escape. That is the knowledge I seek. It has nothing to do with your nightblade."

The dwarf's scarred eyebrows climbed. "You carry that curse?"

"I do."

"Well, that's a bugger." Ena grunted and returned to her darning. "But I suppose we'll take you if you're not near dropping dead right now."

"What?" Ganoven sounded ready to strangle on his own tongue. His forehead flushed nearly as red as the accents on his hose. "Is there to be no negotiation? No consultation? Do *I* get no say?"

"Oh, calm down." Ena chuckled under her breath, just loudly enough that the Aspis agent would be able to hear her across the room. "Try to have *some* dignity. Of course he'll come. We need a second arcanist. This one's skilled and willing to work cheap."

"We don't need two Nidalese," Ganoven insisted. "We have one. Fine. But Teglias is a historian and I'm a scholar of no small accomplishment myself, need I remind you. This is a research expedition, and we're more than capable of doing that research without them. I fail to see why we need *two* of these shadow-besotted spellslingers, especially if we have to pay them separately."

"Because this is going to be a dangerous trip," Ena said patiently, as her needle made quick, expert flicks through the grubby wool toe of her sock. "There's a good chance we won't all come back alive. Now, in your case, that might not cause me much sorrow. But if we lose our only wizard in the depths of some arcane dungeon, why, then I *will* shed some tears, and I'll very much regret not having brought a spare."

While the Aspis agent floundered for a response, Kyril cleared her throat.

"I must ask for some assurances first." The paladin fixed her dark-eyed gaze on the shadowcaller in his silver-stitched robes. "I am a servant of the Inheritor, and I cannot countenance anything that might reflect poorly on her honor. As long as we work together, you will comport yourself in a manner suitable for one of her allies."

Ascaros answered with a quick, indifferent nod. "Fine."

"That easy?" Ena put her finished sock away. Its toe was a knob of woolly scar tissue easily half an inch thick. Isiem couldn't see why she needed to wear boots with socks like that. "Always figured it'd be harder to convert a Kuthite."

"Hardly converting. But we do have some experience with accepting pointless and burdensome orders from Chelaxians," Ascaros said frostily.

"Wonderful!" Teglias's blue eyes twinkled with mischief. "We're just getting started."

Chapter Six
Into the Valley

After a sparse breakfast of fried bread and plum conserve, they left Pezzack. Ena rode a shaggy gray pony; Ganoven chose a showy black steed. The others rode nondescript animals in varying shades of dun and brown.

Not one of their steeds would last out the day. Isiem had conjured them all out of the ether, although he had allowed them to choose their own mounts' appearances. They would not be riding far, and real horses would only have burdened them.

"I thought paladins rode unicorns," Isiem said lightly, watching Kyril climb onto a stolid farm horse who seemed better suited for pulling a beer wagon than carrying a soldier into battle. The Iomedaean had donned a set of plate mail for the road. The metal had been deliberately scuffed to a dull gray, and she wore a plain brown cloak over it to further drab her figure, but despite her efforts to make herself unremarkable, Kyril could not conceal what she was.

Radiance seemed almost to emanate from her: a strength and serenity that spoke of divine certainty. Unicorns were rare even among the holiest paladins, and Isiem had meant his comment in jest, but he really could imagine her riding such a steed. It would suit her perfectly.

"Some do," Kyril replied, patting her conjured horse's neck, "but I've found it uncomfortably showy. It's not always easy to take a unicorn where I need to go."

"You did seem suspiciously comfortable disguising yourself in Pezzack," Isiem agreed, mounting his own shadow-spun horse. Out of habit, he had rendered his in the midnight hues that the shadowcallers of Pangolais preferred. Even its saddle and bridle were silver-trimmed black.

He wished, belatedly, that he'd chosen a less ominous appearance for the beast. It might be seen as a challenge to some of his companions, and that was the last thing he wanted. "That's another thing I thought you had to do: carry a golden sword and a silver shield and inspire the world with your shining example."

Kyril lifted a dark red eyebrow. "You don't know much about paladins, do you?"

"Up until recently, I've not had the opportunity to meet many."

"You're wrong about that, but understandably so. The ones you might have known would have tried to avoid you."

"What do you mean?"

The others were departing, Ena at their head. All around them, the black and red stones of Devil's Perch rose in crooked towers. Somewhere among those eerie wind-carved spires, the strix were keeping a wary eye on Pezzack—and perhaps on them, too.

Isiem couldn't see any of the winged watchers, though. To his eye, the desert sky was a bare, hard blue.

Below that cloudless sky, the land was as desolate as ever. Elsewhere on Golarion, ripening apples were weighing down the boughs of their trees; heavy stalks of grain were nodding in the wind. In fields of rich black earth, turnips and carrots and radishes fattened under drowsy green crowns, while in sturdy whitewashed houses, farmers sharpened their scythes for harvest.

Not in Devil's Perch. The only harvest here would be of scorpions and dust. Although the desert had a flinty kind of beauty, Isiem wouldn't miss its desolation. He had found freedom in western Cheliax, yet he was glad to leave the place behind. A year was enough of his life spent among these stones.

Kyril nudged her heavy draft horse to follow the rest of their party, lagging behind to avoid being overwhelmed by the cloud of dust that their pack wagon left in its wake. That, at least, was drawn by real horses—a pair of handsome red geldings that had been orphaned when their former master met some misfortune in Devil's Perch.

"You served in Westcrown as a member of the Midnight Guard." It wasn't a question, and the paladin kept her eyes on the road as she said it, but neither was it an accusation.

Isiem guided his horse to fall in alongside hers. "I did."

"I was born there. I grew up under Thrune rule. Westcrown was where I had my awakening, and where I began my life as a servant of the Inheritor." She glanced at him, but only briefly. Dust smudged her cheekbones and dotted her brow where it clung to tiny beads of perspiration. Her expression gave away nothing. "There are many paladins in Westcrown. The injustice and the need in that wounded city act as a magnet for those of our calling. But we do our work subtly, because the powers that rule Cheliax today do not tolerate drastic intervention, and we have learned not to draw attention we don't need."

"Were you there when I was?" Isiem asked. It seemed important, somehow, that the answer be 'no.' He didn't like to think he might have worked against her, even inadvertently.

"It's possible." Kyril shrugged. "I left four years ago. But I tried not to cross paths with the Midnight Guard. Most of us did."

"I'm glad you've changed that rule."

She flashed him a quick smile, then urged her horse forward to catch up with the main group. "You're not a Midnight Guard anymore. And you chose to join the resistance, so there might be some hope for you yet."

He let her go, watching her vanish into the dust cloud and reappear on the other side. The sunlight caught her hair, bringing out strands of brightness in the red and sparking a reluctant gleam from her dulled armor. Isiem found himself hoping she would look back, but she didn't.

The wizard smiled ruefully, spurring his own horse toward Ascaros and Teglias, who were riding beside the pack wagon. It had been some time since he'd felt the pleasant discomfort of attraction. A paladin of Iomedae seemed an unlikely object for his affections, but he couldn't deny that he was drawn to her.

There was no sign that she reciprocated his feelings, though, which was something of a relief. It kept things cleaner.

Teglias and Ascaros were engaged in an animated discussion when Isiem reached them. They paused as he came within earshot, but only for a moment.

"His key," Ascaros said, his black eyes alight with more excitement than Isiem had seen in them since their first days in the Dusk Hall. He waved Isiem closer so that he could join their conversation. "The one that opens Eledwyn's stronghold. Teglias says you've seen it."

"I have," Isiem said. "He showed it to you?"

"Of course. I recognized it at once. It belonged to Khorsaveir of the Fangs—one of my forefather's more infamous apprentices, and as his name suggests, one of the first to step into undeath. Shortly after embracing vampirism, Khorsaveir led the assault into Eledwyn's stronghold. He died not long after, and his belongings were stolen by one of the survivors, who sold them secretly to avoid Mesandroth's wrath for the theft."

"One of the pieces he sold was the diamond that's missing from the key's bow," Teglias said. He, too, was dressed plainly for the road, in a belted tunic and breeches under a light cloak of beige cotton. A well-worn pack was bundled behind his saddle, and he wore his scimitar with the ease of long habit. The scholar, it seemed, was no stranger to the adventuring life. "Your friend believes he knows where it might be found."

"It's not far from the path we'll be taking already." Unlike the others in their group, Ascaros had done nothing to deter the curiosity of passersby. He wore the umbral robes and spiked chain of his office openly, and his night-black horse was fairly dripping in onyx and silver. The fearful glances of Pezzack's townspeople, and Ganoven's lackeys, seemed to amuse him. "Seventy years ago, the jewel was lost near what are now called the Trilmsgitt Towers. I think there's a good chance it's still there."

"Why?" Isiem asked.

"Because it was one of my relatives who lost it. Sukorya of the Dusk Hall. She was a formidable sorceress, and she held Silence's mirror before it came to my aunt's mother. The shae spent decades plotting against her, but Sukorya was as canny as she was powerful, and all his schemes came to naught. Until Silence sent her off to hunt an unliving monster in the Backar Forest. He claimed another of my kin had died there—one of Mesandroth's early apprentices, perhaps Khorsaveir himself—and that Sukorya would find answers, and power, in the shade's hoard."

"Instead, I presume, she found her demise," Isiem said.

"Of course." Ascaros's smile was tight and grim. "Silence added another pin to his cloak, and the mirror fell to Misanthe's mother, then Misanthe, then me. But Sukorya had the diamond that belongs to that key, and I suspect it still lies with her bones. Worn as an amulet, it possesses considerable power in its own right, but she was a secretive woman and few knew she had it. Perhaps none, other than Silence. Given that the creature was deadly enough to destroy Sukorya, and Silence has been goading me toward its lair for months, I doubt anyone who might have stumbled upon the monster's haunt by accident would have survived to take the stone. It must be an uncommonly powerful beast."

"I have full faith in our ability to confront the thing," Teglias said serenely, "particularly as we need not destroy it. Just distract it long enough to recover the diamond. The Trilmsgitt Towers are only a few days off the route we'd originally intended to take through the Backar Forest."

"I repeat my earlier question," Isiem said. "Why? Why do we need the diamond at all?"

Ascaros frowned. "Didn't you examine the key?"

Isiem shrugged. "Enough to tell it was magical. And evil."

"And *incomplete*." Ascaros shook his head. "Really, Isiem. The key bears several enchantments, but at least one of them requires the diamond as a key component. It may not even work without it."

"Ascaros believes he may be able to use the magical resonances in the stone to help us locate Fiendslair," Teglias added.

"Oh?" Isiem raised an eyebrow at Ascaros. "And you only mention this now?"

"You said you knew where the lair was. Teglias has since clarified for me that you only *suspect* where it is. From what I've learned of Sukorya, she believed the stone could guide her to Eledwyn's workshop, but hadn't yet made an attempt on it herself when she had her encounter with the beast."

"Do we even know what this beast *is*?" Isiem asked. His horse tossed its head, mirroring his discomfort. "I'd like to know a little more before agreeing to go off on a hunt for mysterious sorcerer-slaying undead."

"Not with any specificity," Ascaros admitted. "It's rumored to have been one of Khorsaveir's creations, but that's all I know, and even that is only rumor. It may not be true. But I believe I'm nearly what Sukorya was, and she challenged the beast alone."

"With fatally unsuccessful results," Isiem pointed out. He was about to add more, but stopped when he saw Ena coming toward them in a plume of desert dust.

The dwarf handled her spell-summoned horse with ease. She spun to a showy stop in front of Teglias, lowering the scarf that shielded the bottom half of her face when the dust had died down enough to breathe.

Teglias coughed pointedly, wiping gritty dust away from his mouth and nose. "Yes?"

"I think we're far enough." She nodded absently at Isiem and Ascaros, still scanning the rest of the group and the landscape around them. There had been no one else on the road since they left sight of Pezzack, and the skies remained empty of even a cloud, but that did not lessen the dwarf's vigilance. "If you two are ready, I'll round up the others."

"Go," Ascaros said, dismounting. He straightened his robes and lifted his pack from behind the black mare's saddle. As he slipped it onto his shoulders, the beast and its trappings vanished into spiraling threads of smoke. Ena flicked the shaggy pony's reins and trotted off to collect the rest of their party.

Pulcher had been sleeping on the wagon, a hat pulled over his face and his wire-rimmed spectacles perched on the hat's brim. He'd taken off his boots and propped his feet over the wagon's side, where his bare toes wiggled occasionally as he dreamed. A piece of straw dangled loosely from his bottom lip, rattling every time he snored. Copple, who was driving the wagon, regarded his companion with an ill-concealed mixture of envy and disgust, and did nothing to warn him when Ena rode up and slapped the taller thug smartly on the bottom of each foot.

"Get up," she said, as Pulcher startled awake. He clapped a hand to his hat, crushing the brim but saving his spectacles, and nearly toppled onto the ground in his surprise. Copple doubled over, wheezing malicious laughter. "We're heading to Molthune."

"I knew that. You didn't have to hit me. We're already riding that way." Pulcher spat the straw onto the ground, put his spectacles back on, and tried to straighten his rumpled hat.

"No," the dwarf said patiently. "We're riding so everyone would see us go. Now if anyone comes to investigate what happened at the warehouse, the townspeople will be able to tell them truthfully that the malcontents who were probably responsible have left Pezzack, riding east. It gives them a little cover, maybe protects them from being accused of complicity. If Desna smiles on us, it might even lure the devilers out to the desert on a goblin hunt. But we are *not* riding to Molthune. Do you have any idea how long that would take? Besides, we'd have to cross all northern Cheliax, and that's more trouble than I want to invite."

"Then how are we getting there?" Pulcher regarded his unsalvageable hat for another moment, sulking, then turned it around and put it on with the crushed brim facing the back.

Ena rolled her eyes. "Walking. Obviously. Get ready."

"What's the plan?" Kyril asked, coming around the wagon's other side. She shook gritty dust from the bottom of her cloak.

"We're heading to Cettigne," Ena answered, checking over her myriad hidden weapons. "Well, not *into* Cettigne exactly. We'll be stopping at a little village outside the city. Some of Ganoven's friends are waiting to meet us with a job offer."

"Merchants," the Aspis agent supplied. "They make a regular run through the Umbral Basin into Nidal once a month, carrying trade goods. The caravan employs hundreds of guards, and they're always in need of more. There simply aren't enough brave souls willing to venture into the shadowlands."

"We're posing as guards?" The dwarf laughed heartily. "Do they know how many time I've been arrested? That's delightful. How much do they pay, these friends of yours?"

"A gold piece per day in Molthune, five per day once we cross into the shadowlands. Mostly they pay in Chelish coinage, but if you prefer another nation's, they'll accommodate. Or pay by weight in silver, if sufficient coins aren't to be had."

"Generous," Ena allowed, still grinning. "For that, I might almost be tempted to stick with the caravan."

"Well, you can't," Ganoven snapped. Unlike the others, the half-elf hadn't protected his head with a hood or hat, and his face was red with sunburn. Coupled with his pointed black goatee, it gave him an infernal look. It seemed to have given him an infernal temper, too. "We're splitting off once we reach the Umbral Basin. You're already under contract, don't forget."

"They won't miss us?" Kyril asked.

The Aspis agent shook his head curtly. "People vanish all the time in the shadowlands. It's why they have to pay the others so much. We'll just number among the disappeared."

Ena cracked her knuckles. "I'd ask whether your friends would miss you, but . . ." She gave Ganoven a smile that would have been cloying on a Taldan courtier.

"Are we ready?" Teglias asked. Quiet as the question was, it cut through the others' chatter immediately. They gathered around the pack wagon, and one by one Isiem dismissed their horses. When only the two red geldings were left, still harnessed to the wagon, the wizard glanced at Ascaros.

Teleporting their companions was a matter of little difficulty; although it was complicated by the fact that neither Isiem nor Ascaros had ever seen Molthune, they had scryed one of Ganoven's contacts the night before, which had enabled them to familiarize themselves with the surrounding environs. Both believed they could reach it. Once that was settled, it was no harder to bring additional people than to teleport themselves. Even the horses were only slightly more challenging. The wagon, however, posed a greater obstacle. Isiem had never tried to teleport such a heavy object, and wasn't sure it could be done. "Can you transport the conveyance?"

"Of course." Ascaros took a delicate silver chain from a pocket and wound it around his fingers. The chain was spiked with innumerable barbs, and they bit into his skin as he pulled it tight upon his hand. Dark carnelian beads threaded upon the chain mimicked the drops of blood that welled from the barbs and trickled onto the silver strand, where they hung suspended.

Isiem nodded toward the chain. "A magnifier?"

"You shouldn't have left Pangolais, my friend." Ascaros spoke softly, raising his bloodied hand to the sky. A spasm of pleasure and pain wracked his features, then faded back into his usual self-possessed detachment. "You turned your back on many useful tools."

"I didn't care for their cost."

"What cost? I have freedom, power, privilege. The only cost I chafe at bearing is the one Mesandroth imposed. The Umbral Court gives much and asks little."

"The boy I knew in Crosspine would have felt differently."

"The boy you knew in Crosspine was a child. And an idiot." Ascaros flicked his hand, shedding the beads of blood in a spray. He unwound the spiked chain, wiped it clean, and tucked it back into its pocket. Then, flexing his wounded fist, he moved toward the center of their group. "From a height the world looks very different, Isiem. I've fought to get here. Unlike you, I don't intend to give it up."

The shadowcaller passed Kyril on his way. From the paladin's stony face, it was clear she'd overheard him. Silently, she went to stand beside Ascaros, never once looking at the black-robed man, while Teglias stayed near Isiem.

Ganoven quickly followed the Sarenite, even as he thrust an imperious finger at his underlings. "Pulcher. Copple. Stay with the wagon."

"Guess that means I'm with you," Ena said with a chuckle, going over to Isiem. She held out a stubby-fingered hand, closing it around his with a grip solid as rock. It was reassuring in its warmth, although Isiem caught himself wishing that it were Kyril holding his hand rather than the dwarf.

It was a foolish thought. A distraction. He dismissed it, focusing on building his spell. Teglias took his other hand, and Ganoven cautiously took the Sarenite's, but Isiem scarcely noticed either of them. He was lost in the magic.

Through the ether, Isiem reached for the seen greenery of Molthune. He conjured the memory of the scene he'd scryed with Ascaros: the dense looming trees of the Backar Forest, its southeastern edge gnawed to blackened stumps by Cettigne's appetite for farmland and firewood. The city itself was visible only as a constant plume of smoke down the Nosam River. Fields of ripening wheat and low, sprawling potato mounds rolled out under tidy farmhouses south of the immense forest, and a broad road traced the river's course down from Lake Encarthan.

It seemed an idyllic, peaceful place, untroubled by the darkness that draped Nidal and threatened Cheliax. From conversations with Ena and Kyril, he knew it was not so—that Molthune, like any nation on Golarion, had its own troubles—but those troubles seemed less intractable, and the perils to Molthune's people less grave, than the dangers besetting its neighbors.

When he had the vision steady in his thoughts, Isiem spoke the word that would finish his spell and stepped through. Distantly he heard Ena grunt and Ganoven suck in a sharp breath, but his companions' alarm registered only at the fading periphery of his awareness. The magic thrumming through his veins was all.

And then it was gone. He stood in a tangle of potato vines, soil crumbling under his feet and the Backar Forest at his side. On a nearby hillside, white-faced sheep growing into their autumn coats stared at him while their shepherd, a boy of fifteen or sixteen years, snored under the shade of a green-burred chestnut tree.

Ena, Teglias, and Ganoven popped out of the air around him, stumbling on the uneven potato rows. The wagon was already there, squared perfectly on the road, the horses in their traces and the Aspis toughs still in their seats. Kyril stood beside the animals, looking down the road toward the far-off city with one hand on the hilt of her sword.

Stronger, faster, more precise. Isiem doubted that he could have teleported the wagon at all, much less so swiftly or with such unerring aim. But Ascaros, with the tools and training of the Umbral Court, had done so effortlessly. It brought a twinge of envy.

The shadowcaller himself waited fifty yards to the side, a part of their group and yet not. The forest's shadows embraced the man, and it seemed to Isiem— perhaps fancifully, perhaps not—that they were made darker by his presence.

The Iomedaean was right, he thought, looking back to the faraway smoke of Cettigne. Molthune was not a paradise. No place touched by Nidal could be.

Chapter Seven
Stories

Ganoven's acquaintances wasted no time. The morning after Isiem's party came to their outpost to the west of Cettigne, their caravan set off for Nidal.

It was an enormous endeavor. Three hundred guards and mercenaries marched together in a patchwork army. Some were bright-eyed youths fresh off their family farms, hoping to earn enough money to buy a proper kit and join the Molthune Imperial Army. Military service was a swift road to citizenship and status in their nation, regardless of one's birth, but the most desirable assignments were reserved for those who had the means to afford them. A man who brought his own sword and shield was a better recruit, and could expect a more competitive posting, than a hayseed who came with nothing but the straw in his hair.

Those wide-eyed younglings brushed shoulders with companies of hard-bitten veterans, destitute adventurers, and gladiators at the ends of their careers. Not all of them were human. Dwarves, half-elves, and even a band of wild-haired centaurs in feathers and face paint numbered among the caravan's guards. Some of their more ordinary companions, meanwhile, bore the facial scars of convicted criminals.

Isiem felt uncomfortable walking alongside those. In Nidal, such undesirables would have been consigned to Zon-Kuthon's torturers immediately after trial, and would likely have been sacrificed within days. In Molthune, however, criminals did not always meet such grisly fates. The nation needed people to realize its expansionist ambitions, and so did not throw their lives away lightly. Some Molthuni murderers, if their crimes were not deemed too heinous, were given the choice to escape the gallows by serving their country. Such a man was forever marked with proof of his crime—it was said the brands on their faces were enchanted to resist erasure—but if he served a period of years in hard labor or military service to repay his debt to the nation, he would be officially forgiven and accepted into society once more.

Pardoning such criminals was more efficient, Isiem supposed, and certainly more humane . . . but he couldn't shake the bone-deep sense that it was terribly unwise. It wasn't the murderers' violence that upset him. He had done worse, as had every one of his companions; even Kyril, sworn to uphold Iomedae's ideals, had likely shed more blood than any gutter killer ever would. But they had done so within the bounds of the law, and the murderers had not. *That* was the violation that troubled him. If a man could not be trusted to obey the laws of his land, Isiem was loath to see him with a sword.

But the Imperial Governor of Molthune felt differently, and so a sizable contingent of branded convicts escorted their caravan to the borders. Isiem tried to avoid them, although he noted that Ena did not.

"They're just people," she said, as they spooned boiled beans from a mess pot at dinner that evening. While some of their fellow guards had brought their own provender for the march, many more had not. The Aspis merchants provided a cold meal in the mornings and a hot one at night. It was cheap, plain fare—heavy on beans and barley, with scarcely any vegetables and even less meat—but it was filling, and it was free. Ganoven, always quick to shave an extra copper, insisted that they eat it.

Isiem took his dented bowl of beans and went to sit with the dwarf at their campfire. It was a calm night, warm for the season, and they'd put blankets on their saddles to make seats around the flames. Teglias was already there, as was Kyril. The paladin had washed her hair, and she wore it loose to let it dry. It spilled over her shoulders and halfway down her back in a cloak of damp curls, the deep red almost black in the twilight.

Ganoven seldom ate with them, and Ascaros never did; neither of them was anywhere to be seen. Pulcher and Copple preferred the company of rougher mercenaries, and had gone to sit at one of the other fires. As Isiem settled on his seat, facing Kyril across the crackling campfire, he was quietly glad for that.

"Just people," Ena repeated around a mouthful of beans. A mild breeze cut through the odors of woodsmoke and horse manure that filled their camp. "Maybe they've made some mistakes, and probably they're not too nice, but I've made mistakes of my own and I'm not always so nice. I don't see a reason to hold that against them, and if we're going to be traveling together—maybe fighting together, maybe my life depending on theirs—I like to know who I'm with. And I'd like for them to know the same about me."

Teglias stirred his bowl's contents without much appetite. "Who are you talking about?"

"The convicts," Ena answered, nodding toward Isiem. "Our wizard doesn't trust them, on account of they've got no respect for the law."

"An important consideration," Teglias agreed, "if sometimes a secondary one." The cleric seemed glad to have something to take his mind off their pauper's dinner. He put the bowl down and leaned back on his blanket-draped saddle, crossing his weathered brown boots with their soles to the fire. The ruddy light took years off his face, making him seem almost as young as the rest of them. "On occasion, greater needs must outweigh the strict proscriptions of the law."

"Not in Nidal," Isiem said.

"No?" Teglias's short brown beard didn't quite cover the wry twist of his lips. "In all the years you lived under the gaze of the Umbral Court, do you mean to say you *never* did anything that would have attracted their condemnation if they'd noticed?"

Isiem shrugged. The question was ridiculous. Of course he had. Everyone had. The Umbral Court set so many traps and snares that no one who wanted to survive a day in Pangolais could abide by every letter of every law.

That question didn't deserve an answer, so instead Isiem tried the beans. They were woefully undersalted.

Only their warmth made them any more appetizing than a bowl full of lumpy plaster paste. He swallowed what he could, then set the spoon aside. "And you?"

"Of course. In my young and wild days, my scholarly pursuits were, I confess, sometimes just an excuse to get into trouble." Teglias's smile widened into a grin. He laced his hands behind the back of his head, stretching theatrically. "I could have been a Pathfinder, you know."

"Would've spared the Church of Sarenrae all sorts of headaches," Kyril observed dryly.

"And innumerable prizes," the cleric said with a mock-offended lift of his chin.

"Really," Kyril said. "Innumerable prizes. As I recall, your greatest triumph in the service of the Dawnflower was hauling home a load of fakes."

"Why don't you tell him that story, Teglias?" Ena said, smirking. "Might as well inspire Isiem to have as much faith in your leadership as the rest of us do."

The bearded Sarenite chuckled. "Oh, fine, twist my arm." He looked at Isiem. "I'm sure you must have heard of Stavian I's purge."

The Nidalese wizard nodded. Nearly two hundred years ago, Stavian I, who was then the Grand Prince of Taldor, had outlawed the worship of Sarenrae in his empire and had declared the Dawnflower's faithful to be traitors. The churches had been claimed for other faiths or razed to the ground, and Sarenites who refused to renounce their religion had fled Taldor, lest they be imprisoned or executed.

"It won't surprise you to know that quite a few Sarenite relics were supposed to have been destroyed during the Great Purge," Teglias said, "or that many of those relics were smuggled to other fates instead. Some were sold on the black market. Others were hoarded inside Taldor.

"One of those hoards was supposed to have been in the home of a wealthy Taldan noblewoman who was arrested and exiled for her faith some years later. Her family was stripped of its name and lost all their assets. Their Westpark townhouse, where the hoard was supposedly hidden, eventually fell into the hands of the Alcedos family. One of the Alcedos scions, Senator Riscaro Alcedos, set up a young mistress in that house.

"Now, rumors of this hoard had been floating around for decades, but the church leadership did not believe it worth investigating until some of the pieces began to trickle out onto the black market. Our agents traced them back to Oppara—and, more specifically, to the Alcedos townhouse in Westpark and the senator's mistress, Zephiba of the Scarlet Veils."

"From the name alone, you can guess what she was like," Kyril interrupted, "and we'll leave it at that, because I don't feel like sitting through Teglias's hours-long reminiscences of her boudoir. I've heard that story once, and that was enough to scar me for life."

"I still hold a flame," the cleric agreed wistfully. He shifted his weight on the saddle. "Well, anyway, back then I was young and brash and boastful, and my superiors either believed my bragging about how I could charm any woman in the world, or—more likely—they just got tired of listening to it. In any case, they packed me off to Oppara, where my assignment was to win

Zephiba's trust and find out whether she had any more of our religious relics.

"To make a long story short . . . I did, she did, and they all turned out to be fakes. Every last one. Zephiba knew the rumors too, you see, and she was as skilled in forgery as she was in the arts of love. The originals had never been there. Wherever that exiled noblewoman hid her treasures, it wasn't in Westpark; Zephiba had no more idea where they really were than I did. But, being a clever woman, she spun disappointment into opportunity. The real relics weren't there, so she made her own. And sold them for an even bigger profit, since she could craft as many fakes as the market would bear." He shrugged. "You can't blame her, really. Sensible courtesans begin planning their retirements early."

Ena chortled. "And that was our revered leader's greatest success: uncovering a bunch of worthless forgeries." The dwarf smushed the last of her beans into paste with the back of her spoon and scraped them out of the bowl into her mouth.

"Yes, well," Teglias said. "The *point* is, I've broken a fair number of laws myself. Some of those laws, I happen to believe, deserved to be broken."

"Not the ones these Molthuni have broken," Isiem said.

"Maybe not, but you don't get to judge that," Ena retorted, "any more than *we* judged *you*." She swallowed and poked the handle of her spoon in the wizard's direction. "Where would you be if we had?"

"Still in Pezzack, I should think," Kyril agreed, "and that would have been a pity."

"I imagine you'd have found your nightblade without me," Isiem said, trying for a levity that might mask his real response.

It didn't work. The paladin caught his gaze and held it, her dark eyes infinitely solemn. "Perhaps," she said, "but that wasn't what I meant. It would have been a pity for your sake. Not ours. The Molthuni are wise: they recognize that a man may be redeemed, no matter how dark his past, by the value and virtue of his life going forward. It's my hope that in traveling with us, and learning from us, you will accept the same possibility for yourself.

"Look at the Molthuni army," she continued. "Everyone who wants to enlist has the opportunity to prove herself. No one is rejected for past misdeeds, or race, or even species. They accept hobgoblins and werewolves, if those hobgoblins and werewolves want to serve their nation. They do not trust foolishly, but they *do* trust, with tolerance and compassion. And because of that, and the strength it gives them, Molthune will become a power on the world stage soon."

It should have been condescending, that speech. Ascaros would have scoffed at it, or replied with insults of his own. But for Isiem, sitting among companions who would have been mortal enemies two years earlier, the half-elf's words struck unexpectedly hard.

The best answer he could muster was a diffident shrug. "We'll see what comes."

"So we will," Kyril agreed.

After that the talk drifted to other things. Ena pulled out a collection of "hoppers" she wanted to show them. They were metal cylinders, small enough that the dwarf

LIANE MERCIEL

could easily fit two into the palm of her hand, with inch-long pins protruding from the top. The bottom of the pin was coated with a reagent, the dwarf explained, which set off a burst of violent heat when it was pressed down and plunged into a compartment of liquid underneath. That, in turn, caused the whole contraption to leap into the air and then explode.

Her attempt to demonstrate one, however, resulted in the cylinder falling over and emitting a damp squeal as vinegary froth spilled from the top around the pin. A weak fizz of air made a *perrrp* noise for almost a full minute, then dribbled off into the mud.

The dwarf shrugged sheepishly and walked over to collect her failed device. "The design still needs some adjustments. But she'll be lethal when I get her working."

"Lethal to whom?" Teglias asked, with a mock-dread that did not seem entirely feigned. He peered at her across the campfire. "Are you carrying those things around in your pack? What if you fall from your pony and they all go off?"

"They can't go off until I put the pins in, and I don't put the pins in until I'm ready to use them," Ena said. "I do have them in my pack, though. I suppose if you shook them hard enough, they might explode. Better pray I don't fall off the pony."

"How does a dwarf get into alchemy anyway?" Kyril asked.

Ena squinted at the paladin. She propped a hand on a stocky hip, bristling with exaggerated indignation. "What do you think of when you think of dwarves?"

"Mountains," Teglias offered. "Gold. Gems. Mines."

105

"Axes and orcs," Isiem said, "and long bloody wars."

Kyril smirked. "Spitting on floors."

"*You*," Ena announced, thrusting an accusatory finger at the paladin, "are a narrow-minded fool beholden to stereotypes. The rest of you, however, are correct. That *is* the realm of the dwarves: mines under mountains filled with gold and gems. Evil orcs skulking in shadowy tunnels, red eyes glowing with greed. And us, a doughty but hard-pressed people, struggling to stave them off with axes to protect all that is ours."

She raised her arms dramatically, then dropped them with a laugh. "Now consider: Torag has blessed us with much more effective ways of cleaving open the mountains than chiseling at them with picks. He has given us the sacred art of *alchemy*. And that can be a weapon, too. A bomb that can blast tunnels through the heart of a mountain can surely destroy a horde of orcs—and can do it without risking the lives of our people in close-quarters combat.

"So we learned it, as we learned all the Father of Creation's secrets, and we kept it close to our hearts. Most other races never even suspect our skill. But it shouldn't surprise you, with a little thought. It really shouldn't."

"Why did you leave?" Isiem asked.

Ena didn't answer right away. When she did, it was with a sigh, and a look away to the empty distance beyond their fires. "Things change."

There was a silence. The noise from other campfires flowed in to fill it. Twenty yards away, a pair of heavily tattooed Varisian knife dancers—sisters, by the looks of them—spun before a spellbound throng of mercenaries. Pulcher and Copple were in their audience, each more slack-jawed than the other. To their right, four dwarves were playing a drinking game with a green-faced farmboy who appeared to be heartily regretting his bravado in joining them.

Kyril cleared her throat. "I'll tell you why *I* left. Because I was born in the Kyonin town of Erages, to half-elven parents, and it doesn't take long for a child to realize when her country doesn't want her kind."

"I thought you grew up in Westcrown?" Isiem said.

"I came to that city later. I found Iomedae there." She glanced down at the hilt of her sword, tracing the emblem on its pommel reverently. "But there were years of wandering before that. Years of trying to find a place and a purpose." When she looked up, her luminous brown eyes caught Isiem's. In them was the same compassion, and empathy, that alternately drew him to her and made him recoil.

The wizard stood, dropping his spoon into the empty bowl. "I'm pleased you found what you sought. Please excuse me. It's late, and I must rest."

He left them by the fire. The night felt colder as Isiem walked back to his tent, although he knew it was only his own turmoil that made it seem so. The merriment of other companies shadowed him to his door; it was a mercy when he let the tent flap fall shut behind him, cutting off their songs and laughter.

A candle was burning on a table inside. Only one, but it was evidently enough light for Ascaros, who sat nearby on a folded blanket, studying a slender book.

Isiem paused by the tent flap, surprised to see the shadowcaller. Although he traveled with the caravan by day, Ascaros had been teleporting himself back to

Pangolais each night. In part, he did it so that he could report to the Umbral Court, but the greater reason was that he didn't care for the discomforts of the road. Until some real demand on his magic prevented the indulgence, Ascaros had informed his friend, he wanted a soft bed to sleep in and a hot bath to wake to, and he meant to have it.

What he hadn't said, but Isiem suspected to be true, was that he also left each night because he didn't trust their new companions enough to sleep in their presence. Paranoia drove Ascaros at least as much as the desire for the comforts of his own bed.

It was a strange world, he thought, where a man felt safer sleeping under Zon-Kuthon's thumb than he did among the green farmlands of Molthune.

Still, the shadowcaller was here tonight, long after the hour when he normally left.

Isiem took his boots off, deliberately knocking them together to announce his presence as he put them aside. "You missed beans at dinner tonight. There might have been a bit of cabbage in there too, somewhere. Possibly. I'm not sure. But there were certainly beans."

Ascaros didn't even crack a smile. He held the book open, sliding it across the floor toward Isiem with a push from two fingertips. "What does that look like to you?"

The book was opened to a page depicting a crude, thick-lined drawing of a monster. It appeared to be a faithful reproduction, but of what, Isiem couldn't tell. The creature stood low to the ground with a long, curved tail like a scorpion's. Lumps bulged all down its misshapen back, but the drawing was so clumsy and stylized that it was impossible to determine whether they were meant to be scales, tumors, or some other protuberance. Five round eyes surrounded a toothy mouth that gaped open in a horrible grin. Two curved pincers hooked from the front of its body, each ending in a mass of furiously scribbled triangles that were, perhaps, supposed to represent claws.

"It looks like some drunk provincial's delirium," Isiem said, pushing the book back. He was careful with it; the tome looked much older than he'd initially realized. Its bindings were peeled and cracking, its pages fragile as onionskin. "What's it *meant* to be?"

"The Beast of the Backar Forest," Ascaros spun the book around on the floor to face himself and picked it up again, setting it on his lap. "It's the only depiction I could find. I didn't even find it, truthfully. Silence told me where to look—in this obscure old collection of folk legends and border tales." He made a face. "The shae is taking great pleasure in baiting me on this subject."

"That thing in the drawing is meant to be undead? How can you possibly tell? It's all blobs and bulges."

"That was the style of the time." Ascaros sank his chin into the heel of one hand, staring at the candlelit drawing. "I can't imagine it's accurate, any more than all those Opparan debutantes are really as chubby and milky-skinned as court painters portray them. They all look like the same woman—and so this beast looks like every other monster to have been captured in a wood-cut two centuries ago."

Isiem crossed the two steps to his own bedroll and sat on the piled blankets, facing Ascaros. "Is there any written description to go along with the drawing?"

"Nothing useful. 'The Beaste of Backar, encountered this our year of 4504 in the Reckoning of Absalom. Slaughtered fifteen men, four horses, two oxen and a dog in a great charnel stinke.' It goes on for three paragraphs, but the only useful information is that the creature apparently was 'clad in the earth of graves' and was so terrifying that all who saw it loosed their bowels. Oh, and it has 'skulls innumerable,' but no head. That part actually makes a bit of sense, though. Khorsaveir was known to be obsessed with the ancient runelords of Thassilon, and they were said to have created undead guardians with multiple skulls. If he was imitating them, or uncovered some bit of their arcana, he might well have made a similarly over-skulled servant."

"That's something to look forward to." Isiem took off his cloak and folded it up to make a pillow, then lay down in the bedroll. "How did they drive it off? The people who encountered it during the Oxen-Slaughter of 4504, I mean."

"They didn't. It killed everyone it could reach. When there didn't appear to be any more survivors, it lumbered off, dragging clawfuls of corpses back into the forest. The witness who reported the encounter escaped by playing dead under the wreckage of his wagon. Later he killed himself, apparently unable to live with the memory of what he'd seen."

"Oh good, even *more* to look forward to." Isiem sighed. "Look, if the book isn't telling you anything useful, stop reading it. Why play into Silence's game?"

"It might be useful." Ascaros closed the book and put it aside, then snuffed the candle. In the darkness, Isiem could hear the shadowcaller climbing into his own bedroll. A whisper of smoke and hot wax lingered in the air. "It tells me that the Beast drags off its victims. That wasn't the only attack. Since then, the Beast has reemerged every few years, slaughtering small parties of travelers and pilgrims, down to the present day. Little else is consistent in the accounts, but it does always seem to take the corpses of those it's killed."

Isiem rolled over, propping his head up on an elbow. "So how do we use that? Zombies? Made to look alive with illusions and loaded with Ena's bombs? We could let it drag them off to its lair, track it, detonate the bombs, and attack immediately after."

"Good, but maybe not good enough. How are we to know if the illusions will deceive it? Undead often sense things differently, and we may only have one chance at it. No . . . to be sure, we must use living bait."

The unspoken suggestion hung heavy between them. Then Isiem said: "I don't think Ena's going to be eager to volunteer as beast bait."

"I wasn't intending to use her."

"Then who did you want to use?"

"It needn't be your concern," Ascaros said softly, after another long pause. "Your new friends would surely object if they knew. They might blame you if you were involved."

"I already am."

"You are not. But you might be, if you keep asking questions. Is that what you want?"

"Tell me," Isiem said. "What's your plan?"

Chapter Eight
Temptations

"Treasure, you say? How *much* treasure?" An expression of almost comical greed washed across Caffoc's face. He hunched closer, dropping his voice to a hoarse conspirator's whisper. "Who else knows about it?"

From the tiny wrinkle of Ascaros's nose, Isiem could tell that the mercenary's breath was uncommonly foul, although he himself was too far away to be touched. Rendered invisible by his spell, he watched their conference from thirty feet away.

The shadowcaller did not recoil. Smoothing his disgust away, he replied: "No one. Except you, me, my friend, and yours. Let's keep it that way, shall we?"

"Yes," Caffoc agreed at once, sinking back onto his heels. He scratched the back of his neck unconsciously, then caught himself doing it and yanked his hand away with a fleeting look of nervous guilt. "Yes. It must be a secret."

The man was an addict. To what, Isiem didn't know, but it was plain that *something* had its hooks deep in his soul. His need and his shame were written in his shaking shoulders and constant twitching. Caffoc picked at himself ceaselessly: he scratched his neck, wiped at his huge beak of a nose, and pinched the peeling skin from his lips—and every time he realized he was doing it, he shot furtive, darting glances at anyone who might have seen.

It was those anxious glances, more than the tics themselves, that betrayed Caffoc's addiction. His guilt and his fear told the tale.

And it was because of that guilt and that fear—and the greed that fed them—that Ascaros had singled the man out for temptation. The Beast of the Backar Forest needed bait, but so did the intended bait himself. A man like Caffoc, who had clearly once been a soldier but had likely lost his position as a result of his weakness and was now desperate enough to march into the Umbral Basin for money to feed his vice, was easy to hook.

"Good," Ascaros said easily. The shadowcaller wore a false face, as he had for almost the entirety of their journey. Once he realized how distrustful the Molthuni were of his true appearance, he'd changed it—and, because versatility was useful and the caravan was large enough to hide it, he'd adopted three separate illusory guises throughout their travels.

Today Ascaros appeared as the least-used of the trio: a sandy-haired mercenary with a deep cleft in his chin and a heavy Taldan accent. "As to how much, we don't know exactly. The creature's hoard must be considerable. It's been in the forest for ages, and no one has ever raided its lair. But, of course, as no one has ever laid eyes on it, no one knows how much gold might be waiting."

"It's a lot, though." Caffoc squeezed the words out in a whisper that sounded like a prayer, not a question. "It must be a lot."

"Surely," Ascaros agreed, putting his hands on his knees as he pushed himself up to stand. "And we'll cut it into equal shares. With four strong arms, I'm sure we can defeat any beast in these woods . . . but we'll need all four. Can we count on your assistance?"

Caffoc's thin red ponytail swept across his shoulder as he nodded jerkily. He wiped at his nose again. "Equal shares."

"Your friend's in, too?"

"He will be."

"Good man." Ascaros clapped the red-haired soldier hard on a shoulder, causing Caffoc to startle and wince. "I'll be back when we get closer to its lair."

The disguised shadowcaller strode away. The caravan was about to start moving again. All around them, mercenaries were pulling up horses' stakes and emptying latrine buckets, while tents collapsed like mushrooms under the heat of a withering sun.

Isiem waited a moment longer, watching Caffoc gnaw his lip. The addict took an indecisive step toward his gathering company, hesitated, and then cursed himself furiously but near-soundlessly and hurried back to his tent, his entire body shaking with suppressed emotion.

Outside that tent, a young male half-orc was trying without much success to scrub a couple of bowls clean with handfuls of grass. Isiem knew, having spied on them invisibly before, that the half-orc called himself

Otter, and that he was Caffoc's ward. The soldier had found him somewhere—where, exactly, Isiem wasn't sure, although he had the impression it had been on a battlefield or near one—and had taken him under his wing, for Otter was incapable of caring for himself.

Whether because of an injury that had rattled his skull or simply because he'd been born that way, the half-orc was slow, suggestible, and earnest as a puppy. He leaped to do anything Caffoc asked of him. In Isiem's first few days with the caravan, Otter had been just as eager to do anything anyone else asked of him, too; the boy had been the butt of some cruel jokes before Caffoc put a stop to that.

But he was strong. Otter looked to be about fifteen or sixteen, in Isiem's estimation, and under his green-tinged skin he had the muscles of a man ten years older. If he'd been born to one of the savage tribes, and trained from birth as their warriors were said to be, he might have a better chance against the Beast of the Backar Forest than his behavior with the caravan suggested.

As Caffoc approached the tent, he slowed and came to a stop partially screened by another mercenary's tent. He could see Otter, but Otter couldn't see him. The man stood there for a moment, tense, his hands strangling one another as he watched the boy. Half-formed emotions darkened his face and passed, like storm clouds blown across the sky.

Then he sucked in a breath, retied the leather thong that held back his lanky red hair, and strode toward Otter, all traces of his indecision walled off behind a stony facade.

"Give me those bowls," Caffoc snapped as he came to the tent. He took them roughly from the confused boy, snatching the clump of stained grass Otter had been holding and tossing it aside. "Get my swords, then take down the tent."

"They're clean," Otter said, quailing from the man's apparent anger. He hunched his shoulders and looked at the ground. "I cleaned them already."

"I didn't ask you that, did I? Go get my swords. Like I *said*." Caffoc shoved the boy toward the tent flap with one hand. There was no real force to the gesture, but Otter stumbled as though he'd been kicked by a mule. He hurried into the tent and back out, clutching a bundle of weapons.

Caffoc yanked the bundle from him and opened it. He took his own sword out first: a plain steel longsword, its leather-wrapped hilt stained with years of use. The other blades in the bundle were a heavy, notched scimitar, evidently of orc make, and a crude long knife, almost a cleaver, with uneven holes punched in the side of the blade. A moth-eaten dog's tail dangled from the hilt like a tassel.

Both of those weapons had the look of trophies. They weren't blades meant to sit easily in human hands. The handle of that goblin-made knife was too small for a man's grip, while the scimitar looked too heavy and ill-balanced for an ordinary human to swing without exhausting himself quickly in battle.

Caffoc gazed at the weapons, chewing his lip again, while Otter struggled to take down the tent by himself. When the half-orc was finished bundling up the canvas and strapping the tent onto its poles for carrying, Caffoc roused out of his trance. "Come here."

Otter obeyed, his head hanging guiltily. He glanced sidelong at Caffoc without lifting his face, as if he feared a scolding for even that much.

The soldier sighed and rubbed the bridge of his nose. "Otter, I'm not angry." He held out the goblin knife, offering it hilt first. "I want you to have this. It's time you had a blade of your own."

"No," Otter said, wide-eyed and worried. He took a stumbling step backward, gaping at the proffered knife fearfully. His shaggy black hair fell over his eyes, making him blink. "You said if I have a knife, people will think I'm a bad orc. They'll hurt me. I don't want them to hurt me. I'm not a bad orc."

"I know what I said," Caffoc muttered. "But it's time now. You have to learn how to fight. I won't always be here to take care of you, and there are times when you'll have to defend yourself."

"I won't," Otter said stubbornly. "I'm a good orc. I do what people say. They see I'm good and helpful and they don't hurt me. I don't want a knife."

"You'll take it, by Asmodeus's iron balls, and you'll damn well learn to use it." Caffoc threw the knife at the boy, who hopped clumsily aside. "I need you to help me fight."

"Fight who?"

"Not who," Caffoc said. "What." He stepped past the boy, shaking his head as he stooped to pick the knife out of the dirt. He plucked a stray leaf from the dog-tail tassel and wiped off the blade. "A monster in the woods. We need to kill it."

"Why?" Otter stared at the knife in Caffoc's hands. He lifted his gaze to the man, repeating his question in the same slow tone. "Why? Is it a bad monster?"

Isiem didn't wait to hear what Caffoc told him. The wizard's invisibility spell was beginning to fail. He could feel the warning tingle of its fading prickle across his skin. In seconds he would be visible to them.

He withdrew from their camp. By the time Isiem reached his own tent, he was once more in plain view.

The tent was already down and packed. Not because Ascaros had lifted a finger to help, but because Ena had bullied Pulcher and Copple into doing it, as she had since the second day of their journey, when she realized that it wasn't going to get done otherwise.

Ascaros, who once more appeared as his true self—no, Isiem reminded himself, not *really* his true self; only the healthy, less-disturbing version that he would have been without Mesandroth's curse—sat on a black horse beside their wagon. He nodded curtly to Isiem when he saw the wizard, then resumed watching the horizon.

Isiem returned the shadowcaller's gesture, although Ascaros was no longer looking at him and didn't seem to notice. The caravan was finally beginning to move, so he conjured his own spell-woven mount. After climbing onto the smoke-gray horse, he fell into place on the other side of the wagon, where he caught sight of Ascaros only sporadically throughout the day.

The memory of Caffoc trying to force the knife onto his half-orc charge gnawed at Isiem. There was no point discussing it with Ascaros, he knew. If anything, the information would merely seal the shadowcaller's resolve. In the judgment of any true Nidalese, the world would be much improved by the removal of a hopeless addict and a dimwitted half-orc. Such weak, flawed individuals only burdened their societies; they were parasites, and like all parasites, best dealt with by being picked off and cast into the flames. And if their deaths could be played for tactical advantage, it was all but a holy duty to see that done.

So went the thinking of the Nidalese, and Isiem knew full well that Ascaros would share those sentiments. But he himself no longer felt that way.

Flawed as Caffoc was, he'd had the compassion to take in a lost half-orc, and the sense of responsibility to protect him from those that would abuse the boy's trust. And slow-witted as Otter was, he had an unswerving loyalty to the man who had saved him, and a prodigious physical strength that would surely be of value to a village smith or Molthuni sergeant somewhere. There were useful traits in both of them, or at least the potential to *become* useful, intermingled with the weaknesses that Ascaros meant to exploit.

Unless Isiem intervened, though, that potential would surely be drowned out by their baser desires. Ascaros, like any Umbral agent, was skilled at manipulating people's worst qualities. Jealousy, anger, fear, ambition: all of those were tools with which the shadowcaller could pry open someone's heart and lay the soul bare. Isiem, who had trained beside him in the Dusk Hall, could do the same.

Appealing to someone's better nature, however, was *not* something they'd ever been taught. Isiem had tried in the past, but every time, he'd failed. He hadn't even been able to turn his own friends aside from fatal folly, and he doubted he'd have any more success with Caffoc.

It was tempting to just tell one of the others about Ascaros's scheme—Ena, or Kyril, or Teglias; any of them would surely handle the matter more deftly than Isiem could—but he wasn't sure where that would stop once it started. They might turn on Ascaros in an excess of righteousness, and Isiem wasn't sure which side he would take then.

Besides, that was the coward's way out. Better he should handle it himself.

He turned the problem over in his mind while watching the yellow fields and heavy-boughed orchards of Molthune roll past their caravan. Occasionally, they rode past flocks of fat beige sheep or a scattering of angular-hipped cows grazing on a hillside, always tended by one or more of the rough-coated collies that seemed ubiquitous in this part of the world. Some of the dogs were red and white, others splashed with tan; all of them were beautiful, and keenly intent on their work.

None of the animals paid the caravan much mind, but the locals who watched them did. Whether farmers or shepherds, the Molthuni kept their distance, and they watched the Aspis caravan warily. Everything about the farmfolk said that they wanted no trouble, and that they expected nothing else to come from meddling with foreigners.

Their stares pricked at Isiem's conscience. Finally, after they passed a young mother who called her children in from apple-picking to clutch them close as the caravan passed, he could bear it no longer. Wheeling his horse around, he rode back toward Caffoc and Otter.

The red-haired soldier pulled his horse's reins back when he saw Isiem approaching. They had never spoken; while Isiem had spied on them several times, he had always done so unseen. Now, as he rode to them openly, Caffoc drew away warily, his mouth a thin line and his nostrils flared. Otter didn't catch on to his guardian's discomfort until Isiem was within arm's-reach, but he started visibly when he did.

"Is there trouble?" the half-orc asked. He gawked at Isiem's near-white hair, pale complexion, and deep gray robes. Although their inky color was faded by his time in Devil's Perch, the garments were distinctly Nidalese in cut, and the severity of their lines was emphasized by the sparing silver accents that suggested piercings in the cloth. Even to one who did not recognize their provenance, the effect was unsettling.

"There is not," Isiem assured him, although he looked at Caffoc when he said it. "I only want to talk."

"We've nothing to say to the likes of you." Caffoc tried to urge his horse past Isiem's, but the animal shied away from the wizard and refused to go forward. Otter looked uncertainly from one man to the other, staying to the side.

"Perhaps not," Isiem said, "or at least not yet. But I have some things to say to you."

"About what?"

"The Beast of the Backar Forest. You will do your young ward a disservice by asking him to stand against it. He trusts you, and you would send him to his death." Isiem kept his attention on Caffoc; he did not give Otter so much as a glance. But he saw the addict's eyes flick toward the half-orc, saw the pain that flitted across the man's thin face, and knew he'd hit his mark.

"Are you sure of that?" Caffoc asked weakly, dropping his gaze to the ground.

"For centuries the Beast has lived in that wood, slaying entire companies at will and leaving no survivors. Unless you and your young friend are heroes out of song, yes, I'm sure."

"We're not," Otter broke in. From the suddenly defensive jut of the half-orc's lip, it seemed he thought Isiem was mocking them with the suggestion. "We're not heroes. We're just people."

Caffoc's head tipped forward. His thin, seamed face was a study in conflict: self-loathing, desperate need, and recognition of his own weakness warred with whatever better angels his nature could conjure. Isiem didn't know which way the man would fall, and he doubted that Caffoc knew either—but after a tortured stretch, the red-haired soldier swallowed, glancing sidelong at his young ward.

"That we are," he muttered, turning his horse away from Isiem's. This time the animal obeyed him willingly, eager to move away from the unnerving encounter. The wizard could scarcely hear him above the animal's relieved snort, so quietly did the man speak. "Just people."

Without another word, Caffoc moved away. Otter followed him, casting a troubled glance over his shoulder at Isiem. The wizard waited a moment longer, then returned to his own party, still clustered loosely around the wagon. It did not appear that anyone else in the caravan had cared to eavesdrop on their conversation, nor that his absence had attracted much notice from his own companions, but Ascaros gave him an inquisitive look as he fell in beside the shadowcaller.

"Your plan won't work," Isiem told him. "The addict's backed out. We'll have to do this the hard way."

Chapter Nine
The Hunt

I wish you hadn't told me about that half-orc and his addict friend," Ena grumbled as she funneled colorless fluids into a row of round bottles. After filling each one, the dwarf inserted a slender pin into the top of each bottle with the care of a jeweler setting a priceless diamond into her life's masterwork. "It makes it much less fun to complain about how *I've* got to do all the dirty work now."

"Very sorry," Isiem said without looking up from his spellbook. It was hard to read by the soft white light of his floating glow-globe, particularly as he'd sent it to shine over Ena's work and was sitting on the shadowy periphery of its illumination, but he had little alternative. Dawn was still two hours away, and they needed to be off before the rest of the camp awoke. After dealing with the Beast of the Backar Forest, Teglias hoped to continue separately into the Umbral Basin, and none of them wanted to be followed by the curious or greedy when they broke off from the caravan.

Ena didn't answer. When she'd filled the last of the dozen bottles she'd brought, the dwarf rose from her squat, pulling each arm over her head in turn to stretch away the stiffness. She rubbed her eyes with the backs of her fists and looked over to Isiem. "You still reading?"

"No." He closed the compact book and tucked it back into a pocket. The words of magic were etched in his mind. If he shut his eyes, the wizard could almost see them, written in incandescent gold on the inside of his eyelids. He let the glowing sphere wink out. "I'm ready."

"Then let's not waste time." Ena slid each of her newly prepared bottles into a padded carrying case. She slung the case over a broad shoulder and led Isiem away from the caravan and into the woods.

The trees of the Backar Forest closed around them almost as soon as they stepped off the road. Twenty yards past its periphery, there was no hint that any civilization existed in the world. Although it was well into autumn, and the farms they'd passed had been nearing harvest, there was no sign that the wood's wild growth was slowing for winter's approach.

Broad-leaved brambles with tiny black berries wound around the thinner trees' trunks, while spindly shrubs with pointed grayish needles crowded the scant spaces between them. The forest's low, damp hollows were thick with skunk cabbage and threaded with glimmering ribbons of water; its hills and rises were green with wilder tangles of vegetation. As dawn began to filter through the autumn trees, it shed a misty gray haze across the layered loam of past years' leaves.

Isiem had never seen any forest so verdant. It was easy to imagine fairies dancing across its dawnlit boughs, or satyrs romping through the forest's riotous fertility. Much more difficult, he thought as he picked his way clumsily through the undergrowth, to imagine an undead monster lurking in this place so full of life.

For almost half an hour they walked through the wood without speaking, accompanied by the trills of unseen birds and the babble of hidden creeks. The rich green-brown scents of moss and fallen leaves enveloped them, punctuated occasionally by a pungent note of crushed skunk cabbage.

Ena worked her way through the forest methodically as dawn melted into morning, casting from side to side like a hound following a scent. She tied the ends of her weatherstained blue cloak around her waist to keep the garment off the wet earth and tucked her trousers into her boots. Forgoing any notions about trying to look dignified for the deer and squirrels, Isiem quickly emulated her precautions.

Other than the odd mutter to herself when she came across something she didn't like, Ena made no sound in the forest. Even her footfalls were nearly silent, in sharp contrast to Isiem's constant snags and blunders. He hadn't expected a dwarf to have any real skill in the woods, but she did, and her ease left him both envious and mystified.

Just as Isiem was plucking his sleeve off another bramble—somehow he'd gotten the cloth wrapped around thorns on all sides of the vine, a feat of baffling ingenuity—Ena held up a hand, signaling that she'd found some sign of their quarry.

Isiem approached. The scarred dwarf stepped aside, pointing a booted toe to the patch of earth that had drawn her attention.

Under the broad, veiny leaves of two nearby skunk cabbages was a patch of withered ground. A fine web of dead white roots, brittle and impossibly fragile, lay over the earth like frost that refused to melt. Isiem stooped to touch them, and found that they'd been completely drained of moisture.

A few feet away, obscured by undergrowth and visible only while looking sideways near to the ground, the wizard noted several grayish, shriveled stems just barely poking out of the damp earth. Wrinkled black shreds clung to their tops: skunk cabbage leaves, dehydrated almost past recognition. The dead plants appeared to have been pulled upward by some unearthly force, drained of life, and abandoned in the mud. While new growth had sprouted around the remains, nothing had touched the dead things themselves. No animal had eaten them; not even mold blemished those wizened black leaves.

"Bit unnerving," Ena said, straightening and moving to the left. "It continues this way, and the other way, too. Looks like a circle." She paced back across the arc, this time in a straight line, measuring her steps. "Thirty or forty feet across, by my estimation. What would do that?"

Isiem shrugged. He knew of nothing that would make that circular blast of death, but that meant little. The world held stranger creatures than he could imagine. "Some type of life drain, maybe. Ascaros suggested it was a wizard's creation. It may have aspects of different undead bound together."

"Or it might be something completely unique." The dwarf chuckled humorlessly and moved forward through the wood.

Three more times she stopped, twice to point out similar circles of long-dead vegetation, the third time to note a badly rusted suit of chainmail that had sunk deep into the mud beside a sparkling creek. Yellowed bones poked out of the chainmail, and withered hair matted the moss beneath it. Although time and weather had stripped the corpse of its flesh, its bones did not appear to have been disturbed by any scavenger.

The remains were in a sorry state, and it was impossible for Isiem to determine what had killed the chainmail's wearer. He couldn't even tell if those half-buried bones had once been human. But he felt a prick of apprehension as he walked away from the bones. In this place, so full of life and its hungers, *something* should have dragged away a limb to gnaw or stolen that hair to line a nest. That the corpse had lain undisturbed for so long suggested they were facing a profound desecration—and that was a frightening prospect.

"You're not going to tell me what killed him?" Ena asked when she saw Isiem leave the bones. "I was hoping you'd have a spell for that."

"None I know," the wizard replied. The spells he had readied were only able to confirm what he'd already guessed: even if the chainmail's wearer had been slain by some arcane force, no magic lingered in those old bones now.

"Well, that's useless," the dwarf said, although there was no heat to it. She walked on another half-mile, veering from side to side, then stopped and picked up a long deadwood stick. Poking the loam ahead of her, Ena continued until she found a suitable spot, where she paused and dug a narrow, shallow hole by stabbing the stick into the ground and wiggling it in circles. She dropped one of her glass bottles carefully into the hole, then covered it up and went on. A few yards later, she buried another.

"Are we that close?" Isiem asked. The dwarf only had a dozen or so traps; he doubted she'd be setting them if she didn't think they'd catch prey. "Should I tell the others to come?" They had left the others with the caravan, partly to deflect possible pursuit and partly because they were not sure where, exactly, the Beast lurked in the forest. By now the rest of their party would have filtered into the wood in twos or threes, each group leaving half an hour after the others and searching along a slightly different course.

Ena dug another hole and planted a third device, arranging them along the arms of a rough V that funneled toward the path she and Isiem had taken to approach this point. Using a shirtsleeve, she wiped a smear of mud off her brow. "Unless they've struck better sign on their own, yes. You can tell them that I anticipate we'll draw the beast out at nightfall."

"Do you think it fears the sun?" Many undead creatures did, but Isiem hadn't considered that the Beast of the Backar Forest might be among them. It seemed a glaring design flaw, and he wouldn't have expected an intentionally constructed undead to share it.

"I think there's a fair chance of that. We're near its lair—those blasts have been converging in this direction, and there've been old and new ones overlapping for about a hundred yards now—but it hasn't come out to greet us. Not while the sun's still shining. "Anyway, its choice to lurk in this particular forest in the first place suggests it might not care for daylight. There's not much here to draw undead. Not many humans around to feed on, no graveyards, no sites of historical atrocities as far as anyone's bothered to record. What's left?" The dwarf thrust a stubby finger at the surrounding wood, turning a slow circle to emphasize that they were hemmed in on all sides. "All these trees, and year-round protection from the sun."

"And you intend to lure it out," Isiem concluded with a sigh. "At night. Where it will probably have the advantage on us even if it isn't hindered by the sun."

"That's about the shape of it," the dwarf agreed. "Do you have any spells you want to lay down for our ambush?"

"Not particularly. I expected that it would come after us first."

Ena snorted and thrust her stick back into the ground. "If we had to rely on you, it would." She shook her head in exaggerated derision. "Wizards. Here I thought you were supposed to be masters of planning and plotting, and you can't even lay a trap for a pile of bones in the woods."

"Not until it's a little closer, no." Isiem plucked a small compass from his pocket. Its face was a flattened cabochon of polished bloodstone framed in spiky steel. The compass's needle was sharply serrated on both sides, as befit a creation of Zon-Kuthon's torturous faith.

Ascaros had loaned it to him, and Isiem had agreed with its necessity, but the wizard still found it deeply uncomfortable to hold Kuthite magic. The thing felt treacherous as a scorpion in his palm. The Midnight Lord was not known for his kindness to apostates.

Inwardly wincing, outwardly tranquil, Isiem nicked a finger against the needle's point. He squeezed a bead of blood onto the compass face, splashing more crimson onto the red specks and striations that mottled the dark green stone. Immediately the needle began to spin, faster and faster, revolving on the bloodstone until Isiem whispered: "Ascaros."

The needle stopped, pointing south-southwest. A second drop of blood caused it to resume its twirling, until Isiem said: "Teglias." And then, a third time: "Ganoven." With each name, the needle stopped abruptly, pointing southward in a slightly different direction. Each of his named companions carried a compass similar to his own, and the steely needle located them unerringly.

When the needle stilled on the last one, Isiem focused a thread of magic into the bloodstone. *We are here*, he sent into the stone, following it with a carefully surveyed image of their position in the forest. As Isiem woke the compass's magic, the blood he'd spattered onto the stone sizzled and hissed, burning off in curls of iron-scented smoke. *North. Ena has found the Beast. Join us.*

The last of the blood burned away. A dusting of ash clouded the bloodstone's gloss and dulled the needle's serrations. Isiem blew the ash away, silently relieved that the compass had gone inert so quickly, and returned the bauble to his pocket.

"They're coming?" Ena asked, leaning on her stick. She'd stopped digging to watch the wizard work, but once he put the compass away, she strode another few yards north to bury her next trap. "You told them where to find us?"

"I hope so. If the compass works as it should."

"You are *so* bad at reassuring me," the dwarf muttered, thrusting the stick into the wet earth and churning it around.

An hour later, Ena had buried all the traps she'd brought. The dwarf melted back into the woods, scouting ahead, while Isiem waited for the others to join them.

They came in a scattered trickle: Teglias and Kyril first, then Ganoven with his thugs, and finally Ascaros, alone, stone-faced and jarringly out of place in his stark Nidalese attire.

When they arrived, Kyril's lips were tight with frustration, and her cloak had picked up so many new snags that the cloth looked fuzzy. Ganoven sucked the back of his left hand as he came up the last rise; the skin was reddened with a crosshatch of scratches, as if he'd tried to backhand a bramble for its insolence in pricking him. Isiem wondered if the Aspis agent was actually stupid enough to have done that. It wouldn't have surprised him.

The rest of them seemed to have come through the forest none the worse for wear. Pulcher had a pink daisy tucked behind one ear, apparently unbeknownst to him. Isiem stared at it for a moment, puzzled as to which of their companions could have been frivolous enough to plant the flower on the man. The twinkle in Teglias's eye, and his not-quite-suppressed smile, suggested that the Sarenite cleric might have been the prankster.

"What is that idiotic thing?" Ganoven snapped when he finally left off nursing his injured hand long enough to notice Pulcher's decoration.

The towering thug just blinked at him in blank confusion while, beside him, Copple tittered behind a pudgy hand. Visibly irritated, Ganoven rose onto his toes, snatched the nodding daisy from behind the man's ear, thrust it in his face, and then hurled it into the mud. "*That* thing."

Pulcher stared at it for a while. His spectacles slid slowly down his nose, and he pushed them back up with a sausage-thick finger. After a long deliberation, he grunted and stepped past the flower. "I didn't put that there."

"No, of course not," Ganoven snapped. "It must have been your fairy godmother who planted it there. Maybe she thought it would finally make use of all that dirt between your ears."

Teglias coughed into a hand, both to interrupt them and to hide a chuckle. "These woods *are* known to be filled with fey," the cleric said gravely, his mirth betrayed only by a slight wrinkling at the corners of his eyes. "Some of them have quite childish senses of humor. They might be amused to see us turning against one another so easily."

"Well, we're not here for them," Ganoven said stiffly. "We're here for the Beast." He turned to regard Isiem. "You claimed you'd found it?"

"Ena did," the wizard replied.

"I did," the dwarf agreed, stepping out of a nearby bush and brushing stray leaves from her cloak. Ena was less than ten feet away, yet Isiem had had no inkling she was there. He wondered how long she'd been hiding.

Ena plucked a clinging bramble from her sleeve and released it gently, leaving no pull in the cloth. "It's not far from here, but not as close as I'd thought, either. We'll have to lure it out to get it across my traps."

"*We* will?" Ganoven objected.

"I will," the dwarf amended, giving him a caustic look. "Wouldn't want you to have to do any extra work. You might get the idea we expected you to help."

"You're the one who chose to plant your traps in the wrong place," the Aspis agent said.

"That I did, and I'm glad I did." Using her scavenged walking stick, Ena carefully scuffed the loam around one of her traps. Its silver pin had become a shade too exposed, jutting out from the surrounding dirt. "The earth is desecrated where that creature lairs. Up there, my traps might have detonated the instant I buried them."

"Did you see the Beast itself?" Isiem asked.

Ena shook her stubbly haired head. Foreboding shadowed her eyes. "I didn't, and I don't much want to. It *stinks* around the lair. I'm not sure why the smell doesn't carry farther. It should. It's worse than the smell of sickness, worse than rotten meat . . . it's a *wrong* smell. The Beast is undead, all right. Nothing else reeks like that. But no, I didn't see it. Just the spongy stinking earth and bones around the hole where it's hiding."

"Nightfall, then?" Kyril asked. "You'll lure it out and lead it here?"

"I will," Ena said. "You'd best be ready for it when I do."

The hours until sundown passed in tense silence. Kyril prayed silently, her longsword bare and gleaming across her lap. Pulcher and Copple amused themselves gambling with knucklebones; neither of them seemed the slightest bit concerned about what they might face in the wood. Both of them cheated constantly, and neither noticed. Ganoven paced back and forth, muttering the words to a simple force spell over and over under his breath, like an unprepared actor desperately rehearsing his lines in the last minutes before curtain rise. The incantation was accurate, to Isiem's mild surprise, but if the Aspis agent kept repeating it, he was going to waste it on empty air.

"Calm yourself," Isiem told the man, looking up from his cross-legged perch on a mossy log. "Your spell is correct. Now relax, and wait. If you're too tense, the magic will fail."

Ganoven stopped, visibly startled that he had been addressed. As soon as he recovered from his surprise, though, the half-elf's lip twisted up in a sneer. "Do you think I'm a *complete* novice?"

Isiem shrugged. He returned to his own meditations, sending his consciousness outward to the fading warmth of sunlight on the trees' upper leaves, the gentle riffle of wind through the hanging vines, the low smells of damp earth and moss. In Nidal he had learned to meditate through times of absolute terror, and while he had discarded many other Kuthite teachings since entering his exile, that one he had kept. It was too useful to forget.

After a time he opened one eye, just a sliver, to see Ganoven seated on a stump ten yards away. The bearded half-elf was imitating Isiem's cross-legged posture and measured breathing, and while his attempt was stiff and awkward, he appeared to be making a real effort.

Inwardly Isiem smiled. He closed his eyes and went back into the haven of his own thoughts.

The last of the daylight dwindled through the screening leaves and vanished. Violet twilight seeped in, cool and moist. An unseen chorus of nocturnal frogs and crickets sprang up, singing to herald the coming night. It was pastoral, tranquil—and painfully evanescent.

"I'm going in," Ena said. The dwarf had pulled her hood up. Cloaked in its drab fabric, she was all but invisible in the gathering gloom. "Be ready."

As she left, Isiem wove a protective ward around himself. The spell formed a nearly invisible shield of force around him; with luck, it might deflect blows aimed his way. A shimmer in the night air told him that Ascaros had done the same. A moment later, Ganoven followed suit, his spell stuttering briefly before solidifying around him. Their other companions took no precautions, as far as the wizard could tell.

"I can't see," Pulcher complained. He pulled off his spectacles and rubbed the greasy lenses against the front of his jerkin, smearing them even more hopelessly. "Can't fight if I can't see."

"Be still." Ascaros stepped out from the shadows, ignoring the tall thug's flinch, and touched the man's forehead with a small agate. He did the same to Copple, who shivered as well as the shadowcaller's spell settled over him and rubbed his eyes in wonderment.

"Well, isn't that a thing," Copple mumbled hoarsely, turning around in a circle and gawking at the trees and bushes. "I can see!"

"Of course you can, you ninny." Pulcher tightened the chinstrap of his open-faced helm and checked his bracers, then picked the hammer up again and gave it a few practice swings. "What did you think the spell was going to do, make you pretty? Hurry up and strap on your shield. Who knows when that dwarf'll be back, or what she'll be trailing when she comes."

"Do you need help with the darkness?" Ascaros asked Teglias. The shadowcaller seemed unnaturally tranquil, his face a white mask in the deepening night. That very stillness was a sign of the man's turmoil, Isiem knew; it meant his concentration was slipping on the illusion of normalcy that masked his true, withered face.

"No," the bearded cleric answered calmly. His hands stayed folded on the hilt of his scimitar, its point driven into the loam between his feet. "No, I think I can handle the night."

Whatever Ascaros meant to say in response was cut off as Kyril raised a hand abruptly. A halo of ghostly blue flame blazed up around her longsword, bathing the paladin's face with holy light.

"It's coming," she said.

Chapter Ten
The Howl

Even as the paladin spoke, Isiem heard the crack of breaking tree limbs. The earth bucked under his feet, suddenly as treacherous as the deck of a storm-tossed ship. By his side, Pulcher fell, losing his grip on his hammer's handle. The big thug scrabbled after it on his hands and knees, grabbing at clumps of skunk cabbage for purchase and throwing dignity to the wind.

Isiem didn't blame him. An onrushing roar filled his ears, growing louder by the second. From the way it reverberated in his head, pushing the insides of his skull outward like wine overfilling a skin, he wondered if it was a real sound or some horrid magic of the Beast's. The backs of his eyes ached from the pressure; purple spots swam across his sight. And still the ground churned and thrashed, adding to his dizziness. Not fifty yards away, mighty trees snapped like toothpicks and crashed down, but the sound of their breaking was nothing against the skull-splitting clamor in his head.

Then it stopped, and a deep, steady rumbling took its place. Ena's traps exploded in the earth, shattering into useless geysers of glass and steam long before their intended target was anywhere in view.

Pulcher got unsteadily back to his feet, wiping mud and blood from a long cut across his hairline. Ganoven, looking past the rest of them into the forest, blanched white. Kyril, beside him, murmured a toneless prayer. The aura of holy fire around her sword flickered like a candle in a draft, then blazed up brighter than before.

The Beast had come.

Isiem smelled the thing before he saw it. At first all he could make out visually was a strangely lumpy shadow looming amid the trees, its head level with their highest branches—but the stench of the Beast was immediate and overpowering. One instant, he was breathing clean forest air. The next, he choked on a foulness so wet and thick that it was like sucking in lungfuls of cold, rotting blood.

He heard Pulcher drop back to the ground, retching; he heard the absurdly quiet plop of the man's spectacles falling into the mess. But he didn't turn or look away, because by then the Beast had smashed enough of the surrounding trees to show itself in the early moonlight.

It was more like a moving hill than anything that should walk. Twenty feet high and nearly as wide, the Beast of the Backar Forest was a monolith of chains and bones and worm-eaten cloth, all packed together by damp, reeking dirt that, Isiem was certain, was what remained of the flesh from its constituent bodies.

It had the rough shape of a scorpion, but it was covered in such a carapace of caked decay that he could barely tell. Skeletal arms and legs bristled from its sides like a porcupine's quills, dwarfed by the enormous bone pincers that clacked in front of the thing. Along its back—if that word could even apply to such a creature—a triple row of decaying human heads gaped and giggled. More skulls were strung along its long, lashing tail; the last of them had a grisly, glistening white spike jutting out of its jaws.

Some of the heads were still fresh enough to have filth-matted hair and skin. Others were bare bone, their craniums packed full of dirt that wept through their eye sockets and trickled from their nostrils. Each was attached by a skeletal hand grasping it through the holes where the spine had once attached to the skull's base, and each was animated into an unholy mockery of life.

They gibbered and screeched and laughed, sometimes all at the same time. Their jaws, attached only by strings of dried gristle, flapped constantly in meaningless idiot speech. None of them had eyes; several had been dented and crushed in so badly that they no longer had faces. Isiem had no sense that any of the heads were aware of their surroundings, much less able to think or control the creature that wore them.

But *something* in that mountain of filth had enough rudimentary intelligence to chase Ena. The dwarf came hurtling through the undergrowth ahead of the Beast's pincers, zigzagging around tree trunks and somersaulting down hillsides with desperate skill. Bouncing back to her feet, the bruised and battered dwarf charged straight at the hollow where she'd laid all her traps—and where not one of them was left to help her.

The adventurers scattered, even Kyril, fanning outward in their retreat. Standing their ground in the face of the Beast's trampling fury would have been worse than useless. Their intended ambush was ruined, and the thing would have crushed them without slowing an inch.

Only Ascaros had the presence of mind to do more than scramble out of the way. He blew a wisp of dried spidersilk at the Beast as he darted aside. The fragile strands dissolved on his breath, sparkling in the air—and then reappeared, made a thousand times thicker and stronger by magic. A net of tenebrous webbing, large enough to entangle even the Beast of the Backar Forest, erupted around the undead monstrosity's lower quarters.

The Beast slowed to a grinding stop, dragged to a halt by Ascaros's web. It thrashed at the sticky mess with its pincers, but succeeded only in further ensnaring itself. Several ropy strands strained and snapped, but the bulk of the web held fast. The decapitated heads on the creature's back moaned and babbled in broken chorus, their unseeing eyes and unthinking mouths rolled toward the sky.

Seeing his enemy pinned, Teglias raised his holy symbol in one hand, holding the other flat so that his palm faced the Beast. His voice stern and filled with righteous wrath, the cleric called upon his goddess's power. A beam of blinding sunlight lanced from his open palm, so brilliant it left ghost-streaks seared across Isiem's vision,. The holy light blasted away dirt and bones and squealing fragments of chains, leaving a black-edged hole in the Beast so big that Pulcher could have put his foot through it.

It was impossible to tell if the searing light had *hurt* it, though. The creature showed no flicker of pain, only the same near-mindless ferocity. It lurched in the webs again, releasing another wave of eye-watering stench, but remained unable to tear free.

Kyril hesitated only a second before swearing, thrusting her longsword back into its sheath, and grabbing her bow instead. In one fluid movement she nocked an arrow and loosed it, burying the long ash shaft in the Beast's earth-filled side. Again, however, the unliving thing made nary a grunt or whimper to show it was aware of any injury.

"This isn't good enough," the paladin growled. She dropped the bow back over her shoulder and drew her sword again. Once more, fire leaped out to sheathe the blade. "I can't hurt it from here. I'm going into the web."

Isiem, preoccupied with his own spellcasting, didn't reply at once. Instead he spread three fingers in a fan and pointed them at the Beast. A stream of fire burst from each of his fingers, scorching through the tangled webs to lash the undead creature with fiery whips of gold and crimson.

And then he *couldn't* answer, because the Beast struck back at them all. The chains embedded in its body shot out, shedding flakes of rotten flesh and bone, and burst through the shadowcaller's web in a hundred thrashing vines of metal.

A bladed chain stabbed through Teglias's calf, yanking the cleric into the mud and ruining the magic he'd just begun to shape. Another slammed into Copple's face, punching out teeth and a mouthful of blood.

Howling, the tattooed thug dropped his sword and fell to his knees. Two more chains swung at Isiem, high and low, but he threw himself to the side and his shield spell managed to deflect their glancing blows.

Ena wasn't as lucky. One of the animated chains wrapped around her waist, whipping around the dwarf again and again until her hands were bound to her sides. At the end it thudded a clot of gristle and steel into her stomach, knocking out her breath. With a final heave, the Beast hoisted the kicking dwarf into the air, dragging her over her companions' heads toward its own web-snared bulk.

It pulled at Teglias, too, hauling him toward its crushing pincers. The cleric seized onto the gnarled root of a nearby tree and clung to it, white-knuckled, until the chain ripped bloodily loose from his leg. Ashen-faced, the Sarenite gulped breaths of agony and relief. The Beast had torn flesh from him, but it did not have him.

It only had Ena, and it hugged her close to its stinking side, pushing the side of her face into the filth next to its rows of moaning heads.

"Oh, no," the dwarf said, staring wide-eyed at a lolling head that returned her stare with a vacant, chittering smile. Her booted feet scuffed uselessly against the dirt and bones beside her. "No, no. Don't let it take my head. Don't let it, you bastards. You can't. You *can't!*"

"If you had let me use the addict and his idiot, your friend might still be safe," Ascaros muttered to Isiem. The shadowcaller rubbed something between his fingers, whispering another incantation. Isiem caught a whiff of licorice and recognized the magic just before it took hold of him.

Time slowed. The Beast's chains drifted rather than whipping forward, as if they were pushing through clear treacle instead of air. Each drop of blood that fell from Copple's cheek or Teglias's gouged leg or the countless cuts on Ena's face and body seemed to float through the night like a dark bubble, and when each drop struck the ground, Isiem could see every ripple and mote in the splash.

But not everything was slowed.

Kyril plunged past the wizard at full speed, leading with her fiery longsword as if it were a lance. Pulcher had staggered back up and dragged his enormous hammer out of the mud. Vomit stained the front of his shirt and spattered the blocky hammer's hilt, but the big man's grip seemed steady.

Before either of them could bring their weapons to bear, though—before they even reached the fringes of the shadowcaller's web—the lolling heads on the Beast's back turned their faces to the sky and shrieked in unison.

Their cries made no sound, but a rolling wave of force erupted outward from the Beast. Ghostly white, it billowed over the woodland with the delicacy of a jellyfish enveloping its prey, and its touch was just as deadly.

Plants shriveled instantly as the wave of death touched them. Insects dropped from the air, their stiffened wings suddenly pulled down by the hollow anchors of their shells. A puff of something like frost brushed over Isiem's skin, and then he too felt the wrenching, incredible agony of the Beast's magic sucking the life from his body.

It was like a blast of wind on the most brutally cold winter night he'd ever experienced—or, equally, like standing in front of a fiery inferno so ravenous that it pulled the breath from his lungs. Isiem couldn't breathe. He couldn't blink. It was impossible to move, to think, to *feel*. There was only the Beast's hunger wrenching at everything that made him alive.

And then, somehow, it faded. The magic released its grip.

Air rushed back into Isiem's lungs, raw but exhilarating. He was still alive. His fingers were stiff and wrinkled and white, but—with an effort—they moved. Barely. He was *alive*.

But he couldn't get up. He couldn't even lift his head out of the dirt. Magic was an impossible dream; the spell stored in his rubied ring might as well have belonged to Mesandroth himself for all the good it would do. All he could do was lie among the dead dry plants and wait to die himself.

As the wizard lay there, helpless tears trickling from the corners of his eyes, he heard Teglias's voice rise in a broken croak. The words were weak and distorted; Isiem couldn't make out the exact nature of the chant, although he recognized it as a prayer.

Wobbly as it was, the incantation held together. A second wave of force roiled through the spell-burned forest, this time a warm gold rather than ghostly pale. Sarenrae's blessing infused them with new life, pushing back the killing numbness of the Beast's hunger. It could not restore the dead—the plants and insects remained inert, beyond the reach of the Dawnflower's revival—but it renewed the strength of the living.

Isiem pushed himself shakily back to his knees.

The first thing he saw was Kyril. The half-elf didn't seem to have been seriously slowed by the undead howl; she had reached the Beast and was hacking at the heads on its back with mighty sweeps of her fiery sword while dodging the clumsy attacks of its one free pincer. Cleaved skulls and shattered chains, set alight by holy flame, showered around the paladin in a messy halo.

Their other companions had been hit harder. Pulcher and Copple stayed on the ground, moaning and only half-sensible, even after Teglias had healed them. Isiem couldn't see Ascaros at all; he didn't know whether the shadowcaller had abandoned them, gone invisible, or simply moved out of view. Teglias slumped against the bloodstained roots of the tree that had saved him, already preparing his next spell.

Ena, still latched to the Beast's back by her robe of chains, had sustained the worst hurt. Isiem couldn't tell if she was unconscious or dead. Blood seeped from her nostrils and darkened her clothing under the chains. Skeletal hands had risen from the depths of the Beast's body and begun digging at the dwarf's neck, working their bony fingertips into her flesh in an apparent effort to pull her head off her shoulders. Several of them had already wormed their way under her skin, and more dug in each second.

Isiem couldn't hurl fire at the Beast without killing Ena. Nor could he strike it with ice or lightning; the destruction wrought by such elemental forces was as imprecise as it was impressive. If it were Copple or

Pulcher, or Ganoven, he wouldn't have hesitated, but Ena . . .

His safest options were weak ones, unlikely to save her in time. The dwarf's fate rested with Kyril, and the blazing fury of the paladin's sword. The most Isiem could do was help.

He could do that, though.

Forcing himself to inhale slowly, Isiem repeated his chant, loosing a second fiery streamer at the Beast. Teglias added his own prayer to the attack, piercing through the red and orange of the wizard's spell with a lance of blinding white light. The dual assault blasted skeletal limbs and dirt-caked chains off the monstrosity. Its web-snared pincer went black and brittle, then burst apart in the heat.

The Beast staggered. Kyril hacked into it with renewed ferocity. The paladin threw all her strength into every swing. Beads of perspiration dripped from her brow, glittering like diamonds in the white light of her sword as they fell. Her blade hacked through the chains binding Ena, cutting through the squealing metal as if it were butter, yet she could not get her friend free. More chains rose up to entangle the unconscious dwarf, and more bony hands grabbed her close. And even as Kyril slashed them away, the skeletal claws continued to tear at Ena's neck.

Then the Beast's back arched up convulsively. Percussive cracks rattled through its body as bones shattered inside and outside the monolith. The skeletal arms grabbing at Ena cracked apart like eggshells; the fingers embedded in her neck drew a necklace of bright blood as they broke under her skin.

Amid the trees, Ascaros winked back into view abruptly. It was his spell that had saved her.

Kyril didn't waste any time. She threw her shield aside and grabbed the dwarf, slashing at the remaining chains as she pulled Ena forward. Her blessed blade screamed through the steel, and as soon as she'd torn Ena free, the paladin leaped away from the Beast and ran. The webs clung to her legs, but with Ascaros's spell lending her speed, the paladin was able to jerk free.

Once Kyril and Ena were clear, both Isiem and Ascaros hurled fireballs at the lumbering Beast. The wizard's was a blue-edged ball of scarlet flame, improbably vibrant in the night; the shadowcaller's seemed a colorless shadow of the first one, its hues washed out and tinged with gray. Both struck with brutal force, and between the two fiery blasts, the Beast collapsed in a stinking heap. The remaining webs burned around it, hiding its bulk in a shroud of fiery lace.

It was over. They'd won. The Beast had fallen, and they'd lost none of their own.

Their victory was as complete as Isiem could have hoped for, and yet he felt more fear than joy. The sight of Ena helpless in chains on the Beast's back, her throat ringed in blood and her face ashen as if she was already among the undead, tarnished any real sense of triumph he might have felt.

Deadly as it had been, the Beast of the Backar Forest wasn't even their primary target. It had only been a means of getting there. They would likely face greater dangers in their pursuit of Eledwyn's nightblade. Some of their number might not return. Isiem had known that from the beginning, of course, but seeing Ena slip into Pharasma's grasp—and then, narrowly, out of it—made the knowledge suddenly more real, and more painful.

He had friends again, which meant he could lose friends again.

Could, and almost certainly would.

Chapter Eleven
The Gifts of the Dead

As Teglias tended to their companions, Ascaros strode to the fallen Beast, pulling a curved steel knife from his belt. Kneeling beside it, he yanked away handfuls of sticky charred webbing and sank the knife deeply into the undead creature's side.

Isiem joined him silently, trying to ignore the carrion stench that burbled up from the Beast's innards when Ascaros plunged his blade in. The smell wasn't as intense as it had been while the monstrosity was fighting; the loss of its animating magic seemed to have also dispelled its unearthly foulness. But it was still a hill-sized pile of crushed and decomposing corpses, and it still smelled like one.

The reek did nothing to deter Ascaros. The shadow-caller clambered atop the felled Beast and began yanking at the bones that protruded from its carcass. He tossed aside skeletal arms and bony legs, using them as levers to pry away the dirt and layers of ancient, rotted flesh that made up the monster's body. Skulls broke away and jounced down the Beast's lumpen flanks as he worked.

"What are you doing?" Isiem asked, covering his nose.

"The older bodies are deeper in," Ascaros grunted, leaning hard on a jutting leg bone to split off a chunk of chain-studded earth almost as large as he was. He kicked it off the Beast's side, causing it to tumble down and crash to pieces against the forest floor. "Buried. Under newer victims. Sukorya won't be that far in . . . but she's deeper than any of these. Are you going to help?"

There didn't seem to be any alternative. Isiem grimaced, wishing he'd brought gloves. His were still with the luggage, unhelpfully stowed wherever they'd left the pack animals to prevent them from being run off or slaughtered by the Beast. "I suppose."

"Use the bones," the shadowcaller advised. "It keeps your hands cleaner. Slightly." He thrust a long bone between two of the decapitated heads and broke off another slab of dirt and carrion.

Isiem bit his tongue and began his climb up the Beast's back. The dead creature's body was spongy-soft beneath his hands and feet. It left a sticky reddish-brown residue on his palms and boots, and every time his weight pressed into it, another puff of stench erupted from the accursed thing.

"We could just wait until Pulcher and Copple are back on their feet, you know." He tried not to inhale as he spoke. It was fruitless; he could taste the Beast's rancid filth coating his tongue like poisoned oil. "Let them do the manual labor."

"I wouldn't trust them to recognize what we're after," Ascaros said, "or give it up if they did." The shadowcaller stopped his digging to grab Isiem's wrist and haul the wizard up beside him. Even with all he'd chipped away, there was more than enough room for them to stand side by side on the Beast's back.

Looking down from the crest of the creature's body, Isiem could see that the corpses making up the inner layers did indeed appear to be older than those of the outer shell. The newly unearthed bones were stained a deep yellow-brown, and uncounted years of grinding pressure had forced them into oddly sculptural contortions. Each corpse had been balled into a fetal position and then compacted into a gnarled knot, its bones abraded smooth on their outer surfaces but cracked and rough inside.

None of them had heads anymore, but many of the corpses still had scraps of clothing and other personal relics wedged between their compressed bones. One of those, Isiem realized with an unpleasant thrill of recognition, wore the remains of a Dusk Hall master's robe. The once-gray fabric was so clotted with the crusted effluvia of decay that its color and cut were impossible to identify, but the distinctive shape of its spiked buttons gave it away.

Isiem tugged Ascaros's sleeve and pointed down at the skeleton he'd noticed. "Look. It's in a shadowcaller's robe."

Ascaros had to step to the side and crane his neck to see what Isiem indicated, but once he did, his face twisted with a kind of terrified excitement. The shadowcaller skidded down the Beast's side toward the balled skeleton, using a leg bone from another unlucky victim as a drag pole to slow his descent. Upon reaching it, he knocked it free of the dead abomination and pounced on the skeleton like a cat seizing upon a crippled mouse.

With nary a shred of sentimentality for his ancestor's remains, Ascaros kicked the bones apart, then stooped to rummage through the rotted cloth that had been compacted in their midst. He pulled two filthy rings from the skeleton's fingers and untangled a long chain, its spikes crusted in carrion-stinking dirt, from its midsection. Several other objects, all unidentifiable beneath their thick coats of detritus, dangled from the chain.

The shadowcaller dropped the whole thing into a small sack, along with both of the rings, and tied it shut. He poked at the bones a while longer but soon lost interest. Without another word to Isiem, he walked away from the fallen hulk of the Beast.

"What'd you find?" Pulcher called. The big man was sitting up on the ground, groggy but evidently restored to his senses. Blood and mud crusted half his face and stiffened his short hair into wild spikes. Judging from his squint into the darkness, the spell that had granted him sight had evaporated.

"My revered great-aunt," Ascaros replied curtly. He paused for a step and conjured a buzzing white spark into the night. The spark hovered over his palm, then darted between the tree trunks, staying just close enough for the shadowcaller to see. He followed it into the woods, never once glancing back to see if the others were coming.

"Good to see he values our company after all we've been through together." Ena croaked a pained, mirthless chuckle. The dwarf was lying on a pile of dead leaves, her head propped up by a folded cloak—Kyril's, not her own. Isiem couldn't see Ena's cloak anywhere, and suspected that the paladin had discarded it as beyond repair. "Did he get his diamond?"

"I think so," the wizard replied, climbing down from the Beast's lifeless bulk.

"Is he going to run off with it?"

"I hope not."

"Me too. I'd chase him down, but . . ." Ena gestured to her assorted wounds. A nasty line of bruises encircled her throat. More bruises left dark splotches tattooed across the fire scars on her scalp. From the way she winced when she moved, it seemed there were other injuries hidden under her light leather and chain. "He chose his moment well. I'm not going to be chasing much of anything for a while, I don't imagine."

Despite her poor condition, the dwarf seemed to be in decent spirits. She chortled feebly at Isiem's expression when he neared. Her voice was still hoarse from her near-strangling by the skeletal hands. "Worried?"

"I was."

"I'm touched." Ena shifted so that she could peer into the night after Ascaros. "Do you think the diamond might kill him? He seemed to think it was an awfully ominous piece of work. Cursed, even. Maybe someone *should* go after him. For his own sake as much as ours."

"I don't doubt the stone is dangerous," Isiem said, "but Ascaros has had a good deal of experience evading his ancestor's snares. I doubt the rest of us would help him much on that front."

"I suppose you'd know best," Ena said, plainly doubtful. She turned her head as Kyril approached them.

"We're heading for the Umbral Basin in the morning," the paladin said as she neared. She scowled in the direction of Ascaros's disappearance, then turned back to Isiem and Ena. "I suggest you rest while you can. It will be harder once we enter the shadowlands." She wrinkled her nose, eying Isiem. "Rest, and bathe."

"Not in that order," Ena added, sweetly helpful, as the paladin left to check on Ganoven.

"Yes, thank you," Isiem said irritably. "I really *was* worried about you, you know. Although I'm beginning to wonder why."

"Because your only other friend in this group's a selfish bastard who'll run off with a sack of cursed corpse-loot while the rest of us are still patching up our wounds after his last idiotic scheme. That'd be my guess." Ena's expression softened, though, and she lifted a hand to offer a conciliatory little wave, grimacing at the effort. "And I really was touched. Now go take a bath."

"Where do you propose I do that?"

"There's water by the camp." That was Ganoven, who was standing on decidedly unsteady feet. Under his neat black beard, the half-elf's face was deathly pale. Torn leaves flecked his clothing, but for once the normally fastidious Aspis agent seemed not to notice. Weariness roughened his words. "I'll show you. Come."

The Aspis agent struck a spark to his lantern and led Isiem through the forest, following a series of marks notched into the trunks of redsap trees. It was obvious why Ganoven had chosen them. Their sap, a garish crimson, stood out so brightly against the trees' silvery-pale bark that it was easy to spot even by the sweeping light of Ganoven's lantern.

The trail of slashes went on for a quarter-mile or more, winding across creeks and rises. Isiem had expected Ganoven to call his underlings to accompany them, but he never did. They walked in solitude through the wood. Around them, crickets and frogs sang a nocturnal melody, falling silent when the two-legged intruders passed and then resuming when they had gone by.

At first, Ganoven was quiet, but when they'd put enough distance between themselves and the site of the Beast's death, he glanced back at Isiem.

"You've never been to the Umbral Basin, have you?" the half-elf said.

Isiem shook his head. "It's not a place we often have reason to go."

"Nor we." Ganoven's thin, pinched lips quirked to the side in a humorless facsimile of a smile. His black eyes followed the lantern's light, steadfastly avoiding the dark areas of the wood. "Trade through the valley is profitable, to be sure, and leading that caravan is a prestigious post. It's difficult work, shepherding so many superstitious and bellicose fools through the shadowlands into the realm of the Midnight Lord. Then negotiating with the Nidalese . . . well, it has a reputation for challenging our subtlest minds. For a time, I myself thought of attempting the task. I had the opportunity once."

"Why did you decline?"

"A post opened in Egorian. I chose the capital over the caravan. I've always considered myself more a scholar than a man of action; the choice seemed obvious." The half-elf had lapsed into his habitual condescending tones, but then he shrugged and shook them off, continuing in a surprisingly reflective manner. "I may have made a mistake in that."

"How so?" Isiem asked.

"I was useless against the Beast. Useless." The lantern trembled in Ganoven's hand, throwing shivers of light and shadow against the trees around them, but his voice remained steady and unsparing. "When it charged us, when I saw it . . . all the words of magic I'd been practicing just vanished from my head. I couldn't have conjured a spark to save my life. I *didn't*. The rest of you brought the monster down, but I had no part in it—because I had never seen anything like that in my life. I had never *imagined* such a thing."

Isiem remained silent, unsure what the man wanted. Plainly Ganoven wanted *something*—he doubted the Aspis agent was the sort to confide in anyone casually, and they had hardly been cordial before—but his aim was still unclear.

"My inexperience made me useless," Ganoven continued, altering his course to the left as they passed another slash-marked tree. His lantern was burning low, its smoky yellow glow shrinking steadily around them. "It will, I'm sure, be worse in the Umbral Basin."

"Do you propose to turn back?"

"No." Ganoven gave the Nidalese a sidelong glance. "I want your help preparing. We're both men of learning, practitioners of the arcane. Our arts are the same. But while I may be a master scholar, you have more practical experience."

"You want me to teach you to fight," Isiem said flatly. He didn't relish the prospect. His own lessons in magic had been filled with fear and pain. As an exceptional student, he had been spared the worst of his fellows' suffering, but the Dusk Hall remained a dark place in his mind. It was not an experience he was eager to revisit, particularly in Ganoven's company.

He could hear the whickering of horses, and the gurgle of a night-cloaked brook, not far off among the trees. They were nearly to the stream. "On the eve of entering the Umbral Basin. A little late, don't you think?"

Ganoven shrugged. He set the dying lantern on a fallen log as they reached the water. In a clearing to the west, Teglias had begun setting up their camp. "We're not in the valley yet, and we're not dead. It's not too late."

A single tent stood among the tethered horses. The sight of it filled Isiem with immense relief and an equally great, bone-deep weariness. All he wanted out of his life at that moment was a bath and a chance to curl into a lumpy bedroll under that travel-stained canvas roof. He still reeked of fear and sweat and his climb up the Beast's decomposing bulk, and every sinew in his body ached with exhaustion.

But Ganoven was right. They could ill afford to enter Fiendslair with one of their wizards so poorly prepared. And he needed to learn some new spells himself. Demons were known to be impervious to many common methods of attack. Unusual techniques, like Ascaros's bone-cracking spell, or the specialized magics devised by Nidalese shadowcallers who had fought beasts from the far planes for millennia, were more likely to succeed.

Isiem sat on the log beside the failing lantern, beckoning tiredly for the half-elf to join him. "The light will die soon. Let's practice while we can."

Late the next morning, reunited, they made for the Umbral Basin. Ascaros had returned sometime before dawn, withdrawn and preoccupied; the others had trickled in after daybreak. Their physical wounds were healed, although a pall lingered over their travels. While the wild beauty of the forest around them was vibrant as ever, it was overshadowed by memories of the horror they had so recently seen and apprehensions of those that waited ahead.

They didn't follow the road. Kyril suggested going back to the caravan and entering the Umbral Basin under the protection of its numbers, but Ascaros had dismissed that idea impatiently. "Our destination lies north, near the foot of the Mindspin Mountains," the shadowcaller had said. "The caravan is taking a southern route. Unless you want to spend twice as long in the Umbral Basin as we must, we'll do better to strike out on our own."

"Do you believe you can find it?" Teglias had asked quietly. "The entrance to Fiendslair is said to be hidden."

"It is," Ascaros had replied, "but Sukorya's jewel will show us the way."

That had hardly been enough to satisfy the Sarenite, but it was all the shadowcaller meant to give them. When Kyril and Teglias asked to see the diamond, he showed it to them only briefly, and away from the rest of their company.

Whatever they saw in the stone, it was enough to silence both the paladin and the cleric. Both of them returned to the group with tight mouths and hooded eyes, and neither spoke of what they'd seen.

Their reaction solidified Isiem's discomfort. As soon as they resumed their journey on flesh-and-blood pack mules and spell-woven palfreys, he angled to confront his friend.

"You're certain it's Sukorya's diamond?"

"Completely." Ascaros's steed was ahead of Isiem's; all Isiem could see of his friend was a dark gray cloak crowned by curly black hair. There was a curtness to the shadowcaller's words that made it clear, even past his refusal to slow down, that he did not wish to discuss the subject.

Isiem didn't care. He spurred his horse alongside Ascaros's. "How do you know?"

The shadowcaller reined his ebon horse back, casting an acid glance at his friend. "I suppose it's possible that the Beast of the Backar Forest might have digested more than one shadowcaller in its day, true. But even granting the perpetual murders and betrayals among my kin, Sukorya's diamond would be impossible to mistake."

"What is it?" Isiem asked.

"A cursed thing, like all their treasures." Ascaros fumbled at the neck of his cloak with a black-gloved hand. After a few seconds, he pulled up a spiked chain of antique make. Among the baubles hanging from the chain was an elaborate egg-shaped case of silver.

Every inch of its surface was worked into whorls and curlicues evocative of knotted chains and claw-like manacles. Smooth black onyxes and cabochons of smoky quartz dotted its design in the timeless Nidalese fashion. A serrated line along one side of the egg, and tiny hinges on the other, suggested that it could be opened like a locket.

Ascaros detached the silver case from the chain, palmed it for a moment, and then tossed it at Isiem with a flick of his wrist. "Examine it yourself, if you like. Just close the case before you return it. I don't much like looking at the thing."

"Is it dangerous?" Isiem peered at the case in his hand. It did not gleam in the leaf-dappled sun. Instead, its dull gray metal absorbed the light, giving nothing back. Up close, its designs were more disturbing than he had initially thought, suggestive of bodies wrenched in torment rather than empty chains. Or perhaps that was only how they appeared *now:* the lines seemed to move in his peripheral vision, contorting into new patterns the instant they were out of sight.

"Only if you try to use it. Or look at it too long." Ascaros's horse quickened its step, responding to his mental command rather than any physical cue. The shadowcaller avoided looking at the silver case in Isiem's hands, but he gave his old friend a wry smile as he rode away. "You were always good at resisting those lures, though. I hope the knack hasn't left you."

Hesitantly, Isiem eased the case's clasp open with his thumb. The metal was oddly cold in his hand. A moment earlier it had felt ordinary against his skin, but a chill seemed to breathe from its heart as he opened it.

Inside, something sparkled. It was bright—far too bright to be casting back reflected sunshine. Its radiance came from within.

The wizard cupped his hand around it reflexively, trying to hide the brilliance before it drew his companions' eyes. He wasn't sure why, but somehow it seemed vitally important that no one else see what the case contained. Only after he'd wrapped the case in a fold of his cloak, dimming its light, did it seem safe enough to continue. Cautiously, keeping the case cupped in the thick gray fabric, Isiem pried its lid open completely.

A diamond shone inside. Easily the size of a quail's egg, it had been cut into a pillowy, soft-cornered cushion that refracted its facets endlessly into a rainbow-laced hall of mirrors. It was flawless, as far as Isiem could see, except for a single dark crystal trapped at its core.

There was something troubling and hypnotic about that flaw. The crystal was no natural hue: it was scarlet as fresh-spilled blood, and at the same time an utter, lightless black. Color and un-color slid across its surfaces. Sometimes, impossibly, both at once.

And it was evil, profoundly evil, so much so that gazing into it caused Isiem's jaw to clench and set his teeth to trembling.

The Nidalese was no stranger to malice. In his time, he had murdered friends and betrayed them. He had spoken to demons and stared into the void from which shadowbeasts came; he had loved a Chelish diabolist and trembled blind before the Black Triune. Only the night before, he'd faced the Beast of the Backar Forest and dug into its corpse.

But he had never touched evil like what lay within that diamond.

He closed the case with shaking hands and spurred his horse to catch Ascaros's. Wordlessly, he thrust the silver egg back at the shadowcaller, who took it with a taut, knowing nod. Only after Ascaros had clipped it back onto its chain and dropped the case under his shirt, removing it from view, did Isiem take a full breath again.

"How can you stand having that next to your skin?" he asked, shuddering.

"The gifts of my kin," Ascaros replied, lifting one shoulder in a scant shrug. "This is no worse than their others. So, you agree: it's the key to Fiendslair?"

"I didn't delve that deeply into the stone," Isiem admitted. "I didn't dare. But I fear you are correct. It is the key to Fiendslair."

Chapter Twelve
The Valley of Nightmares

No clear line separated the shadowlands from the ordinary world.

The change crept up on them slowly, hour by hour, as they rode east out of Molthune. The sky became grayer, bit by bit, as the clouds thickened into a perpetual overcast. Wildflowers grew more sparsely among the creeks and bushes, and those that persisted lost their vivid hues. Red poppies' petals shifted to a faded, tired pink. Sun-yellow dandelions lightened to soft cream. And all of them, in the end, became the same stark white, while the grass around them darkened to shadowy gray.

The strangeness dampened conversation. No one wanted to speak, anyway. Sound behaved oddly in the shadowlands: a whisper could carry for miles, while a shout might die abruptly in the air. It was eerie enough hearing the steady clop of their horses' hooves distorted; no one wanted to hear their own voices warped. They rode in silence, watching the world's colors drain away.

Night came early in the shadowlands. When it was too dark to ride safely, Teglias signaled a halt. It was only midafternoon—or it should have been—but days were abbreviated by that cloud-smothered sky, while nights stretched long and cold.

Isiem and Ganoven conjured ghostly lights to illumine the campsite as the others set about raising tents and watering the pack mules. On a whim, Isiem attempted to make his light emerald-green, but was unsurprised when it manifested as a hazy white instead. The illumination was barely half what it should have been, and the shadows cast by that crippled glow seemed deeper and more menacing, as if the darkness were offended at his temerity in trying to break its grip.

"There's something wrong with my spell," Ganoven grumbled, eying his wisp of a light.

"Nothing is wrong with your spell," Isiem said. "The wrongness is in this place."

"Can it be countered?"

Isiem shook his head, sending a second floating ball of light to shed its radiance over Copple and Pulcher while they hammered tent stakes into the rocky ground. A third circled around the other side of the tent, aiding Ena as she unpacked their bedrolls. "No more than the shadow over Nidal itself can be. Perhaps less: the shadow recognizes its masters there. Not here."

"Dimmed light spells don't worry me," the dwarf grunted while hauling armloads of bedrolls into the tent. "If that's the worst the Umbral Basin throws at us, I'll count us lucky. Blessed, even."

"It won't be," Ascaros said softly. He had dismissed his summoned steed but had not come to join them in the wavering circle of light. Instead, he stood at its periphery, a silhouette against the darker night. One of his hands was poised near his throat, and silver gleamed across his white knuckles: the chain that held the spell-locked case of Sukorya's cursed diamond.

Teglias cleared his throat. "Should we set a guard?"

Ascaros's shrug was barely visible, a ripple of fabric in the shadows. "If it soothes you."

"I'll take first watch," Kyril volunteered immediately. She had just begun to loosen the first buckle on her armor, but she clacked it back into place and straightened. "It's no hardship."

"I'll take third," Ena said resignedly, "and that *is* a hardship. But not as bad as the middle watch. So that one's yours." She pointed midway between Pulcher and Copple, leaving it entirely unclear which of them she meant. The two of them immediately set to quarreling, while the dwarf chortled under her breath and finished unpacking what they'd need for the night.

The Aspis thugs argued all through their meal of salt fish and barley porridge, resorting to pointed glares and "accidental" shoves when Ganoven ordered them to drop the discussion. They hadn't settled who was taking the middle watch by the time Isiem retired to his bedroll. The sound of their bickering, only barely muffled by his pillow, continued as he dropped into slumber.

Regardless of whether it was Pulcher or Copple who eventually lost that argument—or whether they just kept arguing until it was time for them to both sit the watch—everyone was still alive when Isiem woke the next morning.

The day was gray and gloomy, and a constant veil of drizzling rain shrouded them as they gathered their belongings in preparation for venturing deeper into the valley.

The Umbral Basin was not a deep valley. It was a broad, shallow bowl that sloped down from the feet of the Mindspin Mountains at such a gradual incline that in another place, less obviously cursed, it might have been mistaken for flat land. Opaque gray fog filled that bowl, and even from a distance, it was plain that there was nothing natural about the mist. It was thicker than smoke, immobile as stone. Wind did not touch it, and it lingered long into the morning and then into afternoon, as the weak sun labored above them and they rode steadily toward the fog.

"I have heard stories of a black storm that rolls through the Umbral Basin and twists reality in its grip," Kyril murmured as they crested another low hill to see the shadow-filled valley below. The blurry suggestions of trees and boulders were barely visible through the fog, more as amorphous patches of deeper gray than as anything their eyes could identify. "Is this it?"

Isiem shook his head. "The fog's danger is more prosaic. Horses might stumble on unseen stones and break their legs. Traveling companions get separated. It's easy to lose sight of landmarks, or the road, and wander aimlessly in the valley. Then night falls . . . and the deadlier dangers come."

"Does anyone live in there?" Ena stood in her stirrups, pushing back her hood and craning around her shaggy pony's neck as if that would enable her to peer through the fog. "Villages, towns? *Any* kind of civilization?"

"Not that I've ever heard," Isiem said. "In Pangolais they teach that no one, not even a shadowcaller, survives in the Umbral Basin for long. Certainly no one would believe that a peasant could survive there. But there are many people who have an interest in hiding from the Umbral Court, and many in the Court who have an interest in keeping dissenters cowed. So it's possible that someone might have tried to eke out a living in the valley, and equally possible that the official histories might choose to assume them dead without any real proof."

"Would you have done it?" Kyril asked, pushing back her damp hood. Curiosity shone in the half-elf's dark eyes. "When you were desperate to flee Nidal. Would you have tried hiding in the Umbral Basin, if that was the only chance of escape that you had?"

"No," Isiem said. His hair was beginning to come loose again, so he unknotted the leather thong that held it back and retied it. "I wanted to escape, not die."

"There are a thousand and ten ways to die in Pangolais," Ascaros agreed quietly, "but very few to leave the Umbral Court's control. If there were *any* chance of escape through that pass"—the shadowcaller nodded toward the black rift in the mountains ahead—"those rumors would have run through Nidal like wildfire. But no one has ever spoken of the Umbral Basin as anything but doom."

"Charming," Ena grumbled, eying the paladin as she settled back onto her saddle. She shook raindrops from her cloak with a pronounced shiver. "Doom. I'm glad you asked about that. I feel *much* better now."

Ascaros shrugged, fingering the spiked silver chain that trailed down his shirt. "We shouldn't have to spend a full night in the valley. Sukorya's stone will lead us to Fiendslair, and I will open the hidden gate as soon as we find it. We might have to ride into the night, but we won't have to sleep in the Umbral Basin."

"That's nice," Ena said. "Not that I could sleep here anyway, but I appreciate the thought."

They rode a little faster after that, but only a little. The mist rose up to their saddles as they descended into the valley, and then up to their necks. The pack mules balked in dismay at entering it, although Ascaros's shadowsteed was undisturbed by the clammy, blinding fog.

It made for an unnerving journey. Isiem was constantly on edge, certain that he'd just seen some faceless foe creeping toward them, only to realize that it was an illusion created by the swirling movements of the mist.

He wasn't alone in his unease. All of them rode close together, as if proximity would protect them from whatever might lie unseen in the distance. Pulcher muttered a steady stream of profanity-laced prayers under his breath, and the handle of his hammer never left his ham-sized fists. The fog clung to the lenses of his spectacles no matter how many times he tried to wipe them clean. Copple swiveled to and fro in his saddle, squinting into the fog with fruitless paranoia. Sweat beaded on the short man's doughy brow and, mingling with the drizzling rain, dripped from his coarse black sideburns. Perspiration stood out on his forearms so that the colorful tattoos etched across his skin seemed to be melting.

But when they finally stumbled across concrete evidence of a menace in the mist, it was not at all what Isiem had expected.

Directly ahead of them, the fog parted abruptly, as if blown aside by an impalpable wind. The rains, too, ceased. Five blackened shacks stood in a circle on the barren ground. Four of them were barely large enough to hold a man standing upright with his arms at his sides. The fifth, at their center, was twice the size of the others and far better made. Its logs had been arranged in elaborate braidlike patterns, whereas the others looked like giant piles of kindling, thrown together with nails hammered in wherever two pieces of wood chanced to cross. It seemed a minor miracle that any of them stood upright.

All five were built entirely of warped, sooty black logs, such that Isiem initially assumed they must have been damaged in some great fire.

When he got within twenty feet, however, he could see that assumption was wrong. The stony earth around the buildings was neither scorched nor littered with cinders; it was the same dull lead gray as the perpetually overcast sky. Colorless grass and near-leafless saplings grew not far away, and they showed no sign of having been burned.

The logs hadn't been touched by flame. They had been petrified—not just the wood, but the nails that had been hammered into the logs, and even the straw and mud that had been used to caulk the fist-sized gaps within the walls. And whatever had done it had turned them not to drab ordinary stone, but to glossy black obsidian.

"What magic is this?" Kyril breathed. She dismounted from her horse, tossing its reins back across the animal's neck.

"None I want to meddle with," Ena replied darkly, crossing her arms. "I'll stay just where I am, thank you. Or better yet, leave."

Kyril ignored the dwarf. "There's something inside the central building." Pushing her cloak back from her sword arm, she approached cautiously. The fog seemed to respond as she did, creeping closer with every step the half-elf took. Foggy tendrils snaked back through the outer ring of shacks, blurring their burnt black edges. "I don't think it's alive."

Ena eyed the mist warily, reaching for the crossbow that dangled from a saddle loop just behind her thigh. "Oh, good. Let's run through our options then, shall we? It could be undead. Or a trap. Or demonic, that's always a solid choice. Shadowbeastie of some kind, there's another. Or—"

"No. It's something else," Kyril interrupted. "Something hanging from the ceiling. Ornaments or talismans of some kind, perhaps." She drew her sword a few inches from its sheath. Its blade shone, in defiance of the cloudy sky, as she called upon her goddess's power. Briefly the half-elf closed her eyes; when she opened them again, it was with a grimace of distaste.

"Well? What are they?" Ena inquired. "Hams? *Demonic* hams?"

"This is no time for jokes. Wizard, come and look." Kyril waved over her shoulder with a gloved hand. "I sense evil from whatever lies in there, although I can't say what to make of it."

Isiem approached and peered past the paladin. Sleek black objects, their size and shape vaguely reminiscent of lemons, dangled from twisted ropes hung from the apex of the largest shack's ceiling. They were just visible through the holes in the walls where the warped logs leaned away from each other. Between them, pale knotty ropes drooped in semitranslucent loops around a larger, round object in the center.

"Can you tell if all of it's evil?" he asked.

Kyril nodded. "The central building more than the others. Whatever's inside more than the shell. But yes, all of it. All of them." She drew her sword again, fully this time. The steely blade blazed with a halo of blue flame, as it had when she faced the Beast. Its brilliance threw her features into sharp relief, making her seem more a marble statue than a living woman. "Shall I come with you?"

There was no sense turning down help. "Please."

Together, they walked toward the ring of black buildings. The earth was strangely dry here, despite the ever-present fog and the recent rain. It crunched underfoot, breaking apart into brittle fragments of cracked mud. A ten-foot circle of empty ground surrounded the shacks where the gray-hued grass and feeble saplings could not, or would not, grow.

Each of the shacks had a narrow opening in its walls, just large enough for a man to squeeze through if he turned himself sideways, that faced the central hut. A fist-sized hole punctured the center of each shack's ceiling. The sides of the holes were worn smooth on top, but crusted with dark dried residue in ripples along the sides and bottoms. Footprints were visible in the chalky gray dust on the hutches' floors. They looked like they'd been made by bare human feet with broad, splayed toes. A faint odor of blood and vomit wafted through the blackened buildings, so slight that Isiem wasn't sure it was really there.

Otherwise, the shacks were empty. Seeing nothing else, Isiem went on to the larger hut in their middle.

Blood spattered the hard-packed dirt floor under that eerie roof of braided obsidian. Congealed and caked in layers, it was nearly an inch thick in places. Some was old, some was new, and much was mixed with dried strings of ichor that Isiem couldn't identify. The vomit smell came from that rippled crust of gore, although mercifully the hut's gap-riddled sides allowed the wind to dilute the odor.

Up close, the walls of this hut did not seem to have been built by human hands, but rather somehow grown as an organic whole. The obsidian logs that composed it had been bent and woven around one another like strands in a wicker basket, but they had no apparent ends. Each flowed seamlessly into the next, again and again, in a fashion that unpleasantly recalled the dizzying shifts in the engraved silver of Sukorya's jewel case.

Above the bloody floor, between those eye-wrenching walls, the ceiling curved to a gently pointed apex. There, suspended seven or eight feet from the ground, a bizarre and bulbous cauldron hung.

It was Nidalese work. Isiem recognized that immediately. A wide web of spiky black iron and obsidian served as the cauldron's framework, supporting an inner lining of milky, blue-tinged white membrane.

The inner lining sagged through the iron, bulging out from the metal's grasp.

Tubes of similar membrane, these slightly thicker and more opaque, connected to the cauldron's base and looped up to gaps near the shack's ceiling. It was these that Isiem had glimpsed from the outside. He had thought they were ropes, then, but now he could see that they were rinsed, bleached coils of preserved intestine. Each of the tubes ended in a smooth, podlike obsidian bulb with a conical tip.

"What is it?" Kyril whispered tensely.

Isiem started. He had forgotten she was there. "I don't know," he admitted, taking a step closer. There were footprints pressed into the softer parts of the bloody muck inside the hut and around its entrance. These, too, looked human, and it appeared that who- ever had made those tracks had been dragging some bulky burden along with them.

"The Splinter Men," Ascaros said. "This is where they feed, and are born." He had approached from the opposite side of the clearing. The shadowcaller's face looked like a waxen mask, and from that Isiem knew he was deeply troubled by what he'd seen among the buildings. If Ascaros was too disturbed to maintain the illusion of normalcy, they were in grave danger indeed.

"I don't know what the Splinter Men are," Kyril said.

"You would have heard rumors, surely, among the other guards in the caravan," the shadowcaller said. "Bands of marauders in the Umbral Basin who wear rags over their soot-smudged skin. They murder men with black knives as their victims sleep. It's said that their mouths are stitched shut, and that they never utter a word."

"I heard stories like that, yes," the paladin said doubtfully. She lifted her sword toward the obsidian structures, and its holy flame flared bright. Isiem imagined that the coiled intestines twitched away from the light of that divine fire . . . but that *was* only his imagination. Surely it was. "I heard a lot of other stories as well. Do you mean to say this one was true, and that such creatures live here?"

"They don't *live* anywhere," Ascaros said. "The Splinter Men are dead things walking. This is where they feed. The splinters driven into their mouths prevent them from consuming anything that their master does not give them. That cauldron dissolves their victims into the only sustenance they can take. Its feeder tubes force apart the splinters and spew the contents into their throats, like a mother bird regurgitating worms for her young.

"Sometimes, when their numbers are too few, they capture living people and force the tubes into their mouths, and thus create new Splinter Men from their victims." He gestured to the cauldron and its connected intestines with a hand that blurred in the air. A suggestion of gray bone was evident in that blur, like the outline of a fish glimpsed through rippling water. Isiem darted a sidelong glance at Kyril, wondering if the paladin had noticed the shadowcaller's illusion beginning to come apart, but her demeanor revealed nothing.

"Who's their master?" she asked. "And where are these Splinter Men now?"

"Their master is long dead. He was another of my revered ancestors. And yes, like the others, he was seeking immortality when he created these monsters. Their method of feeding was meant to transfer the victim's soul and consciousness into the bodies of those who consumed him. I don't think it worked quite as intended, but since my ancestor was one of the first to be destroyed and digested, we can't effectively ask him." Ascaros's smile was a tight white line. He was regaining control of his illusory mask, though; his black curls had regained greater definition and his face appeared fully human again. "As for where the Splinter Men are, I have no idea. Out hunting, I would presume. They'll return when they have another victim."

"Will that victim be alive?" Kyril asked.

"I don't know," Ascaros replied, "and it hardly matters. We don't have time to be distracted with such things."

"Saving the life of an innocent is not a distraction," the paladin said stiffly.

"No, but this discussion might be," Ena called from where the others were still grouped with the horses. "You'd better get back over here. Something's coming through the mist."

Chapter Thirteen
The Splinter Men

The Splinter Men came through the mist like black-clad wraiths, silent even down to the soundless slap of their feet.

They looked alive, almost. Their pale skin and expressionless faces were little different from those of living Nidalese, and if there was a whiff of old blood and chill earth to them, it was no worse than might cling to any gravedigger. But the burning hunger in their dead black eyes betrayed them, and the splinters driven like wooden stitches through their lips told their name.

Isiem had hoped there might only be four Splinter Men, corresponding to the four empty shacks ringing the central hut, but the gods did not choose to smile on him there. At least a dozen of the maimed murderers streamed toward them, dragging two other bloodied, apparently insensible people. Through the dense fog, Isiem couldn't see if their victims were alive or dead, but in either case the two of them hardly looked able to stand up on their own, let alone offer any resistance. They'd be of no use in a fight.

The Splinter Men seemed to think the same, if they thought anything. Twenty yards away, they let their victims fall to the ground. Focus returned to their hollow eyes, and they raised their heads like blind men hearing music. An awful yearning contorted their dead faces as they turned in wordless unison toward Ascaros.

They said nothing. No threats, no demands. Abandoning their victims, the Splinter Men simply rushed toward the shadowcaller with their long knives drawn. The blades were sickle-shaped shards of obsidian, eight to ten inches long, and did not seem to have any handles. The Splinter Men gripped their knives by the bases, slicing open their hands so that cold black blood darkened their palms and ran down their wrists.

Although the Splinter Men seemed singularly fixed on Ascaros, the others stepped into their path. Pulcher, Copple, and Kyril formed a rough line to meet them, while Teglias tried to wrestle his balky horse around to face the oncoming mob. Ena raised her crossbow, sighted down the oaken shaft, and fired at the Splinter Man in the lead. The bolt caught him in the chest with a meaty thud. The dead man staggered, rocked by the impact, but steadied himself and kept coming. The dwarf nudged her pony backward, slotting another quarrel into her crossbow.

Fire rushed out to greet the Splinter Men. Ascaros hurled a ball of shadowy flame at the stitch-lipped undead, bowling them over in a burst of blinding light and heat. Before they could recover, Isiem hit them with a second fireball from another angle. The Splinter Men ignited swiftly, their arms and legs draped in flickering scarves of flame and their faces melting like tallow masks. Silently they burned and fell back into the mist, never issuing so much as a moan.

More climbed over their thrashing bodies, stamping out the flames with their bare cold feet and leaving their companions inert in their wake. Ganoven, his jaw knotted tight in concentration, raised his hands toward the oncoming undead. A bolt of virulent yellow-green acid flew from his fingers, reflecting brightly against the obsidian blades of the Splinter Men before slamming into the lead one's head. The sizzle of bubbling flesh sounded strangely loud in the fog; a moment later, the stomach-turning smell hit.

Stumbling and sightless, the Splinter Man kept coming, even as the left half of his face sagged and dripped down his chest in gooey rivulets. Chunks of bone sloughed off his skull as the acid consumed it, and through the widening socket of his dissolved left eye, Isiem could see that the interior of the dead man's skull was completely empty.

He couldn't see it for long. Pulcher's hammer came swooping down to crush in the Splinter Man's hollow skull. The dead man crumpled, slumping to the ground, but then the rest of them were on the front line, their black knives raised high. One grabbed at Copple, dragging the shrieking man sideways in his saddle and slashing a red gash across his thigh. Another hacked wildly at Kyril, but the paladin's horse danced nimbly to the right and the half-elf drove her boot into the Splinter Man's face, snapping his head back.

Others closed in, but by then Teglias had gotten his snorting, kicking steed back under control. Gripping the reins tightly in one hand, the cleric lifted the other to the sky. Wan gray sunlight coalesced around his upthrust hand and intensified, gathering strength until it seemed that the full fury of the sun had been summoned through the Umbral Basin's fog.

It erupted from the cleric's hand in a nova of white-gold radiance, searing away the mist instantaneously and incinerating the Splinter Men where they stood. Isiem felt the sunlight as a flash of warmth across his skin, just hot enough to verge on unpleasantness, but to the undead it was devastating. Not one of them was left standing when the brightness cleared enough for the wizard to see again.

"That was easy," Ena said, surprised. "We're not even scratched. Other than Copple, who doesn't count." She removed the bolt from her crossbow and slung the weapon back on its saddle loop, then nudged her pony over to take a look at their fallen foes.

"I fear it might not be so easy as that," Ascaros said. He had gotten ahead of her, and was peering down at the nearest of the Splinter Men.

It was the one melted by Ganoven's spell. While Copple winced his way through wrapping a crude bandage around his thigh, Isiem joined the others studying the dead creature. His face was a mangled ruin, scorched by Teglias's divine fire and bubbled by Ganoven's acid bolt. Cratered splash marks dotted the grayish skin of the Splinter Man's neck and continued down to his chest.

He was dead, completely dead, and parts of him looked like they'd been dead a very long time. Under the thicket of splinters that riddled his lips, the flesh was parched and dry. His fingernails were cracked, missing in places, and mazed with a dark web of dirt. The eye that hadn't been melted by acid was a flabby, desiccated orb, wrinkled and mushy as an apple left in the cellar too long.

Whatever the man's name had once been, whichever nation he'd hailed from and whoever he'd once known or loved, he was nothing but a corpse now. Isiem had already turned, ready to walk away, when he heard Ascaros suck a hissing breath through his teeth.

The Splinter Man was moving. His fingers were twitching. His lips trembled behind their hundred cruel piercings. The shrunken eyeball vibrated in its socket, and above it the dead white threads of his eyelashes shook as though he were trying to blink his vision clear. He moved to sit up.

Swearing, Pulcher smashed his hammer into the Splinter Man's head, knocking the thing back down like a rag doll. Acid-softened flesh splashed into the air, and the Splinter Man stopped moving. But all around them, unseen in the mist, Isiem could hear the others beginning to stir.

"Immortality," Ascaros whispered. The shadowcaller sounded on the verge of hysteria. He took a step back from the corpse, beckoning for his shadowsteed to come near. "They wanted immortality, and this is what they made. Monsters who cannot be killed."

"What do you mean, can't be killed?" Pulcher hefted his hammer, tossing it six inches in the air and letting the haft slap back into his palm. He pointed the weapon's bloodied head at the crushed Splinter Man. "I killed it. It's dead."

"Afraid not," Ena said, tapping her pony's flanks to urge the animal alongside Ascaros. The dwarf's eyes were wide, and she snapped her head up in alarm at the increased commotion of the Splinter Men getting to their feet around them. "It's *not* dead. None of them are. Kyril, get back here. There's no time to see to the fallen."

The paladin had already started into the mist, trying to find the Splinter Men's discarded victims, but she stopped upon hearing her name. "What do you suggest?" Kyril asked sharply, turning as the dwarf addressed her.

"For us to not get lost in the mist, first off," Ena said. "Beyond that, I'm open to ideas."

Kyril's sword was blazing once again, and she seemed to regard that as conclusive proof that their enemies were not defeated. Her scowl was ferocious. "We've struck them with fire, acid, and Sarenrae's holy light, and they're not stopping."

"We run." Ascaros climbed into his saddle, not waiting to see if the others did the same. He tapped his heels to the shadowsteed's sides, turning eastward—at least Isiem *thought* it was eastward; he couldn't be certain through the valley's haze—toward something only he could sense. The silver links of Sukorya's chain gleamed between his clenched fingers. "To Fiendslair. If the wards around the place don't keep out the Splinter Men, the gate itself surely shall. These creatures might not have existed when Eledwyn built her stronghold, but she would have warded herself against all Mesandroth's underlings. And these are, in some way, his. They were drawn to the magic of her diamond." He grinned. "Or his blood."

"Let's go." Kyril wheeled her dapple mare around. Her horse rushed to follow the shadowcaller, forgetting its earlier unease around the spell-spun mount. "And pray you can find it before the Splinter Men run down our horses."

The next hours passed in a blur. The mist closed in around them, wet and cold and blindingly thick, as though guided by some hostile mind that did not intend to let them escape. It was impossible to see their surroundings, their direction, anything. Even the shapes of their companions, not twenty feet away, were dim blurs in the fog. Isiem couldn't tell which one was Ascaros, or whether the shadowcaller knew where they were going. All he could do was lower his head against his gelding's neck, trust he was following the right blur, and pray that they reached Fiendslair before his spell gave out.

The drumming of their horses' hooves was impossibly loud, a desperate driving percussion to nowhere. It wasn't the only sound, though. The slap and crash of the Splinter Men's pursuit surrounded them, echoing eerily from all sides.

Grunts and growls and bestial panting breaths floated through the haze, and even though the dead men had never uttered a sound when Isiem could see them, he was entirely convinced that the cries of the chase were theirs. It was impossible to say how close they were: it might have been ten feet or a thousand.

Pulcher's horse was the first to go lame. It twisted an ankle on something unseen and went down hard, throwing the big man into the fog. He came up cursing, clutching his shoulder, and searching fruitlessly for his bow and helm. Even if they'd had time to mount a real search, though—and they didn't, not with the Splinter Men hounding their heels—it would have been hopeless. There was no finding anything in the mist, and the sun was going down.

"Get on, you idiot." Copple turned his horse back to his stranded friend. His face was deathly pale, and sweat beaded on his brow. The wound in his leg seemed to be causing his significant pain. But he clenched his jaw and stayed behind, waiting.

Swearing incessantly, Pulcher clambered up behind the tattooed man, grabbing him around his ample waist. Under other circumstances, the sight of the mismatched Aspis thugs clinging to the overburdened horse might have been funny; as it was, Isiem just hoped they didn't lose the second beast too quickly. It was struggling under Pulcher's weight, and he doubted it would stay up for long.

Not a minute after they'd left the lamed horse behind, its screams pierced the mist, along with the wet noise of knives sinking into living flesh.

"It might buy us time," Kyril murmured grimly, but from her tone it was clear she didn't believe it would be much.

"How are they that close on foot?" Ena gasped. "We've been riding for *hours!*"

No one had an answer, or the breath to give it. Darkness was coming down on them fast, and the ghostly lights they'd conjured were little help. The mist caught their illumination and turned it from diamond to pearl: bright, and beautiful, but utterly opaque. Soon they rode in a bubble of blind, reflected whiteness, while the misty night stretched out infinitely around them.

Then Teglias's horse went down. Kyril circled back to collect the cleric, but there was no saving his gelding. Moments later, Ena's stout shaggy pony began to falter.

"We've got to stand and fight," the dwarf growled, dismounting from her pony. She refused to leave the animal, though, looping a rope through its bridle and coaxing it to follow them after she doubled up on Isiem's conjured steed. Relieved of its burden, the shaggy little pony gamely fought to keep up. Its ears flattened at the shrieks of Teglias's horse in the distance. "Outrunning them isn't working."

"*No*," Ascaros snapped. The shadowcaller was far forward of them all. Isiem could see nothing of him, not even the suggestion of a silhouette reflected in the fog. "We're nearly there."

"How much farther?" Ena demanded. Her pony was weakening, and it seemed to make the dwarf angrier. She gripped the rope with both hands, staring across the stained hemp as if she could renew the animal's failing strength by sheer force of will.

"Soon," Ascaros insisted. "Soon."

It was hard to imagine, harder to believe. Isiem couldn't see anything through the cloud of diffused light around their group. If salvation lay ahead, it was well hidden.

But then he became aware of a new sound: a shrilling, jarring, jagged vibration, like a steel file scraping against the long bones of his body or a slow shot of lightning through his veins. It was less noise than sensation; Isiem didn't hear it so much as he felt it, and what he felt wracked him worse than pain.

Unsettling as it was for him, it was far more terrible for the Splinter Men. The eerie chorus of their chase broke apart, interrupted by spastic cries of fear and woe. Flashes of green and white fire flared through the fog, accompanied by the nightmare percussion of cracking bones. The slap of the Splinter Men's footsteps slowed, although it did not stop.

And now Isiem could see something cutting through the mist ahead. A wedge-shaped slash of crimson light bled through the blanketing whiteness. Odd, interlocking geometric shapes rotated and spun in the radiance, as if the light were being projected through cut-outs in a screen. *Sukorya's case,* Isiem thought, and indeed the ghostly images in the light had the same mind-wrenching impossibility as the angles and shapes inscribed on that case. The lines refused to come together correctly, and they changed uncomfortably at the periphery of his vision.

The fog receded where the red light reached. Against that newly empty patch of darkness, the largest of those geometric outlines brightened and steadied. It traced an impossible form, all warped curves and fractured angles stretching into dimensions that Isiem couldn't follow. The smaller shapes—which seemed to be only extensions of the same shape, somehow, connected across those same dimensions of impossibility—collected inside it, piling atop one another in denser and denser layers until finally, mercifully, there were too many lines to distinguish and they melted into an ill-defined crimson glow.

Its light washed across the mute faces of the Splinter Men, standing in a rough semicircle two hundred feet behind them. The dead men were completely motionless. They stood as if in a trance, their black knives dangling forgotten at their sides. Some dripped fresh-spilled horse's blood. Mist skirled about their feet in curling wisps, but it was the only movement around them.

"The gate," Ascaros said, stepping out of the foggy night to stand before the pulsing portal. Sukorya's case was in his hand. The silver shell had cracked open just slightly, and red light oozed from it like blood from a brawler's mouth. "I was right: its magic holds them at bay. But it will not hold forever, and when the portal closes, they will be free." He held an open hand out to Teglias. "Give me the key. Let us enter Fiendslair."

Kyril glanced back at the Splinter Men. Their upturned faces were red with reflected light, their eyes empty and pitiless. She scowled, putting a hand to the hilt of her sword as she strode toward the disorienting gate. "Into Fiendslair it is. We don't have any choice, do we? We can't go back. There's only forward."

Chapter Fourteen
Fiendslair

Red light swallowed them.

The world shifted under their feet, but Isiem saw none of it. Hot air blew across his face, and cold, and a breath of damp wind that smelled of musty spices and sour wine. It left a clammy coating on his skin, which lingered as the crimson glow finally softened and gave way to an ordinary lack of light.

He raised a finger. Light blossomed around it, a brilliant hibiscus pink that changed to an equally vibrant emerald green after the first few seconds. The wizard nodded slightly, satisfied that the colors of his magic worked as he willed. Wherever Fiendslair was, it wasn't the Umbral Basin.

They stood in a five-sided chamber walled in smooth brass. A circle of runes crawled across the floor under their feet. The living horses were still with them, crowding the room uncomfortably, but the spellsteeds had been dispelled. Reflections of Isiem's floating light danced across the polished metal, refracted into a thousand tiny, verdant suns. It was beautiful, but it was the only thing in the room that was.

Five doors stood in the chamber, one in each of the mirrorlike walls. The doors were as dull as the brass was bright, for each of them was made of flesh.

Scaly, spiny, or oozing with ichor, each door seemed to have been made of the flattened and contorted carcass of a demon. Isiem recognized the curling stripes and smoke-scented fur of a brimorak, the mangy hides and goatlike horns of a half-dozen spite demons pressed together, and a slaggy, melted face, coated in a thick layer of masking slime, that he thought might be an omox.

As Isiem studied the amorphous visage, trying to determine if it was indeed such a formidable fiend trapped inside, its sagging eyes suddenly blinked. Ena's shaggy pony threw its head back in alarm. The pony retreated to the center of the room, where it huddled with the other animals and whickered nervously at the fiendish doors on all sides.

"They're *alive*," Ascaros hissed.

"Why yes, so they are," Teglias said. He approached the omox door, stopping two feet away with his hands clasped professorially behind his back. The cleric leaned down, marveling at the trapped demon, and Isiem waved his light toward the door to better illumine it for them both. "Yes, of course."

The omox's slimy eyes squinted painfully as the light drew near. It tried to turn its squashed face away, pulling back under the layers of viscous greenish-pink ooze that constituted its body, but it was as trapped in its position as a butterfly pinned under glass.

"What do you mean, 'of course'?" Kyril asked. She frowned at the demonflesh door, flexing a mailed fist as if she wanted to smite it then and there. "How long did you say this place had been abandoned? How many centuries? And these things still *live*?"

"They're demons. They do not age, they do not die. Unless you kill them . . . and there's no reason to kill these. They'd lose their efficacy if they were dead." The Sarenite moved on to the next door, which was fashioned from some spiky fiend that Isiem didn't recognize. Its body seemed to be composed of thousands of fine white bones, like a fish's skeleton, with innumerable glowing crimson eyes scattered among them.

"But as long as they live, they are considerably more durable than wood or stone. Impervious to many forms of attack, resistant to magic, virtually impossible to break down with ordinary weapons—you can see the advantages. I would wager that whatever enchantment keeps them alive and imprisoned in this state also enables them to heal whatever damage they *do* suffer." The cleric uncorked a small bottle of water and, before anyone could stop him, flicked a few droplets onto the door of red eyes and white bones.

The blessed water bubbled like acid, eating a handful of tiny holes into the fiend's flesh. The door shuddered violently, as if it had been kicked; the crimson eyes scattered among its bones quivered and bulged. A dozen tiny mouths, which Isiem had not previously noticed, opened across the door's surface and shrieked soundlessly through the white needles of their teeth.

Behind Teglias's back, Kyril and Ena exchanged an uneasy look. Pulcher muttered a village prayer, and although he got most of the words wrong, nobody laughed at his mistakes. They were too busy watching the fiend. Confirming Teglias's hypothesis, the wounds caused by his holy water healed within a minute, leaving no trace of damage on the door.

"Well," the cleric said to Ascaros, capping his vial of holy water and sliding it back into a pocket. "I'm satisfied to be right—and a little apprehensive about what that means. Which way shall we go?"

"I have no idea," the shadowcaller admitted. He handed the key to Fiendslair back to Teglias, then tapped the silver case that held Sukorya's diamond. Its glow had vanished the instant they passed through the portal; the stone appeared to be inert. "This offers no guidance. And while I am aware of *what* Eledwyn did, I know very little about *how* she did it, or how her workshop was arranged. All the stories that survive of this place came from Mesandroth's lackeys, and none of them worked here."

"Then we'll go exploring." Teglias pocketed the key with a wry smile. "I'm not too old for adventure yet."

"*I* want to know how we get out of here again," Pulcher grumbled, turning in a slow circle and scanning the demonic doors.

"Easy," Ascaros said. "Just channel a thread of arcane magic into the runes on the floor here. The mechanism is simple from this side."

"But I don't have any magic!"

Ascaros gave a shark's smile. "Then you'd do well to stay close to those of who do, wouldn't you?"

Ganoven snapped his gloved fingers, pointing imperiously at Pulcher and Copple. The latter was in the middle of drinking a potion for his wounded leg, but he finished it hurriedly and massaged the life back into his slashed thigh as his superior turned on them. "You two, get out your bags. The *special* bags."

Copple managed a serviceably smart salute. Being in this room seemed to have unnerved him as much as it had the horses; his brow was shiny with sweat, and he seemed more deferential than Isiem had ever seen the man. "Yes, sir."

The tattooed thug wrestled a saddlebag off their uneasy, sidestepping packhorse with some difficulty. Eventually he got it open and pulled out two bulky sacks of quilted red-and-black cloth. He handed one to Pulcher and slung the other over his own back.

Each bag was stitched with three horizontal bands of looping copper wire, by which Isiem recognized the enchantment that they bore. That particular technique was employed by a cabal of Chelish wizards who specialized in outfitting merchants undertaking risky expeditions; he had often seen similar bags being packed and unpacked in the market square of Pangolais. Such bags could hold far more than their outer dimensions suggested, and the quilted ones had the additional property of being able to isolate their contents into separate compartments.

The sacks represented a substantial investment. The Aspis Consortium must truly have believed there was something valuable to be found in Fiendslair.

"We'll begin with the spite demons," Teglias decided. "The weakest demon is likely to guard the least dangerous portion of this place, wouldn't you agree? That should give us a sense of how the rest of our expedition is likely to go."

He gestured to the door covered in patchy fur. Goatlike hooves and sinewy legs had been folded at excruciating angles to make it. The bearded heads that rolled slot-pupilled eyes at them were wrenched backward and sideways on necks that had to have been snapped in multiple places.

But they lived, somehow, and two of their curved black horns jutted out to serve as an apparent handle.

With only the slightest hesitation, Ascaros took hold of those horns and pulled.

At first, nothing happened. The shadowcaller pulled harder. Tendons stood out on his wrists and neck as he strained, and the trapped spite demons snarled and spat uselessly in their flattened prison, but the demon-flesh door did not budge.

Then some ancient magic in the door stirred fitfully back into service. A tiny, whirling blade, no greater in circumference than a silver coin, spun out from the top left corner of the door and carved along its side. A bright red ruby shone in its center, illumining its serrated silver edges. Those silver edges slashed through flesh and bone as the circular blade spun along the door's outline, spraying a fine mist of demon blood across the near walls where it passed. Judging from the deep discoloration of the brass in a two-inch stripe along those walls, this had been a regular occurrence in days long past.

Once it was cut free, the door pulled open easily, trailing thin ribbons of gore and loose hair. Ascaros swung it open wide enough for everyone to see through, then paused.

Beyond it stretched a ten-foot-wide hallway. Reliefs covered its gently curved walls, depicting floral vines and lush gardens with a fineness of detail that Isiem supposed must be a mark of elven crafting. Frosted lamps hung from the ceiling, their wide glass bowls supported by copper chains worked to resemble climbing mandevilla. The amber-hued light that glowed in the depths of their bowls was very faint, doing little more than softening the shadows that filled the hall. Several of the lamps seemed to have burned out over the centuries, and gave no light at all.

At the end of the hall, twenty feet ahead, was an elaborate archway filled with dim and misty light. More carvings wound around the arch, again resembling some type of flowering vine, although Isiem could not identify the species from where he stood. The fluid music of a fountain echoed down the verdigrised hall, its serenity startling after the chamber of demonflesh doors.

"Eledwyn *was* an elf," Ascaros said, eying the ornate lamps dubiously. "I suppose it's possible she wanted to have some part of this place resemble her homeland."

"Possible," Ena said. "But likely?"

No one had an answer to that. After a minute stretched away in uncomfortable silence, Ganoven waved his henchmen forward. "Time is wasting. Fiendslair might have an infinity of it, but the Aspis Consortium does not."

"Me first." Ena pushed past Pulcher and Copple, holding up a hand to keep them back as she crouched to begin her survey of the amber-lit hallway. The Aspis thugs were only too happy to let the scarred dwarf go ahead of them. Pulcher dropped his immense hammer and leaned on it like a walking stick as Isiem sent his floating light forward to assist Ena.

Working fastidiously, the dwarf probed the deeper recesses of the wall carvings with a long, angled steel stick tipped in a tuft of dusty wool. Amber light twinkled across the sweat beaded on her stubbly scalp. Occasionally, in response to nothing Isiem could discern, she paused to examine the floor. It took her the better part of ten minutes to cover the twenty feet, but after satisfying herself that no traps lurked in the hallway, the dwarf stood up and nodded to the rest of them.

Then she crouched again to approach the archway, peering through its green-streaked bronze leaves into the next room. She stayed there, totally motionless, for almost a minute, then slowly withdrew.

"It's a garden," she reported, sliding away her tools. "Or it was."

"Was?" Kyril echoed.

Ena shrugged. She went over to her pony, patting its soft brown nose to reassure the worried beast as it snuffled into her shoulder. "I suppose it still is, mostly. Go look for yourself. It seems safe enough. I'll watch the horses."

"Fine." The paladin readied her sword and moved forward, cat-light on her feet. Again, Copple and Pulcher seemed quite content to let someone else take the lead, although this time they followed begrudgingly a few steps behind. Ascaros came after them, weaving a protective spell around himself as he walked, and Isiem did the same as he fell in alongside his old friend.

The faint, sweet fragrance of white flowers drifted through the archway at the hall's end. There was a bitterness alongside it: the earthy scents of loam and leaf-rich forest soil, layered with countless years of death and renewal. It reminded Isiem powerfully of the Backar Forest.

And, indeed, it seemed that Eledwyn had kept a forest of her own in this strange place. Past the archway, an enormous oval-ceilinged chamber held a garden so wild it scarcely fit that name. Enormous trees towered thirty feet above the ground, their roots covered by mossy blankets and spindly yellow mushrooms. White-skinned saplings grew in the spaces between them, as did dense patches of crocus and feathery ferns. High above them, an enchanted sun shone: a globe of burnished gold that traveled on a silver track around the ceiling, carrying its light across the artificial sky. It was a magnificent work of magic; its artistry took Isiem's breath away. And after all these years, it still worked.

That sun no longer charted a steady course, however. In places the track had been bent or blackened as if by some fiery explosion. Whatever had caused the damage had left no other scars; the forest had likely grown over any destruction in the chamber's lower reaches. But on the ceiling, nothing hid the marks of that long-ago blast, and when the golden sun passed over the ruined portions of its course, its enchanted light faltered and failed.

There were dead spots in the forest beneath the longer stretches of damaged track, where no light reached the plants to sustain them. Frilled shelves of mushrooms dotted the great trunks that lay sideways across the dead lands like half-buried bones, but otherwise they appeared to be devoid of life.

Elsewhere, peculiar new forms of life flourished. As Isiem left the others to their own explorations and ventured deeper into the wild garden, he saw the source of the babbling he'd heard earlier: a marble fountain, its sides bearded with green-gray moss, that fed a spider web of creeks throughout the forest.

The wizard's boots sank deep into the soft loam as he approached the nearest of those streams. Nothing else had left any tracks on the land, but there were things living in the water. He saw their pale blurred shapes flit away from his presence, but after several minutes of standing very still, he saw one hovering under a submerged tree root.

It was a curious creature, about the size of his palm and so white that it was virtually translucent. A carapace of soft chitin covered its body, which resembled nothing so much as an oversized flea's. Its four faceted eyes were an opaque reddish-purple and moved freely at the ends of jointed eyestalks.

"What *is* that?" Kyril asked, stepping carefully over a curly-headed fern to join the wizard. As she neared the stream, the insectlike creature in the water darted away, vanishing downstream.

"I have no idea," Isiem said. "Some of the fishmongers in Nisroch keep snails in their tanks to eat algae. Perhaps these things—whatever they are—serve a similar purpose in the streams?"

"Seems like it would have been easier to use fish." The paladin raked a stray lock of reddish hair behind a slightly pointed ear, glancing over her shoulder at one of the dead spots in the forest. "Then again, fish might not have survived this long. The birds didn't."

"Birds?" Isiem echoed.

"There were songbirds here originally. Generations of them, maybe. All dead now, though. Ena found the bones, all piled up together under some of the trees a little ways to the west. We're not sure what killed them, but it looks like they all died around the same time, and it was a long time ago." Kyril nodded toward the sparkling creek. "Those water bugs are the only animals that seem to have survived all these years."

"I'm surprised anything did. Have you found anything else?"

"Yes. It's . . . some kind of sculpture, I think. Teglias is studying it, but he asked for your help. I came to find you so that you could take a second look." Extending a gauntleted hand to guide him, she led the wizard through the forest garden along a curving path that was barely visible under centuries of unguided growth. Once the path had been paved in flagstones, but time and tree roots had pushed many of those slabs aside, while others were completely covered by dead leaves and live ones. It was visible only as a wavering line of sparser vegetation in the wood, and as scattered stones amid the greenery.

The sculpture at the end of the path, however, had not been touched by time. It was an immense work of living wood, fifteen feet high and ten across. Innumerable trees and vines had been woven together by magic so that their overlapping trunks and branches formed an intricate knot of multicolored strands. Smooth silver bark twined around fibrous gray and shaggy dun; glossy olive leaves brushed gently against red-throated white flowers and fragrant lilac. The interaction of all the disparate plants, creating a design that varied unpredictably in the center but came to four symmetrical compass points at the perimeter of the circle, suggested wildness and absolute control at the same time.

It was a wonder. Isiem had never seen its like.

Teglias, Ascaros, and Ganoven were studying the circle of branches intently, while Pulcher and Copple sat off to the side trying to crack open some nuts they'd found in the forest.

"Ena's gone to get the horses," the Sarenite said when he saw them. "We'll keep them here while we explore the rest of the complex. It seems safe enough. There's water here, and grass by the streams."

"What is this?" Isiem asked, motioning to the immense living sculpture.

"The Circle of the Four Gates," Teglias answered. "An ancient symbol, and an obscure one. It's mostly forgotten nowadays. But in earlier ages, it was used by some druidic sects to represent the natural world." The cleric pointed to the flowers that blossomed at each of the four compass points: red, yellow, blue, white. They were all different species, but they had clustered together so that each group of flowers was the same size as the others. "The flowers mark the classical elements: fire, earth, water, air. The plants within represent the wild variety of life that flourishes within the embrace and interaction of those four elements. Each design is subtly different, depending on the sect and the individual druid, but that much of the meaning is always the same."

"Does it do anything?"

Ascaros lifted one shoulder in a shrug. "It seems to maintain the air and water in this place. I suppose it might have some influence on that enchanted sun, as well. If it does anything else, it's beyond me to tell. You're welcome to examine it yourself, if you like."

Isiem did, but could tell little. He wasn't familiar with the magic undergirding the sculpture. The druidic arts had always been foreign to him. In Nidal, such mysteries were considered the domain of primitives, or mystic cults like the albinos of the Uskwood, and were little studied in the arcane schools of Pangolais or the hushed temples of Zon-Kuthon. He *felt* the magic in the symbol, stirring sleepily under his probing spell and running through each leaf's green veins, but he could not unravel its meaning.

Defeated, he shook his head and stepped back. "It's druidic, I can tell that much. But no more."

"I believe your friend is right," Teglias said. "It maintains the balance of elements in this place that allows the garden to live. The important thing, in my mind, is what it tells us about Eledwyn. This was a woman who valued the natural world, and who chose to make her sanctuary a garden, going so far as to enlist the aid of druids in crafting it. Clearly she was not entirely evil."

Ascaros snorted. "I can see you've never met a Nidalese druid, Teglias. In the Uskwood, they honor nature by watering their gardens with human blood." He shook his head. "Don't go looking to redeem Eledwyn. Use her weapon or don't, but don't kid yourself—you're fighting evil with evil."

The Sarenite started to speak, then subsided with a small inclination of his head. "I suppose that's wise. If there are no objections, we'll rest here tonight and see what else there is to be found on the morrow. It'll be faster if we split up. Kyril and Ena will go with me. Ganoven, take your men. You two together." He pointed to Isiem and Ascaros.

"It's safer if we all stay together," Kyril protested.

"It's *safer* if we find what we came here for and get out quickly," the cleric said. "None of us is a novice, and in any case, we haven't seen anything more dangerous than water bugs and a few unpleasant doors in here."

"I agree with the cleric," Ganoven said, stroking his tidy black beard. "It's far more efficient to canvass the place in a single day, then regroup just before we leave." From the glint in his eye, and Kyril's answering scowl, Isiem surmised that the paladin shared his thought: the Aspis agent just wanted a chance to loot the place without the others seeing.

"*I* think you're being a stupid greedy idiot," Ena said, eying Ganoven as she returned with two of their horses. "But I can also see you're bent on it. Fine. At least I should be out of blast range when you inevitably blow yourself up."

"I'm so glad you agree," the Aspis agent said, unruffled.

"Ascaros," Teglias said. "Do you still have those compasses?"

"Yes." The shadowcaller opened his satchel, removing the bloodstone compasses he'd distributed before they went into the Backar Forest to hunt the Beast. He handed compasses to Kyril, Teglias, and Ganoven. The last he did not keep for himself, but offered to Isiem. "I trust you all remember how to use them? Each communicates with the others and will guide you to them. For a small price in blood."

"I remember," Isiem said. He noted that this one's needle was silver, not steel like the others', and that there was a rune at its center that the compass he'd used previously did not possess. The wizard wondered why Ascaros wasn't keeping the compass for himself, but he accepted the needled stone and slid it into a pocket. It rested cold and heavy against his leg, its needle pricking into his thigh. He turned it around, which made it only slightly less uncomfortable.

If any of them stumbled into real danger in Fiendslair, the compass was unlikely to save them. It took precious seconds to use, and it required a level of concentration that a panicked man might not be able to muster. But it might be useful before that, if they had enough warning to know.

"Good," Ganoven said. "Then it's settled. Tonight we rest. Tomorrow we find this nightblade."

Chapter Fifteen
The Laboratory of Demons

Ganoven and his thugs were already gone by the time Isiem arose the next day, and Teglias's group was leaving. Ena gave Isiem's shoulder a brief squeeze as she departed; Kyril nodded in wordless farewell.

"Good luck," Teglias said. "Try not to get eaten, and be sure to give them indigestion if you do." And with that, they, too, were gone.

Isiem assumed it was morning, although that was only a guess. The garden's artificial sun moved along its track at a speed that seemed to approximate a day's length, but it never rose or set, and there was nothing else in Fiendslair that had even that tenuous connection to the world outside. The natural cycle held no meaning here; Isiem strongly suspected that Eledwyn's workshop existed outside Golarion altogether.

A covered pot of porridge sat by the embers of their cookfire. Isiem lifted the lid and looked inside. Oats, raisins, a smudge of honey. Kyril had prepared that meal, he guessed—the paladin had a distinct sweet tooth, and had never been able to abide plain porridge—and probably Copple had been the one who'd scooped out most of the raisins and all but the faintest whiff of honey for his share.

But there was more than enough left for him. He hesitated, wondering if he should save some for Ascaros . . . but the shadowcaller wasn't anywhere to be seen, so he had probably already eaten his fill. And if not, there was no telling when he'd be back.

Isiem took the whole pot, and was just finishing it when Ascaros came back through the trees. "Ah, you're finally awake."

"Indeed." Isiem put the pot aside and closed his spellbook. He'd studied while he ate, imprinting the words of magic carefully on his mind and storing another teleportation spell in his ruby ring. Without knowing exactly what they were likely to face, it had been difficult to choose the spells that might be useful, but he was accustomed to that. It was the wizard's daily lot. "What shall we explore?"

"One or another of the demonflesh doors, I imagine." Ascaros's illusory face twisted in an expression of very real disgust. "Ganoven cut through the brimorak door before you woke up. I don't know what he found past it, but it might be prudent to find out. He was a little too eager to run off on his own yesterday."

"Of course he was," Isiem said dryly. "He's here to find weapons, and weapons are vastly improved by surprise. Particularly if the enemies you want to surprise are Chelish devilers, and your not-entirely-trusted allies are Nidalese who might be in league with those devilers. It's entirely predictable that he'd want to leave us behind. It will be even more predictable if he tries to backstab us on the way out."

"Quite so," Ascaros agreed. "But *I* didn't come here looking for weapons. I came to find out how I could cheat death. As such, I'm not especially interested in getting myself killed during the search. Tends to negate the point."

"We agree entirely." Isiem collected the satchel that held his traveling spellbook and a few other necessaries. Shouldering the satchel, he followed Ascaros through the garden and back to the circular brass room.

Both the spite demons and the brimoraks were still bleeding when the Nidalese arrived, suggesting that some of the companions had just passed through. The brimoraks' blood boiled away upon contact with air, leaving a foul sulfurous smell in the room.

The demonflesh doors did not heal instantly after being cut open. Their flesh took a minute or two to mend back into a solid seal, allowing a door to be used by several people before it closed. The delay was likely excruciating for the demons—their agonized, squashed expressions certainly suggested as much— but the builders of this place had not been much concerned with their pain.

"Now's our chance to spy on them," Ascaros said mischievously, poking at a sliver of exposed bone from a brimorak's severed finger. The wounded creature snarled at him, its bestial face flattened and voice muted by the magic that held it trapped in the shape of a door. "The door's open. It's a golden opportunity to take them unawares."

Isiem eyed the bleeding door dubiously. Tendrils of raw pink flesh were beginning to adhere to the walls around it as the demons' broken bodies healed, renewing the airtight seal around the chamber. They didn't have long to decide; their best chance might already be past. "Really?"

"No." Ascaros jabbed the bone back down vertically into the brimorak's finger, eliciting a final soundless squeal, and turned away. "I *am* tempted to catch them stealing, because I know they are, but not enough to forgo my own explorations to do it. We'll take the door of bones."

"What are those things? I don't recognize them."

"Vermin." The shadowcaller pulled hard on the handle of warped bone that jutted out from the mass of fiends. Another tiny blade whirred out, shearing through the fine white bones around the door's edges with a high shrill noise. It sliced through a blinking red eyeball as well, spreading the viscous, crimson ocular fluid across another six inches of bone and wall.

"Ostovites," he continued, stepping back as they waited for the door to open. "Mindless, vile little parasites that have barely any bodies of their own. Instead they dig into their victims' bodies, then soften the bones with their saliva and pull them out so that they can peel them apart and weave them like wicker strands in a basket. Except they never make anything so sensible as a basket; they just build themselves demented attempts at arms and legs that barely function well enough for them to crawl to their next unfortunate prey. The best of them look like crippled starfish. The rest . . . well, being smashed into a door of eternal suffering is likely a considerable improvement on their own architectural skills."

The whirling blade retracted back into the wall. The door was free, framed by a fine dust of ground bone.

Isiem pulled it open and sent his floating light ahead. Its bubble of illumination passed over dusty tables and cobwebbed chests, freestanding wardrobes crowded with acolytes' robes, and eight narrow beds on iron frames. Their mattresses were wrinkled and shrunken, their blankets faded by time, but on the whole, the room was remarkably well preserved. Behind the demonflesh door, it appeared, this place had been empty and sterile for centuries.

"Eledwyn's assistants?" Isiem stooped to lift the lid of a wooden trunk at the foot of a bed. More clothes were tucked inside, along with a pair of pale green candles that smelled mustily of sage, a small gold incense dish, a necklace of irregular aventurine beads, and a few pages of faded, barely legible script. He rifled quickly through these last items—mnemonics and study aids. "They were worried about possession, poison, disease."

"It seems likely," Ascaros agreed. "Fiendslair is far too large for a single person to have managed, and the assistants would have had to sleep somewhere. And yes, of course they'd be concerned about such things. Demons are demons, and it's a fool who forgets that." He rummaged through the clothes hanging in the wardrobe. They all appeared to be of the same simple cut, although the gray-green robes were in several different sizes.

Isiem moved to the next trunk. It held a few more personal effects and ritual paraphernalia from the same esoteric religion, but nothing that struck him as being of great interest. The two after it were similarly unrevealing.

The fifth one was different. The lid of this trunk was tipped back, propped up by an overflowing heap of tangled chains, collars, and other restraints. Most of them did not appear to be made for human forms. Some were inscribed with sigils that Isiem recognized as paralytic spells; others contained links of verdigrised copper and were adorned with milky quartzes to neutralize the bound creature's poison. All were damaged in some way, although a few seemed to have been partly repaired.

"Chains for demons," he murmured, disentangling one such chain from a set of four interlocked manacles. Bubbles of dried ichor were faintly visible on the interior surfaces where they'd corroded the ancient steel. Isiem traced them with a pale fingertip, wondering what fiend had left those marks.

Ascaros came over. "Is there anything else?"

"Those books." Isiem nodded toward a stack of three yarn-tied notebooks piled next to the trunk. "Repair notes, perhaps."

"One would think Eledwyn would have been able to afford better books for her underlings. These look like schoolgirl's diaries." Ascaros picked up the top notebook and riffled through its pages. After a few seconds, he frowned, closed the book, and picked up the next. "I can't read any of this. It's all in Elven."

"Well, take them anyway." Isiem began sorting the chains into neat piles on the nearest bed. "I'll prepare a translation spell tomorrow. It should at least enable us to determine whether it's worth the trouble to translate all of them."

"If only they'd thought to include some pictures." Sighing, Ascaros bundled the books up and tucked them into his satchel. "Have you found anything else interesting?"

"Not unless you're fascinated by prayers to nature spirits."

"I'm mildly curious as to why anyone would bother. But no, can't say I care beyond that." Ascaros helped extricate the last few sets of cuffs and chains. He chose a few of the smaller pieces to carry away. Isiem did the same, trying to vary his selections to encompass the widest possible range of restraints and intended targets. After packing them into his satchel, he led the way back out to the central brass room.

The brimorak and spite demon doors were bleeding again. So was the omox, although that one had nearly healed shut under its drying line of ichor.

This time, after raising an eyebrow at Ascaros and receiving a tiny nod in return, Isiem grabbed a brimorak's bent blue-gray leg and hauled that smoking door open. Dripping gobbets of boiling blood, it pulled aside to reveal another long hallway, narrower and less elaborate than the one that led to the forest garden.

Unlike that ornately designed hall, this one held no metalwork or carvings, and while it was lit by enchanted lamps, these were simple globes of frosted glass hung from braided ropes. Several of them, like the lamps in the other hall, seemed to have lost their magic over the ages; their spheres were dark and lifeless.

A series of rune-scribed silver plates were embedded in the floor. The flowing letters etched into those plates lit up as Isiem and Ascaros neared them—or, at least, some of them did. Others, drained by ages of neglect, stayed inert.

"Trap?" Ascaros asked, staying near the door.

Isiem shook his head and continued down the hall. "If Ena has already been here, she would have disabled it or marked it. If she hasn't, I would expect Ganoven's idiots to be plastered across the walls. As neither of those things has happened, I must conclude there's no trap."

"Impeccable reasoning." The shadowcaller followed, amused.

As he stepped on the first of the lit silver plates, Isiem heard a faint hissing sound. White smoke billowed from a second, matching plate that faced downward from the ceiling. He froze, wondering if his blithe assumption about the lack of traps was going to prove fatally wrong . . . but the smoke drifted harmlessly past him. The fragrance of cedarwood and incense lingered, and nothing else.

More smoke fell from the ceiling as he crossed the next silver plate, and the next, and the next. Some of them did indeed prove inert, but most seemed functional, although few produced the sizable plume of the first. A trail of cloudy white followed Isiem through the hall, doubling in Ascaros's wake.

Through the haze of fragrant smoke, Isiem saw a large circular room ahead. An enormous oval dome of clear glass, itself large enough to serve as a small room, filled the chamber's center. Smaller glass bubbles, hundreds of them, lined the walls. Their curved surfaces reflected the hallway's light like so many bulbous eyes in the shadows.

The light globes that hung from the ceiling in here were broken—not merely dark, as some of the ones in the hallway had been, but smashed into saw-toothed fragments. Several were melted and dimmed with a bubbled lace of soot. Robbed of their magic, the room was dark except where Ganoven's spells and his minions' lanterns created small, shifting pools of illumination.

Other things were with them in those pools. From across the room, Isiem saw Ganoven lift a dangling, cat-sized creature out of a curved glass tank in the wall, stuff it into a metal cage, and drop the cage into one of the compartmented sacks he'd brought. A moment later, he pulled out another tank and reached into it with gloved hands, snatching out two smaller creatures that went into a second cage. Pulcher sat cross-legged on the floor, clumsily teasing a bit of yarn in front of another creature that was loose in the room.

Ascaros cleared his throat. Startled, Pulcher dropped the yarn. Ganoven's head snapped up, and an apprehensive, guilty look flashed across his face before he shook it off and put on an oily smile.

"You surprised us," the Aspis agent said.

"I can see that." Shaking the last of the white smoke from the hem of his shadowcaller's robes, Ascaros crossed the circular room. Isiem followed, glancing at the glass dome in the chamber's center as he passed it. The floor underneath the dome was worked into a series of concentric ovals in different colors of metal and stone. Among them, Isiem recognized silver, iron, ink, glass, salt, and amethyst in myriad shades of purple and swirled lavender. Protective magics, all of them. They warded against everything from deceitful illusions to fire and acid, while both the inner- and outermost rings were inscribed with runes to contain fiends.

There was nothing else in the dome, though, while there *were* things in the glass tanks near the back of the room. The skeletons of rats, cats, and other small animals sat in those prisons, along with droppings that had dried to rocks and the dust of their last meals. Greenish-gray mold and white-tufted fungus covered their bare little bones.

As Isiem walked by, his floating light bobbing over his shoulder, one of those skeletons stood up and looked at him.

It was a turtle. Mold furred its shell, obscuring its original colors and patterns underneath a coat of dull gray. Tendrils of ropy white fungus braided around its skeletal legs and muzzled its dead bony beak. Eight chitinous, serrated legs clattered along the under- side of its shell. From a crack in that shell sprouted a monstrous, fleshy set of jaws on a long stalk, like some horrid green-veined flower. The turtle's eyes were long gone, but the black pits that remained were undeni- ably fixed on Isiem's approach, and as he stared at it in momentary shock, the dead creature lifted a stubby leg at him and pawed at the front of its tank. Its toes looked like tiny human fingers, and they left smudged greenish prints on the glass.

"Remarkable, isn't it?" Ganoven trotted over, his bearded face split in an ingratiating smile. "They aren't really *alive*, of course, but they do seem to be capable of basic responses. They can walk, and they move toward food or water, although they can't seem to ingest any of it. They move away from extremes of heat or cold, and if something damages them, they scuttle away upon being exposed to it again. So they are capable of learning, as well as reacting on instinct."

"What are they?" Ascaros asked. Around them, more of the dead creatures were stirring. Rats and cats and patchy-feathered birds, bald but for a few stray plumes that poked through their moldy bones, had risen onto their fleshless feet and were watching them through the glass. Every one of them was deformed in some way, with malformed appendages, extra heads, or strange vegetal growths protruding from their bodies, and all had the same eyeless jawstalk growing from somewhere in their bodies. Fibrous strands connected their bones like puppet strings of misplaced sinew. The room echoed eerily with the sound of their scratching at the tanks.

"Not undead, not possessed, and not truly alive. Beyond that, we don't quite know," Ganoven admitted. "My spells have some limits."

"Evil?" Isiem raised an ivory eyebrow at the half-elven man. "Surely you can sense *that*."

"Evil . . ." The Aspis agent gave a reluctant, concessionary shrug. "No, actually. I mean that I don't have a way of sensing it, not that they aren't. Or are, for that matter."

"Well, who isn't," Ascaros said, with a lopsided little half-smile. He pulled on a kidskin glove and traced his fingertip across the surface of the turtle's tank. It snapped at his hand, and he stepped away, his smile deepening slightly. "Vile little things. These are what you were putting into that sack when we came in?"

Ganoven's mouth opened, and he hesitated, then nodded briskly. "Safely contained, of course."

"Yes. Safely contained. Like that one?" The shadow-caller gestured to the creature that Pulcher had been baiting with his bit of yarn. It was a cat, as fungus-ridden and skeletal as the others. Hair-thin fangs filled its empty eye sockets like ingrown eyelashes, gnashing softly at nothing. Only a bit of striped orange fur on the tip of its tail and across the knuckles of its paws hinted at the dead cat's original appearance.

"It's my pet," Pulcher said, sulky as a chastened child. "Been alive for a thousand years, how many people have a pet like that? I named him Sparky. Ganoven said I could have him."

"Sparky," Ascaros echoed, musing. "Yes. Appropriate." He pointed at the offending cat and murmured a word, and although Isiem recognized the spell and knew what was coming, he still flinched as a hissing stream of fire erupted from the shadowcaller's hand to annihilate Pulcher's skeletal pet.

Sparky burned swiftly, mold and bone and fragile cartilage going up in a rush of popping flames. The jaw-stalk that had been hiding inside its ribcage lunged out, belching bitter smoke as it burned upward from throat to teeth. Wider and wider the mouth pulled, until the top of the head collapsed under its own weight and tumbled back into the smoke and was lost from view.

For an instant, Isiem thought he heard words in that billowing belch of smoke. Threats, curses, imprecations in some inhuman tongue—the meaning of it eluded him, but the *intent* was clear. Hatred, and a promise of vengeance.

Or so he thought. It took only seconds for the skeleton to burn away, and almost as soon as he imagined there were words amid the snapping sparks, the tiny conflagration was gone.

Pulcher, once he recovered from the shock of being so narrowly missed by the shadowcaller's spell, turned a furious glare on Ascaros. A red flush crept up the sides of the big man's neck, darkening his ears. "Why'd you do that?"

"Do what? Burn Sparky?" Ascaros asked, his apparent boredom belied by a malicious twinkle in his dark eyes. "Because I wanted to see if the smoke would kill you."

"Why you—" Pulcher began to lumber to his feet, but Copple grabbed him around the waist and pulled him back to the ground. Gasping viciously and clutching at the leg that the Splinter Men had slashed, the chubby thug nevertheless managed to warn his friend off with a furious shake of his head.

"*No*," Copple hissed, "not now."

"Not ever," Ascaros said calmly. He crossed to where the two thugs sat sprawled on the floor. Ostentatiously ignoring Pulcher's hate-filled stare, he poked at the cat's charred bones. "You should thank me. And you should see Teglias for a curative spell. While I certainly *hope* I acted swiftly enough to prevent you from catching Sparky's contagion, I can't be sure. Therefore, I suggest you explain your stupidity to the cleric in case I was too late."

Pulcher's flush had drained from him as the shadow-caller spoke. By the time Ascaros finished, he was pale. "Do you think I'm sick? With the mold?"

"I think you should run off and see Teglias," Ascaros said with a small shrug, still studying Sparky's remains. "Or not. It's entirely your choice. Since your stupidity can, once again, only kill you, it's of no great concern."

"You're a bastard, you know that?" Pulcher got back to his feet. Glancing nervously at the skeletal creatures trapped in tanks all around them, he edged toward the hallway's entrance, then hurried away, with Copple hobbling and cursing at his side.

When his lackeys were gone, Ganoven wiped perspiration from his brow. The sudden realization of how much danger he'd put them in, and Ascaros's fiery show of force, seemed to have unnerved the Aspis agent badly. His arrogance had evaporated, leaving him white and shaken. "I should apologize for letting him—"

"You should," Ascaros agreed, "but I don't care to hear it. It doesn't matter anymore. I trust you will not be removing those cages from their sacks until we leave this place."

"No, no, of course not," the goateed half-elf said hastily. "That would be very foolish."

"Yes. It would." At last Ascaros turned away from the cat's charred bones, fixing Ganoven with an icy smile. "Very foolish. I'm glad we agree. Now perhaps you should go see whether your lackey is better at following my instructions than yours. I would hate for him to get lost looting another room instead of going to Teglias promptly."

Ganoven nodded jerkily and went to the hallway, all but fleeing from the Nidalese. Once he was out of sight, Ascaros let out a long, angry exhalation and dropped his pretense of calm.

"That *idiot*," he fumed. "That thundering, colossal, dung-brained *idiot*. Those cages he's using probably aren't even enchanted. It would serve him right if they all die of plague once he pulls them out of the sack. All of them, all his entire consortium of idiots. They must all be unfathomably stupid to have entrusted anything of importance to that lackwit."

"Enough," Isiem said. "It's done. We'll take precautions in the future, as they can't be trusted to take their own."

"Killing them now would be a good start," Ascaros said.

Isiem shrugged. He had no love for the Aspis agents, and they no longer seemed much of an asset to the expedition. It was possible that Kyril might disapprove of their deaths . . . but they were not good men, and she seemed to have few qualms about striking down the unjust. Nevertheless, he felt no urgency to deal with them now. "Do you know what afflicts these beasts? Do you really believe it's a plague?"

"I don't know," Ascaros admitted. "I'm not sure what to make of all these bones." He returned to looking at the charred cat, and Isiem joined him.

The little creature had burned fast and hot, although it was impossible to tell now whether that had been a result of its bones' age and dryness, a property of the mold that grew upon it, or something else altogether. Little remained but a few blackened fragments and a suggestion of caustic foulness that prickled at his nose.

"Did you hear something in the flames when it burned?" Isiem asked.

The shadowcaller gave him a blank look. "Such as?"

"Words. A voice, maybe. Anything peculiar."

"No." Ascaros turned on his heel, walking past the rows of glassy cages to leave the smoky chamber. His silhouette was distorted by the great dome in the center, which shrank his reflection, then stretched it, then squashed it down again. "Nothing."

And that, Isiem knew to a certainty, was a lie.

The cythnigots, Eledwyn had written, *are minor parasites among their kind. Nothing more than nuisances to the great powers of the Abyss, they lurk in stinking sulfur swamps and prey upon the weakest demons they can snare. They hurl themselves against every spellgate I open, flinging themselves mindlessly at me like sand crabs washed up onto the shore with every wave.*

Feeble as they are, they may prove useful. At least as a starting point.

Isiem closed the book gently. He closed his eyes, too, and rested a palm flat on the smooth, clear dome that occupied the chamber's center. The glass was cool under his skin. Tranquil. It conveyed nothing of the horrors that must surely have taken place under its shield.

"What did you find?" Ascaros asked.

"A beginning." Isiem held up the notebook. It looked the same as the ones in the apprentices' room: slim, unassuming, bound in plain grayish green. But no apprentice had recorded the thoughts captured on those pages.

The writing was in a small, precise feminine hand uninflected by emotion. Beautiful as the archaic script was, it did nothing to hide the ugliness of its writer's work, nor had she made any attempt to soften her deeds. Her recordings contained no suggestion that such hesitations had ever crossed her mind. The clinical coldness of the notes, which had detailed so many horrors in the previous pages, spoke of Nidalese training; Isiem recognized it even across the chasm of centuries.

It was Eledwyn's notebook. He was sure of it. And whoever she had been before coming under Mesandroth's thrall, there was nothing but ice in her soul by the time she'd written these lines.

"A beginning to what?" Ascaros lowered the sheaf of papers he'd begun to sort through.

Isiem gestured toward the cages of deformed, fungus-tufted bones. "This."

"If you know what they are, say so," Ascaros said impatiently. "Now is no time to be cryptic."

"These creatures were infected with Abyssal parasites," Isiem said. "Something called cythnigots. Apparently, in their native habitat, they insinuate themselves into the bodies of demons and, eventually, kill them. Eledwyn summoned them to begin an early stage in her experiments. She thought some of their abilities might be transferable to other purposes."

"What abilities, and what purposes?"

"That I don't know, and I'm not being cryptic. I haven't read that far."

"Then I suggest you get to it."

While Isiem reluctantly returned to Eledwyn's note-book, Ascaros eased open another drawer recessed in the wall between rows of bone-filled glass cages. Like the glow-globes in this chamber, and the silver-plated hall that led to it, the magic that had once locked these drawers had failed in places. Some of them slid out easily, while others remained secure.

The Aspis agents hadn't touched those compart-ments—having tried two and found them locked, they'd given up on the rest—but it had been a trivial matter for Isiem and Ascaros to determine which enchantments were failing. A cantrip told them where the magical auras were weakest, and there they focused their efforts.

In one of those drawers, they'd found Eledwyn's notebook and the sheaf of loose pages that Ascaros had examined. Isiem had taken a glance at those himself, and had seen that they were lists of imports into Fiendslair: furniture, food, plants and livestock, spell components. Eledwyn or one of her underlings had possessed a particular fondness for sweet spices; they'd spent a small fortune on cinnamon, cloves, and nutmeg.

No doubt there were clues to be found in there somewhere, but they'd take time to tease out—time that none of them wanted to spend in Fiendslair. While Ascaros fiddled with the remaining drawers, Isiem returned to his reading.

Eledwyn's world enveloped him in its precisely mea-sured horrors. He read her tally of sacrifices: caged beasts infected with cythnigots and observed until their deaths, summoners' gifts offered in supplication to greater Abyssal powers, four apprentices consigned to the void for stupidities or disloyalty.

He read, too, about the knowledge she purchased with the blood of others. Both those secrets and the blood that bought them could have overspilled a sea, and the final count went far beyond the pages of one slim book. But it was enough for Isiem to grasp, however dimly, the enormity of what she'd done. Somehow, Eledwyn had crystallized the power in blood into a new form—a magic that recalled the obsidian huts of the Splinter Men and the lightless curves of Nidalese nightglasses, but that had a purpose more alien than either.

And she had not used human blood to do it. She had used the deaths of demons.

"I think I have it," Ascaros said softly from the other side of the room. Awe and fear and uncertainty tangled all together in his voice. A sleek white drawer rested between his hands, its edges curled into fanciful representations of vines, or perhaps deformed bones.

"Have what?" Isiem asked.

"The nightblade," Ascaros said. "One of them." He held it up.

It was a sliver of obsidian, or so it seemed at first glance, like a more delicate version of the Splinter Men's knives. Its shape suggested a wide compass needle, similar to the ones on the bloodstones Ascaros had handed out earlier. The nightblade's handle was a curve of plain silver, slightly smallish in a way that suggested it might fit a woman's hand more readily than a man's, although it seemed to rest comfortably in Ascaros's grip.

As he studied it more closely, however, Isiem could see that the nightblade was anything but simple. Its glossy black blade had the same lightless infinity in its depths that he remembered from the nightglasses of Nidal, and there was a flicker of crimson along its edge that recalled the hellish glow of Sukorya's diamond and the gate into Fiendslair.

The sight of it brought the taste of bile to his tongue. "'One of them'?"

Ascaros nodded. He lowered the nightblade, wrapping it back in its shroud of black cloth. That, too, called unpleasant echoes back from Isiem's childhood. Nightglasses were kept the same way. "The only one in here. It was in a case with empty loops made to hold more. I imagine there are others. Bigger ones, judging by the difference in loop sizes. There were three gaps in the case, so that suggests at least two more blades exist."

"Where would they be, if not here?"

"I don't know. Perhaps they were destroyed when Fiendslair fell. But we have one. If they can manage to share, our allies' work here is done." It was hard to tell whether Ascaros was elated or disappointed by the prospect, but there was a current of *some* tense emotion running through his words.

"Maybe," Isiem said. He tried to stretch the weariness from his shoulders, with very limited success. The ache seemed to go deeper than his bones. "I don't hold much hope of that, myself. Let's go back. We should talk to them."

Chapter Sixteen
Haunted

They found the camp in a tumult.

Their horses were dead, all of them. The tale was easy enough to read from their carcasses: one by one the animals had stooped to drink from the streams that wandered through Eledwyn's enchanted gardens, and one by one they'd been seized by the bony white insects that lived in the water. Not one of their beasts had been spared, not even the pony that Ena had fought so heroically to save from the Splinter Men. It lay alongside the others, its shaggy mane cut short where it touched the water.

It was less clear how the insects had killed them, for nothing was left of the horses' submerged heads and necks but bare bone. Every morsel of hair and flesh had been stripped away; not a fleck of blood dimmed the diamond clarity of the streams. The scuttling bugs had even crawled into the horses' skulls to clean out any tiny clinging scraps of brain matter.

From the shoulder up, the bodies were undisturbed, each lying next to the others in a perfect line. They lay so close that their sides touched. But below the water line, all that remained was fresh white bone, so pristine it seemed to have been cleansed by magic.

The earth beside the streams was unmarred by any signs of struggle. Crisp, calm hoofprints traced each animal's path down to its final drink. The precision of the row made it clear that magic was involved.

"But whose, and why?" Isiem wondered aloud.

"Whose spell, you mean?" Kyril wiped her hands as she walked away from their little cluster of tents. The paladin's face was drawn and grim. Flecks of ichor clung to her dark red hair. "Originally I would have guessed the water bugs', but now I'm not so sure."

"Why?"

"Because something's wrong with Copple." She beckoned for him to follow her back to the tents. "He and Pulcher came running to us while we were still in the other room, yelping something about poisonous fungus smoke. I don't know what your friend said or did to them, but he had both of those poor men in hysterics. Teglias examined them, and didn't find any signs of curses or disease in Pulcher, but when he looked at Copple . . ."

They were almost to the tents. The Aspis Consortium's was the largest of the three, although Ganoven had ordered his underlings to set their bedrolls outside its door. Pulcher sat on his, whittling mechanically at a stick that he didn't seem to see. His spectacles had slid down to the bottom of his nose, but he never pushed them back up. The bedroll beside him was empty, and

Kyril stepped over it as she held the tent flap open for Isiem to enter.

Inside, Copple lay on a pair of saddle blankets that smelled strongly of horse. His shirt was soaked with sweat, but his face was peaceful and his chest rose and fell in the easy rhythms of untroubled sleep. His trousers had been pulled down to his knees, exposing an angry, purplish line where the Splinter Man's knife had cut him.

Teglias was kneeling near the sleeping man. As the Nidalese wizard stepped into the tent's canvas dimness, the Sarenite moved aside. "Ah, Isiem. I'm glad to see you."

"Kyril said something was wrong with Copple."

"Indeed. I've eased him into sleep so that we can discuss it without troubling him." Teglias gestured to the man's wound. "Tell me, what do you think?"

Isiem squinted at the slash. It was grossly discolored, but there was no visible crest of pus. He touched it tentatively. The flesh felt oddly fibrous to his touch, compressing stiffly under his finger, but there was none of the heat or swelling he would have expected from an infected wound. "Poisoned, maybe."

"Perhaps. This wound was healed twice. I saw Copple drink a potion when we arrived, and I healed it myself when he came to me today . . . but while that drove back whatever is troubling him, it clearly was not a cure. He's been deteriorating since." The cleric's blue eyes were grave. "Does your companion know whether the Splinter Men envenom their blades?"

"I'll ask."

Isiem made his way back out to the garden. It was nearing night, or the closest thing to it in this artificial place. The golden sun that shone overhead was turning toward the farthest reach of its track, and their campsite was falling swiftly into shadow.

Ena had built a campfire and was just returning to it with a kettle of water. From the angle of the dwarf's approach, Isiem could see that she'd gone far afield to get water from a stream where she wouldn't have to look at her dead pony. She'd been crying.

"I'm sorry," Isiem said. That seemed terribly inadequate, but he didn't know what else to say. He would never have imagined that Ena, prickly and practical as she was, might be reduced to tears by the loss of a pony.

The dwarf scowled and dashed a sleeve across her face. Her eyes were puffy and red, but dry. "It's nothing. Horses die. People, too. There's no use crying about it."

It didn't sound like she believed that, but it sounded like she wanted to. Isiem inclined his head and left her.

Ascaros was in the Nidalese tent. The shadowcaller sat crosslegged on his bedroll, a jumble of chains and collars lying in a ring of agates and tiny mirrors around him. A second, larger circle of aventurine and melted green candle stubs surrounded the first one. Two white candles sat on opposite ends of the shadowcaller, each just within arm's reach. One was lit, the other not, although its wick was blackened and the wax vanished slowly as if it were being consumed by an invisible fire.

As Isiem pushed open the tent flap, allowing a gust of sage-scented smoke out of the tent and fresher air in, Ascaros opened his eyes. "Did you tell them about the nightblade?"

The wizard shook his head. "Between Copple and the horses, the time didn't seem right. Have you had time to learn anything about it?"

"Some. I've only begun my divinations, but the initial results are . . . puzzling." Ascaros tapped the glassy black blade, which rested almost hidden in a fold of the blankets by his bedroll. "Its enchantments are incredibly complex. Summoning, binding, a touch of enthrallment. Some aspects of healing. None of its magic, however, speaks to death or destruction. I'm beginning to think that it's not the nightblade itself that's a weapon, but what it made. Or summoned."

"Perhaps the other pieces will give us some insight." Isiem pointed to the array of shackles that Ascaros had taken from the apprentices' room. "Anything on these?"

"Not much more than you might have guessed by looking at them." The shadowcaller shrugged. He lifted a jade-studded steel manacle on a thin finger and held it over the unlit candle, where the flame would have touched it if there had been one. Fleeting images danced along the inner curve of the metal: distorted glimpses of demonic forms, a faceless figure in gray-green robes with its arms upraised, a great glass dome with flashes of lightning trapped inside. Isiem couldn't make out the rest; the pieces of the vision were too fast, too small.

Ascaros lowered the manacle. The illusory cascade vanished. "They captured demons and experimented on them. They captured humans and experimented on them, too. Sometimes both at once. The shackles kept their victims docile while they did their grisly work. Some of it was very grisly indeed. They wanted to achieve immortality—and that meant testing mortality. In every way they could imagine."

Isiem was silent for a moment, weighing those words. From the look Ascaros gave him, he knew the shadowcaller was thinking the same thing: a Nidalese mind could imagine many, many ways to test how easily a creature died.

But they had not come to dwell on Eledwyn's long-ago sins. "Did you find anything that might help with Mesandroth's curse?"

"No. Although I've begun to understand why it was laid. Eledwyn spent a considerable amount of time trying to find ways to make possession work for her goals. It doesn't appear that it ever did."

"I don't believe it did, no. She wrote about it." Isiem flipped through the notebook. It took a moment for him to find the passage he wanted, but when he did, he held the slender gray-green book open carefully.

"Possession," he read aloud, marking the words with his thumb as he went, *"will not serve our ends.*

"The possessed die faster, not slower. Demons burn through borrowed flesh without care. Introducing undeath does not resolve the problem, and as subjects invariably go mad between the two transformations, this method is useless for preserving the mind and soul in flesh.

"Working the other way, we find no better results. A human soul can be forced into a demonic body, but soon takes on characteristics of the shape it holds. Demons are too strong in their identities: taking their bodies compromises the soul. Even over short periods, the pull is too strong for the mortal mind to resist.

"We must go older and deeper, to things that are not so set in themselves. We must follow the cythnigots' trail."

"What do you suppose that means?" Ascaros asked.

Isiem closed the notebook and tossed it onto his bedroll. It landed with a soft thump, seemingly too light to carry the weight of what was written within. "That their early experiments—the ones you showed me in that manacle's vision—didn't work. Possession wasn't a road to immortality, with or without the touch of undeath. So she looked elsewhere. Somewhere deeper in the Abyss."

The shadowcaller's face twisted into a grimace. "If Eledwyn gave up on undeath, then her further lines of research are unlikely to help me."

"There might be indirect aids," Isiem said. "She might have known of other apprentices who continued that line of work."

"Scant consolation, but I appreciate that you're trying to offer me any." Ascaros snuffed the lit candle and put both white tapers back into a small black box, along with the agates and minuscule mirrors. He left the aventurines, green candles, and twists of burned sage, Isiem noted. They looked like the same ones the apprentices had kept. "What are the rest of our companions doing?"

"Worrying about Copple and mourning our horses. I don't suppose you have any insights about either?"

"I'd mourn the horses before Copple, too." Ascaros shrugged. "No, I don't have any idea what befell either of them. I do wish the water bugs had eaten Ganoven's idiot before our animals, though. The horses were useful."

"A sentiment shared by many." Isiem paused. He flicked a fingertip toward the nearest knot of dried, sooty-ended sage. "Is there a reason you've put out the apprentices' herbs and stones?"

"For safety, of course." Ascaros's smirk was mirthless. "From what, I don't know. But they did."

"I see," Isiem said, although nothing was further from the truth. He withdrew from the tent, letting its flap fall shut behind him.

Ena had a pot of porridge boiling over the tiny fire, but it didn't seem that anyone was much interested in eating. Nor did it seem like the dwarf had much interest in cooking: Isiem could smell the scorched grains from his tent twenty feet away. Ena had never burned their porridge before, but she wasn't even pretending to watch the pot now. She stared past it, to the glimpse of the creek that was visible between the screening trees and the slumped outlines of their dead horses, their bodies fading into the artificial night like a line of dusk-blurred hills on the horizon.

He paused beside her, wanting to say something, but in the end he swallowed his words and went on to find Kyril.

The paladin was sitting by the water, twenty feet upstream from the dead horses, sharpening her weapons. A lantern hung from an angled pole that she'd driven into the stream bank. It swayed gently over her head, drawing ripples of fire from her dark red hair.

"Ascaros knows nothing about what's afflicting Copple, or how our horses died," he said.

Kyril nodded, keeping her gaze on the knife in her hands. She drew the sharpening stone across it in swift, sure strokes. "That's about what I expected, although it would have been nice to be wrong. Well, no matter. It's in Teglias's hands. Better rest while you can."

"While you stand guard alone all night?"

She glanced up at him with a bit of a smile. It made his throat clench. "I'm waiting to see if the water bugs come back. I've got my hook and my net. I'll spend the night fishing if need be."

"Do you expect you'll need help?"

The half-elf's smile deepened, but she shook her head. A suggestion of perfume drifted past, carrying a breath of unopened honeysuckle buds and crisp green leaves. Isiem couldn't tell if the fragrance was Kyril's or the garden's, but it was intoxicating. "It's not worth losing spells over," she said. "You need your sleep."

Accepting her dismissal with a bow, Isiem returned to his tent.

Ascaros was asleep in his bedroll, snoring softly through the wizened leather of his nose. His illusions usually lingered a while after he dozed off, but the spell had clearly reached its end. Isiem turned away from his companion and pulled his blankets close, but it was impossible to get comfortable. He had tried to fix the memory of that green and subtle fragrance in his mind, hoping its beauty might fend off the ugliness of all that had happened to them today, but other thoughts kept pushing it away.

The wizard had never been given to imagining vivid pictures as he read. Indeed, he'd always had difficulty doing it when he tried. That inability to visualize had been a blessing during his studies in the Dusk Hall, and he had thought it would be the same for the apprentice's notebook. But it was not so.

Unwanted images filled his head as he lay restless on his pillow. A brimorak in rune-carved chains, shrieking as boiling blood gushed from its gurgling throat. Four goat-horned spite demons with their limbs broken and interlocked in a flattened pinwheel pattern. A man slowly dissolving into the gooey shapelessness of an omox, flesh and bone melting into slime while his terrified eyes, untouched, fell loose from his skull and floated in the puddle. Isiem saw them all in flashes and fragments, one sliding into the next with the perfect unreality of dreams. Throughout the cascade of horrors, the gentle music of the stream flowed: a sanctuary from all the evil Isiem saw, and yet touched by evil itself.

He wasn't sure if he *was* dreaming, or if he was somehow envisioning those awful sights while still awake. They seemed more like things remembered than ones imagined, but he had no such memories of his own. Surely they hadn't been among the phantasms Ascaros had showed him in the manacle—had they? His thoughts were murky, muddled; only those alien images seemed clear.

And then a shout ruptured the artificial night, and the muzziness vanished like a pricked bubble.

Ascaros startled up from his bedroll. Without his illusory face, he was a ruin of a man in those blankets, his mouth a pucker of yellowed teeth. "What's happening?" he hissed, the words deformed by his lack of lips.

"I don't know." Isiem threw back the tent flap and looked outside just as Kyril rushed past their tent, long hair flying loose behind her. She'd taken her boots off while she waited by the water, and her feet made white flashes in the gloom. The paladin's sword blazed bright in her hands, scattering shadows in her wake.

Isiem grabbed his satchel of spell components. "Cover yourself," he said to Ascaros as he ducked out of the tent. "Your real face is showing."

Without waiting to hear the shadowcaller's response, he hurried toward the Aspis Consortium's tent. Kyril was already there, Ena and Teglias with her. Ganoven stood shivering in the grass, wrapped in a elaborately embroidered Osirian robe that stopped just above his skinny knees.

Lying on the ground between them all, pale and delirious under his woolen blanket, was Copple. The garish tattoos on his arms writhed with the unnatural twitching of his muscles. His eyes were wide, totally white, and unseeing. The cords of his throat bulged as if he were being strangled by invisible hands. Spittle flecked his lips, which moved in continuous, inaudible whispers.

"He just started screaming," Ganoven said, nearly as white-faced as his stricken underling. "Then he said something else—it was all garbled, I couldn't make it out. And then he started flopping around like a hooked fish. He's been whispering the whole time, but I can't make any sense of it."

"It's not Taldane," Kyril said. She seemed calmer than Ganoven, or at least more controlled. With a smooth motion, the paladin sheathed her sword, snuffing its divine flames. "It's not any human tongue. He's speaking the tongue of demons."

Ganoven flinched. "Copple? Copple doesn't know anything of the sort." He cast an alarmed look at the paladin. "What's he saying?"

She shrugged. "I don't speak it. I just recognize the sound of it."

"Let me." Isiem drew a pinch of soot and salt from his satchel, rubbed them together, then touched his dusted fingertips to his left ear and Copple's lips in turn. The man's flesh was cold and stiff as a corpse's. He kept gasping those strange, choked whispers even as Isiem's magic carried his mutterings to the wizard's ear.

The strangled words Isiem heard weren't in Pulcher's voice, though. They weren't in a male voice at all. It was a *woman's* voice he heard, sweet and almost childlike, whispering in the tongue of demons.

"We come for you, sinners. We come. Your spells cannot save you, your smoke cannot shield you, your prayers will give you no refuge. There is no escape. We come." Hearing his own voice translate the whispers in his mind was eerie, and for an instant Isiem had the uncanny sensation that the woman speaking through Copple spoke through him as well. A clammy, alien feeling lingered in his mind like an echo of each word he uttered.

Unnerved, he ended the spell, wiping the dust from his ear as hastily as if it were poison. He raked his fingers through his hair, scrubbing away the spell's imaginary residue.

"Was that all he said?" Teglias asked. His blue eyes were sharp with curiosity, and his gaze stayed fixed on the wizard.

"It's as much as I cared to hear." Isiem closed his eyes briefly, willing the unpleasant memory away. "It isn't his voice. There's someone else speaking through him. It sounds like a woman, but its mind is . . . other."

Even as the wizard said it, though, Copple's frantic whispers slowed to a trickle and then stopped. The man's chest rose suddenly, causing Ganoven to start in alarm again, then sank as he exhaled a deep, shuddering breath. His eyes rolled back down, although they remained unfocused under fluttering lids. Whatever fever seemed to have him in its grip relented, and the tension drained out of his muscles.

The others watched uncertainly. No one spoke; the only sound was Copple's labored breathing gradually returning to a normal rhythm.

Then Ascaros joined them, his footfalls rustling through the garden's long-dead leaves. The shadow-caller had donned his formal shadowcaller's robes and restored his masking illusion. Curly black hair, as thick as it had been in his youth, framed his handsome scholar's face. His body seemed hale and strong, untouched by any shadow of the grave.

He carried Sukorya's diamond enclosed in its silver case. As he reached Copple, the shadowcaller let the spiked chain rasp through his fingers, dangling the case two feet above the unconscious thug's face. It revolved slowly in the air, but nothing more than gravity and its own momentum seemed to be moving it, and eventually it stilled.

Ascaros cocked his head at the case, looking puzzled and slightly worried. "There's none of Mesandroth's magic in him."

"There isn't any, or there *wasn't* any?" Kyril asked. "Whatever was in him seems to have passed. Perhaps it's just gone now."

"I suppose." Ascaros withdrew the diamond in its case and tucked its chain underneath his robe. As always, Isiem was silently relieved when the thing was out of sight. "What was he saying earlier?"

"Threats and warnings," Isiem replied. "He said our spells and prayers wouldn't save us, and that our smoke could not shield us. He spoke with a woman's voice, but the language was that of demons, and the mind behind those words was not human."

"I doubt he was talking to us," Teglias said with a frown. "The reference to 'smoke' seems unlikely to be directed at anything we've done. More probably it has something to do with one of the original features of this place. Those smoke-producing plates in the halls, perhaps, or some other aspect of the work done in Fiendslair. Didn't you say you had found dried sage among the apprentices' belongings, or candles infused with it? That might have been the smoke the speaker meant. Something used for curative or purifying purposes. Something that couldn't protect them."

"It could have been a haunt," Kyril suggested. "Many people died badly here, and it's not unheard of for the traumatic memories of the dead to find voice in the living. That would explain why it was a woman's voice, as well, if it was her death that created the haunt."

The Nidalese exchanged a look. Ena caught it, and frowned at them both. "What?"

"There were many traumatic deaths here," Isiem said. "Some might easily have become haunts."

"But you don't think that's what happened." The dwarf squatted on her haunches, pulling up a few blades of grass and shredding them in as dramatic a display of frustration as Isiem had ever seen her make. When the last blade had been reduced to damp green fluff, she tossed it irritably at Copple. "Is he up yet? Can we ask him?"

As if on cue, Copple's eyes drifted unsteadily back into focus, then locked onto the dwarf's face. He bolted up to a sitting position, gasping in panic. "What happened?"

"Don't tell me you don't remember," Ena muttered. She dusted grass flecks from her thighs and stood, enormously resigned. "Fine. Let it be a mystery for the ages. Hopefully one that *stays* a mystery for the ages, because I'm going to be bitterly disappointed if it happens again tonight. Or tomorrow. Or the day after that. Note that I'm not counting any more days, because I don't intend to be here any longer. Two more days and I'm gone. I hate this place."

"I don't remember," Copple gasped feebly. His hands twitched in the grass as if he were trying to cling to its reality.

"I just told you not to tell me that," Ena said crossly. "I'm going back to bed. The rest of you can tell me if he says anything sensible." Stomping with each step, the dwarf departed.

Copple turned his head, watching her go. When she was beyond his limited sight, the pudgy man looked back at the rest of them, still bewildered as a child. "Please . . . I don't remember anything. What happened to me?"

"It doesn't matter," Kyril said. She patted his shoulder reassuringly, then froze for the slightest of instants before her look of gentle concern returned. The paladin stood, checking her sword and glancing around their encampment one last time. "Sleep if you can. We have another day of work ahead. And then, gods willing, we can all leave this place behind."

Copple nodded weakly and relaxed into the grass. Isiem turned to leave, Kyril close beside him; Teglias remained behind with Ganoven a little longer to keep watch over the recovering man. As they neared the Nidalese tent, the paladin grabbed at Isiem's sleeve.

"He isn't well," she whispered. Her eyes were alight with something he couldn't quite identify—fear, and anger, and whatever it was that drove paladins to throw themselves against the great evils of the world. At that moment, Isiem thought, Kyril looked like a hunting hound that had just caught the scent of a lion. She was straining to leap to the chase, even as she wasn't sure she wanted to catch the beast she'd detected.

The intensity of her alertness alarmed him far more than her words. But he answered dryly, trying to downplay it: "Yes, I'd rather gathered that."

"More than what he said, or what we saw. When I touched his shoulder, I felt it, and by the blessing of Iomedae, I *sensed* it. There is an evil in him that was not there before." Kyril let go of his sleeve, but she stayed close. Her perfume took hold of him again, and now it was clearly hers: linden and green honeysuckle, blending subtly into the sweetness of the garden. It was a strange contrast to the grimness of her words. "It didn't just poison his mind, Isiem. It's in his flesh. And it's still there."

Chapter Seventeen
Discoveries

No one slept well that night. Their haggard faces and fatigued movements the next morning told the tale: not one of them had rested after Copple's peculiar episode. His wound's discoloration had diminished by the time they broke camp, and he said his leg didn't pain him anymore, but no one seemed to take much reassurance from that, least of all Copple himself. It only served to underscore that some unknown power had indeed touched him.

Their collective mood grew even darker when Ena reported that their food supplies were spoiled. Somehow the twice-baked hardtack had gone sour and soggy overnight. Their sacks of oats were fuzzed with green mold, and their dried sausages were soft and slimy brown under furry white-specked coats. The similarity to the mold on the skeletons that the Aspis company had taken was too close to miss, and the three of them received a number of hard glares from the others. Nothing else had been contaminated, only their food—but all of it was ruined beyond repair.

"It's not natural," Pulcher muttered. He clutched his arm where the stick he'd used to haul water back to camp had slipped and bruised him, worsening the injury he'd sustained when his horse threw him while fleeing from the Splinter Men. Teglias had declined to heal the injury, saying it wasn't serious enough to warrant magical treatment, and that refusal, as much as the pain itself, had put the big man in a foul mood. "None of it's natural."

"Of *course* it's not natural," Ena snapped. "This was all fine when I put it away after dinner. Now it's rotted worse than a deviler's heart and I don't even want to keep the bags. Burn it. Burn it all. I can't abide mold."

Kyril shook her head. "We don't have time for a bonfire." She looked to Teglias and Ascaros, who had been experimenting with purification spells from the time Ena had first told them about the spoilage. "Can you remedy it?"

"I don't care if they can." The dwarf scrunched her wide nose. "I'm not eating it. After seeing it all slimy like that, how could you? Eeugh."

"It's resistant to our spells, anyway." Ascaros abandoned the sacks of verminous oatmeal and slimy sausages. "We *can* purify it, but it rots again within minutes when I do it, and half an hour when the Sarenite uses his magic. Given the unnatural speed with which the contamination returns, I would not advise eating this food even while it appears wholesome."

"I'm trying very hard to convince myself that I don't need to panic about being in a demented wizard's laboratory where the doors are made out of tortured demons and people get possessed while sleeping and all our food is cursed to spoil overnight," Ena said. "You aren't helping."

"We'll finish today and leave," Kyril said firmly. "Find whatever you want to find today; we're not staying any longer."

"You don't think that's overreacting?" Teglias said. "Nothing that's happened so far has actually been harmful. Unsettling, yes. Unpleasant. But not *harmful*. We've come a long way for this opportunity."

"It was harmful to our horses," Ena said, crossing her stocky arms. "And I, for one, am inclined to view that as a lesson. We thought the water bugs were harmless and they weren't. What else are we mistakenly assuming won't hurt us in here? What else are we overlooking until it lulls us into getting our heads chewed off?"

"I don't take chances when it comes to demons," Kyril said, nodding in agreement with the dwarf. "Overreaching is what gets people killed, or worse. Plainly *something* can reach us, and we can't easily counter that magic. If it were up to me, we'd leave now. It's only out of respect for all you've sacrificed to come here that I'm willing to stay even one extra day. But after that, we go."

Teglias inclined his head in reluctant acknowledgment. "Then we'd best make use of the time that remains. We haven't finished cataloging what lies behind the omox, and we haven't even touched the seraptis."

"We'll finish the omox first," Ascaros said crisply. "Whatever dangers might be there, we've already been exposed to them, and they haven't killed us yet. The same can't be said for whatever waits behind the seraptis door. So that's what we'll do—and we'll do it together. No more splitting up. Not after this."

Ganoven scowled at the shadowcaller, but no one voiced any disagreement. Even if they'd had food, Isiem thought, no one would have wanted to eat; certainly he wouldn't have been able to force much past the knot of turmoil in his stomach.

They gathered their gear and filed back to the chamber of demonflesh doors. Once there, Kyril took hold of the corroded harpoon embedded in the omox's squashed body and gave it a heave, starting the slow process of opening that door.

When the serrated blade had finished slicing away the omox's tortured flesh, the oozing door swung open to a reveal silver-plated hallway similar to the one Isiem had seen the previous day. Kyril led the way down, keeping a hand on the hilt of her sword. Copple followed, damp with nervous sweat, while Pulcher kept muttering curses and rubbing the bruise on his arm.

Glow-globes flickered uncertainly on their chains, casting staccato swells of light and shadow across the curving walls. Here, too, smoke issued in unsteady spurts from some of the ceiling plates as the adventurers crossed below. And once again, the veil of smoke cleared to reveal an enormous oval-shaped chamber dominated by a great glass dome in its center and walled in by smaller glassy tanks.

This room had sustained worse damage, though. A massive web of cracks splintered the glass of the central dome; a hole large enough for a human to step through gaped in its the middle. Fist-sized chunks of glass made a boulder field of the concentric rings on its floor. The glow-globes around the dome appeared to have exploded as well, leaving only inert, jagged stumps on blackened chains hanging from the ceiling. It appeared that Mesandroth and his underlings had been far more thorough in their destruction when they'd swept through this quarter of Fiendslair. Perhaps they'd released whatever was in the dome to do their work for them.

Several of the tanks along the walls were smashed as well, and more glass sparkled along their floors like scattered diamonds. The remainder were much larger than the tanks that had held the fungal skeletons of rats and cats in the previous room. These were sized for sheep, calves—even people. Their dry bones, clad in desiccated shells of skin and brittle hair, littered the gleaming compartments.

With its illuminating globes destroyed, the room was utterly dark. But Ganoven and Isiem had both conjured light spells to illumine the party's progress, and their radiance afforded a fleeting view into the bubbles as they passed. None of the human skeletons wore any clothes, and they appeared to have been quite elderly when they'd died, as they all had long, tangled gray hair. Unlike the remains in the other room, these had no furry coating of fungus.

Some, however, bore other marks. Many had scarred and knitted bones that spoke of recovery from surgical wounds. A few were missing neatly severed limbs. Others had been altered in ways Isiem couldn't fully comprehend. Their bones had been molded like soft clay, and pieces of other creatures had grown into them. There were no graft lines, as he might have expected to see on a golem; rather, the changes seemed to have come into them organically.

"The later experiments?" he murmured to Ascaros. The shadowcaller glanced at the human skeletons and nodded once.

At the end of the room, a small bronze door stood to the right, while a broad archway led straight ahead to a rectangular chamber that appeared to be a combination of library and dissection room.

"We haven't opened that," Kyril said, nodding toward the bronze door. "It's locked. Not with an ordinary lock, but with magic. We couldn't figure out how to get through yesterday."

Enormous claws had gouged deep rents in that door, but it didn't seem that they'd been able to break through. Eight raised panels adorned the door, each of them densely inscribed with arcane runes. The lettering was in an archaic form, but the traditions of Nidal had been so faithfully preserved through the ages that Isiem could still understand them with little difficulty. They spoke of all-consuming fire and shattered bone. He traced his fingertips across the sigils, wondering what secrets they held.

What had caused the damage to the door was less of a mystery. A jumble of razor-sharp horns and bones, held together by withered scraps of dry purplish skin, had been pushed into a pile against the wall nearby. Whoever had moved the bones—presumably his companions—had lifted the creature's skull up to crown the pile, and Isiem easily recognized the horned head as that of a kalavakus.

Dismantled as it was, Isiem couldn't tell what had killed the fiend. Apparently anticipating his question, Kyril shook her head. "Corrosion holes and spell burns on the skin, a couple of penetrating wounds that might have come from a blade or a horn. There's more of that greeny-white mold on the bones, too. But what killed it? I couldn't conclusively say."

"Nothing else in this room that might have done it?"

"Only whatever might be behind that door. Do you think you can open it?"

Isiem let his hand fall back to his side. He hadn't studied the lock carefully, but it didn't strike him as particularly complex at first glance. Quite simple, even. But that wasn't his first concern. "It seems a sturdy door, and its inscription suggests it's guarding something of importance. Are you sure you want it open?"

"No," Kyril replied, tipping her chin surreptitiously toward Teglias and Ganoven. "But I'm sure they will."

The others had continued to the rectangular room ahead. Isiem left the bronze door and approached the new room cautiously, his light spell floating over his shoulder.

The first sight that greeted him was a line of three ironbound dissection tables. Each bore countless stains on its reddish wood: blood, ichor, corrosive slime. All were studded with fist-sized eyebolts to serve as anchor points along the sides and corners. Coils of steel chain, thicker than Isiem's wrist, dangled from some of those bolts.

Shelves lined the walls around the tables, each burdened with innumerable bottles of alchemical reagents and specimens in jars. Most of those jars held organs or severed body parts floating in cloudy brine, but a few held entire creatures shrouded in swirling smoke, not liquid. Lesser demons, Isiem guessed; none appeared to be of this world.

While demons' signs of life were less obvious than mortals', the wizard nevertheless had the unshakable sense that the fiends trapped in those smoke-filled jars were sleeping, or in stasis, rather than truly dead. Isiem had seen enough death in his time to recognize the leaden, absolute slackness of a body whose soul had flown, and he didn't see that same surrendered stillness in these.

"This is where we stopped yesterday," Teglias said, gesturing to the shelves of bottled demons. "With them, and with those books." He pointed past the dissection tables to the two long desks at the very end of the room, framed by a pair of bookcases that were piled high with scrolls and dusty, black-bound tomes.

From twenty feet away, Isiem recognized the silvered mark on the backs of those books and froze, gripped by remembered fear. A step ahead, Ascaros stiffened as well.

Mesandroth's mark shone on the flat black covers, alongside the ancient sigil of the Umbral Court and the identifying runes of a dozen lesser arcanists, midnight clerics, and necromancers. Most were Nidalese, a few Ustalavic, the rest from countries that had fallen under the march of time and had their names forgotten.

"Ghasterhall," Ascaros murmured, approaching the bookshelves with a measured tread. A ghostly light winked into existence on a nearby candle, shedding its light over the pages. "The Whispering Way." He paused, one fingertip hovering over the spine of a scaled book spotted in feathery yellow mold. Slanted, sinuous letters ran over its bindings; the way they were formed suggested that they had not been scribed by any human hand, nor meant to be read by human eyes. "This one, I think, might even be from Ilvarandin, if such a thing can be imagined. Eledwyn cast a very wide net."

"For what?" Teglias asked. He made no move to approach the bookshelves; it seemed all those grim old pages unnerved the Sarenite more than the bottled demons did. Wisely so, Isiem thought. The texts on those shelves were an astonishing collection of writings by the great evils of the world, and those scholars or fools who had sought to preserve them.

"Death. Undeath. Summoning. Shaping. All the ways that flesh can be bent and unmade and reformed . . . and all the places that life comes from, in all the forms it can take, in this world and others." Ascaros drew out one of the chairs and seated himself at the left desk, drawing out one of the books that bore his ancestor's sign. It was locked, as were many of the others, but when the shadowcaller pressed his thumb to the silver bindings, the lock opened with a curiously loud click. Black dust limned his thumbprint for an instant, tracing its whorls and lines, and then vanished, leaving both the shadowcaller's thumb and the book's bindings clean.

"Is that what you came to find?" the cleric asked.

"It might be," Ascaros replied without looking up. "It very well might be."

"Just take them all," Ganoven urged. He beckoned an unenthusiastic Copple to hold his enchanted sack open. "Drop them in the bag and we'll move on. There's room. You can have an entire compartment to yourself. Two, if you like. Keep what you want when you've had time to sort through it. We'll sell the rest."

"That would not be wise." Ascaros glanced briefly at the tattooed thug, then dismissed him with a minute curl of his lip and returned to browsing the black-bound book. "Artifacts of power have their own wills and ways, and they are seldom kind to the imprudent. Many would argue that what is written in these books would corrode the soul, and what we've seen of Fiendslair suggests that is true. I will take what I need, and only that. Even that is a risk." He smiled into the pages, a mirthless and inwardly directed expression. "As for selling these texts . . . No. I doubt you'd like the buyers they'd attract."

"Nor would we," Kyril said, in a tone that brooked no further discussion. "We'll leave you to your reading, and we'll take none of those books for ourselves. *None* of them," she emphasized, touching her sword hilt meaningfully as she looked at Ganoven.

"Are you *threatening* me?" the Aspis agent asked, puffing up in disbelief.

"Not unless I have to. But I *am* trying to ensure that you respect the threat posed by these books. I don't recognize those sigils, nor their authors, but I know the name of Ghasterhall. That's nothing we need to take back with us. It's nothing the world needs at all." The paladin stepped away from the library, flicking a final look of distaste over its tumbled heaps of books and scrolls. "We came for a weapon. Let's find it, and go."

"Bronze door?" Ena suggested. "I'm just dying to know what's behind it that made someone, or something, try so hard to rip it down."

"Fire, if I read the runes right," Isiem said. "Raw, elemental flame."

"Oh." The dwarf sighed in vast disappointment, rubbing a hand over her stubbled pate. "That hardly seems worth the bother. Well, let's open it anyway. Maybe they meant the fire of . . . diamonds. Huge, enormous diamonds that flash with fiery brilliance. It could be metaphorical, right?"

"I'm afraid that's not likely," Isiem said. "Warding runes tend to be fairly literal."

Ena threw her hands into the air. "Fine. *Fine.* Shatter my dreams, crush my hopes of finding anything remotely worthwhile in this blasted place. You're worse than Teglias."

The cleric cleared his throat. "Tell me when you're ready to open it," he said to Isiem. "I'll prepare a protective spell."

"Thank you." Isiem inclined his head to the Sarenite and went over to examine the bronze door more closely. The inch-deep scratches clawed into its face interfered with his reading of the runes, but nonetheless he was soon able to confirm his suspicions. The metal was enchanted to withstand incredible heat, and to do so for prolonged periods: hours at a time, if not days. Isiem touched its scarred bronze tentatively, fanning his fingers over the door before daring to make any contact. He couldn't feel even the slightest warmth.

A secondary enchantment, nearly as powerful as the first, enabled the door to lock firmly into place and hold fast against eruptions of incalculable fury. Modern Nidalese magic used the same symbolic inscriptions as that centuries-old door, and it was clear that the door would be impossible for anything weaker than a god to force open once it locked.

And yet the lock itself was almost nothing.

"What is it?" Ena asked, squinting warily at Isiem's expression.

He moved aside, extending a hand to the circle of sigils that served as the door's arcane seal. "This lock. It's . . . I could have opened this after a year and a half at the Dusk Hall. When I was a child barely past my first cantrip, I could have unlocked this door. Easily. It's enchanted to be extraordinarily resistant to brute force or mundane lock-picking, but it opens easily to the proper magic."

"Good thing whatever clawed at it didn't have any." The dwarf paused, looking mildly alarmed as a new thought occurred to her. "Or do you think it did? Could this be a trap?"

"I have no way of knowing. Do you still want this door open?"

"We've come this far," Teglias said. "It would be foolish to stop short out of baseless speculation. We have no reason to believe anything unpleasant waits on the other side."

"Except fire," Ena muttered.

"Except fire," the Sarenite agreed, "and that I can counter, if you will allow me."

Isiem bowed his head and pressed his hands together as Teglias raised his holy symbol over the wizard to begin the spell. Warmth flowed over him, slow and rich as honey, and settled into his skin. There was no heat to it, nor cold, only a pleasant, soothing languor, accompanied by a sense of assurance that the world meant him no harm.

It was an illusion, of course, but Isiem allowed himself to take solace in it for a few short seconds until Teglias finished his incantation and lowered his golden emblem.

Then he exhaled, gathered his focus as he had been taught to do in the Dusk Hall, and turned to the claw-scarred bronze door. Keeping his own magic ready, the wizard unlocked the spells that bound that fiery door shut.

Almost before he had finished unraveling the last of its arcane bonds, the bronze door slid into the wall to its right, revealing a square compartment that measured five feet to a side.

It was an incineration chamber. The gray stone of its walls were rippled with scorch marks, while the ceiling was seared solid black. A dusting of grainy ash and charred bone fragments flecked its floor.

Most of the compartment, however, was occupied by a dead man dressed in the same gray-green robes that Isiem had seen in the apprentices' closets.

The man had been dead for a very long time. His skin was the color of old parchment, flattened against his skull and desiccated to the point that it was impossible to identify his features. Soot and ichor stained his back and the outside of his sleeves, suggesting he had hunched forward to protect himself from a blast at his back. The cloth over his lower torso was brown and stiff with dried blood. Ancient as the wound was, the sheer quantity of the blood loss suggested that had been what killed him.

The corpse's hands were knotted protectively in the pit of his stomach. Holding his breath, Isiem leaned into the ash-gritted compartment and forced the dead man's fingers open. Up close, he could see that the corpse's teeth were bared in a yellowed grimace, and that whatever had clawed into his torso had not only exposed his ribs, but crushed several of them. One, completely severed, had fallen to the floor underneath his body.

Something about the contorted position and the evident agony in which the man died suggested that the dead man's tortured grin wasn't just the expression of a mummified skull, but that the apprentice had actually died with his face clenched into that grimace of determination.

What could he have wanted to protect so badly? It seemed obvious that the apprentice, mortally wounded, had fled into this incineration chamber to hide from the kalavakus. Whether he had intended to immolate himself rather than allow the demon to kill him, or had merely hoped that the heavily enchanted door would prove a sufficient barrier to hold off the fiend, was something Isiem would never know. But one way or another, he'd meant to take refuge here—for himself, and for whatever he was holding.

Wincing in anticipation, Isiem broke the last of the corpse's stick-brittle fingers and let the hidden object tumble from its dead guardian's grip into his own. He closed his hand around it hurriedly and pulled back from the compartment, seized by a sudden claustrophobic dread. Only after his breathing had steadied, and he felt somewhat more like himself, did Isiem open his hand to see what lay in his palm.

It was a key.

Chapter Eighteen
The Seraptis Door

After Isiem retreated, clutching the key, Pulcher hauled the mummified apprentice out of the incineration chamber. Ganoven cataloged the dead man's belongings, but unless the Aspis agent had a hidden talent for sleight of hand, it did not seem he found much. The apprentice had died possessing nothing more than the clothes on his back, and those only barely; the stiff, shredded robes fell away from his bones as soon as Pulcher moved the body.

Those bones were profoundly discolored, and although Isiem couldn't tell whether their chalky yellowy-gray appearance was caused by the incineration chamber, the sheer passage of time, or anything else, the wizard couldn't shake a suspicion that something had poisoned the apprentice down to the core of his being.

But kalavakus demons were not known to have venom, and in any case, no poison had been necessary to kill the unfortunate man. Kyril winced when she saw the corpse's condition under those ruined robes. She lifted a smashed arm to show the rest of them. "It's a wonder he lived long enough to climb into that chamber. Look at this. Broken arm, slashed legs, crushed ribs. How could he possibly keep standing?"

"Desperation can give a man strength," Ena said. "For a while."

"That's a lot of desperation." Kyril glanced at Isiem as she gently returned the corpse's arm to some semblance of a resting position. A red curl fell over her brow, tumbling across her right eye. "What was he holding?"

Wordlessly, Isiem held his hand out to her. The key, an outwardly simple piece of cut steel, lay across his palm. It pulsed with magic against his skin, but it bore no ornaments, no inscription. Other than the blood dried on its handle, there was nothing about its appearance to suggest it had any significance at all.

"The seraptis door," Teglias murmured.

As he spoke, the incinerator's bronze door slid back out from the wall, closing off the compartment with a loud clang. Pulcher, who hadn't been looking at it, jumped visibly at the noise.

Isiem, who had, scarcely concealed his own flinch. He was tenser than he'd realized. "I thought you said you hadn't touched the seraptis."

The Sarenite shrugged. "Almost true. We did open it. But it only opens onto another door, and that one we couldn't pass. The key that let us in here did nothing. I had thought to try it again with Sukorya's diamond, but now I think this must be the proper key instead."

"Why?"

It was a moment before Teglias answered. For an instant, the cleric's eyes seemed to lose focus, as if he were racking the deep recesses of his memory for a near-forgotten detail. A pensive frown formed on his lips. "I . . . am not certain." He pinched the skin between his eyebrows and massaged it between his fingers, closing his eyes. "Perhaps it was something I saw in its design."

Isiem touched the man's wrist. "Is something troubling you?"

"No. No, I'm fine." With a shake of his head, Teglias opened his eyes and moved away, stepping carefully over the chunks of glass that littered the chamber's floor around the broken central dome. A thousand tiny, distorted reflections moved across the facets of the larger chunks, following him. "Just tired. I didn't sleep well last night."

"I don't think any of us did," Ena said. She, too, looked concerned, but her tone remained brisk. "Do you want to go in?"

Teglias nodded, clearing his throat. "Yes. We must go on. We still haven't found the nightblade."

"Let's get to it, then," Ganoven said, abandoning the apprentice's rag-clad bones. Annoyance twisted his habitual sneer deeper than usual. "There's little profit to be had here, since our sorcerer has decided we're not to be trusted with any of those books."

"You aren't," Kyril muttered, not quite under her breath. She shifted her scabbarded longsword to a more accessible angle and headed back across the room, stepping around the bigger pieces of glass and crunching the smaller shards under her boots. "If we're doing this, let's get it over with. Best to be ready. The kalavakus might be dead, but it wasn't the only demon in here, and I doubt it was the only one Mesandroth freed."

Summoning her own divine light around the end of an unlit torch, the paladin led the way back toward the demonflesh doors.

"Ascaros, are you coming?" Isiem called.

"I suppose I must," the shadowcaller replied with a pronounced lack of enthusiasm. He rolled up the yellowed scroll he'd been reading and returned it to its leather case with the care of a new mother handling her infant. As he slid the case into his satchel, Ascaros nodded pointedly toward the receding glow of Kyril's torch. "We agreed to stay together, after all."

"That we did," Isiem said. "Do you need help carrying anything?"

Ascaros shook his curly-locked head. "The Aspis Consortium isn't the only source of storage enchantments. My satchel can carry what I need."

"*Is* it what you need?"

"I think it might be. Part of it. This is some of Mesandroth's early work; it dates to when he was still refining his curse, and had not yet laid it on his own bloodline. Some of his original sources are here, too. If I can follow his reasoning and see what he did, I might be able to unravel the magic." The shadowcaller's fingers stilled over the silver buckles of his satchel, hovering reverently upon the cold metal. Then he shook off that momentary trance and resumed piling more books into the seemingly infinite depths of the bag.

Isiem watched him work, guarding his own misgivings. He did not doubt that the world would become a more perilous place with those books' secrets released from their imprisonment in Fiendslair. But the nations of Golarion had survived those threats once before, and would survive them again, and the secret libraries of the Umbral Court were a far safer place for them than an Aspis auction table would be. Short of destroying them—and Isiem wasn't sure he could do that, even if he'd wanted to—this seemed the best course.

By the time Ascaros had finished transferring Eledwyn's collection to his own keeping, Kyril's light was long gone. In its absence, the cracked and blood-stained hulk of the main room's central dome seemed full of menace; the glass cages around it, littered with bones of gray-haired victims, were repositories of ancient misery. He was Nidalese, and he should have had no fear of shadows, but Isiem found that he didn't want to walk past any of them in the dark.

"A locked door shouldn't be enough to stop a demon," he said.

"Why? Because some of them can teleport?" Ascaros asked wryly. "Not in here." He motioned to the walls that enclosed them. Only vague curves and lines were visible in the limited light of their spells. Above them loomed the silhouettes of bookshelves, shaggy with loose paper. "The creators of this place warded it against such magic. Perhaps it was meant as a pre-caution against escaping fiends; perhaps it's simply a natural side effect of this space existing outside the world. Regardless, one cannot fold space or travel across the planes here. Any attempt to do so results in violent failure. The only way out is the way we came in: through the brass room."

Isiem rubbed his ruby ring uneasily. He had seen no signs of such enchantments himself, but if Ascaros was correct, his stored teleportation spell was worse than useless. "So much for contingency plans. How do you know?"

"I tried it soon after we arrived, thinking I might want to have a ready escape if Fiendslair proved more dangerous than anticipated. I didn't test the spells on myself, obviously. I'm still alive. But there's a pulverized water bug in the garden who can attest to the dangers of attempting to teleport in this place. The magic bends in on itself, collapsing in places and stretching unpredictably in others. I killed the bug before I sent it, but the rebounding magic macerated the corpse completely. Nothing would survive that."

"When were you planning to tell me?"

Ascaros slung his satchel over a shoulder. Although he'd packed at least a third of Eledwyn's library into it, the black leather bag showed not the slightest bulge, and it didn't seem to weigh any more than its usual ten pounds. "When you expressed an interest in teleporting."

"And the others? When would you have warned them?"

"The same." The shadowcaller's black eyes were piercing and pitiless. "If they didn't mention it to me before they tried, and they hadn't the sense to test it themselves, they would have gotten what they deserved. Shall we go?"

Taking the lead, Isiem motioned for his glowing sphere of light to float forward. It circled around his shoulders, casting infinite reflections along the glass tanks in the main room, as they left the experimental chamber and returned to the demonflesh door. Fresh ichor still stained the door and the walls around it; the trapped fiend had only just begun to heal back into place. The wizard pulled it open and the two of them stepped through, rejoining the rest of their party in the brass room.

They had already cut open the seraptis door. The maimed fiend stared hatefully at them from her confinement. Her long black hair was a tangled net around her face and torso. Strands of it caught in the crimson slashes that crisscrossed her arms. Those red wounds gnashed futilely at the adventurers, opening and closing convulsively like so many ravenous mouths.

None of the companions, however, paid the trapped demon any mind. Their attention was focused on a second door that stood thirty feet down a straight, smooth corridor behind her. The new door was a perfect circle of steel brushed to a matte gray finish by innumerable tiny, crosshatched scratches. Other than a single pinprick of black in its center, it was entirely featureless. Contrary to Teglias's uncertain suggestion, nothing about the door's design suggested the apprentice's key should fit.

"Ah, you're just in time," the cleric said as the Nidalese came to the seraptis door. "May I have the key?"

Reluctantly Isiem handed it over. The Sarenite pressed the key to the tiny hole at the door's center, which dilated to accept it. A moment later, the steel spiraled back in, flowing like water to engulf the key completely. A soft, almost musical click sounded, and the door released the key as it rolled smoothly into the wall.

Beyond it was devastation.

Blood painted the walls of the bronzed hallway ahead. Moldering bones, pulverized so badly that they looked like gravel, had been heaped high against the newly opened door. As the steel slid aside, they tumbled through in a clattering avalanche. More lay shattered on the floor amid the wrinkled, stiffened rags of apprentices' robes.

The silver plates that lined the floors and ceilings of the previous corridors were repeated in this one as well, but here they had been ripped out of their housings and used as weapons to crush and dismember the unfortunate apprentices. Thin coils of fragrant white smoke leaked out of the gaps in the ceiling where the disks had been, casting a partial shroud over all those ancient dead.

Earlier, Isiem had wondered if Eledwyn's apprentices had escaped the fall of Fiendslair, since they'd only found the single body in the incineration chamber. Perhaps, he'd thought, they'd managed to evade or outrun the fiends that Mesandroth had freed to wreak havoc upon them.

Now he knew it was not so. They had died here, all of them. And they had died horribly, clawing at the uncaring steel door even as one of their own number locked them in, quarantining them along with whatever terror had brought them down. It hadn't been the kalavakus, or at least not the same one whose bones they'd found outside the incineration chamber. Death had come upon these people from behind, and had departed the same way.

And the apprentice who'd escaped had promptly locked himself in the incinerator.

"I think, perhaps, it might be wiser not to venture down this hall," Ascaros murmured from the back of the suddenly silenced gathering, as Teglias withdrew the key and passed it mutely back to Isiem.

"Seconded," Ena said.

But Teglias shook his head, and Ganoven was already beginning to wade through the bones with his underlings in tow.

"We will not go back unless we must," the Sarenite said, although he extended a hand to stop the Aspis agent's progress. "Kyril, do you sense any evils ahead? Anything that might pose an immediate threat?"

"No." Tension hardened the paladin's shoulders, and she kept her gaze riveted on the smoke-veiled distance, speaking in clipped tones. "But you already know I have great difficulty picking out individual evils here. This entire place is so permeated with malevolence that it fogs my prayers. If it's not a demon, I'm not likely to see it."

"Happily, it's demons we're concerned with," Teglias said. "Ena, do you see any tracks?"

"In the bones, you mean? Do I see any tracks of huge hideous monsters trampling through the rubble of these poor dead souls? Well, obviously *something* stomped them pretty thoroughly. But somehow I'm guessing that's not what you meant." The dwarf scowled as she moved to the fore, kicking a papery-skinned skull back toward them. Its withered nose and leathery scalp bumped across the shard-strewn floor, stuttering its course to the side. The skull came to rest against

Teglias's boot, staring at him with gaping sockets and a lipless grin. After a moment, the cleric pushed it aside gently with a toe.

"No," Ena growled as she crunched across the bone pile. She stopped at the edge of Isiem's light, partially engulfed by the sweet white smoke that fell placidly from the ceiling, and peered into the gloom ahead. "No, I don't see any tracks. But there are demons up this way." The dwarf paused, then added: "They're behind glass, like the people and animals in the other rooms. I don't think these ones are dead, though."

"But they're trapped?" the Sarenite pressed.

"Far as I can tell."

"Then they should pose no danger to us. Let us proceed." Matching deed to word, Teglias continued into the experimentation room. His robes whisked through the weak white smoke. Ganoven hurried after him, while the others followed with more foreboding.

Ena was right: the room at the end of this hall mirrored the others, with an enormous glass dome at its center and smaller tanks recessed in the walls, save that these walls were pierced by multiple dark archways. About half the tanks were cracked and empty; the others remained intact. But where the previous chambers had held the skeletons of cats and sheep and humans, these were filled with fiends. And they were not just bones.

Demons plucked from every layer of the Abyss sat in those glass bubbles, caught in stasis like so many monstrous flies in amber. Isiem didn't recognize all of them—the Abyss spawned an infinite variety of abominations—but he knew enough to be awed and horrified by the scope of Eledwyn's collection.

Goat-horned spite demons and blue-gray brimoraks were caged next to squat froglike demons with lopsided secondary faces grinning toothily from their midsections. A swarm of ostovites were imprisoned around the partly consumed body of a gaunt, black-bearded man; the little fiends, caught in the act of extracting and reshaping their victim's bones, flurried around the corpse like misshapen, pink-tinged snowflakes. Beside the ostovites was some hideous thing that resembled a gigantic, gas-bloated corpse, its greenish skin bulging with pockets of effluvia. Fanged tentacles coiled around its swollen body.

Many of the imprisoned fiends were not whole. Like the human and animal skeletons in the previous chambers, they showed the scars of grisly experimentation. While the denizens of the Abyss had always been unpredictably horrific in their forms, Isiem was sure that some of the bodies he saw were grafted together from multiple fiends. Some had human heads and limbs—deformed, discolored, or boiled smooth in acid and lye, but unmistakably pieces that had been human once. Their bodies were crisscrossed with lines of white scar tissue angled in ways that no mere needle and thread could manage.

"How many of these do you think it supped on?" Ascaros asked, walking down the line of enchanted cages. The distorted reflection of his face, ghostly over the bodies of trapped fiends, followed him down the row. "How many of these bled for the nightblade?"

"Of these?" Isiem canted his head to one side, studying the swarm of ostovites. "None, presumably. These appear to be alive. Those Eledwyn took for the nightblade did not survive."

Ena looked from one to the other in confusion. "What are you talking about?"

"Speculations. Only idle speculations." Ascaros stopped in front of a spider-faced fiend whose chitinous body was surrounded by a ring of fleshy, suckered tentacles. While a demon could easily have such a chaotic form on its own, the ridges of scarring at the base of each tentacle indicated that these had been added by other hands. "This place really is a marvel of cruelty. All of it."

The dwarf stared at him. "Don't dodge the question. Did you learn something about the nightblade from Eledwyn's books? You're talking like you know something we don't."

"We have a nightblade," Isiem admitted. "At least, we think we do."

The dwarf's eyes bugged out. She gave a sharp, humorous laugh. "I'm glad you saw fit to share that information with the rest of us." She held up a calloused hand as the wizard began to open his mouth. "No, don't make excuses, I don't want to hear them. Just tell us what you know about the thing. What is it? What does it do? Is it as deadly to demons as we'd thought?"

"Not directly," Ascaros said. "I'm not entirely sure what it is or how it works."

"Well, what *do* you know?"

The shadowcaller motioned to Isiem. "What did the book say?"

"That it 'slices through the flesh of space.' That it's 'a lodestone whose call and creation is blood,' and that its purpose was 'to summon to feast the spirits that have no souls.' There's more, but those are the lines I recall."

"That's lovely," Ena snarled. "Practically poetry. What does any of it mean?"

"We're not sure," Ascaros answered. "What we are *guessing* is that Eledwyn crafted her nightblades using some of the same magics that Nidalese arcanists have used for centuries to make nightglasses—magical mirrors used for testing students and summoning shadowbeasts—and that she imbued them with the blood of fiends. Her writings indicate that she collected the essences and effluvia of the fiends she tortured and killed in this place, concentrated them into this blade, and used it to draw out powers that demons feared. A combination of lodestone to find them and sacrifice to entice them, I believe. Ultimately, it's a tool of summoning."

The shadowcaller paused, glancing at the nearest glass cage. A clean-shaven woman's head leered back at him, dangling from the chest of a raw-fleshed demon like a grotesque pendant. "That much I'm fairly certain we have right. What's less clear is how, or if, the nightblades were connected to the rest of this work. She told Mesandroth that demons were too inhospitable for human souls, no matter how their bodies were altered in attempts to accommodate. But other creatures, she claimed, might serve better."

Ena followed the shadowcaller's look and grimaced at the grafted demon. Deliberately, she squared her stance away from it so that she wouldn't have to see so much as a reflection in the corner of her eye. "What other creatures? These . . . hybrids?"

Ascaros shook his head. "I don't think so. I think these are her failures. Eledwyn's notes say she was looking for something that preexisted demonkind—the embodiment of some ancient, ancestral memory of fear she found lurking in the most ancient fiends' thoughts—and she used sacrifices of demons' blood to lure them out. But what was she luring? On that, your guess is as good as mine."

"She went looking for the enemy of her enemy," Isiem added, "but we don't know what she found. Her writings came to an abrupt end soon after she used the nightblades to summoned it—whatever *it* was."

"Because Mesandroth destroyed her laboratory, or because of what she summoned?" Ena asked.

The Nidalese shared a look, and then Isiem cleared his throat uncomfortably. "It could be either. Or both."

"Monsters used to slay monsters," Kyril said. She surveyed the ranks of horrors around them with a slow shake of her head. "We can't use that."

"No," Teglias agreed. A shadow seemed to pass across his clear blue eyes. "That particular folly has led men into ruin too many times. If summoning more monsters from the Abyss's bowels is truly what the nightblade does, it's useless to us."

"Maybe to you, but not to me," Ganoven said. He turned a black glare on Ascaros. "I'll overlook that you apparently found a nightblade and didn't see fit to tell the rest of us until now. I'll *even* overlook that you make all these claims without offering to let us test the artifact ourselves. But I came here to retrieve a nightblade on behalf of the Aspis Consortium, and I mean to have one."

"Then get one," Ascaros said indifferently. "There are at least two others in here somewhere. But I'll not give you the one I've found. The Sarenite can have it, if he wants it. You can't."

Ganoven stiffened and puffed up in outrage. Isiem, wanting nothing more than to put the entire conversation behind him, moved on before the Aspis agent could explode.

The shadowed archways all seemed identical, so he made for the one directly across the room, circling around the dome.

That dome had been cracked by innumerable hard blows and smeared with dried blood and flecks of shredded skin. The legacy of destructive experiments, Isiem guessed. Most likely these had been more tests of whether demonic grafts could protect human flesh from various forms of magical assault . . . and judging from the residue, the answers had been decidedly negative.

Jeweled sconces surrounded the dome. On the wall behind them, wands of wood and bone and polished stone had been mounted in a display case. Bloody fingerprints smeared the glass cover, and the wands had been knocked loose into a jumbled heap along the case's bottom, but whoever had flailed so desperately at the wands hadn't been able to get a single one free.

The case wasn't locked. It had only an ornamental brass latch, and although its hinges were stiff with disuse and crusted gore, it creaked open on Isiem's first try. The wands tumbled out as soon as he lifted the cover enough to allow them. They filled his hands with glass and copper, fiery jacinths set in gold, pale blue quartz mazed with white lines of frost. Each one was a work of art. A quick cantrip let Isiem see their auras, revealing that, together, they represented enough destructive power to level a small town.

Not a single one of Eledwyn's wands held a mote of protective or curative power. They were all designed for pure destruction. Some of the wands held raw elemental magics; others contained layered spells meant to be released simultaneously or in quick succession, which Isiem could not identify as easily. What little he could discern, though, both raised his estimation of Eledwyn's inventiveness and made him glad that the woman was long dead.

"Ah, finally! Something that might salvage this sorry expedition," Ganoven said behind him.

Isiem started, thinking that the Aspis agent meant the wands, but a glance over his shoulder dispelled that notion. The half-elf was looking past him to the rows of demons' cages—or, more precisely, to the gemstone that gleamed in the center of each one.

Unlike the glass tanks in the other rooms, each of the demons' bubbles was adorned with a single precious stone. The smallest gem was the size of a quail's egg; the largest was bigger than Pulcher's fist. They ranged from perfectly colorless diamonds to chrysoberyls and tourmalines in impossibly vivid shades of yellow and azure. Individually priceless, the collective value of the stones would have stolen the Ruby Prince's breath.

And yet . . .

"You can't take those," Ascaros said coldly.

Ganoven spun on his heel. "Why not? I've about had it with your—"

"You fancy yourself a wizard, don't you?" The shadowcaller gestured contemptuously to the cage nearest the Aspis agent. It held a single brimorak, trapped in stasis with wisps of smoke rising from its nostrils. The gem set in its bubble was a radiant blue-green apatite affixed squarely between the demon's red eyes. "Look at that cage. Tell me: what purpose does that jewel serve?"

"I don't know," Ganoven snapped. "I don't care. You say the nightblade is worthless because it's too dangerous to use. Fine. These gems will repay the Consortium for the money we've wasted on this goblin hunt. If they're as valuable as they look, we might even turn a profit."

"Or you might get your idiot self killed. I'd shed no tears over that, admittedly, but it doesn't mean I intend to let you take me with you. Why do you suppose fiends need jewels in their cages when sheep and rats did not? No, wait, perhaps that one's too hard. Let me ask an easier question: why do you suppose these fiends are in *stasis*, when all the other cages we found had only moldering bones inside?"

"Because the jewels are holding them," Ena said, fingering her crossbow as she eyed the chartreuse flashes of a nearby chrysoberyl.

"Precisely!" Ascaros gave the dwarf a sardonic clap. "The demons are in stasis, and the *reason* they're in stasis is because the jewels are anchoring that spell. Remove them—if you even can—and you'll break the enchantment that holds them in place. And then, I imagine, we will all be briefly but intensely sad."

Ganoven hesitated, then shook his head stubbornly and smoothed a ruffled hair back into his goatee. "It's a brimorak. Come, have *some* courage. We came here prepared to fight demons. This is a minor one, and it's trapped. We have every conceivable advantage, and you want to cringe away from *this*?"

"That's a fair point, as far as it goes," Ena conceded. She unhitched her crossbow and fitted it with a bolt.

"Indeed." The Aspis agent nodded toward Pulcher.

With a mighty heave, the big man brought his hammer crashing down on the curved glass tank. It shattered immediately, sending splinters of glass flying. Ganoven scrambled after the chunk with the embedded apatite, while the others tensed, weapons and spells readied to assail the brimorak.

But instead of lunging at them or trying to escape, the demon collapsed. Its striped, bluish hide paled to a chalky, poisoned gray; its crimson eyes went dead black and shriveled into its skull. The sulfurous yellow fangs dropped out of the demon's mouth, replaced by a netting of mold and mildew that itself withered and died in seconds.

Almost before the last chunks of glass had stopped rolling across the floor, the brimorak had collapsed into a pile of dust, fur scraps, and fungus-spotted bone.

"That . . . is not what I expected," Kyril said, lowering her sword. Beside her, Ena almost dropped her crossbow in surprise.

"The gem's unscratched," Ganoven announced with considerable relief, holding the chunk of glass up triumphantly. Apatite was a fragile stone, and that impact had been hard enough to chip a diamond. "And it seems that demon wasn't so dangerous after all. Let's do the rest, eh?"

"Demons don't age." Kyril stood staring at the pile of fungus-spotted bones. She spoke as if she were trying to persuade herself of the statement's truth. "So what killed the brimorak?"

"Looked like some kind of disease," Ena offered. The dwarf started toward the brimorak's shattered cage, then hesitated, stopping ten feet away. "A disease that could kill something that wasn't even really alive."

"Something linked to the nightblade?" Isiem asked, turning to Ascaros.

The shadowcaller paused, then nodded reluctantly. "It's possible. The mold does look similar to the cythnigots we saw in the first room. A modified version, perhaps. Or an unrelated experiment in defeating demons by disease."

"Then the bones are valuable too," Ganoven said. He snapped his fingers. "No dreadful blood-lured monsters involved, just fungus. Copple—take those bones and put them in your bag. If there's a plague that can do that to a demon, imagine what the Worldwound crusaders would pay for it. Something like that could drive the demon hordes back to the Abyss without costing a single human life. Why, those bones might be worth more than all the gems in this room put together."

"I don't want to get a plague," Copple protested, hanging back at the edge of the room.

"It doesn't affect *people*," Ganoven said impatiently. He glanced at Ascaros. "Does it?"

The Nidalese sorcerer shrugged. "I've only begun to dimly apprehend the outlines of what Eledwyn tried to do here. But a significant part of her work *was* centered on hybridizing humans with demons. I'd hate to make any promises about what the fungus would or would not affect."

"I'm not touching it," Copple declared.

"Fine. We'll just take the gems. I already have those cats, anyway. I'm sure they'll serve." Ganoven pointed to the next glass cage, which held the flurry of frozen ostovites. "That one next."

Licking his lips, Pulcher moved to the ostovites' tank and shifted his sweaty palms on the handle of his hammer. With a last glance back at the rest of them, the big man hoisted the weapon and smashed it into the glass.

It, too, shattered, and as the chrysoberyl in its center tumbled free, the tank's ostovites blanched to a dead white. Isiem could *see* the life drain out of them, and it went with breathtaking speed. In the span of two heartbeats, they lost all color, went stiff and brittle, and were covered by a fine fuzz of mold. Then the mold withered, puffed out gray spores, and died, and the ostovites' pock-riddled bones broke apart into gritty fragments around the dried corpse of the man they'd been eating.

Pulcher's jaw dropped. "This is *easy*," he said, and swung his hammer into the next tank without waiting for anyone else to react.

Again the cage cracked apart under his first blow, and again the binding gemstone—this time a ruby, bright as fresh-drawn blood—went spinning away in a glittering penumbra of broken glass.

But this time, the creature that emerged from the broken tank did not wither or die.

It attacked.

Chapter Nineteen
One of the Lost

The fiend spilled out of its broken cage in a spreading halo of slime. An overwhelming aura of evil, as palpable as a cloud of poisonous fog, engulfed the room as the creature unfurled its writhing tentacles, opened the fang-filled maw that slitted through its swollen belly, and slid toward the explorers with astonishing speed.

That tide of crushing malevolence hardly seemed to touch Ganoven or his underlings, but it washed over the rest of them like a physical malaise. It wrenched at Isiem's stomach, besieging him with an overwhelming sense of spiritual nausea. Jeweled wands spilled from his nerveless fingers, clattering across the floor.

From the corner of his eye, he could see Ascaros hitting his own head with the heel of a hand to drive it out, Kyril clutching her midsection and gagging, and Teglias grinding his teeth desperately against the sensation. And even as they strove to overcome the disorienting wrongness of the creature's presence, it closed the scant distance to the group.

The fiend was a thing of horror. Its bloated flesh was a kaleidoscope of unholy pregnancy and disease. Each bulge that rippled across the fatty dunes of its mid-section contained a new half-formed infection: some malformed spawn or living disease that wriggled in a yolk of orange pus.

As he gazed upon the fiend, reeling from the skull-crushing grip of its aura, Isiem was filled with the dizzy certainty that what he saw swimming in its flesh would soon be slithering through his.

Hadn't the thing looked different in its cage? More . . . human, somehow? He couldn't seem to grasp any solid memory, but the general *sense* of it had been human, surely. A face, an arm, an ear. He had seen those things. Hadn't he?

And hadn't this entire stronghold been dedicated to warping mortal flesh? What writhed before him, Isiem was suddenly sure, was not some alien creature summoned from the poisoned seas of the Abyss, but the remains of a once-ordinary person. He knew it—and he knew that he was doomed to join it. Its spawn would wriggle through his flesh like worms, consuming him while he lived and transforming him into a mindless host like the thing now pulling toward him.

Paralyzed by the thought, Isiem could do nothing but stand frozen as the fiend snaked a tentacle around his knee and dragged him toward it, or itself toward him. The grotesque maw in its middle opened into a saliva-stringed smile, and he couldn't even flinch at being devoured.

Then fire roared past him, slapping his face with its heat and singeing the ends of his loose white hair, and Isiem snapped out of his daze.

Ascaros's fireball struck the fiend with incandescent fury, burning through the purulent coat of ichor that protected the thing. Smoke and slimy vapor filled the air, shrouding the creature's monstrous form and breaking the hypnotic horror that had paralyzed Isiem.

The wizard scrambled away, yanking off the tentacle that gripped his leg. Blood soaked his robe where the tooth-lined tentacle had torn at his skin, but he hardly felt the pain through his adrenaline. The creature's skin was unpleasantly fibrous and knobby with tumors under its coating of viscous slime; Isiem wiped his hands frantically against the floor as soon as he'd gotten loose, preferring to scrape off his own skin rather than leave it coated with that foulness.

Through the smoke he could see Kyril charging at the fiend, sword ablaze, and Ena racing to reload her crossbow. Behind them, Teglias huddled on the ground, clutching his head against some unseen assault. Ascaros's staff, raised high in one hand, was limned with the incandescent beginnings of the shadowcaller's next spell.

But Ganoven was nowhere to be seen. A blur in the smoke on the far side of the room might or might not have been Copple—it was impossible to be sure through the faltering light and the distorting reflections of the room's myriad glass cages—and Pulcher was backed up to block one of the archways, his hammer held level before him as if he were covering someone else's retreat.

They're abandoning us.

The realization came with a sting of anger almost strong enough to block out the fear. Of *course* the Aspis Consortium agents were abandoning their erstwhile allies. They had their jewels, their scavenged skeletons; they had enough of a profit that they didn't *need* companions anymore. So they'd flee back to safety, shed false tears over their allies' sad sacrifice, and keep the extra shares of the treasure.

If they lived. Isiem was abruptly disinclined to let them. Already on his hands and knees, he rolled into a sitting position, grabbing desperately at the wand that had fallen closest to his fingers. It was made of cloudy white glass banded in bright gold, and although Isiem wasn't sure exactly what it did, he recognized Sarenrae's sun emblazoned on those gilded bands and hoped the Dawnflower's holy flame would prove lethal to this fiend.

His hopes were answered. The power of the gods answered his clumsy call, seizing his fumbling attempts at grasping the wand's magic and forcing them into deadly focus. White light gathered in the wand's core, intensifying each time it passed a golden band until it stung tears from Isiem's eyes. Squinting against the wand's brilliance, he pointed it blindly in the direction of the fiend.

Sunfire erupted from the wand, punching through the tentacled beast in a searing line. It let out an ululating cry, hammering its knotted tentacles against the ground in fury and pain. The light seemed to hurt it worse than the burning did; the thing's single eye squeezed shut and, weeping viscous tears, pulled back into the soft folds of its body.

Then Ascaros released another spell, hammering the fiend with a second fiery blast. As soon as the magic left the shadowcaller's fingers, Isiem scrambled toward his friend, grabbing at the remaining dropped wands as he fled. He pushed one of the wands into Ascaros's hands, not bothering to check which it was. "They've left us. The Aspis agents. They've gone with the treasure and left us to die."

A scowl twisted Ascaros's face. He took the wand and shoved it into his robe, turning to squint at the smoke-shrouded doorway. From the look on his face, Isiem knew exactly what his old friend was thinking: he was gauging whether he could engulf their fleeing comrades in another burst of flame before they escaped. "Not if we kill them first."

"But the demon—"

"To hell with the demon. I'll let it drag my soul down to the Abyss if it means I get to spit on Ganoven's bones before I go."

In front of the doorway, Pulcher had fallen. His head was snapped back at an impossible angle, and his arm had been ripped off at the shoulder. The sluggishness of the blood spilling from that ghastly wound made it clear that the man was already dead.

Between the dead Aspis agent and where the two Nidalese stood, Kyril had closed on the fiend and was hacking at it with her blue-haloed sword. Isiem couldn't see Teglias or Ena in the confusion, but he guessed the paladin was defending them both. Her blessed blade cleaved through demonflesh with shocking ease, hewing off great steaming chunks of gristle. The wounded fiend let out a shrill, ear-rending shriek of surprise and pain—

—and darkness descended upon them all.

Absolute confusion fell upon them with the blackness. It was impossible to see anything. The floor was slick with slime and blood. Smoke and screams choked the acrid air, bouncing erratically off the glass tanks and enormous dome in the chamber's center. And through it all, the fiend's aura of sickening malevolence continued unabated.

Isiem still had a grip on Ascaros's sleeve, the only point of certainty he could find in the chaos. They had no chance of finding the original entryway in this mess, not while blind. It was on the far side of the chamber, separated by too much distance and danger. To reach it, they'd have to rush past the enraged fiend in the dark. Hoping that the nearer door was where he remembered, and that Kyril's goddess would see to her servant's safety, he dragged his friend along with him as he hobbled toward the unseen exit.

Before he'd taken more than a few steps, he heard screams and the gnashing of inhuman teeth. The cries were so high-pitched, so shrill with terror and pain, that Isiem couldn't begin to identify them. He hesitated, on the cusp of turning back, but Ascaros yanked him forward. A flare of agony went up Isiem's wounded leg; he stumbled, gasping in the blackness.

"Keep going," the shadowcaller rasped. Now it was Ascaros pulling him onward, forcing his unsteady feet over rolling chunks of glass. "Keep going until we're out of the dark."

"Then what?" Isiem whispered. His leg hurt unimaginably. Worse, he could feel something moving in there, stretching his skin and compressing his muscles as it wriggled hot through his flesh. He put a hand to his thigh and immediately regretted it: whatever was in his wound pressed up against his hand, pulsing violently as if to taunt him with its presence.

It was *alive*. He swore, glad that the darkness prevented Ascaros from seeing the tears that stung his eyes. Nidalese did not cry. Above all they did not cry for pain, or fear, or even for having fiendspawn incubating in their bodies . . .

"Then we'll make a plan," Ascaros answered. "For vengeance, and survival."

They were nearly out of the darkness, Isiem guessed. Hoped. The sickening sensation of the fiend's presence was relenting, and the glass underfoot seemed to be tripping him less often.

Behind them the screams had stopped, although the noise of the fight went on. In the relative quiet, Isiem said: "I think it infected me with something. I can feel it moving around inside."

Ascaros didn't hesitate. "We'll deal with that, too."

At last they emerged into a lesser gloom. Isiem's little light appeared again, illumining their surroundings in its subdued yellow glow. Empty glass cages surrounded a small open archway ahead. Although the thrashing of tentacles and the thrum of Ena's crossbow continued behind them, and the stench of burned demonflesh still stung Isiem's nose, this little corner of the room seemed almost peaceful. The dust of centuries lay undisturbed on its glass tanks.

"Give me your leg," Ascaros said. Taking his spiked chain in one hand, the shadowcaller laid the other on Isiem's thigh. The demon's venom pulsed up in response, sending a fresh stab of agony through the wizard, but this time Isiem gritted his teeth and tried to keep the pain off his face. The cloaking darkness was behind them; he had to be Nidalese once again.

At the end of Ascaros's prayer, a wave of magical cold shivered through Isiem's body. Zon-Kuthon's healing had never been gentle—its chill was akin to a splash of icy water used to revive a flagging victim on the torture table—and yet it had never hurt quite *this* much in all the hundreds of times he'd been subjected to the Midnight Lord's touch.

The venom in his body raged against the healing. It burned and fought so viciously that its thrashings were visible through flesh and skin and cloth—and then it ripped through Isiem's thigh, bursting outward in a stinking fountain of poisoned pus and blood. The wizard collapsed on the dusty floor, clutching his mangled leg. He bit his lip desperately against the screams that fought their way up his throat. Ascaros's voice, steady and measured in the cadences of renewed prayer, registered only as a faraway echo in his mind.

But the surge of healing that accompanied the prayer was very real. It dispelled the fog of suffering from Isiem's thoughts and brought him back to himself. Shakily, he stood, averting his eyes from the mess that the demon's poison had made of his flesh on the floor. His leg was steadier. Not whole—not exactly—but close enough.

"Can you walk?" Ascaros asked urgently. Somewhere in the darkness, a concussive boom was answered by a hail of shattering glass and a new inhuman roar. One of the other tanks' occupants, it seemed, had been awakened from its long sleep.

"Yes," Isiem said. The tatters of his robe were wet and unpleasantly sticky against his skin, but that discomfort was of no consequence. "We should go back. They need help. It sounds like something else has been freed."

"Good." Ascaros spat, wrapping his spiked chain around his hand to tighten it into a neat loop. He tucked it into a pocket and put on the flayleaf bracelet that he'd worn in Barrowmoor, a seeming lifetime ago. "Maybe it'll take care of Ganoven for me."

"He's not the only one in danger," Isiem said. "Kyril's out there. Ena. Teglias. They're all fighting in that darkness. We have to help."

"No, we don't. They might all be dead already." Ascaros scowled. "Let's get out of here. Then we can check on them safely."

"How?"

"I'll tell you when we're safe," the shadowcaller snapped, striding away from the continuing noises of battle. "*Come.*"

Isiem hesitated. His companions *were* still in danger, whatever Ascaros said, and he didn't want to abandon them.

Yet he could not see how charging blindly into battle would result in any better outcome than it had the first time. The fiend had every advantage in its conjured darkness; Isiem wouldn't be able to see it to target with his more precise spells, and he dared not sweep the entire area with destruction, not while his friends were somewhere in there fighting.

Suicide is not bravery. It was an old adage in the hinterlands of Nidal, where farmers and fisherfolk quickly learned not to contest the edicts of their shadowed overlords. But as Isiem followed Ascaros, retreating from their comrades' fight, he found himself thinking: *cowardice is not wisdom, either.*

It was too galling for him to bear. As soon as they were through the doorway, he seized Ascaros's shoulder and demanded: "How are we going to help them?"

The shadowcaller pushed his hand away impatiently. The illusion that guised him in false health did not affect touch; Ascaros's shoulder felt bony as a skeleton's under the tenebrous cloth of his robe. But his strength, somehow, was far greater than Isiem's. "The compass."

Isiem touched his pocket. The magical compass was there, heavy and unyielding against his thigh. Its needle pricked dully against his palm. "What of it?"

"The one you hold is master to the others. The Umbral Court created it, and it carries all the hallmarks of their paranoia and lust for control." Ascaros snorted. His hands, curled with remembered hatred, were ivory claws around his staff. "The compasses do more than allow each to locate the others. With the master, you can spy into their carriers' thoughts. You'll know where they are, what they see, what they think." He drew a breath. "If they're alive, and in need of help, we'll go to them. If they're dead, you may thank me for preventing you from having thrown your own life after theirs."

Unless our cowardice is the reason they're dead.

It would do no good to say that, though. Taking a moment to collect his thoughts and gird himself for the prospect of drawing upon the Umbral Court's magic, Isiem turned away from the shadowcaller and looked around the hall they'd stumbled into.

Unlike the stark sterility of the previous chambers, this one was puddled with condensation and choked by strange vegetation. The air was humid, uncomfortably warm, and smelled of vegetal decomposition; the purifying magic that sustained the rest of Fiendslair seemed to be weaker in this portion of the complex. Demons' bones, rotted and yellowed by the passage of time, rose from the surrounding plant life like fossilized nightmares. Few bore marks of violence, but many were spiderwebbed by threads of pale green fungus.

Ahead, the walls were riddled with the mouths of more tunnels opening onto the corridor where Isiem and Ascaros stood. In contrast to the symmetrical organization of the previous halls and chambers, these sprang out unpredictably, connecting at uncomfortable angles and uneven heights. They looked more like diseased growths than the result of any systematic plan, and they hardly seemed to be creations of the same mind. If there had ever been any sense of order beneath the chaos, it had long since been overgrown.

"What happened here?" Isiem murmured, even as he withdrew the compass.

Ascaros looked around as well, grimacing. He drew his arms across his chest, gathering his robes away from their surroundings. "The touch of the Abyss, I'd wager. A gate that was opened too often and too long, a rift between planes, or perhaps something subtler. Some corruptive influence on the mind of this place's creator. I don't know. But *something* of the Abyss has tainted this place, and its presence is much stronger here."

"Much," Isiem agreed, stepping forward to get a quick look down the hall. He didn't want to be taken unawares while entranced by the compass's magic.

Where Fiendslair's light globes still functioned, the rampant vegetation was thick and lush. Emerald-green moss covered every available inch, even garlanding the flowering vines that crowded around the lights. In other corridors, the lights had been dead so long that generations upon generations of wan mushrooms and luminescent fungi had grown up over the remains of whatever plants had originally colonized those halls.

Much of the plant life, whether it grew in light or darkness, had an unhealthy appearance. The flowers on those vines were the mottled pink and purple of badly beaten flesh, and their petals were fringed with tiny green teeth. They swayed on their vines, snapping at any movement in the air. Some of their flower buds had an eerie resemblance to eyeless, wormlike heads. Around them, the other plants seemed to be wilted, or misshapen, or rotting on the stem—and yet they were all incredibly fertile, even denser than the thickets of the Backar Forest, for all that they seemed to be strangling one another with their roots.

It was hideous, and hideously disturbing. But nothing he saw seemed to pose an immediate threat. Wiping sweat from his palms, Isiem withdrew from the riot of diseased vegetation and hefted the needled compass in his hand. "How do I use it?"

"The same way that you used the others."

"Why aren't *you* doing it?"

Ascaros sighed theatrically at his suspicion, although Isiem had the distinct impression that the shadowcaller was amused at being asked. "Because you're the one who cares, and you wouldn't believe me if I told you they were well. Or dead. Better you should see for yourself. Don't you agree?"

"Yes," Isiem answered grimly. He pricked a drop of blood with the compass's serrated silver needle. "Kyril," he said, focusing a thread of magic into the device's speckled green stone, as he had in the Backar Forest.

The blood sizzled into colorless smoke. It rose around him in widening curls, filling the humid air until it obscured his sight entirely. Within seconds, the dense mist shifted and became transparent. What he saw—and what he *felt*—through that enchanted haze was not his own reality, but for a moment eclipsed it.

Kyril couldn't breathe. She'd killed the demon, but it was killing her, too, with poison that gnawed at her gut and dug into her ribs like a hungry parasite. Ena was a lead weight on her back, insensible and maybe dead. She couldn't let go of the dwarf, though. She didn't have any other companions left in this hellish place.

Teglias was gone, and she worried that he might not have fled of his own volition. He'd looked right at them as he ran from that fight, and there had been no recognition in the cleric's blue eyes. She feared the worst: that his will might have been dominated by some fiend's. Because that would mean not only that they'd lost their friend and ally, but that there was another demon in this place they had not slain.

Praying to Iomedae to grant her strength, Kyril kept running down the glass-strewn corridor. With one hand, she kept a tight grasp on Ena's wrists around her neck, holding the unconscious dwarf onto her back like the world's least practical cloak. In the other, she held her gore-smeared longsword, even though she knew she didn't have another fight left in her.

She had to try, though. That was a paladin's duty: to always try.

The demonflesh door was before her. The seraptis's white flesh was fused to the walls and showed no signs of recent maiming, so either none of her companions had fled this way, or they were far ahead of her. Whichever it was, she and Ena were alone for the time being.

Perhaps Iomedae had smiled on her servant, and they were something close to safe.

Carefully, she lowered Ena to the ground and pressed the back of her hand to her companion's bloodied brow. The dwarf was burning with fever and chattering in delirium, but she was alive. Kyril allowed herself a sigh of relief before she scanned the hallway one last time, then heaved down on the seraptis door's handle.

As the blade whirred out, cutting the seraptis's flesh free, Kyril folded her hands over her wounded abdomen and prayed to the Inheritor to force the demon's venom from her body.

Isiem severed the link, shuddering. Torture rarely fazed him; since childhood, he'd mortified his friends' flesh and his own. But having endured that burning venom's reaction to healing magic himself, he found that he could not bear to watch Kyril suffer the same.

"Ena and Kyril are alive," he told Ascaros, staring at the compass's scarlet-speckled face. "They've just reached the seraptis door and are about to pass through. The dwarf is badly wounded, and the paladin not much better, although she was preparing to heal herself when I broke the connection. I believe they killed the fiend that injured them, although Kyril seemed to fear that others might be in pursuit."

"And the others? Did you see any sign of Ganoven or his minions?"

Isiem shook his head. "No, nor of Teglias. Kyril seemed to think they were alive, though. She was worried that Teglias might have been possessed. They slew the demons that they freed, but there may yet be something in this dungeon with us." He steadied the compass in his palm and, steeling himself, pricked his finger again. "Ganoven."

Blood-spawned mist swirled over his sight, and through it he entered the Aspis agent's mind.

Ganoven was furious. And afraid.

Pulcher was dead, and it had been an ugly death. He didn't know where they were in this infernal labyrinth, and he didn't know how to get out. He didn't even know if they were alone in this place. Maybe the paladin had killed that last demon, and maybe it had killed her. He hadn't lingered to find out.

Everything was *wrong* here. The halls were more like tunnels, twisting and unexpectedly cramped and overhung with dripping vegetation. It was nothing like the neat, orderly corridors and symmetrical arrangements they'd passed through previously. He'd followed Teglias out of the demons' chamber, assuming the cleric must know something he didn't about the layout of Fiendslair, but now he was beginning to think he'd made an awful mistake. The Sarenite had vanished long ago, and Ganoven was entirely lost.

And now this.

"What do you *mean* you've lost the skeletons?" he shouted at Copple. His voice echoed longer and louder than it should have in the plant-choked halls. The half-elf scowled, crouching slightly in discomfort. He hadn't intended to make quite that much noise, and he didn't like this place, with its alien fungi and predatory vines. Greenery should *stop* sound, not amplify it—but everything was wrong in these halls, so why shouldn't the plants be, too? One of those plants, he was fairly certain, had actually tried to *bite* him. That rip in the shoulder of his coat hadn't been torn by thorns.

Of course, Copple didn't notice, fool that he was. The pudgy man quailed, dropping the quilted sack and covering his head with his arms. "I'm sorry! It must have happened in the panic while we were running!"

"Did you open the sack?" Ganoven hissed, venomously soft.

Copple blinked at him through the absurdly garish tattoos that decked his arms. "No. I—I don't think so. We were running, I couldn't have."

"Did you take them out?"

"No. No, I didn't. You have to believe me!"

No, I don't, Ganoven thought, but he didn't gloat about it. That would have been unbecoming. Instead he contented himself with a sneer. "Then how could they have been *lost,* hm? Do you mean to suggest the skeletons got up and walked out of your sack of their own accord?"

They could have, a small treacherous voice whispered in his mind. *They did walk. If they could do that, why couldn't they have climbed out of the sack?*

The Aspis agent pushed those thoughts aside. "Never mind. You say you didn't open the sack, yet the skeletons are gone. Very well. We will correct your mistake later. Do you have the gems, at least?"

"Y-yes." Copple began to fumble for them, but Ganoven cut him short with a wave.

"No, no, leave them as they are. I should hate for you to lose them as you did my skeletons." Ganoven used his thumbnail to crack the wax seal on another potion and downed it with a grunt. Healing magic flowed through his veins, erasing the last of the bruises and burns he'd suffered from that horrible fiend in the tank. Copple watched him hungrily. The idiot had squandered all his own potions on minor ailments earlier in their journey, leaving him with insufficient magic to cure the wounds he'd sustained in that scrap. But at least he had the sense to keep his mouth shut. Ganoven had no intention of rewarding the dolt's shortsightedness with more potions, and even Copple wasn't stupid enough to ask.

"Come," Ganoven said, tossing the empty bottle aside and peering around. The eerie jungle that had swallowed these halls was quiet; there was no indication that any imminent threats approached. This was their best opportunity to escape, before whatever had eaten their former comrades came looking for another meal. "Let's go."

Again Isiem extricated himself from another mind. A sour taste filled his mouth; he swallowed it with difficulty. He felt dirty after having been immersed in Ganoven's thoughts, a sensation he hadn't felt after leaving Kyril's.

"I think they're in our part of Fiendslair," he told Ascaros. "Or close to it. They're surrounded by the same tainted, overgrown plants. It's only Ganoven and Copple who are together; I didn't see any of the others. Pulcher is dead. Ganoven panicked and chose the wrong archway during the fight in the dome room, and now they can't find their way out again."

The shadowcaller stretched his arms lazily over his head. "Good. They'll be easier prey on their own. Could you tell exactly where they were?"

Isiem thought back. These hallways were a maze, and he had only a guess as to the Aspis agents' relative position . . . but some of the plants had been familiar in their monstrous deformities, and there was a skull he thought he'd seen before. Beyond that, one of the overgrown statues he'd glimpsed through Ganoven's eyes had looked distinct enough to serve as a landmark.

It had been a curiously ill-defined sculpture, as the Aspis agent passed it, Isiem had wondered if the stone had been deliberately carved into those sagging and shapeless lines, or if the mat of slimy moss growing atop it had dissolved its original form. Only the single central eye in the thing had been clearly drawn—and it was that eye, filled with strikingly intense malevolence, that he remembered most distinctly.

"Maybe," he told the shadowcaller. "They passed a statue that I would recognize if we found it, and I think I might be able to get there."

"Good," Ascaros said. "We'll hit them soon, before they have time to move. So. That leaves only Teglias unaccounted for. Even if Ganoven is wrong about Pulcher being dead, he doesn't have a compass, so it's no use looking for him to make sure. Teglias, however, does."

Isiem nodded and drew a third drop of blood from his finger. "Teglias," he whispered to the compass.

But this time, when the bloodsmoke rose off the speckled stone, it did not clear. The fog lingered for several moments, swirling around his sight, and dissipated without revealing anything beyond its own opaque eddies.

"Strange," Isiem said, wiping the compass clean and returning it to his pocket. "There's nothing there."

"What do you mean, 'nothing'?" Ascaros asked.

"When I tried to spy on Teglias, I saw only mist."

The shadowcaller's dark eyes narrowed. "But you did see the mist?"

"Yes. Is he dead?"

"No. Attempting to contact a dead target causes the magic to fail. The needle doesn't move, and the mist doesn't come. If you see the mist, and it doesn't clear, your target is alive, but he's using magic of his own to hide his thoughts." Ascaros paused. "Or something else is hiding *its* thoughts in him."

Chapter Twenty
The Creator's Blades

"Do you think he's possessed?" Isiem asked. It was a sobering thought. Not only would that mean there was some other fiend loose in this hellish labyrinth, but it would mean that fiend was powerful enough to overcome the will of Sarenrae's dedicated servant.

"Does it matter?" Ascaros was studying the wand Isiem had given him. It was made of hammered copper, dimpled with a thousand tiny hammer blows, and its end tapered to a sharp point. A flat spot along the handle bore a glimmering tracery of Nidalese script, but Isiem couldn't make out the words from where he stood. "We have no idea where he is in this place and we can't trace him with the compass. As we can't find him, and can't possibly influence what might become of him, it's no use worrying about that now."

Nodding minutely at whatever he'd concluded from examining the wand, Ascaros slid it up into his left sleeve and cinched one of the bands around his forearm to hold the copper rod in place. "We'll go after Ganoven."

"Do you think that's wise?" Isiem asked. "The Aspis agents are lost, likely doomed. Ena and Kyril need our help—they aren't safe yet. And if Teglias *is* possessed, then there's something extremely dangerous at liberty in this place."

Ascaros hissed an impatient breath between his teeth. "What was the first lesson you learned in the Dusk Hall?"

"To keep my ears open and my mouth closed," Isiem replied.

The shadowcaller clicked his tongue in annoyance, striding past Isiem into the vine-shrouded corridor. "Fine. What was the *second*? Never take your enemies' defeat for granted. If you haven't piked their heads and burned their bodies with your own two hands, best to assume they're alive and still threats. Overconfidence has been the bane of many a wizard before us."

"Demons have been the bane of many more," Isiem objected. The hall ahead looked unpromising. Puddles of dark water and darker mosses, their surfaces slicked with greasy rainbow films, dotted the floor. Squat mushrooms grew from the walls, hemming in the already claustrophobic space.

"Which is precisely why we shouldn't leave Ganoven to their mercies," Ascaros said, brushing past the lumpen fungi. "Can you imagine what mischief they'd make with him? How easy it would be to tempt him into ruin? Better we should prevent the very possibility. I have no doubt that your friend the paladin would agree. Anyway, if it troubles you so greatly, I'll offer you a bargain. Help me with Ganoven and whatever lackeys he has left to him, and I will devote my utmost efforts to seeing that Ena and Kyril escape this place safely. That's what you really want, isn't it? We'll finish off the traitors, and then we shall see to your friends. Together."

It seemed dubious reasoning to Isiem, but he could see that Ascaros was not about to be swayed from his pursuit. Better, then, to take what concessions he could. "I'll go," he said, "but if we don't find Ganoven quickly, or the pursuit seems dangerous, we'll break off and go back to the others."

"Of course," Ascaros said. "Now, where was the path you thought you saw?"

Hoping he hadn't just made a fool's promise, Isiem moved to an intersection where he could see as many adjoining tunnels as possible. The vision had shown the corridors from a different perspective, and it took him a moment to adjust.

Apart from the faraway buzz of some unseen, half-functioning enchantment, the hall was quiet. Nothing moved, save for the hungry swaying of the toothy vines clustered around the few functional light globes that shone through the warm fog. It seemed as safe as it was likely to get, yet Isiem couldn't shake the sensation of hostile eyes watching them from some-where unseen.

"There," he said, pointing out a three-eyed demon's skull with a wide, curved horn jutting out between its nostrils. With its lower jaw sunk into a murky puddle, the skull seemed to be drooling brown venom through its sickle-shaped teeth. The speckled red flowers around it had grown into bizarre echoes of its shape: they, too, resembled wedge-shaped skulls with scything horns. He remembered the arrangement from the vision, and he remembered the angle from which Ganoven had glimpsed it. "They were above it and to the left. The statue will be some thirty or forty feet down that tunnel."

"I see it," Ascaros said, abandoning the hall he'd begun to venture down. Pushing aside the damp vines that draped the entrance, the shadowcaller strode down the tunnel. Isiem followed, casting uncertain glances backward. The unnatural plant growth in the corridor seemed to swallow up all traces of their passing, as if the creepers and spongy mosses were hungry for whatever little taste of life might linger in their footsteps.

Something worse than vines had struck the Aspis agents, though.

Almost as soon as he entered the tunnel, Isiem heard a man's weeping and smelled the tang of fresh-spilled blood. He eased around the curve as quietly as he could, catching Ascaros by the sleeve to slow him. Together, they peered through a curtain of wormy white fungi.

Copple sat slumped against the statue, shivering violently. Sobs wracked his plump frame. With each heaving breath, bright red blood trickled out through his fingers and spilled across the floor, where the nearby vines stretched out to suck at it with their eyeless pink heads.

The man looked virtually dead. Isiem started forward, but Ascaros grasped his arm to give him pause.

"We came to kill him," the shadowcaller reminded him. "It seems someone else did it first. That is a convenience, not a problem. There's no point healing him."

"I'd like to know who did it while he's alive enough to tell us," Isiem said.

Ascaros shrugged and pulled back into the shadows. With a final glance back at his friend, Isiem approached Copple.

The man looked up as he neared. His complexion was ghastly: dead white on his forehead and the upper contours of his cheeks, livid purple and yellowy-green around the neck and the folds of his double chin. Copple looked like a corpse, all his poisoned blood drained low into his body by gravity.

His eyes were strange, too, their whites stained a pale dirty yellow. But it was when Copple moved his hands, raising them toward Isiem in desperate pleading, that the worst of his wounds appeared.

A rough crescent had been sliced across his stomach, exposing curdled folds of fat and ribboned muscle. Plump egg sacs, hundreds of them, filled the wound. Inside each sac, innumerable white eggs floated like bubbles in a buoyant bath of blood. Some of the sacs had ruptured, evidently torn apart by Copple's own desperate attempts to pull them out of his body, and it was from their broken membranes that the bright blood flowed out and across Copple's lap.

"What *happened* to you?" Isiem breathed.

Copple raised his head feebly. His red-stained fingers twitched across the egg sacs that bulged out of his body, dimpling their membranes inward. He didn't seem to have the strength to rip them open anymore. He barely had the strength to speak; his voice was a labored whisper that Isiem had to strain to hear. "Mother. Mindfogger."

"One of the creatures in the tanks? Is one of those loose in here?"

Copple's laugh was simultaneously dry and gurgling. "No. No, the mother has been free . . . long. A long time. Alone in here with her children. Her children and the dust of their victims."

"The dust of their victims," Ascaros repeated, coming toward them. The shadowcaller's black eyes were alight, burning with intensity. "You mean Eledwyn and her acolytes?"

Copple shook his head weakly. "The demons. The newcomers. Interlopers. She hates them, she hungers, and I feel it, I hear it . . ." Copple dug his fingers into his sparse hair, pulling it outward. The drying blood on his hands made it stick up in wild, red-tufted spikes. Then he slid his hands down again, cradling the eggs that filled his torn belly. "The children sing their hungers to me too."

"Where's Ganoven?" Ascaros asked, scanning their surroundings. "Did the 'mother' take him? What about Teglias? Have you seen him?"

"No." Copple groaned and squeezed his eyes shut. Cloudy tears, yellow with pus, trickled from their corners. "I don't . . . I haven't seen Teglias. Ganoven fled. He left me and ran." He tried to point down a crooked hall, its entrance fringed with torn and weeping creepers, but could only lift his hand a few trembling inches before it dropped back with a thud. "Please help me. I'm dying."

"Yes, you are. How long do you suppose it'll be until those eggs hatch? Not very, I suspect." Ascaros squatted beside the man, observing them intently for several seconds. To Isiem's eye, it seemed that the wriggling threads of life inside the eggs were getting stronger, and that the eggs themselves were growing larger in their sacs so quickly that he could see the swelling as it happened.

They waited another minute or two, watching those translucent filaments take on identifiable shapes. They were tentacled, writhing things, each one misshapen with some unique deformity but all of a type: four long arms around a podlike body that split down the middle to form a nascent maw. In the span of two minutes, they'd grown from half an inch in length to nearly two inches each, and they spilled out over Copple's lap like an apron of bloody bubbles.

"I think we've seen enough," Ascaros murmured. He took out a knife and slashed through the bubbles, one by one, methodically dismembering the spawn inside the eggs as they flailed in their bloody fluid and Copple screamed himself hoarse.

When the last of the bubbles had been eviscerated, Copple lay insensible in a pool of his own blood and clear ichor. His breathing was rapid and shallow, and his color was somehow worse. Even the tattoos on his arms looked like plague corpses. Isiem stooped to help him, but Ascaros pushed him away. Taking one of Copple's limp hands between his own, the shadow-caller invoked a thread of Zon-Kuthon's power to pull the pudgy man back from the brink of death.

It was only a tiny fragment of healing—not enough to repair Copple's ruined insides, barely enough to bring his eyelids fluttering back to awareness—and it seemed almost crueler than letting the poor man die. But the spark of life stayed in him.

Ascaros stood, wiping his hands clean. "Are you ready to finish this?"

Isiem took his eyes off Copple with difficulty. The tunnel where Ganoven had presumably fled would have been obvious even without the pudgy thug's help. Its plants were crushed and broken, and unlike the ones he and Ascaros had trodden on their way here, they were not healing. Florid yellow-red sap, uncannily evocative of bloody pus, dribbled from their snapped stems. It was as if the labyrinth itself had chosen to show them which way Ganoven had run.

The sight did not inspire confidence. But still he said: "Yes."

"Good." Ascaros raised his boot to step over a dying fetal monster, then changed his mind and crushed it under his heel.

"You're going to leave Copple?"

"Of course." The shadowcaller never paused. "He'll serve as a useful delay if anything else comes down this way, and his screams may serve to warn us."

"He might also incubate more demons."

"I'm not sure those things inside him *were* demons. I think there's more going on here than we know. But semantics aside, I don't think he has that much blood left. The egg-laying will likely kill him, in which case the problem solves itself. Now, are you coming?"

Isiem didn't answer immediately. He looked at Copple again. The man seemed to have stabilized, although it was hard to be sure. He drifted in and out of consciousness, twitching his fingers toward the wound in his belly sporadically. That ugly seeping slash remained mostly open, exposing torn flesh and fat, and no doubt causing crippling pain.

If anything came for him, Copple would have no chance to flee. Even if nothing did, he wouldn't be able to walk away alive. His wound was incapacitating, and Isiem could see torn bowel spilling out in its depths. Without additional magic, Copple had no chance at survival.

Kyril would have healed the man, Isiem thought. Ena would have killed him, quick and sure; the dwarf was a more pragmatic sort, and in this place, surrounded by so much danger, she'd keep her healing for herself. Moreover, the Aspis agents' betrayal deserved no greater mercy.

But killing him *would* be a kindness, and it was for that reason, as much as any claims of cold-blooded pragmatism, that Ascaros had healed him. He wanted Copple to suffer. That his suffering could be useful was only a happy accident.

And in another life, Isiem would have let him. Copple had earned his misery.

Mercy, however, meant giving men better than they deserved.

Isiem drew his knife and cut Copple's throat. There was hardly any blood, but it seemed to be enough. Sheathing his blade, he followed Ascaros away.

"That was a waste of time," the shadowcaller said when Isiem caught up. "He would have died soon enough anyway."

Isiem shrugged. A three-way intersection branched ahead of them. The light was weaker down both of the new corridors, with only one faltering glow-globe illuminating each of them, yet the wild tangles of Abyssal flora seemed even more rampant in the gloom. In Fiendslair there was no wind to stir them, but all those snaking vines moved sinuously along the walls, like the tendrils of jellyfish sieving for prey. None of these appeared to be broken. "Which way?"

"You tell me. You're the one with the compass."

Isiem slid the compass into his palm but did not prick his finger to feed it. "Is it so important to hunt down Ganoven? You saw what happened to Copple. There's a fiend loose here, and it took him without a fight. You told me that if there was obvious peril, we'd turn back."

"I did say that," Ascaros replied. "But turning back would be a grave mistake. If this 'mother' is using living men as incubators, it's even more important that we find and finish Ganoven. The fiends in this place won't kill him. They might even help him escape, if they can fill him full of eggs like Copple and spread their filth into the world that way." He gestured to the compass. "Sometimes vengeance has a practical purpose, Isiem."

Resignedly, Isiem pricked his finger. As he forced the blood out, he whispered: "Ganoven."

What he touched through its enchanted mist, however, was no living mind.

He wasn't sure it was *a* mind at all. There was a fleeting sense of confusion, reflected and refracted through a million different angles like an emotion somehow tumbled through a kaleidoscope, or felt by a linked hive of minds at once. A vision of infinite eyes stretched out before him, like a field of daisies where each flower was a disembodied eyeball standing on a stalk of slime. Overhead was a whirling, chaotic sky, stained a thousand different shades of sooty red. Below, he sensed—although he could not see, could not *know*—a sluggish sea of ancient, primordial poison.

Then it was gone, so suddenly that Isiem wasn't sure what he had seen. In its place was the image of an elven woman in gray-green robes, standing outside a summoning circle and shielded by a dome of distorting glass. A black knife flashed, red fire along its edge. The weight of his—*its, their*—body changed. The sea of poison vanished, replaced by a cold glass dome and a floor of rippled stone rings. Different, but no less cruel. New thoughts crept into his head, new magic thrummed in his flesh. Remembered pain wracked him, over and over, an infinity of garbled suffering compressed and imperfectly translated into memory.

In a flash, that was gone, too. Time slid by, an eyeblink, almost nothing. Shattering glass broke its silence, a tall figure striding away in a black cloak, and then—

—*freedom,* and a sudden surge of remembered hate like vomit coming up hot and corrosive and unstoppable in his throat.

Usurpers usurpers hate find destroy usurpers

The black blade flashed before his sight again, limned in crimson flames. In that red, serrated fire, the faces of fiends screamed and burned.

the knife will kill them all

"Isiem. *Isiem.*" A stinging slap awoke him. From the burning on his other cheek, he realized it hadn't been the first. He'd fallen at some point; he lay on the floor, his boots tangled in Abyssal vines. They bit at him ineffectually with deformed flower pods and left stains of nectar—or saliva—on the leather.

Ascaros scowled down at him, his face dark with worry and fear. "Why were you babbling about usurpers?"

Isiem wiped his mouth, kicking the vines away and pulling himself into a sitting position. A sour stickiness coated his tongue. His throat was raspy and tight, as if someone had tried to strangle him. "I think Ganoven is . . . not possessed, exactly, but something close to that. There's something else in his mind. Some *things*. But the compass found him. I wonder if whatever is in him wanted me to see."

"See what?"

Isiem closed his eyes and rubbed his temples helplessly. "I'm not sure. It's old, whatever it is. Very old. The time from its summoning to this world until its escape from Fiendslair was nothing in its mind. And it hails from the Abyss." Unable to bear the taste in his mouth any longer, Isiem spat on the floor. Ascaros raised an eyebrow, and the wizard knew why. Children were taught very early in Nidal not to spit in public, unless they wanted to be spitting blood. It took a great deal to overcome that training.

"So it *is* a demon."

"Maybe." Isiem scrubbed a hand through his hair, then tied the loose ivory locks back again. The memory of hate was burned into his mind, but he didn't think that hatred had been directed at Eledwyn, despite the torture that strange mind had endured at her hands. Its loathing had been aimed at . . . what? The other caged demons? Mesandroth? Someone else? It was all an impossible blur. Frustrated, he shook his head. "Do you still want to find him?"

"Did you see his location?"

"No," Isiem admitted. He cast his mind back through those alien memories. "But Ganoven, or whatever was *in* Ganoven, was fixated on the nightblades." He paused as an idea occurred. "Ascaros—how much location magic do you know?"

Ascaros looked at him in puzzlement for a moment, then understanding dawned. "The nightblades."

Divination magic was rarely reliable, but the ease with which Ascaros had employed Sukorya's diamond to find Fiendslair's entrance suggested that he might have some facility with it. Even the best caster couldn't find an item if he didn't know what he was looking for, which is why he hadn't simply led them straight to the nightblades upon entering. But now that he'd had time to study one properly . . .

Several moments passed before Ascaros answered. His mouth twisted as if the words were bitter as lye between his lips. "Yes. Yes, if the others are close enough to the one we found earlier. They should all have Eledwyn's signature in their magic."

With a slow, reluctant hand, Ascaros drew the spiked chain up from the front of his robes. The silver case containing Sukorya's diamond dangled from its end, revolving in the air. As the case entered its third revolution, a shudder passed through the shadowcaller's body, and the chain vibrated in response. When the vibration reached the egg-shaped case, it split open like a blossoming flower, revealing a slash of crimson light that widened and grew until it surrounded them both in its nimbus.

From it emanated the same overpowering evil Isiem had felt during the opening of Fiendslair, yet it seemed that the pull it exerted on his soul was slightly—very slightly—less. He glanced at Ascaros, wondering if the magic had changed in this place . . . but the question died unspoken, for clearly the shadowcaller was not experiencing the same thing he was.

Sweat stood out on Ascaros's brow, and the illusion that masked his real face faltered, allowing glimpses of the withered man beneath to show through. His breathing fell into the measured, deliberate pattern that students of the Dusk Hall were taught to use when their control began to fail.

The red light shone steady, though. Then, suddenly, it narrowed into a crimson beam, flashed down one of the branching paths ahead, and vanished.

Ascaros wiped his forehead with a sleeve. He did not put the case away, but he lowered the arm that held it. "It isn't far," he said, starting down the path that the scarlet ray had shown. "By the Midnight Lord's small mercy, it's not far."

"What happens when you use Sukorya's stone?" Isiem asked as he accompanied Ascaros down the weed-choked hall. Rivulets of murky water ran alongside their feet, leaving strange curling tracks of slime in their wake. The wizard's sphere of light was beginning to dwindle, so he summoned another, causing a multiplicity of overlapping shadows to cavort amid the poisoned plants around them. "It looks painful."

"It is," the shadowcaller said tersely. He slowed as they reached the end of the hall. A marble archway carved with flute-playing satyrs and dancing nymphs framed the room ahead. Stains from rotten fruit and oozing flowers covered the carvings, causing the nymphs and satyrs to look wounded and leprous. Gloom filled the archway itself, and from its depths came the sound of creaking chains.

Isiem sent his light ahead. The floating sphere illumined a garden of decay. Bulbous mushrooms covered every available surface, sprouting sideways from the walls of bookshelves and frilling the walls with gilled layers of fungus. Most of them were an unhealthy whitish color, splotched with slimy yellow or green, and resembled nothing so much as curling maggots with disturbingly humanlike faces.

Underneath the overgrowth of mushrooms, he could make out the contours of a bed, a desk or eating table—it was impossible to tell which anymore—and a few collapsed chairs. Only one of those chairs remained intact, and it alone was untouched by so much as a spot of mold. A five-foot circle all around it was perfectly preserved and clean of dust. The floor was rich cherry, smooth and freshly waxed; the wisteria vine carved into the chair's wooden back was perfectly preserved, vibrant down to the veins in the leaves and the belled petals on its flowers.

A skeleton sat in that chair, long silver hair flowing down its back like a cascade of cobwebs. It wore gray-green robes in the same hue as the apprentices', although these robes were of finer cloth and interlaced with silver thread. Three jeweled rings glimmered on its bare bone fingers: ruby, emerald, and a great clear diamond with a speck of fractured crimson in its heart. Under its jeweled hand, a pair of black blades rested.

"Eledwyn," Ascaros breathed. From the reverence in his voice, one would have thought it was the elven woman, and not Mesandroth, who was his legendary ancestor.

"It looks like a trap," Isiem said.

"It probably is," Ascaros said. "The question is, why would she leave a trap for *us*? I'm betting she's keyed it to respond to this 'mother' creature, rather than blowing the charge on the first mouse to nibble at her corpse. I'll bet it knows it, too. Why else would the blades still be here after all these years?" The shadow-caller picked his way through the fungal clutter, avoiding as many of the sprouting mushrooms as he could, until he reached the skeleton's side. Bracing himself visibly against an expected magical assault, Ascaros reached into the clean space to lift the treasures from the skeletal elf's hand.

As soon as his fingers touched the obsidian blades, a disembodied, whispering voice filled the chamber. It spoke a tongue that sounded elven to Isiem's ears, although inflected with a strange slurring accent unlike anything he'd heard before. The skeleton did not move, but Ascaros flinched back. "What is it saying?"

Isiem shook his head helplessly. He reached into a pouch of spell components and hastily drew out a pinch of soot and salt, rubbing them together as he rushed through the words that would bring comprehension to his ears. And all the while, the sibilant message slipped by.

"—*our mistake. Take these cursed relics to the bronze chamber, and flee. Immediately. Bring nothing else with you, for I cannot say where they might hide, and nothing that might free them is worth keeping. We thought we had found the death of demons in our nightblade, in the qlippoth . . . but the qlippoth are not simple parasites. They are mad, thinking killers. They cannot be controlled, and all they bring is death. They cannot be allowed to escape. The blades must be denied them. They must. Even my magic is not eternal. Eventually, the wards will fail. The qlippoth are content to wait. When my magic fades, they will take these blades and use them to punch through this complex's defenses, into the world beyond. Take these blades, and the one still in the workshop beyond the brimorak door, and destroy them. Destroy them, if you can.*"

The whispered message ended. Ascaros shook off his paralysis. "Qlippoth," he said. "Interesting."

"You're familiar with them?"

"Not particularly." Ascaros began plucking the rings from Eledwyn's dead fingers. "Only from brief mentions in ancient Dusk Hall texts. Creatures of primordial evil—the original residents of the Abyss, driven out into the deeper darkness by the rise of demons." Cautiously, he reached out and took the two black knives, then retreated from the silver-haired skeleton.

"She said not to take anything from this place," Isiem said. "I only caught the second half of the message, but she seemed quite adamant about that. Whatever these qlippoth may be, the nightblade allows them entry into our world, and Eledwyn didn't want to risk them escaping Fiendslair. She wanted the nightblades destroyed, and the qlippoth sealed in this place like a tomb."

"Then that's what we'll do," Ascaros said, pocketing all three rings. He lifted the flap of his satchel and tucked the nightblades carefully inside. "But I think her personal possessions are exempt from the rule. Whatever holds the mushrooms away from her feet, I trust it also held the nightblade's corruptions from her hands. Besides, I want them."

"Temptation leads men to evil," Isiem intoned solemnly, summoning his floating light back toward the archway.

"I'm already there," Ascaros said smugly, stepping over the layered mushrooms as he turned to leave as well. "So I have nothing to lose. Anyway, we have the blades. Let us be gone."

"No," said Ganoven, stepping into the dim light at the other end of the hall.

Chapter Twenty-One
Reunions

Ganoven didn't look much like himself anymore.

His eyes were vacant and totally white, the irises rolled up to the back of his head. Bloodless slashes crisscrossed his cheeks and forehead, each of them filled with innumerable twitching, mismatched spider legs that flicked back and forth at each other like an ingenue's fluttering eyelashes. The Aspis agent's flesh jumped and bulged with the legs' movements.

Greenish ichor dripped from his nose, eating away his skin in sloughing red furrows. Ganoven didn't seem to notice. He just stared at them with his blank white eyes, while Copple shuffled over to his side.

Copple hadn't survived his throat-cutting. Whoever or whatever had animated his mortal remains had enlarged the slash until it nearly decapitated the corpse. His head dangled across his shoulders, flopping to and fro on gristly strings. The wound in his stomach sagged open, dragged wide by gravity now that he was standing. Fat and viscera spilled down his thighs in a gruesome apron.

But he wasn't a simple zombie. Chitinous claws erupted from his fingertips like the points of spears thrust through dead flesh. Slimy, pulsing muscles like enormous gray worms held his innards together, coming into view occasionally as the corpse lurched between steps. White lines of scar tissue flashed between those ropy muscles: whatever fiend inhabited him, it had been subjected to Eledwyn's reshaping.

"Give me the blades," Ganoven said. His tongue fell out on the last word. In its place, just for an instant, Isiem glimpsed a wriggling stump of muscle that ended in a hagfish mouth.

"No," Isiem replied. Out of the corner of his eye he saw a brief shimmer envelop Ascaros, and knew that the shadowcaller had shielded himself with magic.

Ganoven made a shuddery approximation of a shrug, pushing his shoulders up past his earlobes with a rubbery, boneless ease. His grin was filled with the gleeful clacking of more insectoid legs hanging down from the roof of his mouth behind his teeth. Behind him, the bones of sheep and calves and long-dead men—all the skeletons from the large-animal testing room—shambled into view, held together by more ropy, pulsing tentacles. The cythnigot-infested skeletons that had escaped from Copple's sacks sat astride the larger beasts, clasped onto the backs of their skulls like horrid ivory tumors. Snapping jaw-stalks rose from their bones in nightmare flowers. "Then we'll take it."

Any answer Isiem might have given was lost in the roar of Ascaros's fireball. The shadowcaller's spell engulfed the entire archway, blistering mushrooms and reducing toadstool caps to frayed black parasols. Some of the skeletal calves and sheep blasted apart into fragments of superheated bone, their alien innards sizzling and writhing like snails dropped onto hot coals. Their parasitic controllers spasmed a while longer, flailing at the air, and then succumbed to death.

Somehow Ganoven managed to avoid the fireball entirely. He flattened himself against the floor and shot forward with no apparent effort, dodging the blue-tipped orange flames. Copple made no attempt to do the same; instead, whatever was inside him pulled deep into the corpse's guts, hauling his ripped stomach up behind itself like a castle door raised against a siege.

The dead man's flesh resisted fire better than the skeletons' bare bones had. His eyes burst in the heat, leaving pockets of raw pink in his skull, but he shambled through the flames undaunted, his clothes smoldering over lifeless skin. The skin and muscle of his fingertips retreated slightly as it cooked, revealing more of the chitinous claws that poked through them.

Isiem leveled the gold-banded glass wand at him. Sunfire pulsed through the translucent stone and seared through Copple's body, lighting up whatever unearthly creature was in his corpse. For an instant, it stood sharply defined within his flesh, a headless web of thick misshapen tentacles, and then it exploded through his mouth and ruined gut as a gush of pulpy slime. Copple's corpse sank to the ground, mercifully inert.

The wand went dead in Isiem's hands. Its gold bands darkened to dull brown and its snowy glass turned smoky gray. Its magic was gone.

He tossed it aside just as the larger skeletons fell upon him. Badly damaged by the fiery blast, they nevertheless held together. Yellowed teeth and deformed claws raked at him; bony tails swept at his legs. A rickety human skeleton grabbed at his shoulder and dragged him forward for a bite with its fungus-stained teeth. Desperately, Isiem smashed his elbow into its grin, knocking its head back, but he couldn't evade all of them. He wasn't a fighter, and he went down flailing under their mass.

"Who *are* you?" he heard Ascaros ask over the tumult of clattering bones.

"How unworthy you are," the thing in Ganoven replied. Its contempt vibrated the man's entire body. "How desperately foolish. *You*, whose failings gave rise to the usurpers, whose hubris summoned us to this world of weakness. You ask who we are?"

Isiem couldn't hear what Ascaros said in response, if the shadowcaller said anything. One of the calf skeletons bit him above the right hip with unnaturally sharp fangs. Each of its teeth injected a puff of pale green spores, which sprouted up through Isiem's body with impossible speed. Hairy tendrils and bramble hooks extended from the wound, grabbing at Isiem's arms. Before they could bind him, he grabbed the spore-growths by the fistful and yanked them out of his body, fighting down his own revulsion as much as the wrenching pain. Their roots clutched his fingers, leaving trails of blood and digested flesh across his skin. *His* blood. *His* flesh.

Disgusted and horror-struck, he hurled the clump of twitching foulness across the room. He needed distance, or they'd destroy him.

With shaking, blood-slippery fingers, Isiem took a pouch of silver dust from his pocket and shook it in an uneven circle around himself. A skeletal dog slammed his shoulder with a tail that had mutated into a three-foot-long chain of oversized vertebrae strung on fungal fiber. It numbed the wizard's arm and forced a dent into his circle of powder, but Isiem held his spell intact.

The instant that he closed the circle of silver dust, white light flared within it, and the skeletal creatures assailing him recoiled. They recovered quickly, but now their snaps at him were less accurate, skidding sideways at the last minute as if deflected by an invisible shield.

It gave him room to breathe. Isiem rubbed the numbness from his bludgeoned arm. His hip wasn't bleeding where the skeletal calf had bitten him. A series of tattered punctures showed in his skin where he'd uprooted the fungal growths, but the wound was pale and bloodless.

He'd worry about any lingering effects later. If he survived.

Across the room, Ganoven was engaged in a furious spell battle with Ascaros. Fire and shadow flashed between them, too tangled for Isiem to follow. The Aspis agent was proving far more formidable in this form than he'd ever been on his own. Turning back to the fiend-possessed skeletons in front of him, Isiem tried one of the new spells he'd studied during their journey through the Backar Forest. Murmuring an incantation, he plucked a lump of coal from his pocket and crushed it between his fingers, then tossed the small chunks at the skeletons.

Heat and pressure gathered around them, and the coal turned to shards of razor-sharp diamond in mid-air. They hammered into the skeletal beasts, cracking ancient bone and shredding fungal tendrils. When the glittering spray of diamonds vanished, nothing was left of Isiem's assailants but shattered fragments on the floor.

He turned to help Ascaros. The shadowcaller seemed to be getting the worst of his duel; blood seeped through his shadowcaller's robes in at least three places, and his masking illusion had vanished entirely. The chitinous legs that showed through the rips in Ganoven's face twitched and jerked with something that might have been glee.

Isiem hit the Aspis agent from behind with a scorching stream of fire, then another and another, all three blurring into a twisted orange braid. This time the half-elf failed to dodge. The fiery rays struck him straight in the back, and although the creature in Ganoven's body seemed to impart some resistance to heat, the spell still burned him badly.

He turned a dead-eyed snarl on Isiem. Ascaros seized the opening to snatch the hidden wand from his sleeve. The shadowcaller leveled the hammered copper rod at Ganoven and spoke a word of arcane command.

The Aspis agent froze. His back arched high in the air as he was lifted to his toes by an unseen force, then snapped backward like a rat in a terrier's jaws. The bones in his body cracked in terrible percussion, ripping through his skin from the inside out. Even the insectoid legs in his body stiffened, stretched out rigidly, and snapped apart. When the magic released him, he collapsed to the floor, motionless save for the slow trickle of greenish slime that still spilled from his nostrils.

Breathing hard, Ascaros renewed the illusion that hid his disfigurement and dropped the wand to the ground. Like Isiem's alabaster wand, it had turned dull and worthless; its magic was spent. Isiem tossed him another, this one of gold-chased ivory adorned with innumerable bright jacinths like droplets of congealed flame.

The shadowcaller caught the wand easily and slid it into his sleeve, replacing the exhausted one. He fished a small bottle from his robes, cracked its wax seal with a thumbnail, and drank its contents in a single long swallow. Wiping his mouth, Ascaros looked at Ganoven's fallen body one last time, then pushed the Aspis agent's corpse over with his boot so that the man's sightless white eyes and spider-legged wounds were buried by mushrooms. "Let us be gone from this place."

Isiem nodded. He took out the enchanted compass and wiped one of his bloody fingers across the speckled green stone of its face. "Kyril," he whispered, holding it steady on his palm as he uncorked a potion with his other hand. Almost before he'd finished swallowing the healing draught, the compass's mist rose around him, washing out his reality.

"I don't believe they would do that," Kyril said. Even to her own ears, the protest sounded weak. "I don't. Why would they betray us?"

"The obvious reasons, I'd imagine," Teglias answered. "They're Nidalese." The cleric looked tired and wounded, as they all were, but despite the blood and ichor that stained his robes, he was better off than either Ena or Kyril herself. Whatever he'd fought had not tried him as sorely as their own foes had. The dwarf remained unconscious, even after Teglias had forced his last potion down her throat. Her color was bad, her breathing unsteady; Kyril feared for her survival.

"Betrayal has been bred into them for thousands of years," Teglias continued. His holy symbol had been torn away somewhere in the labyrinth; he fingered the snapped end of its beaded string as he spoke. "They came here seeking prizes for Zon-Kuthon's glory, and they'll let nothing stand in their way. They've already killed Ganoven and Copple. Both of them are evil to the marrow of their bones, and we have to stop them."

"I don't believe it," Kyril repeated, but her conviction faltered with each word. The wizard and the shadow-caller *were* gone. There was no denying that. Sweat dripped from the ends of her hair, spattering on the floor. Some of it took on a crimson tinge as it ran through the crusted blood on her face.

Was it possible that the Nidalese had betrayed them? She wouldn't have been surprised if it were only Ascaros, but Isiem . . .

She had thought better of the man. She had imagined there was some glimmer of virtue in his soul—a spark that might, with careful guidance and encouragement, be nursed into flame.

But Teglias had thought the same. Maybe they'd both been wrong.

"They've found the nightblades. If they leave this place with them, they'll be able to summon all manner of fiends into the world. Creatures worse than demons, worse than anything we've fought here. Worse than you or I could imagine. We have to stop them."

Kyril was wearier than she could remember ever having been before, but the urgency in the Sarenite's voice could not be denied. Nor could the threat he described. "All right," she said, exhausted. "How?"

"They'll have to come back this way." Teglias dropped his broken string of beads and looked around the small brass chamber with its demonflesh doors. "This is the only exit from Fiendslair, so they must come back through the seraptis door."

"It's too tight to fight in here," Kyril said. She started the seraptis door on the slow, bloody process of opening again. "We'll meet them on the other side."

"Be ready for treachery," Teglias said, falling into place behind her.

Kyril put a hand to her sword's hilt, positioning herself more squarely between the cleric and whatever dangers might lie ahead. "I am."

The vision faded. A throbbing headache pulsed behind Isiem's temples. He could feel it pushing at the backs of his eyes. It wasn't just the toll of his wounds or the horror of the Aspis agents' deaths, although that was part of what ached in him. It was a deeper hurt.

He put the compass away slowly, staring at Ganoven's remains amid the charred mushrooms without really registering what he was seeing.

"Well?" Ascaros asked, straightening from his looting of the goateed half-elf's corpse. He'd reclaimed his compass and added a few other baubles to his collection, along with the dead man's purse. A small, detached part of Isiem admired his companion's pragmatism even as he detested the shadowcaller's cold-hearted greed.

"They're alive," Isiem answered. "All three of them. Teglias, Ena, and Kyril. They're preparing to confront us."

"To confront us? Why?"

"Because Teglias has convinced them that we've betrayed their cause and are taking the nightblades for our own nefarious purposes."

Ascaros's pale lips twitched upward in a humorless smile. "If I thought the nightblades could be remotely *useful* for any nefarious purpose, there might be something to that claim. But, as it stands . . ." He shrugged, crushing Ganoven's body deeper into the mushrooms as he deliberately stepped on the fallen Aspis agent's back to leave the overgrown room. "You're quite sure it was the nightblades he mentioned? Not my books of forbidden knowledge?"

"No. Only the nightblades."

"And he spoke of them in the plural?"

"Yes," Isiem confirmed. His heart sank as he said it, realizing why Ascaros had asked. When they'd last seen Teglias, they'd only had the one nightblade. Only the qlippoth, and the Nidalese themselves, could possibly know that they'd recovered two more since. And Teglias wouldn't have been able to discount the possibility of other exits deep within Fiendslair. Only the qlippoth, which had been trapped here for centuries, could be so certain.

"It would be easier to kill them than to argue with them. If, that is, they insist on standing in our way."

"That wasn't what you promised." Isiem nudged Copple's body with his boot. The coils of the dead fiend in him fell out, slippery with caustic pulp, gray and green and grisly, grafted white. Some of those intestinal curls ended in tiny mouths, some in scar-braceleted claws. The stench was eye-watering.

Ascaros, halfway across the room, turned back and grimaced at the smell. He understood the point, though. "I made that bargain when I thought they might want our help. Not when I thought they'd try to kill us on sight."

"It doesn't matter. You made the promise. Honor it."

The black-haired shadowcaller gave him a long look. His thin fingers twitched toward the wand hidden in his sleeve. Then he smiled, not graciously, and offered a second shrug. "You always had more loyalty than sense. Very well. We'll try talking to your friends. *Your* friends, not mine. If you fall, I will leave them. If they attack us, I will kill them. Do you understand?"

"Perfectly," Isiem said. "Thank you."

"You shouldn't," Ascaros said. "You wouldn't, if you had any sense. But, as I said, that never was your strong point."

Chapter Twenty-Two
Crossroads and Loyalties

The demons' chamber was in ruin.

Glass, blood, and ichor made a grisly carpet across the floor, adding an overlay of fresh gore to the centuries-old remains of Eledwyn's apprentices. The only clear space was that trapped within the cracked glass dome at the center of the room. Once the focal point of this chamber's misery, it had become the only place spared from the latest wave of destruction.

Isiem and Ascaros entered cautiously, both veiled behind spells of invisibility. With quiet, careful steps they skirted over the lumpen remains of fallen demons and the shattered glass that littered the ground like icy caltrops.

Kyril was waiting for them. She crouched partway behind the cracked dome, allowing her to use it as either cover against frontal attacks or a shield at her back, depending on how her adversaries approached. The half-elf's hair was dark with sweat, and exhaustion circled her eyes, but her posture was alert and ready.

She was alone. Isiem guessed that Teglias must have remained with Ena behind the seraptis door, leaving the paladin to hold the line.

That caused him a pang of worry for Ena's sake—what might the qlippoth-influenced cleric be *doing* with her?—but it also left him a chance to make his case.

Cautiously, stopping on the far side of the great cracked dome, Isiem let his invisibility slip away. "Kyril."

The half-elf's head snapped up. Her eyes widened in alarm at the sound of his voice, then narrowed as she spotted him. She rose, lifting her sword and shield. "Where's your friend? Coming around to ambush me?"

"Waiting to see whether I'm a fool for trying to talk," Isiem replied. He took a breath, wishing he'd had time to rehearse a better speech. "Teglias isn't himself. He's fallen under the influence of the qlippoth—the fiends that Eledwyn's nightblade summoned. They are very old, and very deadly, and they hate mortal life as intensely as they hate demons. Whatever he told you, it's meant to serve the qlippoth's purposes, not the Dawnflower's. Not yours."

Doubt clouded her eyes. Isiem could see the scales shifting in her head. On one side, years of friendship and the shared respect of compatible faiths. On the other . . . what? A few weeks of travel together? The tentative beginnings of something that might become friendship? And the nagging sense, buried somewhere deep in her mind, that something might truly be wrong here.

"How do you know?" she asked. "How do you even know Teglias is here?"

"Because we've been spying on you." Isiem took the bloodstone compass from his pocket and, resting it flat on his palm, offered it to her scrutiny. "This one is a master to the others. It allows its holder to see where the others are and what their possessors are doing. It showed me that you and Ena were here . . . and it raised my suspicions that Teglias was no longer himself. Take it. See for yourself, if you don't trust my word. Whatever is in him guards him from scrying. It doesn't want its steps to be seen."

"No one does," Kyril retorted, but she lowered her sword and took the compass from him. "How do I use it? To . . . spy." The last word earned a curl of her lip.

"Prick your finger and let a drop of blood fall on the compass face. Then speak the name of the one you wish to see. If he has a compass, and he's alive, you'll see mist. Through it, you'll be able to spy on the lesser compasses' carriers—or not, if they're using their own magic to hide. Try it on either Ascaros or myself, if you wish to see the ordinary result. Or try it on Teglias, if you wish to see what I have."

Eying him with undimmed suspicion, Kyril sheathed her sword and pricked her finger. "Teglias," she said, keeping her gaze fixed on the wizard.

He couldn't see what she did. The compass's magic revealed itself only to its user; to his eyes, there was no mist, no vision, nothing but the curls of smoke that rose from the stone as the drop of blood boiled away.

But Kyril's attention snapped away from him as soon as the smoke appeared. After a second, she thrust the compass back at him, scowling.

Isiem took it. "Do you believe me now?"

"Maybe. It could be a trick. And he might have good reasons for hiding from your spells." She turned on her heel, striding back across the field of bloody glass toward the bone-littered entry hall and the seraptis door beyond it. "But I've seen enough that I'm going to check on Ena. You can come with me if you like."

He did, readying the last of the wands he'd recovered from the case in the experimentation room. Magic hummed through its sky-blue quartz, and he took reassurance from its strength. The muted crunch of glass underfoot told him that Ascaros was following, too, invisibly and at a measured distance. Isiem took heart from that. The shadowcaller was still with them.

But so was something else.

All of you will die.

Isiem froze, the hair on the back of his neck prickling. That wasn't Kyril's voice, or Ascaros's. It wasn't *any* spoken voice.

He whipped around to see a sinuous tentacle flicker away, vanishing around the glass dome behind them. Suckers dotted it, and a glossy black pincer capped its end. Something long and thin extended from the pincer. He didn't have time to see more; as soon as he'd registered that much, it was gone.

Ascaros reacted faster. A fireball bloomed between the shadowcaller's hands, outlining his suddenly visible body in a stark silhouette. Blue-kissed orange fire streaked across the chamber to explode where the pincer had vanished, blasting apart the cracked remains of a demon's empty glass cage and sending a thousand splintered reflections sparkling around the room.

"What was that?" Kyril demanded, whirling. Her sword was out, its edge alight in blue flame.

"A qlippoth," the shadowcaller answered tersely, scanning the smoke and cooling globs of molten glass for signs of his target. "Probably the same one that's influencing Teglias."

"How do you know that?"

"I don't. I'm hoping. We hardly need more than one of these things on our trail." Turning away from the smoke, Ascaros shook his head in vexation and tightened the hidden straps in his sleeve that held the wand Isiem had given him. "Whether it was alone or not, though, I've lost it. I wonder if it only intended to flush me out of hiding."

"If it did, it succeeded," Isiem said. "We should check on Ena."

Kyril nodded, taking the lead once more. The faltering wisps of white smoke that had leaked from the ruined plates in the entry hall were completely extinguished, and the sheer stillness of the corridor added to Isiem's powerful sense of unease. The apprentices' heaped bones bore a few streaks and spatters of fresher blood, shockingly garish in the white glow of Isiem's light spell, that marked Kyril's initial retreat with Ena.

As they crossed between the piles of ancient, pulverized bones, Isiem could see the steel door ahead. Bloody handprints—Kyril's?—tattooed its rim. A crescent of darkness showed the way to the chamber of demonflesh doors, and with it their escape from Fiendslair.

Quickening his step, Isiem sent his floating light forward to illumine the seraptis door. The trapped demon's face scrunched into a familiar, flattened snarl as they approached, but there seemed to be something more than hatred in her glare.

Fear? Defiance? Isiem couldn't guess. Whatever it was, it soon vanished under a muted scream and a mist of sprayed blood as the whirling blade emerged from the door's perimeter and began its gruesome work.

The three of them gathered before it, watching tensely as the silver blade sheared through bone and hair and muscle. Ascaros glanced back at the shadowed hall and the great steel door that still lay ajar behind them. "We should close that," he muttered.

"Then do it," Kyril said, her own attention focused intently forward. "I'm not stopping you."

But the shadowcaller made no move to do so, and Isiem thought he understood why. Child of Nidal he might be, but the darkness of Fiendslair frightened him, too. Something deep and atavistic in his soul was afraid of those unnatural, layered shadows.

There *were* monsters lurking in those lightless depths, and things that would happily drag them off into the dark . . . and it felt so much safer to stand here, in the fragile bubbles of their illumination spells and the comfort of each other's presences, and say that there really was no reason to venture into that terror. There were no threats in view. No need to brave the shapeless horrors of the night and close that gaping door, even if it was only thirty feet away.

"We *should* close it," Isiem forced himself to say. "I'll come with you."

Together they walked back into the darkness. Behind them, Isiem heard the seraptis door slide free.

And then Kyril swore, and something hurtled past them in a blur of yellow cloth, hitting Isiem in the back with what felt like an elbow on the way. The wizard stumbled, and by the time he righted himself to a crouch, the figure had disappeared past the steel door and into the darkness beyond.

He knew who it was, though. Who it had to be. "Teglias?"

"Yes." Kyril's answer was brittle with surprise and defeat. "He just . . . ran. As soon as the door opened. Didn't say a word."

"Excellent," Ascaros said. "Isiem, seal the door. Neither he nor his accursed master will be able to escape once you do."

Uncomfortably aware of Kyril's eyes on his back, but unable to deny the shadowcaller's logic, Isiem pressed the key to the pinhole at the center of the partly recessed steel door. Once again, the hole spiraled wide to accept the key, then poured back in to enclose it as if the steel were smooth-flowing mercury. With a gentle click, the key released, and the door rolled back into its sealed position.

Isiem let out a breath he hadn't realized he was holding. Tension drained from his muscles. The blank solidity of that massive steel door was immeasurably reassuring, and with it in place behind him, he finally turned to see what lay beyond the seraptis door.

Ena was on the ground in the brass-walled entry chamber. Kyril knelt by her side. The dwarf bore no fresh injuries, as far as Isiem could see, but she didn't look good.

Her face had a chalky, grayish pallor. There might have been a hint of green to it, or Isiem might have imagined that, remembering the monsters that the Aspis agents had become. He didn't imagine the shallowness of her breathing, though, or the feverish flutter of her eyelids. Thin white strands of fungus, fine as cat's whiskers, sprouted from what looked like an acid burn across her abdomen.

"She didn't have these before," Kyril muttered, yanking out the fungal filaments and throwing them aside in disgust. She scrubbed her hand against an armored thigh. "What did he do to her? *How?* And how do we get rid of it?"

"It is a disease of the qlippoth," Ascaros answered, joining her and kneeling on the dwarf's opposite side. "At least some of them, anyway. I believe Eledwyn, in trying to devise a plague that might eliminate demons altogether, enhanced or distilled the ability. Perhaps they can pass it to their servants as well."

"Can we cure it?" the half-elf asked.

"We can try. Does your goddess grant you any dominion over disease?"

"Some."

The shadowcaller nodded in acknowledgment, beckoning for Isiem to join them. "Then that is what we'll use. Your prayers against disease, mine against the more ordinary sufferings of the flesh. Isiem, hold her. There may be a struggle."

Gingerly, the wizard held Ena's shoulders down. She was cold under his hands, even through the dirty blue wool of her cloak, and rigid as a corpse. Where the fungus grew, however, her flesh felt disconcertingly soft and mushy, like a peach succumbing to rot.

Kyril pressed a hand to the dwarf's breastbone, beginning her prayer. Radiance spilled from between her fingers and poured into Ena's body, driving back the unnatural chill. The whiskers of fungus withered and collapsed, although the acid-eaten flesh beneath them remained unhealed until Ascaros added his own prayer to Kyril's. The paladin stiffened visibly at the sound of the unholy invocation, but she did not interrupt or object.

Color returned to Ena's cheeks. Groggily, she opened her eyes.

"Gods above," she croaked, focusing unsteadily on Isiem, "but yours is *not* the first face I want to see when waking up." The dwarf struggled into a sitting position, wincing heavily and putting a hand to her abdomen. Despite Ascaros's magic, a palpable bruise remained. "I'd ask what happened, but somehow I'm guessing there's a long version of the story that I don't want to hear, and a short version that goes 'monsters attacked us and we're all that survived.' Am I right?"

"More or less," Isiem allowed. "Depending on your definition of 'survived.'"

"The simple definition," Ena said. She spat on the floor, then sucked in a careful breath and stood up, leaning against the wall for support. "I always like the simple definitions. So. We're all that's left. What's our goal? Getting out alive?"

"Yes," Ascaros said, at the same time that Kyril answered, "No."

"Good, good, I love when everything's unanimous," Ena croaked. The ghost of a smile creased Ena's face. Dried blood cracked and flaked off her chin. "Makes life so much easier. Does anyone want to tell me *why* it's both 'yes' and 'no'?"

Ascaros's answer seemed to be directed more at Kyril than the dwarf. He delivered it with his black eyes fixed, unblinking, on the paladin. "We can escape Fiendslair now. We have all three nightblades in our possession. Teglias and the qlippoth are both on the far side of the steel door, which effectively bars them from leaving this place. We have achieved a greater degree of victory than any of us should reasonably have expected. We've won. What possible reason could you have to linger?"

"I won't leave Teglias." Kyril said it quietly, but there was steel in her voice. "I won't abandon him to that monster."

"You didn't see what happened to Ganoven," Isiem said. The memory of the Aspis agent's transformation was one that he did not expect ever to be able to forget. "It was like he'd been . . . hollowed. Like his skin had been stretched over a framework of horror. I don't know if there was anything of *him* left inside at all."

Kyril frowned at him, fingering the engraved pommel of her sword. "So it's true, then, what Teglias said. You killed him."

"We killed the thing wearing his skin. I'm not convinced it was truly him. I know little of these qlippoth, but whatever their ability to seize and corrupt human hosts, I fear Eledwyn's experiments may have increased them, or blended them with those of demons. What the qlippoth did to Ganoven and Copple . . . that was no ordinary possession."

The paladin's frown deepened. She turned on her left heel, gazing at the demons trapped in their miserable doors. The seraptis's injuries were beginning to knit; congealed blood was giving way to raw pink flesh as the door gradually grew back into place. "All the more reason we must rescue Teglias."

"All the more reason we must *leave*," Ascaros said. "Are you *mad*? Do you realize what will happen if you fall to the qlippoth in there? If they take the nightblades from us and free themselves from Fiendslair? You would doom the world for the sake of one cleric who's probably dead already."

Kyril set her jaw. "It isn't irrevocable. I purified the disease from Ena. I have to try for Teglias."

Faced with the paladin's determination, Ascaros could only gape in astonished contempt. "You're an idiot."

"So am I, then," Ena murmured, "because I'll be going with her." Brushing away the last strands of fungus from her clothing, the dwarf fished around inside the hidden pockets of her cloak. One of her potion bottles had been smashed somewhere in the fighting; she dumped the glass shards from her sodden pocket with a sigh. Another was intact, however, and she drank it with evident relief. A bit more color returned to her face, although she remained unsteady on her feet. "There. Now I'm ready."

"Isiem?" Kyril asked.

The wizard hesitated. At the crossroads of loyalty and self-preservation, he didn't know which way to turn.

He liked Teglias, had enjoyed traveling with the man, respected his courage and learning . . . but if the decision was measured on the scales of pragmatism, there could be no question. Ascaros was right. The chance of saving one man's life—however good and worthy that man might be—was not worth the risk.

But looking at Kyril and Ena, he understood that what was practical didn't matter. Not to them. Loyalty did, and their sense of what was right.

And he was drawn to that, as he had been in the warehouse in Pezzack and a hundred times since. Isiem admired their bravery and their conviction, and in a way, envied it. His own life had no such clear compass.

He was not like them. But he wanted to be.

"I'll go," he said.

"I don't believe this." Ascaros threw up his hands. "Your brains must have boiled away in that desert. Don't ask me to come with you."

"I wasn't planning to. It's better for you to go, anyway," Isiem said. "Take the nightblades away from here. If the qlippoth overwhelm us and escape, at least they won't be able to use those to cut a rift between the planes. We won't risk the world if we fail. We'll only risk ourselves."

A hint of surprise widened the shadowcaller's dark eyes. Ena and Kyril echoed his expression, but neither of them spoke. Only Ascaros voiced the thought all three of them shared: "You'd give the nightblades to the Umbral Court? That easily?"

"No," Isiem said, holding his old friend's gaze. "I am giving them to *you*. You know what the nightblades are, and you know they must be destroyed. They're useless to anyone, including the Umbral Court. There's no profit to be had from them, no meaningful power. They are a failed creation, and they need to be broken before they spill more evil into the world. I can trust you to do that, surely."

"I suppose you can," Ascaros answered. He hesitated, then reached into his sleeve and took out the ivory wand Isiem had given him. Its jacinths glittered under their light spells, their red-orange hues deepened to a sullen, hellish crimson like devils' burning blood. "You might need this."

"I might," Isiem agreed, accepting the gold-chased wand. "Thank you."

"Good luck. Perhaps we'll meet again, although I don't hold much hope for it." The shadowcaller moved to the center of the room, where a faint circle of runes marked the exit. As he focused magic into them, the runes began to radiate a muted golden light, and Ascaros's outline softened in their midst like sea-mist burning away at dawn.

Within moments, he was gone, and the light died softly behind him.

"Well, that was touching," Ena said. She cracked her knuckles and turned to the seraptis door. "Are we ready?"

"Almost." Isiem unsheathed his belt knife and plucked a bit of fleece from his pouch of spell components. He passed the fleece over his knife, and in its wake the cool gray steel of his blade darkened to glossy black with a flicker of scarlet flame at its edge. Its shape lengthened and thinned to a perfect replica of the largest nightblade they'd found, and when the illusion was complete, he tied it to his belt so that the false nightblade swung openly over his hip.

"Bait?" Ena asked, jerking a thumb at the magic-veiled knife.

Isiem nodded. "Past that experimentation chamber, Fiendslair turns into a labyrinth of madness. We'll never find Teglias or the qlippoth in there. Our only chance is to lure them out. And what does the qlippoth want? The nightblade."

"Which it can't get," Ena finished approvingly. "Excellent. So all we're really risking will be our lives. And possibly our immortal souls. Well, that's of no account. Let's go."

Chapter Twenty-Three
One Last Time

One last time, they walked into the darkness beyond the scratched steel door. One last time, Isiem faced the depthless dread of Fiendslair.

They crossed the piled apprentices' bones in single file, Kyril in front with her shield and holy sword, Ena behind her, Isiem in the rear. Along with his false nightblade, the wizard had added a second illusion to their procession: a slight shimmer in the air, suggestive of an invisible fourth person walking alongside them.

The qlippoth had unveiled Ascaros's invisibility once before, and Isiem hoped that the fiend might think they were trying the same trick again. If they were lucky, it might waste its energy trying to attack a man who wasn't there.

If not . . .

He refused to dwell on it. When they reached the experimentation chamber, the three of them fanned out, as they had agreed while forming their hasty plan.

The three of them traced separate, overlapping courses across the smashed bones and glass of the experimentation room. As they walked, each of them stooped to pick through the rubble. Kyril had said that while all the demons' cages had been broken in the fighting, not all of their gems had been recovered. Even for Ganoven and his ill-fated comrades, greed had fallen by the wayside while they were desperate to survive.

But now they were safer—or wanted to create the impression that they *thought* they were safer—and greed might be extremely useful.

Isiem jostled the apprentices' bones with deliberate roughness, tossing them aside as he mimed searching for fallen valuables.

From across the room, Kyril scowled at him. "*Must* you do that?"

It hadn't been rehearsed, but Isiem was inwardly pleased at her improvisation. Being scolded by a paladin only reinforced their guise as looters and tomb robbers. He stood, shrugged at her with theatrical indifference, and kicked a toothless skull in her direction before returning to his looting.

The joy of that momentary teamwork lightened the clammy chill of his dread, but it was all too fleeting. As Isiem came around the curve of the cracked central dome, he glimpsed Ena out of the corner of his eye, and his mood shifted back to tense, silent calculation.

While Kyril and Isiem made a show of robbing the dead, Ena was using her circuit of the room as cover to plant the last of her bombs. She used the apprentices' robes and skeletons to hide her silver-pinned globes, and while that was no doubt a desecration in its own way, it was not one that they meant for the qlippoth to notice. Isiem watched her carefully, alert to the smallest sign that might betray what she was really doing, but the dwarf was as nimble as a Chelish pickpocket, and he never saw a thing.

"Have you got them all?" Ena called, brushing off her knees.

That was the signal that she'd finished placing her bombs. "Not yet," Kyril called back, signifying that she had not spotted the qlippoth or Teglias.

"I think there's one more, maybe two," Isiem said. He hadn't seen them either.

It worried him. This was their only gambit. If they couldn't lure the qlippoth out of hiding, or at least into sending Teglias as its puppet to confront them, then their choices became much starker and much worse: brave the labyrinth of Abyss-touched madness, or turn back and accept defeat without ever having laid eyes on their lost companion.

But then he heard the click and drag of something strange approaching, and hope flared along with apprehension in his chest.

"Kyril. *Kyyyyrrriilll.*" The reedy warble came from a hunched silhouette at the outer edge of Isiem's floating light. It was a distorted mockery of Teglias's true voice, scarcely recognizable. "You came back for me, Kyril. You came *baaacckk*. Come with me now. Come into the dark."

Instead, Isiem waved his light forward.

Like Ganoven before him, the cleric had become a creature out of a ghastly dream. The Sarenite's skin sagged from his skull in a green-gray mask. Wisps of white fungus grew from his temples, twining into his hair. Patches of scabby skin covered his knuckles, and his fingers alternated between long yellow claws and withered stumps with no nails at all.

But he was still undeniably alive. He was no collection of bones, or even as infested as Ganoven. If Kyril could drive out the contagion with her magic, she might yet save him.

Behind the fungal thrall that Teglias had become, the puppetmaster lurked.

It emerged slowly, hovering at the edge of Isiem's light. The qlippoth was a pale, smooth lozenge of flesh, eight feet long and perhaps four across, with a toothy rift in the center. Damp green fungus stained its uneven, continually gnashing teeth, and more fungus streaked the soft slimy blue-pink of its hide. Its eyes were covered in a slick of shimmering, impossible colors, like misshapen soap bubbles that had floated up from a drug-induced nightmare. Long, sinuous tentacles groped the air around it, their sphincterlike suckers flaring obscenely.

Two of the qlippoth's four tentacles were decked with oversized rings or slim bracelets, and a third held a wand of spiraling clear crystal in its pincer. The fiend jabbed its wand into the air in short, sharp thrusts as it approached, and although it was too far for Isiem to have any chance of recognizing the wand's purpose, he saw no reason to risk it.

"It's here!" he shouted to his companions. Kyril had already seen it, and was striding toward Teglias and the qlippoth even before he'd called. Ena skittered back around the dome for cover, raising her crossbow.

One of the qlippoth's horrible shimmering eyes rolled to look in the wizard's direction as he shouted. A second later, its wand followed, swaying in the grip of the glistening black pincer.

Isiem dove to the side, scattering a sparkling spray of pulverized glass, and retaliated with his own spell back at the monster. Flames flew between them: copper and gold from the wizard's hands, a violent swirl of clashing colors from the qlippoth's wand. The fiend's slimy skin bubbled and blistered under Isiem's spell; one of its globby eyes burst. Heat from its own fiery blast washed over the wizard, crisping his ivory hair and sucking the breath from his lungs. The cloth of his robes burned over his back, sweeping agony across his spine.

Caught in the crossfire between them, Teglias went up like a human torch. Fungal spores popped and sparked in the air around him. Yet still he refused to fall, staggering forward, arms outstretched and fingers curled into knobby-knuckled claws.

Despite his own blinding pain, Isiem winced to see the cleric reduced to a shambling zombie. All the man's intelligence and learning, all his morals and lived experience . . . all were swept away under the crush of the qlippoth's control. And that seemed a greater devastation than the fire consuming his mortal shell.

There was only one way to end it. Rolling onto his back to put out his smoldering robes, Isiem tried another spell. His fire hadn't hurt the fiend as badly as he'd hoped; he needed something else. Fishing out a chunk of coal, he crushed it between his fingers and threw a tumult of slashing diamond shards at the tentacled horror.

Before he could tell how effective the attack had been, however, Kyril stepped between him, the fiend, and Teglias in his halo of green-tipped fire. Blessed blue light limned the paladin's sword. Like an avenging angel—more an embodiment of Iomedae's divine wrath than a living woman—she closed on him.

The sight of Kyril's holy grace seemed to drive the corrupted cleric to new heights of fury. His face contorted in rage, Teglias raised his hands and clawed at her with wild rakes of his talonlike hands. The paladin raised her shield to catch them, but she did not return his attacks.

"Pull back," Isiem gasped to her, scrabbling backward on his rump and elbows. Glass splintered under his weight, slashing his palms. The heat coming off Teglias scorched his cheeks and dried his throat. It hurt to breathe too close to the cleric. "Ena's laid the path for us."

Kyril nodded, never taking her eyes off their foes, and began a steady, defensive retreat as Isiem scrambled to stay behind her. Sweat dripped into her eyes and her shield shuddered with every blow she caught, but the half-elf never faltered. She altered her course slightly as she moved backward, angling toward the trail of traps Ena had set.

The tentacled fiend hung back, raising its bejeweled appendages, but the burning Teglias stumbled mindlessly after the paladin. Kyril kept the same measured pace as she gave ground, stepping over loose bones and rolling chunks of glass with sure-footed deftness. As easily as if they were dancing, she led the cleric toward the entryway. Behind her, Ena's crossbow twanged as the dwarf shot repeatedly into the gloom. Each of her alchemically treated bolts exploded with a muted thunderclap on impact, although Isiem couldn't see much of them beyond flashes of silvery blue past the limits of his light spell.

Twenty feet from the doorway, Teglias stepped onto one of Ena's traps. The delicate globe shattered underfoot, spraying blessed water. The holy water hissed into steam as it hit Teglias's wreath of flames, scalding the cleric. He rocked to the left, dropping his fists, and Kyril seized the opportunity. Her fiery sword came around in a blazing blue arc, cleaving a diagonal trail through the steam.

The blade should have buried itself between the Sarenite's neck and his shoulder—a wound that would have been fatal to any living man—but to Isiem's astonishment, it did not. Somehow the impact seemed to be muted. The sword's holy aura diffused around its keen steel edge, blunting what *should* have been a mortal wound into one that merely incapacitated.

Teglias dropped like a felled tree. Immediately Kyril sheathed her sword and grabbed the cleric by the back of his collar, hauling him with her as she broke into an all-out run for the door. *"Go!"*

Isiem rolled back to his feet and hurried after her. They didn't need to kill the qlippoth. They only needed to seal it behind the steel barrier door to cement their victory.

But the fiend knew that too.

It raised a braceleted tentacle. Isiem saw the movement, and glimpsed a flash of blue-white light coruscating around whatever ornament the qlippoth wore. He had nowhere to hide, though, and there was nowhere to run.

A crushing wave of cold slammed into him from behind. It forced tears to his eyes and froze them on his lashes, seared the inside of his throat with freezing air, and sent him sprawling into a heap of ice-glazed bones. His concentration disrupted, Isiem lost his secondary illusion. It was all he could do to hold on to the spell that veiled his belt knife.

Across the room, Ena lifted her crossbow again. Even as she pulled its trigger, the qlippoth sent a second blast of elemental frost to swallow the dwarf. The bolt vanished into the blinding cone of ice, and so did Ena. When the haze of frosty mist and snow fell to the ground, the dwarf fell with it. Red-streaked ice encased the top of her head and ran down the sides of her face like a rippled helm. Her crossbow, frozen solid, tumbled from her hands and broke into pieces on the floor.

Teglias was down as well, and Kyril was close to collapse. The half-elf had managed to push herself up to a sitting position on the ice-slick ground near Teglias, who looked like a three-day-old corpse with his greenish pallor. Blood ran from Kyril's nose and the corner of her lips, and frost crackled in her dark red hair, but she held the strength to summon a spark of healing magic to her hand. It flowed into Teglias, pulling the Sarenite back from the brink of oblivion.

It wouldn't keep him safe for long. The one-eyed qlippoth, seeing its enemies laid low, slithered toward them with horribly liquid ripples of its tentacles. It was badly wounded, its pulpy flesh shredded by the wizard's diamond burst and pocked with fist-sized holes from

Ena's bolts. The jewels on its frosty bracelet glimmered, blue and white and colder than a winter moon . . . but the fiend did not call upon its magic again. Not yet.

Instead, with surprising delicacy, the qlippoth reached forward with a pincered tentacle and snipped the false nightblade from Isiem's belt. Gurgling covetously, it cradled the black knife in the slimy curls of its tentacle, drawing it close to its body for protection.

Then, its precious treasure secured from accidental destruction, the qlippoth gathered itself to withdraw. Ichor dripped from its many wounds, leaving a slug's trail of slime when it pulled back. The tentacle with the icy-gemmed bracelet came toward the injured adventurers again, its enchanted jewels glowing as magic built within.

None of them could withstand another blast. Isiem knew that to a certainty. *He* wouldn't, and he was the strongest among them—which meant he was their best chance at survival.

He loosened the ruby-studded ring from his finger and slipped it into his palm. In his other hand, he readied the wand Ascaros had given him.

Just as the qlippoth pointed its frost-jeweled tentacle at them, Isiem tossed the ring toward Kyril. It skittered noisily across the icy floor, bouncing and clattering against the apprentices' bones, and rolled to a stop a few feet from the half-elf.

"Take it," Isiem shouted hoarsely, leveling his wand at the qlippoth as he spoke. He didn't have to feign his desperation, nor did Kyril have to feign the confusion that furrowed her brow when she turned, painfully, to direct a questioning look at him. The injured fiend paused as well, evidently nonplussed by the wizard's actions, and Isiem filled the breathless gap as quickly as he could. If the qlippoth was in fear of its life, if it was desperate not to spend more uncountable years trapped in Fiendslair, if luck smiled upon him, then maybe . . .

"There's a teleportation spell stored in that ring. Use it to escape this place. You'll never make it out of the Umbral Basin on foot, not with the Splinter Men and the shadowstorms clouding the valley. Your only chance is to take the ring and teleport yourself to safety. I'll follow if I can. *Go!*"

Uncertainly, Kyril reached for the ruby ring. But before she could close her fingers around it, the qlippoth snatched it away. A triumphant snarl contorted its enormous mouth as it slid Isiem's ring onto the one tentacle that didn't already bear a bauble. Gurgling in ugly laughter, it drew upon the magic he'd stored in that band of platinum and small, dark rubies—

—and a fountain of pulverized flesh rained down in the space where it had been.

Mangled tentacles and ribbons of slime, fragments of bone and a few twisted bits of metal—that was all that remained of the qlippoth.

Isiem smiled. Ascaros had been right. Teleportation was a lethal mistake in Fiendslair.

Pushing himself back up to his feet, Isiem hobbled over to Ena. Miraculously, under her icy mask and frost-dusted cloak, the dwarf was breathing. He went through her pockets until he found a bottle marked with the little scribble that Ena scratched on the corks of her healing potions; when he did, he opened it and carefully tipped its contents down her throat.

A moment later, the dwarf's eyelids fluttered open. She groaned. "You again?"

"If it bothers you so much, stop dying." Isiem tucked the empty bottle under one of Ena's unresisting hands and moved away, looking at Kyril. "Will he live?"

"I don't know yet," the paladin admitted. "We need to get him out of here. We *all* need to get out of here. Do you have the key for the barrier door?"

"Yes." He held it up, letting the plain steel glint in the shadows—then paused. "Kyril . . . Teglias is infected. We don't know how badly. If we take him out of Fiendslair, we risk releasing whatever's inside him into the world."

"What other option do we have?" Kyril looked up at him, her face reddening. "Would you just leave him here to die?"

Isiem said nothing. The paladin was letting emotion cloud her judgment, putting a single man's life above the lives of thousands. Teglias was his friend, but it was simple arithmetic—even a child of Nidal could have made the decision. When a finger was infected, you cut it off before you lost the arm.

This was the weakness the Nidalese had burned out of themselves. Isiem had been away from that nation's shadows a long time, but he still had that much. Kyril and Ena needed him to operate the runes that would let them exit Fiendslair. He could refuse to take Teglias, and in so doing remove the burden of guilt from them. The betrayal would be his, not theirs. A mercy.

Isiem stared down at the paladin, at those bright eyes boring into his own.

And decided.

Epilogue

"They tell me I owe you my life," Teglias said, gazing out over the sparkling waters of Gemcrown Bay. He sat in a wheeled wicker chair, a white blanket folded over his lap. Sea birds, tiny as snowflakes from this distance, spun and sparred over the glittering green water. Occasionally one dove toward the waves, skimming over the spray, before spiraling back up to vanish against the sun. "That without your courage and quick thinking, I might have died in Fiendslair. Or, worse, survived as a monster's thrall."

Isiem shrugged uncomfortably, standing behind the cleric's chair. He, too, watched the birds' dance over the sea. Their effortless ease in the air made a painful contrast to Teglias's immobility, but he supposed that was why the Sarenite spent so much time on this balcony. Perhaps it was freeing, in a way, to watch them. "I don't deserve the credit. Kyril and Ena had as much to do with that as I did."

"No doubt," Teglias agreed, wheeling his chair around on the yellow sandstone to face Isiem, "but without you, they would have failed."

"Maybe," Isiem said. He kept his eyes on the white-crowned waves a moment longer before finally, reluctantly, meeting the older man's gaze.

Looking at the chairbound cleric, it was hard for Isiem to feel that their rescue had been much of a triumph. That was profoundly unfair, he knew; certainly the Sarenite had told them, often and honestly, how grateful he was to be alive. Even knowing that, however, he couldn't shake the thought.

Because Teglias had not escaped unscathed. The qlippoth's partial possession—or transformation, or whatever it had been—had exacted a terrible toll from him. Parts of his own flesh had been transmuted into demonic matter, and when the Iomedaeans had purified his body, those portions had vanished along with the rest of the qlippoth's taint.

What could be healed had been, but there was much that no spell could restore. Teglias survived with a sag to the left side of his face, a patchwork of sunken scars on his scalp like ghostly spider webs that stretched from ear to ear, and a persistent inability to use his legs.

It was not that his legs were missing, or even damaged. The muscle was there, the cartilage and bone. But whatever part of his mind or will *controlled* those limbs was gone. It confounded the healers, who could find nothing amiss with his body, and it puzzled the clerics, who had invoked every divine blessing they had.

After the Iomedaeans had exhausted their spells, and the lay healers had gone through their repertoires of herbs and poultices, Kyril had taken him to the country estate of a wealthy sympathizer in Cheliax. There, Teglias could recuperate in comfort, far enough from the outposts of Thrune power to avoid drawing unwanted attention. He could take as long as he needed to regain his strength.

Nothing helped. Nearly a month later, Teglias remained in his chair.

Until now, Isiem had been loath to visit. They had exchanged letters, but as the weeks rolled past, it became even harder for him to muster the courage to see the man. The wait itself had become its own admission of failure. Finally, Kyril had pushed him into coming . . . but he still felt guilty, and then ashamed of that guilt.

"I wish we'd been able to do more," Isiem said, meaning it.

The yellow-robed cleric smiled tiredly down at the blanket in his lap. "I consider it no small miracle that you achieved as much as you did." The setting sun cast the bad side of his face into shadow, letting him look almost whole again.

"It talked to me, you know." Teglias's was thoughtful, almost musing, although a subdued grimness shadowed each word. "The qlippoth. Even before you opened the steel door, it was whispering in my thoughts. I didn't know what it was, or how it was reaching me, but I knew what it wanted. It wanted freedom. It wanted to come into our world. With the nightblade. And it did everything it could to ensure that I'd open that door. Knowing that I was the leader. That the rest of you would do as I said."

The cleric took a breath and closed his eyes, visibly struggling to relax before his control cracked. Wind flapped at the corners of his blanket and rattled the pink-petaled flowers in the vase that the servants had set on a tea table next to the balcony door. Climbing wisteria framed the balcony and hung in fragrant drapes from the latticed arch over their heads; its dappled shade and soft perfume vanished, then returned, as the breezes played around them.

Teglias flattened the blanket under his palms. Gradually, the tension leached from him. "It almost worked. I was arrogant, trusting to my faith in the goddess to protect me. But not even the Dawnflower can protect a fool for himself. Kyril and Ena trusted me. They would have followed anywhere without question, until it was too late. Ganoven was venal, stupid, easily led by his fears and greeds. If you hadn't been there . . . it might have worked."

"But it didn't," Isiem said.

"No, it didn't." When the Sarenite finally looked up, his eyes were clouded with emotion but his face was calm. "What does that tell you?"

"What *should* it tell me?"

"That it wasn't just my life you saved. It was all of ours."

"Not the Aspis agents'." Isiem pushed his windblown hair back from his eyes. "How is the Consortium taking their loss, anyway? Have you heard anything?"

"Did your gambit work, you mean?" Teglias chuckled. A wisteria flower, snapped off by the wind, dropped into his lap. He picked it up, cradling it in his palm. "I would say it did, yes. I wondered, when Ena first told me, why you let your companion take all three nightblades back to Nidal. You let him take Ganoven's belongings, too, didn't you?"

"Yes," Isiem admitted.

"Thereby sealing the narrative that your companion, an Umbral Court agent in high standing, murdered the Aspis Consortium's representative, looted his corpse, and fled back to Nidal with all three nightblades. Where the Aspis Consortium is welcome to come find him, if they wish to try to hold the lords of the Umbral Court to a bargain that they, personally, never struck." Teglias shook his head in grudging admiration and tossed the broken flower away. "Neatly done. And, of course, Kyril was a witness to it, and there's no doubting a paladin's word as to what happened."

"Did they believe it?"

"Naturally. Men like that are always ready to believe that others are as greedy and treacherous as they themselves are. But there's nothing they can do about it. No one wants to risk offending the Midnight Lord's congregation. The Aspis Consortium might not have believed that the nightblade was impossible to use safely, but they will readily accept that it's not worth the cost to reclaim."

Isiem nodded. It was still a gamble whether Ascaros truly would destroy the nightblades instead of giving them to the Umbral Court . . . but he believed the shadowcaller's curse gave him enough respect for the soul-shattering costs of such magic, and enough bitterness toward his shadowy superiors, that he would indeed see those black blades broken. "Then it's done."

"It is done. Our expedition to Fiendslair has been recorded as a conclusive failure. Not nearly as grievous a failure as it might have been, though, which is *not* a fact the annals of history are likely to record." Teglias pushed his chair a little closer. Its wheels clacked on the uneven sandstone. "The question now is: what will you do next?"

Isiem shrugged. A great gray sea eagle dipped low over the bay and came up with a glittering prize in its talons. Trailing a cloud of squawking, squabbling lesser birds who shrieked their envy of its catch, the eagle caught the wind under its black-tipped wings and turned in a swooping curve toward land.

When it was out of sight, Isiem looked back at the Sarenite. "Kyril is thinking of returning to Westcrown. She says the rebellion is truest to its ideals there, and has the best chance of breaking House Thrune's power."

"Do you agree?"

"She would know better than I." The wizard smoothed the sleeves of his robes pensively. The sun was slanting downward over Gemcrown Bay, and the first hints of twilight's chill were coming. Distant, as yet, but in the air. "But I'm not eager to go back to Westcrown. I served in the Midnight Guard there. People will remember me."

"You don't want to be remembered?"

"Not for my work in Westcrown." He'd seen too much ugliness there from both sides. The rebellion had been hard pressed, and had done desperate, vengeful things. And the retaliation, meant to break the rebels' spirits, had been worse. Nothing he'd been a part of in Westcrown was worthy of pride.

"But for something else?" Teglias pressed. "Something better?"

The expectation in the older man's voice gave Isiem pause. Answering in the affirmative, he knew, would mean taking on a burden of hope and responsibility that he was reluctant to accept. He wasn't worthy of such things.

But he wanted to be.

"What would you have of me?" he asked.

About the Author

Liane Merciel is the author of the Pathfinder Tales novel *Nightglass* (also starring Isiem) and the Pathfinder Tales short stories "Certainty" and "Misery's Mirror," both available for free at **paizo.com**. In addition, she has written the independent fantasy novels *The River Kings' Road* and *Heaven's Needle*, as well as the Dragon Age novel *Last Flight*. She is a practicing lawyer and lives in Philadelphia with her husband Peter, resident mutts Pongu and Crookytail, and a rotating cast of foster furballs. For more information, visit **lianemerciel.com**.

Acknowledgments

As ever, I'm indebted to quite a few people for helping this book come to be:

James Sutter and Dave Gross, for their support, encouragement, and occasional threats to light matches beneath a certain balky writer's backside when necessary.

Marlene Stringer, my agent, for her guidance and professionalism.

Peter, for his patience and willingness to talk me off the ledge all the time constantly.

. . . and the dogs, of course, for their continued excellence in providing diversions by finding new and interesting ways of driving me insane.

Glossary

All Pathfinder Tales novels are set in the rich and vibrant world of the Pathfinder campaign setting. Below are explanations of several key terms used in this book. For more information on the world of Golarion and the strange monsters, people, and deities that make it their home, see *Pathfinder Campaign Setting: The Inner Sea World Guide*, or dive into the game and begin playing your own adventures with the *Pathfinder Roleplaying Game Core Rulebook* or the *Pathfinder Roleplaying Game Beginner Box*, all available at **paizo.com**. You can also check out the earlier adventures of Isiem and Ascaros in the Pathfinder Tales novel *Nightglass*.

Abrogail II: Current ruler of Cheliax.

Abyss: Plane of evil and chaos ruled by demons, where many evil souls go after they die.

Abyssal: Of or pertaining to the Abyss.

Arcane: Magic that comes from mystical sources rather than the direct intervention of a god; secular magic.

Arcanist: Practitioner in the art of secular magic.

Asmodeus: Devil-god of tyranny, slavery, pride, and contracts; lord of Hell and current patron deity of Cheliax.

Aspis Consortium: A powerful and unscrupulous international trade organization based in Cheliax.

Backar Forest: A vast woodland in central Molthune.

Barrowmoor: A burial ground for the ancient horselords, chieftains, and tyrants of Nidal. Rumored to be as rich with treasures as it is with curses for those who attempt to plunder it.

Black Triune: The three rulers of Pangolais; some of the most powerful members of the Umbral Court.

Brimorak: Goat-headed demon with a burning sword and hooves.

Cantrip: A minor spell or magical trick cast by an arcane spellcaster.

Cettigne: Molthuni city-state.

Cheliax: A powerful devil-worshiping nation.

Chelish: Of or relating to the nation of Cheliax.

Cleric: A religious spellcaster whose magical powers are granted by his or her god.

Crosspine: Small village in the southern Uskwood.

Cythnigots: Parasitic, fungal form of the ancient Abyssal creatures known as qlippoth.

Daemons: Evil denizens of Abaddon who exist to devour mortal souls.

Dawnflower: Sarenrae.

Demoniacs: Those who seek power through the worship of a demon lord.

Demons: Fiendish denizens of the Abyss, who seek only to maim, ruin, and feed on mortal souls.

Devil: Fiendish occupants of Hell who seek to corrupt mortals in order to claim their souls.

Devil's Perch: Inhospitable region of mountains and desert in northwestern Cheliax. Home of the strix.

Diabolist: A spellcaster who specializes in binding devils and making infernal pacts.

Druid: Someone who reveres nature and draws magical power from the boundless energy of the natural world (sometimes called the Green Faith).

Dusk Hall: Academy in Pangolais where initiates are trained as shadowcallers through study of both wizardry and the dark worship of Zon-Kuthon.

Dwarves: Short, stocky humanoids who excel at physical labor, mining, and craftsmanship. Stalwart enemies of the orcs and other evil subterranean monsters.

Egorian: Capital of Cheliax.

Elven: Of or pertaining to elves; the language of elves.

Elves: Long-lived, beautiful humanoids who abandoned Golarion millennia ago and have only recently returned. Identifiable by their pointed ears, lithe bodies, and pupils so large their eyes appear to be one color.

Eye of Abendego: Enormous permanent hurricane southwest of the Inner Sea.

Fiends: Creatures native to the evil planes of the multiverse, such as demons, devils, and daemons, among others.

Galtan: Of or relating to Galt, a nation embroiled in constant revolution

Ghasterhall: A haunted library in the Ustalavic city of Virlych, also known as the Palace of Travesties. It acts as headquarters for the Whispering Way.

Goblins: Race of small and maniacal humanoids who live to burn, pillage, and sift through the refuse of more civilized races.

Golarion: The planet on which the Pathfinder campaign setting focuses.

Half-Elves: The children of unions between elves and humans. Taller, longer-lived, and generally more graceful and attractive than the average human, yet not nearly so much so as their full elven kin. Often regarded as having the best qualities of both races, yet still see a certain amount of prejudice, particularly from their pure elven relations.

Half-Orcs: Born from unions between humans and orcs, members of this race have green or gray skin, brutish appearances, and short tempers, and are mistrusted by many societies.

Halflings: Race of humanoids known for their tiny stature, deft hands, and mischievous personalities.

Hell: Outer Plane of evil and tyrannical order ruled by devils, where many evil souls go after they die.

Hellknights: Organization of hardened law enforcers whose tactics are often seen as harsh and intimidating, and who bind devils to their will. Based in Cheliax.

House of Thrune: Current ruling house of Cheliax, which took power by making compacts with the devils of Hell. Often called the Thrice-Damned House of Thrune.

Ilvarandin: A legendary evil city located deep below ground.

Inheritor: Iomedae.

Inner Sea: The vast inland sea whose northern continent, Avistan, and southern continent, Garund, as well as the seas and nearby lands, are the primary focus of the Pathfinder campaign setting.

Iomedae: Goddess of valor, rulership, justice, and honor, who was a herald of the dead god Aroden before passing the Test of the Starstone and attaining godhood herself.

Kalavakus: Powerful, 7-foot-tall purple demons known for the horns that cover their bodies. They work as the Abyss's slavers, guards, and mercenaries.

Kobold: Small reptilian creatures that dwell in underground warrens, scheming about world conquest. They believe themselves to be cousins to dragonkind and deserving of similar reverence.

Kuthite: Worshiper of Zon-Kuthon; of or related to the worship of Zon-Kuthon.

Kyonin: Forest kingdom seen as the elven homeland and largely forbidden to non-elven travelers.

Lake Encarthan: One of Avistan's largest lakes.

Lamashtan: Worshiper of Lamashtu, the goddess of madness, monsters, and nightmares.

Mendev: Northern crusader nation that provides the primary force defending the rest of the Inner Sea region from the demonic infestation of the Worldwound.

Midnight Guard: Nidalese spellcasters—primarily shadowcallers—loaned to the Chelish military.

Midnight Lord: Zon-Kuthon.

Molthune: Expansionist nation in central Avistan, ruled by a military government overseen by nine General Lords. Perpetually at war with it's northern neighbor, Nirmathas, which declared its independence from Molthune almost six decades ago.

Molthuni: Of or relating to Molthune, or a citizen of that nation.

Necromancy: School of magic devoted to manipulating the power of death, unlife, and life force, such as creating and controlling undead creatures.

Nidal: Evil nation in southern Avistan, devoted to the worship of the dark god Zon-Kuthon after he saved its people from extinction in the distant past. Closely allied with devil-worshiping Cheliax.

Nidalese: Of or pertaining to Nidal; someone from Nidal.

Nightglass: A magic item useful in the summoning and binding of creatures from the Plane of Shadow.

Nisroch: Major port city of Nidal.

Omox: Foul demon made of living, fetid slime.

Oppara: Coastal capital of Taldor.

Orc: A bestial, warlike race of savage humanoids from deep underground who now roam the surface in barbaric bands. Possess green or gray skin, protruding tusks, and warlike tendencies. Almost universally hated by more civilized races.

Osirian: Of or relating to the region of Osirion, or a resident of Osirion.

Ostovites: Small, bony parasitic demons that cannibalize their hosts in attempts to create better bodies for themselves.

Outer Planes/Outer Sphere: The various realms of the afterlife, where most gods reside.

Paladin: A holy warrior in the service of a good and lawful god. Ruled by a strict code of conduct and granted special magical powers by his or her deity.

Pangolais: Capital city of Nidal, situated deep in the Uskwood.

Pathfinder: A member of the Pathfinder Society.

Pathfinder Society: Organization of traveling scholars and adventurers who seek to document the world's wonders.

Pezzack: A town of rebels and outcasts on the northwestern shore of Cheliax; extremely isolated from the rest of the nation.

Pezzacki: Of or pertaining to Pezzack; someone from Pezzack.

Pharasma: The goddess of birth, death, and prophecy, who judges mortal souls after their deaths and sends them on to the appropriate afterlife; also known as the Lady of Graves.

Plane of Shadow: A dimension of muted colors and strange creatures that acts as a twisted, shadowy reflection of the "real" world.

Ridwan: Nidalese city that is a religious center for the faithful of Zon-Kuthon.

Rokoa: Strix title for a tribe's spiritual leader; a wisewoman or shaman.

Ruby Prince: Khemet III, the Forthbringer, current ruler of Osirion.

Runelords: Seven Thassilonian governors who ruled that ancient empire after the death of First King Xin.

Sarenite: Of or related to the goddess Sarenrae or her worshipers.

Sarenrae: Goddess of the sun, honesty, and redemption. Often seen as a fiery crusader and redeemer.

Scroll: Magical document in which a spell is recorded so that it can be released when read, even if the reader doesn't know how to cast that spell. Destroyed as part of the casting process.

Second Ashes: Tragic fire resulting from civil unrest in Pezzack.

Shadowbeasts: Monsters summoned from the Plane of Shadow.

Shadowcallers: Nidalese casters who train in both arcane magic (like wizardry) and divine spellcasting as priests of Zon-Kuthon.

Shae: Intelligent natives of the Plane of Shadow who lack definite form.

Sorcerer: Someone who casts spells through natural ability rather than faith or study.

Spellbook: Tome in which a wizard transcribes the arcane formulae necessary to cast spells. Without a spellbook, wizards can cast only those few spells held in their minds at any given time.

Strix: Race of winged humanoids who dwell in the mountains of Devil's Perch in northwestern Cheliax. Hostile to outsiders and regularly antagonized by Chelish miners and settlers encroaching on their territory.

Taldan: Of or pertaining to Taldor; a citizen of Taldor.

Taldane: The common trade language of Golarion's Inner Sea region.

Taldor: Formerly glorious nation that has lost many of its holdings in recent years to neglect and decadence. Ruled by immature aristocrats and overly complicated bureaucracy.

Thassilon: Ancient empire which crumbled long ago, once located in northwestern Avistan and ruled by seven runelords.

Torag: Stoic and serious dwarven god of the forge, protection, and strategy. Viewed by dwarves as the Father of Creation.

Umbral Basin: Pass between the Mindspin and Menador mountains on the border of Molthune and Nidal. A dangerous and shadowy crossing, risked by only the most prepared merchant caravans.

Umbral Court: The ruling council of Nidal.

Undead: Once-living creatures animated by dark supernatural and spiritual forces.

Undeath: The state of being undead.

Uskwood: Nidal's central forest, said to be haunted.

Ustalav: Fog-shrouded gothic nation.

Ustalavic: Of or related to the nation of Ustalav.

Varisia: Frontier region at the northwestern edge of the Inner Sea region

Varisian: Of or relating to the frontier region of Varisia, or a resident of that region. Ethnic Varisians tend to organize in clans and wander in caravans, acting as tinkers, musicians, dancers, or performers.

Westcrown: Former capital of Cheliax, now overrun with shadow beasts and despair.

The Whispering Way: Secret organization dedicated to undeath and immortality.

Windspire: Traditional strix roosting place near Pezzack.

Wizard: Someone who casts spells through careful study and rigorous scientific methods rather than faith or innate talent, recording the necessary incantations in a spellbook.

Worldwound: Constantly expanding region overrun by demons a century ago. Held at bay by the efforts of the Mendevian Crusaders.

Zon-Kuthon: The twisted god of envy, pain, darkness, and loss. Was once a good god, along with his sister Shelyn, before unknown forces turned him to evil. Patron god of Nidal.

Torius Vin is perfectly happy with his life as a pirate captain, sailing the Inner Sea in search of plunder with a bold crew of buccaneers and Celeste, his snake-bodied navigator and one true love. Yet all that changes when his sometimes-friend Vreva—a high-powered courtesan and abolitionist spy in the slaver stronghold of Okeno—draws him into her shadowy network of insurgents. Caught between the slavers he hates and a navy that sees him as a criminal, can Torius continue to choose the path of piracy? Or will he sign on as a privateer, bringing freedom to others—at the price of his own?

From fan-favorite author Chris A. Jackson comes a tale of espionage and high-seas adventure, set in the award-winning world of the Pathfinder Roleplaying Game.

Pirate's Promise print edition: $9.99
ISBN: 978-1-60125-664-5

Pirate's Promise ebook edition:
ISBN: 978-1-60125-665-2

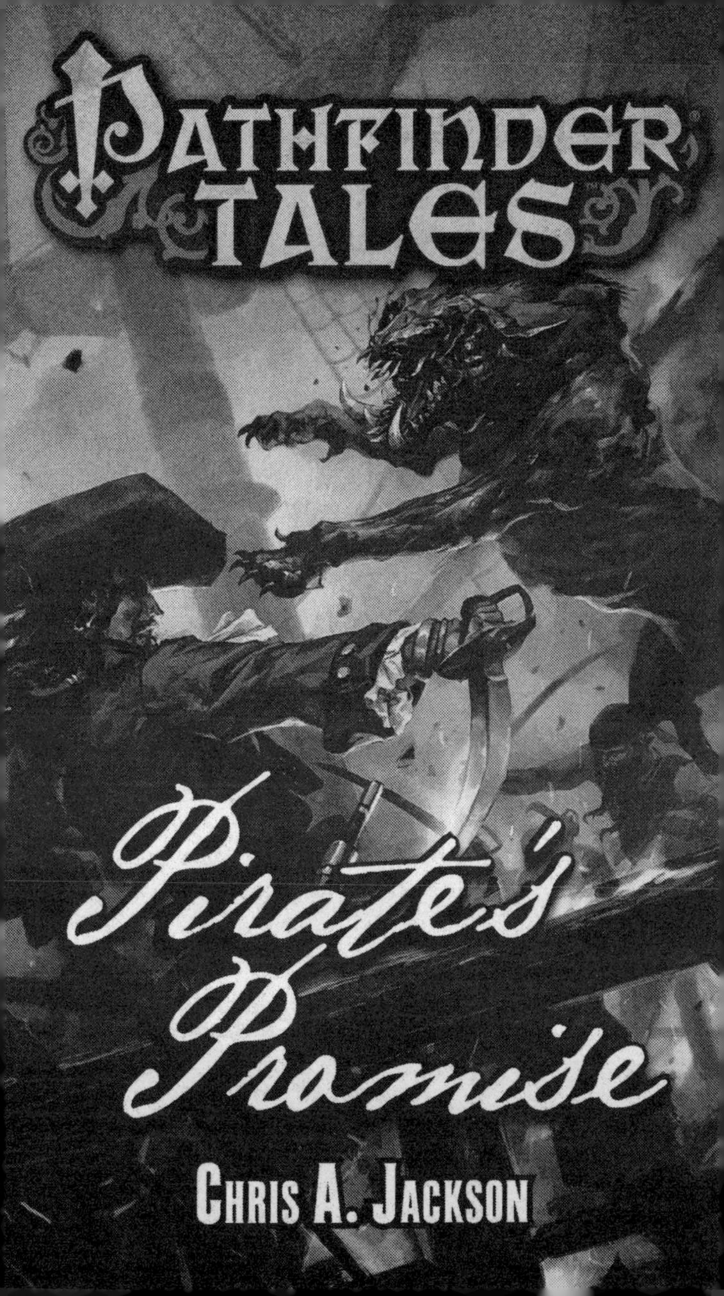
Pathfinder Tales
Pirate's Promise
Chris A. Jackson

When the leader of the ruthless Technic League calls in a favor, the mild-mannered alchemist Alaeron has no choice but to face a life he thought he'd left behind long ago. Accompanied by his only friend, a street-savvy thief named Skiver, Alaeron must head north into Numeria, a land where brilliant and evil arcanists rule over the local barbarian tribes with technology looted from a crashed spaceship. Can Alaeron and Skiver survive long enough to unlock the secrets of the stars? Or will the backstabbing scientists of the Technic League make Alaeron's curiosity his own undoing?

From Hugo Award winner Tim Pratt comes a fantastic adventure of technology and treachery, set against the backdrop of the Iron Gods Adventure Path in the award-winning world of the Pathfinder Roleplaying Game.

Reign of Stars print edition: $9.99
ISBN: 978-1-60125-660-7

Reign of Stars ebook edition:
ISBN: 978-1-60125-661-4

PATHFINDER TALES

Reign of Stars

TIM PRATT

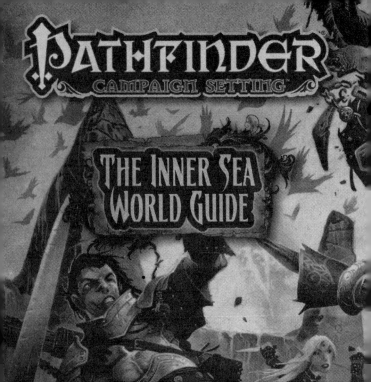

PATHFINDER
CAMPAIGN SETTING

THE INNER SEA
WORLD GUIDE

You've delved into the Pathfinder campaign setting with Pathfinder Tales novels—now take your adventures even further! *The Inner Sea World Guide* is a full-color, 320-page hardcover guide featuring everything you need to know about the exciting world of Pathfinder: overviews of every major nation, religion, race, and adventure location around the Inner Sea, plus a giant poster map! Read it as a travelogue, or use it to flesh out your roleplaying game—it's your world now!

EXPLORE YOUR WORLD!

paizo.com